"*The Orphan Sky* is a culturally intoxicating, emotionally gripping, and dazzlingly original book. It is Sergei Rachmaninoff's Piano Concerto 3 meets Khaled Hosseini's *The Kite Runner*. I loved it!"

—Mona Golabek, pianist, actress, author of *The Children of Willesden Lane: Beyond the Kindertransport— A Memoir of Music, Love, and Survival*

"This is one of the best novels I've ever read about a woman's struggle. There is both the dark, and the light, and Ella Leya braids them perfectly."

—Nina Barrett, owner of Bookends & Beginnings

THE

ORPHAN

SKY

ELLA LEYA

Copyright © 2015 by Ella Leya
Cover and internal design © 2015 by Sourcebooks, Inc.
Cover design by Archie Ferguson
Cover image © YuliaPopkova/iStock

Sourcebooks and the colophon are registered trademarks of Sourcebooks, Inc.

Published by Sourcebooks Landmark, an imprint of Sourcebooks, Inc.
P.O. Box 4410, Naperville, Illinois 60567-4410
(630) 961-3900
Fax: (630) 961-2168
www.sourcebooks.com

Library of Congress Cataloging-in-Publication data is on file with the publisher.

Printed and bound in the United States of America.
VP 10 9 8 7 6 5 4 3 2 1

In memory of my mother, Jane, and my son, Sergey—your dreams continue…

THE CAUCASUS REGION, 1970s

DISTANCE IN MILES

0 5 10 20 40

S.S.R. | SOVIET SOCIALIST REPUBLIC
A.S.S.R. | AUTONOMOUS SOVIET SOCIALIST REPUBLIC

N
W E
S

DAGESTAN
A.S.S.R.

SOVIET SOCIALIST REPUBLIC OF

AZERBAIJAN

BAKU ★

*SEE INSET
AT LEFT*

IRAN

CASPIAN
SEA

PART 1

CHAPTER 1

California, June 2002

Music seemed to flow out of the painting. Piano arpeggios in scarlet layers. Violin pizzicati in gold and silver brushstrokes. A dark D minor progression of chords sweeping by, trailed by a velvety soft harmony in white. Flutes spilling nostalgic blues and violets into the ever-changing palette of Rachmaninoff's *Piano Concerto no. 3*.

I could see and hear music again; I could surrender to its colors and passions. Something I hadn't been able to experience in twenty years. Since I buried my heart in the past. Since the sea of my destiny took me far away from the land of my childhood and washed me ashore, an empty shell without the trace of a pearl.

The painting was exhibited at the Pacific Design Center in Los Angeles, on loan from the National Art Museum of Azerbaijan. The *Times* art critic praised it effusively in his article:

> *The application of broken colors, mineral-based pigments, and silver; the dramatic Caravaggio-like shift from dark to light; the mystical objects depicted in the tradition of ancient Persian miniatures—all these induce an extraordinary emotional effect. The painting—signed Maiden Tower—is a true masterpiece, created by an artist who possesses brilliant technique and unconstrained imagination.*

And what everyone who's seen it wants to know is this: Who is this great master?

I knew. The moment I entered the showroom and saw the canvas, I knew.

Maiden Tower, obscured by the large crowd of spectators, dazzled by the relentless camera flashes, rose from the darkness of the stormy sea, fires breaking out of its sliver-like windows. A lonely princess— half human, half bird—standing on its crown, her wings reaching into the dome of the wakening sky.

And, appearing from behind the clouds, drowned in Caravaggio's light, the face of a girl.

My face.

Many years ago, I sat for Tahir in a dingy, dark Kabul hotel room. With the roar and the flashes of artillery tearing up the sky outside. With the moon—the only source of light—peeking in through the grimy window. I can still smell the paint, trace Tahir's strokes in the air. Painfully familiar, even after all this time.

A group of visitors, obviously VIP, approached, led by a short, stocky woman in a pink Chanel suit. I'd seen her before. The editor of a glossy magazine, *Azerbaijan Today*, published here in Los Angeles, and the curator of every Azeri event in America. She cleared space for her group, positioned herself firmly on her crimson stilettos, and began to speak in heavily accented English:

"Ten thousand years ago, the evil Shah of Darkness conquered the Land of Azerbaijan and ordered the building of a tower from the bottom of the Caspian Sea. When the tower reached the sky, every maiden was taken from her parents and locked inside to wait for the night of her wedding to the Shah. Darkness swallowed our land for many years until one morning when birdsong wakened the people of Azerbaijan. Fluttering vermilion feathers, the Firebird soared over Maiden Tower, leading the sun back to its rightful place in the firmament of the sky."

The Legend of Maiden Tower—a tale from my childhood

promising a triumphal finale at the end of a long struggle. Encouraging one to stand up to darkness and strive to reach for the skies. Something I had failed to do.

It was after five p.m. when I pulled onto the southbound 405 Freeway, together with the thousands of Angelenos heading back to their safe enclaves. Mine was Laguna Beach, a quaint California village of fishermen, artists, and jet-setters, lost between sunburned rocky canyons and the blue infinity of the Pacific Ocean. An ideal escape for someone running from the past.

I opened the door to my lonely villa and went to my spare room, empty except for the baby grand Bösendorfer buried in the corner under a thick cloak of dust.

How long had it been since I'd even touched it?

I wiped off the dust, lifted the lid, and stroked the keys, invading the mournful silence of the black-and-white keyboard. Playing the melody of the first theme from "Allegro ma non tanto." Rachmaninoff's *Piano Concerto no. 3*.

Wakening the shadows.

CHAPTER 2

Soviet Azerbaijan, May 1979

By the time I turned fifteen, Communism had become my religion.

Of course, at the time, it would not have occurred to me to make any comparison of Communism to religion—the latter being Communism's most despised ideological rival in the battle for the souls and minds of the Soviet people, a battle that had begun in 1917 with the victorious Great October Socialist Revolution.

Temples of Communism with crimson banners and flags arose from the ashes of burned mosques, churches, and synagogues; hammers and sickles and red stars replaced crescents, crosses, and stars of David; and the philosophical doctrine of the Communist Party of the Soviet Union became the one and only source of truth. And God? Well, we had Lenin.

As a member of Komsomol—the Youth League of the Communist Party—I worked tirelessly with the younger kids, educating them in the high principles of Communist ideology. And for that, I was rewarded with the most wonderful task—to administer the Sacred Oath of the Lenin Pioneers to Baku's finest ten-year-olds.

The morning of the swearing-in ceremony, on May 6, 1979, couldn't have been more glorious. Just the day before, the gusty wind Khazri swept through Baku, scouring every crevice, leaving behind air so pristine that it sparkled in the ginger sun like my mama's favorite crystal vase.

"Azerbaijan, Azerbaijan,
You are a rose in the sun.
The blood your sons and daughters shed
Turned Soviet banners crimson red."

I sang, together with the soon-to-be Lenin Pioneers, who packed the vast marble-and-granite 26 Commissars Memorial, ecstatic with anticipation of the ritual that was about to commence. Short, tall, thin, brown, blond pigtails, brunette porcupine haircuts. They were as different as the people of our country. But with their red Pioneer ties, dressed in white cotton shirts starched to perfection—the boys in neatly pressed black woolen pants, the girls in black woolen skirts and white knee-high socks—their differences disappeared, and they became a living image of the Soviet Union itself.

"Azerbaijan, Azerbaijan,
You are a diamond in the sun.
Your glory shines near and far,
A jewel in the crown of the USSR..."

I strutted to the center of the square and took my place of honor next to the memorial depicting a slain Red Commissar coming back from the dead, his Herculean torso breaking out of the ground, an eternal flame blazing in his mighty hands. A symbol of the invincible power and triumph of Communism.

My own grandfather was a Red Commissar who gave his life for the bright future of our country. He died heroically in World War II and was posthumously awarded the Soviet Union's highest honor—the Order of Lenin. His name—Comrade Badalbeili—would remain engraved forever in the history of Soviet Azerbaijan.

I locked my eyes on the eternal flame. The remains of the Red Commissars lay underneath my feet, their blood flowing through the blue-and-red veins of the torch, fueling our faith. And their souls lived among us, guiding us to the gates of the Communist paradise.

I recited, first in Azeri, then in Russian—both the official languages in Soviet Azerbaijan: "In the presence of my comrades, I solemnly take this pledge."

A chorus of a thousand voices echoed mine: "In the presence of my comrades, I solemnly take this pledge."

"I promise to stand by my comrades in danger! I promise to protect my Motherland from Western imperialism!"

The granite bas-relief showed the execution of the Red Commissars in all the agony of their final moments—their life-sized figures maimed, blood gushing from their wounds, their faces frozen in blind determination.

"I promise to be fearless! With my life I will prove to be worthy of my Motherland! My Motherland—a garden of a country with no gods and kings. No rich and poor. Only happy Soviet citizens," I pledged, embossing every consonant. "I promise to spread the ideals of Communism to the corrupt Americas, to Africa and Asia, to the Moon, Mars, and Pluto! How lucky I am to be born in my Azerbaijan! Soviet Azerbaijan!"

The brass of trumpets filled the Memorial, followed by the crisp beat of snare drums. I lifted high the crimson velvet banner, its golden hammer and sickle shining in the sun. At the head of the procession, I marched through the Alley of the Fallen and out of the Memorial Park.

The ceremony over, the crowd of new Lenin Pioneers thinned rapidly. Many boarded buses taking them back to their remote districts. The rest left with their parents.

I lingered in the shade of a cypress tree. Blossoms waved at me from everywhere, shimmering with pearls of dew: purple clusters of hyacinths swelled across the flower beds; orange-red petals burst out of the pomegranate trees; bridal veils of silver-white jasmine wound near my feet, filling the air with the sweet scent of glory.

I had everything I'd ever wished for: my place in my Soviet Motherland and my other source of glory—my music. My piano.

One of Azerbaijan's rising star pianists, I was a week away from the final round of the national competitions. A win there would take me to Budapest to represent my country in my first international piano competition. The very thought of the future made everything look bigger and more vibrant. The glazed-blue sky stretched wide and uninterrupted except for a tiny chiffon cloud fluttering away. And my city sprawled around me—an ancient amphitheater descending all the way down to the turquoise of the Caspian Sea, with kilometers of golden sand beaches and boulevards of chestnut and cherry trees. I squinted and slowly, blissfully inhaled.

"You disappointed me, Leila."

The words hit me like hailstones. Comrade Farhad.

He was nineteen, four years older than me. Tall, with a full head of iron-black hair, the dark skin of a highlander, and deep-set eyes the color of a starless night. They could pin you to the ground. As could his words, always communicated in a loud, commanding voice. He spoke that way because he sometimes slipped into stuttering—a defect he had been working to overcome.

I first met him in the summer of 1978, when I arrived along with youth from the Pioneer Organization of Cuba at the seaside Camp Chaika, where Comrade Farhad worked as the head counselor. He welcomed us with a stirring speech at the opening flag ceremony, teaching us to become true masters of our lives, encouraging us to seek continuously the "next great Soviet purpose," and inspiring us to expand our needs beyond ourselves. Charismatic, dependable, and alluringly impervious, he seemed to embody my grandfather's revolutionary passion, the same passion that once ignited thousands of Azeri proletariat to follow my grandfather in the storming of the oil barons' bastions. Comrade Farhad definitely possessed the same magnetism. From that moment on, the girls could not stop talking about him, about how handsome and masculine he was.

A few days later, an accident happened in the camp. The underground gas reserve exploded, causing the structure that contained the kitchen and dining hall to collapse. Thankfully, it occurred in the early morning hours while the campers were still asleep in their cabins. Calm and self-controlled, Comrade Farhad immediately lined up the camp population by the flagpole. Everyone was accounted for, except for the cook's helper. Ordering us to stay in

10

place, he sprinted to the site of the explosion and returned a few minutes later with the injured old woman in his arms. She cried, chanting through her tears: "Allah give you joy and happiness. You saved my life, son."

Comrade Farhad had been elected Secretary of the 26 Baku Commissars District Komsomol Committee and in the evenings took classes at the Baku State University, majoring in the history of Communism. I was astonished when I received a phone call from him six months after I first met him. He introduced himself, asked unassumingly if I remembered him, and then invited me to join his committee as a junior member.

"You disappointed me, Leila," Comrade Farhad repeated. "Your deliverance of the pledge left me c-c-cold." The last word betrayed him, and a tinge of pink traveled across his face.

"But, Comrade Farhad, I practiced for months."

"Practicing is not enough. To be a true Communist, you must live and breathe the morals and principles of Communism."

I frantically retraced every word of the pledge, every emotion I experienced while delivering the lines. All seemed fine. I tried so hard to be the best, to rise to Comrade Farhad's expectations.

"I have a few minutes before the meeting at Baku City Hall," he said. "Walk along. We'll have a conversation. A vital conversation that will steer you in the right direction."

Comrade Farhad himself was going to walk with me. My eyes still swelled with tears, but my heart was dancing the *lazgi*.

We left the 26 Commissars Memorial Park, passed the Mirza Fatali Akhundov National Library, and turned toward Oilmen's Boulevard. All in silence. It was Saturday afternoon, and the streets were bustling. Barefoot boys played soccer in the middle of the road. An occasional car had to slow down to avoid running over the ball or hitting a kid. Some drivers cursed angrily at the boys; others stopped to watch the game and cheer the players. When the ball rolled close to Farhad, he unexpectedly charged ahead. With the dexterous skill of a soccer forward, he passed every player on his way, faked the goalie out of position, and kicked the ball. It rolled between two buckets that served as the goal. The crowd burst into applause. Comrade Farhad gave me a barely noticeable smile, and we continued. In silence. When was he going to start talking?

A foamy, cocoa-colored puddle spread across Zevin Street. A flock of women in chadors crouched down on the sidewalk. Shouting, laughing, rocking back and forth, they soaped a large Farsh rug decorated with camels chasing pheasants across its verdant field.

"You've missed two committee meetings this month," Comrade Farhad said. "Is there any explanation?"

"But, Comrade Farhad, haven't you read my letter?"

"What letter?"

I felt as if the warm wind Gilavar had just blown away the sand sinking beneath my feet. "The one in which I told you about the competition."

"What competition?"

"The Budapest International Piano Competition that will take place next March. And I'm one of the three finalists to compete for the honor to represent our republic."

"Oh, yes, I remember now. And I'm proud of your music accomplishment, Leila. But you can't use your music as an excuse to disregard your primary responsibilities—your Komsomol duties. And that's what I must talk to you about. Disloyalty starts with the small things—missing Komsomol meetings, wearing fancy jewelry with religious symbols."

Horrified, I checked my fingers for rings and my ears for earrings. Nothing.

Oh no! My ankle bracelet! A silver thread with a tiny blue bead—a *gozmunjughu*. A traditional Azeri guard against evil eye. I had it hidden inside my sock but the bead showed a little.

"And recently you've been posing and giggling in front of the cameras," Comrade Farhad said, his voice dripping with distaste. "Like some sort of a royalty...*an oil princess.*"

True. I *was* sort of oil royalty. That's exactly what Papa liked to call me—"my oil princess." But it never struck me as anything negative. The opposite, actually. My papa was one of the most important oilmen in Azerbaijan. He hunted for the treasured crude oil reserves beneath the Absheron peninsula. And whenever he found a new well and the oil fountain gushed up from under the ground, he brought me to the field to let me dip into the black gold and leave my handprints stamped forever on the derrick.

"The handprints of a future virtuoso, our own Fre-de-ric Cho-pin," Papa had said a week before when a TV news program taped the ceremonial opening of a newly discovered oil field. It sounded so funny the way Papa pronounced the name of my favorite composer and pianist—leisurely, one syllable at a time, as if reciting a poem. That's why I giggled, and the camera caught me.

"Playing piano and showing yourself off in public won't make you a valuable member of Soviet society. It won't," Comrade Farhad said. "Hard work and dedication will. You're a lucky girl, Leila. You come from a most illustrious family of highly accomplished Communists. Your oilman father. Your mother, the surgeon. Your grandfather, Honorable Comrade Badalbeili. How many people do you think have a street in Baku named after their grandfather? Very few can pride themselves in having such an advantageous upbringing."

I could hear a trace of sadness in Comrade Farhad's voice. I knew nothing about his family, other than that he was born in an *aul*, a mountain village, and raised by an aunt in a communal apartment in Black City, Baku's industrial neighborhood. And through every season, he wore the same pair of black trousers, shiny from too many pressings.

A wave of guilt swept over me. "Comrade Farhad, more than anything else I'd like to prove my worth to society. Please give me a chance."

He stopped, his eyes narrowed, evaluating me. The whiff of Papa's aftershave reached my nose. The sign of masculinity, just like the black specks of beard around his lips. I drew it all in, stealthily, little by little, until I felt like a sprout bursting out of its sheath.

"All right. I will give you a task. A very important task." Comrade Farhad unlocked his briefcase and rummaged inside until he retrieved a yellow notebook. He leafed through the pages. "Here it is. Listen attentively. A few blocks from here, in Old Town, a new shop opened last week. The one with the green door. Near the Maiden Tower. The address: 33 Ashuglar Street. I've received an urgent warning that the owner is an American mole. And the shop is a cover-up for anti-Soviet activities. The mole uses a highly sophisticated scheme to lure in the youth of our neighborhood, contaminate them, and then spread the cancer throughout our city. We must stop him."

To catch and expose a Western spy—there was no higher feat for a Soviet citizen. We knew the Americans had their secret cells planted in our society, posing as merchants, teachers, even members of the Communist Party. They lurked, waiting for the first opportunity to strike. That's why we always had to be on guard, watch vigilantly for any suspicious behavior, and report it to the authorities. Now I had a real chance to trap an American vermin and become a hero. To rise to Comrade Farhad's expectations. To impress him.

On the other hand, an assignment of such magnitude could distract me from my preparation for the piano competition in Budapest. I dithered, shifting from foot to foot, my heart beating inside my ears. What to do?

Comrade Farhad, tapping his fingers on his thigh, let out a sigh of impatience.

I lifted my hand in salutation. "I swear to show myself deserving of the special task you've given me."

He returned the salutation. "This is the chance you've asked for. This is your chance to regain my trust. Report to me every Tuesday. Congratulations. The mission is yours."

He shook my hand, squeezing my fingers in a firm grip. Leaving my palm slightly wet. "See you around, Leila."

Poised and assertive, planting his feet in wide steps, he crossed busy Communist Street and disappeared inside the lace arch of Baku

City Hall. But not before throwing a furtive look back at me over his shoulder.

Inspired, I wanted to act right away. To prove to the whole world that I was worthy of Comrade Farhad's choice. The clock on Baku City Hall showed quarter to two. I had more than two hours before my piano lesson. And Maiden Tower, with its nest of anti-Soviet activities, was just around the corner.

The jagged edges of Maiden Tower's crown cut into the sky.

A creepy, damned place. Baku folklore had it that the old woman who lived in the Tower's basement and took care of the grounds was the maimed soul of one of the maidens imprisoned by the Shah of Darkness a thousand years ago. People called her the Immortal.

The legend said that if the Immortal's eyes should meet mine, I would first lose my hair. Then I would go blind. At the end, I would inherit her damnation—be buried alive.

I had never actually seen her. Those few who did claimed the Immortal had rooster-like yellow eyes emitting dreadful flames.

Thankfully, my destination—33 Ashuglar Street—was located a few blocks before Maiden Tower. I spotted it at once.

A screamingly green door. As if someone had hurled a bucket of paint from afar, leaving a fat blot in the middle and random splatters thrusting their clutches around the door like the tentacles of a giant sea monster.

A shoe merchant exited next door, carrying a large basket loaded with traditional Azeri leather-and-brocade slip-ons, *charigs*, their curled-up toes gleaming in the sun like precious gems. He placed the basket in the middle of the sidewalk, retrieved a pack of Kazbek cigarettes from his trousers, and stuck one between his teeth. Striking a match against the wall, he lit his Kazbek, leaned against the threshold of his store, and stared in my direction.

On a narrow, busy street in broad daylight—where could I hide? I slowed down, settling into the tempo of the "Adagio sostenuto" from Beethoven's *Moonlight Sonata*. I planted my steps in rhythm with its lamenting melody, stopping at the end of every eighth measure to look at store windows. All the while, I kept my focus on the green door.

What was inside? What did a spy's nest look like? A dark basement with a single bulb swinging from the ceiling? A figure hunched over an iron desk, turning the knobs of his radio, transmitting our top national secrets to his handlers in America? Did he have a gun?

I kept ambling back and forth…back and forth…while watching cautiously for any sign of action around the green door.

There was none. Merchants from adjacent shops and their customers all went about their own business. No one but me seemed to care about 33 Ashuglar Street.

Instead, I was gradually becoming the center of attention. Negative attention. The men seated under the vines of the *chaikhana*, teahouse, smacked their greasy lips with a vulgar *tztztz* and cackled every time I passed by. A fat grocer with a shaved head and black stubble on his face threw a lewd three-finger gesture at me and whispered, "Hey, *gözəllik*, beauty, come to my basement. I give you ten rubles." And he rubbed his crotch.

I darted away, crossed the street, and entered a fabric store. There I found a surveillance spot behind a shelf piled with silks. I examined the fabric bolts slowly, one at a time, unfolding them, feeling the texture, laying the silks against my skin without taking my eyes off the target.

It didn't take long before the green door opened, and a young man stepped out.

No, he was too young to be called a *man*. More like a lanky teenager, with long, wavy chestnut hair reaching his shoulders. The way he was dressed—in dirt-streaked, bell-bottom jeans and a loose white shirt embroidered with flowers—made him look like a foreigner and completely out of place on a Baku street. What a strange way for an undercover agent to disguise himself. Wasn't a spy supposed to blend in with the environment?

The boy closed the door behind him and remained still for a

moment, deep in thought, as if making sure he hadn't forgotten anything. His face—thin and sun-kissed—seemed strangely familiar. A high forehead, a few stubborn curls hanging over his large, deep-set eyes, thick eyebrows, as if sketched in one sweeping stroke of charcoal, reaching from the bridge of his nose to the edges of his temples. And the wide, slightly asymmetrical mouth, moving in some silent dialogue the boy was having with himself, adding a touch of quirkiness to his refined, intelligent face.

I had definitely seen him. But where?

"Are you looking to buy a silk *parça*, *qız*?"

A middle-aged saleswoman with henna-dyed red hair rushed toward me, a servile smile on her face. Before I had a chance to say no, she tugged on the end of one of the rolls, and a waterfall of cerulean and indigo silk poured onto the floor in shining folds.

"Made for your skin, *qız*. Swear, as if you were my own daughter. Buy five meters and sew a dress with a long, pleated skirt. Boys will sweep the floor under your feet with their eyelashes, take Allah as my witness. Are you listening, *qız*? Or are you counting flies in the air?" The saleswoman pursed her lips.

"I'm, uh, sorry, but I'm not looking to buy. I don't have money with me today."

"*Sonra mənim vaxt sərf etməyin.* Then do not waste my time." She waved her hand dismissively.

Outside, the boy was walking away, his bare feet slapping against the pavement, raising little puffs of dust. He stopped at the *kutabkhana*, bought a pile of steaming *kutabs*—crepes filled with meat and herbs, took a huge bite, and disappeared around the corner.

I decided to take my time and count to ten. *One, two, three...* With each count I became more energized, driven by the significance of my task. Before I reached *seven*, I charged across the street, slightly opened the green door, and squeezed through.

The door slammed shut behind me with a sinister D-F-G-flat triad. Too fast. Too tight. Darkness splashed into my eyes and drew me into a bottomless hollow of night. Was it a trap?

Something flickered in the distance, dressing the darkness in a soft veil of blue. Out of the blue came an explosion of sounds followed by the seamlessly expressed melancholy of Chopin's "Ballade no. 1." My fingers traced the melody on an invisible keyboard—my usual way to connect with the music, to feel its emotions on my fingertips. I touched the keys softly, as if gliding my hands through water, but the musical notes kept slipping between my fingers like bubbles, waltzing away in the blue radiance.

My hands brushed against the walls as I moved through a long, narrow corridor. Three steps down, the corridor opened into a small room, its floor and walls overlaid with ancient rugs, their diamonds, rosettes, and sprays of vine spinning in a slow trance.

A Rapsodija radio gramophone, the source of Chopin's nostalgic "Ballade no. 1," rested its bulk on four skinny legs. A tamed fire dragon waved feeble tongues behind the iron screen of the hearth, adding to the illusion of timeless harmony reigning in the air, fragrant with something sweet and tangy. Black currant maybe?

Leaning against the wall, Leonardo da Vinci's *Mona Lisa* smiled at me, alive with the shadows of the dancing fire dragon. I came closer. The painting *did* look like *Mona Lisa*, except there was no landscape in the background. Only bare canvas, placed on a table next to an oil lamp with a tear-shaped glass.

Piles of books covered the rest of the table. The books looked as old as the rugs, proudly wearing frayed leather and gold bindings. One of them, a large volume, lay open. In the dim light, calligraphic verses written in Azeri curled across the pages like coral snakes. Underneath the verses were faded Islamic miniatures depicting Layla and Majnun. I leafed through the book, a legendary twelfth-century love şer penned by Azerbaijani poet Nizami Ganjavi.

"Young and innocent, they savored the violet-scented wine of first love and became deeply intoxicated… Oh, first love's wine, how can any heart resist your bittersweet taste…"

I picked up another book wrapped with a leather flap and released the flap carefully. It was a sketchbook with images of old

Baku streets, painted in brilliant colors, entwined with gold, surrounded by exquisite calligraphy. Under one of the miniatures—of
Maiden Tower—a few handwritten lines:

> *Once upon a time, when the evil spirit of darkness reigned*
> *over the Land of Azerbaijan, hiding the sun inside his*
> *underground caves,*
> *When the orphan sky peered at the Caucasus Mountains from*
> *the black dome of sorrow,*
> *When the rain shed its tears of ice upon the barren earth...*

A ghazel. As suspended in time as the rest of the room. Was this
really a spy's nest? Or was I inside some medieval troubadour's castle
that had been locked away from the world for centuries?

A glissando, three dreamy chords, and the spectacular finale of
Chopin's "Ballade no. 1." Then silence, invaded only by the crackling fire and the whispering of the turntable's needle against the
recording. I tiptoed to the gramophone to turn it off, stopping in
a slim alcove stacked floor to ceiling with music albums. Rows and
rows of them, neatly lined up against the wall. One album in front
had a dated photograph of a handsome young man in a tuxedo on
its cover and the title written in English: *Vladimir Horowitz Plays
Chopin*. The album sleeve was empty. I hesitated, then slipped it
inside my bag as material evidence of the American connection.

Time to leave. I dashed through the corridor, grabbed the
doorknob, threw the door wide open, and—*Allaha şükür!* Thank
God!—almost fell on my face in sun-splashed Ashuglar Street.

CHAPTER 3

I made it just in time for my piano lesson.

Not good enough. According to Professor Sultan-zade, to be "just in time" was about as good as not being there at all. She wanted her students outside her rehearsal room at least a half hour early. Like lambs waiting to be slaughtered, we paced between the marble bust of Comrade Lenin and the iron railing with the winged horses, listening to the broken musical passages, occasional slaps, and angry shrieks flying out of her lesson-in-progress, guessing which one of her torture techniques she would inflict on us today.

Professor Sultan-zade, the chair of the piano department of the Baku Conservatory of Music, was a dedicated advocate of Soviet pedagogy based on the motto of a former Russian Empire generalissimo, Alexander Suvorov: "Hard training, easy combat." In affirmation of her hard training, her students had been steadily gathering prizes at competitions all over the world. I was accepted into her class at the age of ten after winning second place in a regional competition and being classified as a "potential national treasure."

The Soviet Union did treasure its classical musicians and ballet stars above all other achievers. Sergei Prokofiev, Dmitri Shostakovich, Aram Khachaturian, Sviatoslav Richter, and the prima ballerina of the Bolshoi Theater, Maya Plisetskaya. All highly revered by the Kremlin and the Soviet people, they formed the cultural Olympus of our society. It had become my goal to reach that summit, and to do so I had learned to sacrifice.

Four hours of daily piano practice left me out of the social life in my old school, and I graduated from the eighth grade with neither friends nor the skill of making them. Last autumn, I began my first year at the specialized Asaf Zeynally Music College, where the education catered to the individual music talents of its students. The academic subjects, even though obligatory, had been moved into the background. In my case, the fact that Professor Sultan-zade herself had taken me under her wing meant even fewer academic demands—flexible attendance in classes and almost guaranteed good grades.

I mounted the long, oval staircase and rushed to the rehearsal room. Ear to the leather-upholstered door, I heard nothing but daunting silence. The previous student, a girl with a flat round face that seemed on fire every time she exited the room, had gone. I waited a few seconds for the clock to announce four thirty, took a deep breath, and knocked on the door.

"You may come in, Leila."

Professor Sultan-zade, tall and arid in her usual dark maroon dress, black stockings, and hair pulled back in a bun, leaned against the wide-open window. The smoke from her cigarette danced with the breeze in and out of the room.

"You obviously had important business to attend to," she said sternly.

"I…I was actually here, waiting to come in."

"Czerny, *The Art of Finger Dexterity*." She pronounced her verdict, took another puff of the cigarette, and turned away as if she had lost interest in me.

For the next hour and a half I played Karl Czerny's fifty most difficult études, addressing every aspect of piano technique—clear passages, chords, double octaves. I actually loved those études, because in them, unlike most of the piano material used for the development of technique, I had found inner dynamics and understated beauty.

But Karl Czerny wasn't the instrument of torture. The metronome was. Every time Professor Sultan-zade finished with a cigarette, she threw the butt out the window, lumbered to the piano, her stilettos screeching with every step like unworn military boots, and slid the weight down the pendulum rod to speed the metronome up to the next tempo. By the time I reached "Étude no. 33," with its arpeggios in the left hand and chords in the right, I couldn't even look at my hands. I felt dizzy.

"Good effort today." Professor Sultan-zade patted my shoulder at the end of the lesson, my wrists swollen and my fingers burning as if they had crossed the Sahara Desert.

"Excuse me, Professor." I retrieved the empty American album sleeve. "Today, I heard the most remarkable interpretation of Chopin's 'Ballade no. 1.'"

"Who is the artist?"

"Vladimir Horowitz," I read.

"*That person* was a traitor," she whispered, her mouth so tight it looked like an old scar. "If you want to have a career in music—and you very well might have one—then don't be stupid. *Never* tell anyone what you just told me. And I'd better call your parents too."

She grabbed the album cover from my hands and threw it into the fire.

Why would Professor Sultan-zade, who treated every written or recorded musical note as life's most precious gift, burn Chopin's album? What harm could Chopin's music cause, even being played by a very bad person?

On my way home, I rehearsed the explanation I would give to my parents. How Comrade Farhad gave me an assignment and how I took my chances and went behind the green door.

And the things I wouldn't tell them about. The way Chopin's "Ballade" made me feel, Mona Lisa's painting, the boy…

Aladdin.

Yes. That was it. He looked exactly like Aladdin—slender and boyishly agile, with long, curly brown hair, almond-shaped sapphire eyes, a faraway look on his thin face. A barefoot alien from the past.

As I turned onto my street, I heard the familiar *şikayətlər*, complaints.

"What have I done, Allah, to deserve your curse?"

Aunty Zeinab. In her usual place—in the middle of our court-yard, next to the lemon tree. Her hands on the tops of her massive hips, the layers of skin on her neck folding and unfolding like the bellows of an accordion, she cried to the heavens: "Why did you give me a donkey for a husband? Why? The son of a whore is a drunkard, a gambler, and an adulterer. Let him fall in a pit and die."

Aunty Zeinab could be a tigress, but her heart was made of sweet jasmine *şərbət*, syrup. We were not blood-related, but our families had a fifteen-year history together, going back to a day in the delivery room of the Baku Railway Hospital. My mama had just finished giving birth to me when she spotted a blue, motionless baby thrown on a waste tray for hopeless newborns. The only medical staff, a tired midwife, hovered over unconscious Aunty Zeinab, choosing to save her over the baby. Mama cut my umbilical cord, slid off the surgical table, reached for the newborn, and began spanking, rubbing, and twisting her until the baby inhaled her first breath and joined me in a scream. With two dark, hairy infants in her arms, Mama stumbled to Aunty Zeinab's table.

"Which one is mine? They look the same," Aunty Zeinab cried.

Mama studied the babies, realized that she didn't have the answer, and fainted next to Aunty Zeinab. Later, she recalled seeing a beauty mark above my belly button before cutting the cord. How many times had we heard that story?

Mama didn't have milk so Aunty Zeinab insisted on nursing me. Every morning she took two tram rides from her tiny communal dwelling on the edge of the city to come to us. Luckily, an apartment downstairs in our building became vacant, and my papa, using his connections within City Hall, secured it for Aunty Zeinab's family.

"Good evening, Aunty," I said, hoping to sneak past her. It was a custom to call our family's close friends aunts and uncles.

"Daughter, sweet daughter of my heart." Aunt Zeinab clutched me in a hug, pressed against her soft belly. From under her arm, I noted Uncle Zohrab, her husband, peeking from behind the kilim that hung at the entrance to their apartment. Taking his chances, he tiptoed behind Aunt Zeinab's back and out of the courtyard.

I loved Uncle Zohrab. One quarter the size of his wife, with a smile that never left his face, he was kind and caring; he'd never even hurt a lizard. Zeinab and Zohrab were second cousins, and they continued a family tradition of artisanship that started almost five hundred years ago with the creation of masks for medieval mystical spectacles, later shifting to doll making for *kilim arasi*—puppet shows played between folded carpets.

I loved watching them work. With his large, robust hands, Uncle Zohrab mixed clay and water into a paste, molded and fired the paste into unglazed porcelain figures, and applied skin color to each. And when they lay on the table, indifferent and cold, Uncle Zohrab's hands performed magic—illuminating the porcelain figures' faces with exquisitely human expressions.

Then Aunty Zeinab dressed the dolls in traditional Azerbaijani costumes—silk pantaloons and chemises, velvet skirts trimmed with golden braid, brocaded knitted jackets, chiffon veils, bracelets, buttons, and pendants made from gems, copper, and silver. Their bisque dolls were national treasures, exhibited and exported to the West. We heard that only millionaires there could buy them.

But their masterpiece, Almaz the Doll, stayed home in the permanent display at the Baku Museum of Fine Arts. With her emerald eyes, smooth olive skin, and fiery red hair, she was a precise replica of their daughter, Almaz, my milk sister, whose life Mama had saved.

Gently, I squirmed out of Aunty Zeinab's embrace. "Aunty, is Almaz home?"

"Yes, rose petal, she is. With Allah's help, how have you grown to be your noble parents' pride, while my flesh-and-blood is nothing but a gossipy thorn?"

"Gossipy" was exactly why I needed to see Almaz. As Aunty Zeinab liked to say, "Before a rooster started his crow in the faraway Khizi Mountains, Almaz already knows how many eggs his hens have laid."

Almaz and I grew up inseparable, sharing our secrets and dreams. We learned to swim in the Caspian Sea and to climb Besh Barmag, the sacred Five Finger Mountain. A pair of *jorabs*, multicolored socks, everyone called us.

And then she changed. Overnight. Changed so drastically that I thought a wicked dervish had stolen the best friend of my childhood and replaced her with a vain, empty-headed double. Our paths diverged. While I divided my passion and time between my Komsomol responsibilities and my music, Almaz sweltered in the Turkish baths, gathering gossip. She even became bored with studies and dropped out of school after the eighth grade. Mama came to help, enrolling her in a prestigious nursing program that would provide her with useful skills.

Maybe the change was the result of Almaz's bad birth. She suffered from epilepsy. Twice I witnessed her shaking as violently as if possessed by witchcraft. Mama even taught me how to prevent her from choking during the convulsions.

I moved the kilim aside. "Can I come in?"

Inside, the air was humid, the floor wet. Almaz sat astride a towel on the kitchen table, painting her toenails cherry-red, her long, damp hair spilling over her bronzed back and bare breasts. She had nothing on but a pair of black panties trimmed with red lace. A henna snake coiled around her leg all the way to the knee.

"How was your date?" she asked without lifting her head.

"How do you know?"

"The whole town knows." She paused and scratched her temple with the tip of a red thumbnail. "A match made in Communist heaven. Comrade Leila and Comrade *Aži Dahāka*."

Aži Dahāka—a mythical serpent-dragon that spits out fire—was a nickname Almaz gave to Farhad after she heard him speak at a Komsomol rally.

She was jealous. I would be too if I was in her place. Six months ago, Aunty Zeinab surprised all of us when she betrothed Almaz to Chingiz from the third floor, a beanpole with gold teeth, an unevenly shaved pea-sized head, and lethargic cow eyes. He loitered around the neighborhood, the sleeves of his nylon shirt rolled up high, trying to look like a diligent laborer. In truth, he hadn't worked a single day in his entire twenty-five years and lived shamelessly off his childless uncle, Ali Khan. Like a flatworm.

"I need to ask you a question," I said.

"Wait." Almaz blew on her toes. "What is it?"

"Have you heard anything about the new shop near Maiden Tower with the green door and—"

Like an iguana, she slid off the table, scurried toward me, and sealed my mouth with her hand, the beads on her bracelet pressing hard against my cheek. "Where have you been? The whole city has been talking about it. It's a *music shop*. But not for real. The owner is an offspring of the Immortal."

"The Immortal?" My heart dropped.

"Yes, can you believe it? And just like her, he is a wicked sorcerer. He sells poisonous music records from the black market." Almaz's eyes glistened darkly, her voice lowered to a whisper. "If you listen to his music, your skin will turn into fish scales."

Clusters of dirty clouds raced across the starless sky like a pack of hounds loosed from their chains. I counted the steps; only sixty-three to go along the narrow balcony and then up the stairs to our apartment on the fourth floor. But there was definitely someone following me.

The Immortal?

27

I glanced back. Nothing except my shadow trailing behind. Was it fear that made me feel as if my shadow was improvising? Stepping on my feet, trotting ahead of me, crawling up the walls, slowly enclosing me. The words of an ancient curse whispered in my head, turning to acid in my stomach.

From the dome of a moonless sky
The dead maiden's evil eye
Casts a spell upon a soul
Who wanders all alone.

The Immortal's hex. A punishment for entering the green door.

In panic, scared of my own shadow, I ran toward a tiny beam of light flickering at the end of the balcony where, to my total humiliation, I bumped into Chingiz. He leaned on the railing, smoking a cigarette.

"Is somebody after you?" He puffed smoke into my face.

"Nobody."

"Nobody means—a ghost. So you've been running from a ghost. Oh, there she is."

I anxiously turned in the direction of his pointed finger.

"Got you!" He soundly slapped his thigh and brayed like a donkey. His gold teeth glowed in the night, and his eyes ogled me with a malignant, unmovable stare.

I dipped into my pocket to retrieve the key and opened the door to our apartment. Actually two doors. An exterior heavy oak door identical to those of the rest of the apartments. And a bunker door, as I called it. A year ago, Papa brought a brigade of workers who spent an entire week setting the solid steel door and fortifying it with German locks and bolts sturdy enough to protect the treasures of the Hermitage Museum.

It may not have been the Hermitage, but our apartment did resemble a museum. The largest unit in the building, it had four rooms altogether: a sitting room with a vaulted ceiling and arabesque tapestries on the walls; my parents' boudoir, furnished with the Versailles bedroom set of Louis XVI (not the real one, of course, but a magnificent handmade replica); my room, airy with a balcony, split by a screen into a bedroom and my music rehearsal space; and Papa's pride, the smoking room.

It was filled with so many interesting things: his X-shaped wood-and-brass throne with an eagle's head, perched on carved lion's feet, a dragon-wrapped chandelier, emitting shadows instead of light—a gift from Chairman Mao in 1973 when Papa visited China with a Soviet delegation; a dagger studded with massive rubies, suspended in front of a Persian rug hanging against the wall. Papa liked to joke that he had found it in Genghis Khan's hidden tomb.

With Papa, I never knew if he was joking or not. He was an avid—no, compulsive—collector. He hunted his treasures the way he hunted his oil reserves. Fanatically. But if you asked him, he'd just shrug and laugh. *A little hobby*, he called it. And why the bunker door? *Just to keep safe the biggest treasures of my life, my beautiful wife and daughter.*

Why did my family live in such luxury? Why was my papa allowed to acquire and display his riches instead of using them for the common good? Why did I myself preach the equality of our Communist society to the younger generation?

Because that was the normal way of life in Soviet Azerbaijan, something I never would have thought of questioning. There were common citizens and there was *Nomenklatura*—the ruling class of Communist Party members, who held key positions in government, industry, and culture. To become a part of *Nomenklatura* was an ultimate ambition of every Soviet citizen.

I was born into it.

"I thought we'd miss you," Mama said without taking her eyes off her mirror. Dressed in a beige evening suit, she was applying her neutral lipstick. Her only fake means of beautification, as she called it. She didn't need more. Her natural colors mixed into a bouquet of spring. She had the eyes of the morning sky, and the sun seemed to get stuck in the silk of her hair. Today she allowed it to swing freely in the air. So different from her usual professional hairdo—a braid wrapped around the top of her head designed to add a sense of gravity to her youthful face with its skin as transparent as Carrara marble.

I had received none of Mama's gifts, except for her petite frame. I was all Papa's daughter. Our hair was as black and stubborn as mattress springs. We usually wore out at least one ivory comb a month. Mama bought the combs a dozen at a time at a small shop on Torgovaya Street. The owner, an Armenian craftsman with a bald, pear-shaped head, always swore the next batch of his combs would last a lifetime. But I didn't believe it. I doubted there was an elephant romping through the jungle anywhere with tusks strong enough to tame our hair.

"What happened today?" Mama dropped the lipstick into her snakeskin clutch, snapped it shut, and raised her eyes at me. She spoke with a flat voice, usually reserved for a negligent nurse or the reckless parent of a little patient. "So, Leila, what have you gotten yourself into?"

"Nothing to worry about, *Mamochka*. It's about a Komsomol assignment."

"An assignment that involves carrying anti-Soviet material?"

"Of course not. I mean yes. The anti-Soviet material is the evidence. You see, Comrade Farhad has chosen me for this very, very important task."

"What kind of important task?" Papa came in, freshly shaved, wearing a linen suit and his signature canary tie. He was as dark as if he bathed daily in a Baku oil well. His mane still shone inky black, but a gray mouse had run through his square-shaped little mustache. Tall and trim, he resembled the cypress tree outside my window, swaying in rhythm with the wind, grasping the essence of the earth with its powerful roots.

"It's a secret, Papa."

"Secret? Secret between you and Comrade Farhad?" Papa poured himself a cognac from the bar and took a sip from his glass. "I like the fellow," he said, enjoying his drink. "He's ambitious, knows what he wants and how to get it. Who knows, maybe someday you'll make a nice couple. I wouldn't mind having a son like Farhad."

Papa winked, wrapped his free arm around me, and plopped a kiss on the top of my head. I drew in the aroma of Papa's tobacco mixed with cologne, the same cologne I'd detected on Comrade Farhad earlier. My head spun a little.

"Don't plant those seeds in her head," Mama said with an air of casualness, but I could tell by the presence of a low overtone in her voice that Papa's words had struck a wrong chord.

She slipped into her new pumps, exactly the same shade as her suit—always a perfectionist—and turned to me. "Your Komsomol commitments are vital and beneficial, but your music comes first. Don't get distracted from your piano practice, no matter how wonderful Comrade Farhad is and how important his assignment is. You hear me?"

"I can handle it all. Don't worry. Where are you going?"

"Comrade Bagirov's nephew's engagement." Papa rolled his eyes and twitched his head in Mama's direction. "It's all part of being married to a celebrity."

Half joke. No one doubted who wore the tiara of celebrity in the family, but Papa did feel proud of Mama's accomplishments. She was one of just a handful of women to rise in a society in which women, even though they had taken off their chadors—black Islamic veils of modesty—fifty years ago, still very much lived in the shadows of their husbands, with their triumphs limited to the kitchen. As a *hekim*—a surgeon-healer—with a heart of gold and hands of silk, Mama was a well-known person. On the streets of Baku, total strangers rushed over to her, breaking into tears, kissing her hands, blessing her over and over for bringing their little loved ones back to life.

Mama grew up in an orphanage in a small village and came to Baku to study medicine at the Academy. She supported herself by working as a cleaning nurse at the hospital—the same hospital where she would later become the head of the pediatric surgery department. Papa, the only son of Azerbaijan's great Communist hero, spent his childhood in our fancy apartment, raised by his widowed mother.

They met in the emergency room where Mama was doing her medical internship and where Papa was delivered with a brain concussion, several broken bones, and cuts all over his body, the result of a motorcycle crash. They got married a month later. "Your mama tamed the wild beast in me," Papa liked to complain. She did, for the most part. But Papa still had quite an explosive temper. A common joke among his friends was that he owed his success in discovering new oil fields to the power of a roar that could shake the earth and make fountains of oil spurt from under the ground.

"The usual story." Papa creased his forehead and raised one bushy eyebrow then the other so they seemed to leap off his face. "Your mama gets invited, and I tag along. I'm just a chauffeur here."

"Is that why you are wearing a linen jacket to a black-tie party?" Mama played along.

Safe territory. Papa liked being different. Liked to disregard and even break rules and traditions, as if still rebelling against the Black Widow, as Mama called his mother. An old woman in black who never smiled and pinched my forearm every time I attempted to laugh—that's how I remembered her. She died before I turned six.

Her oval photograph hung in Papa's smoking room between two pictures of her husband, Comrade Badalbeili. In one of them, my grandfather, still nearly a boy, rode a big white horse at the head of the Bolshevik brigade in 1920. In the other photograph, taken in 1943, he resembled Generalissimo Stalin. The same thick mustache and a general's trench coat with a row of medals and orders.

Unlike my ideologically zealous grandfather, my parents were *social* Communists. Highly dedicated members of the Party, they worked tirelessly in their professional capacities on behalf of our country. Deep inside, I always questioned whether their

Communism was anything more than a comfortable and gratifying routine, a way of maintaining a status-filled life in their social and professional establishments.

"I cooked your favorite *chykhyrtma*." Papa pressed his fingers together and brought them to his mouth. "Ummm...delicious."

"Thank you, *Papochka*."

"Anything for you, *qızım*. Whatever you need, just ask your papa."

He finished the cognac, wiped his mustache with the back of his hand, and scooped me in his arms. "I love you, my precious *brilyant*, my diamond," he said, kissing me on the forehead and rubbing his scratchy cheek against mine.

"I'm ready, Mekhti. Let's go." Mama wrapped a silk *kelegayi*, scarf, around her shoulders. "And you, Leila, don't waste precious time. Warm up dinner and get to your practicing."

Sometimes I thought she envied my closeness with Papa. But every time I tried to tell her how much I loved her, she stopped me: "The more you say 'I love you,' the less you mean it. Words are cheap."

Cheap or not, I yearned for them.

Mama followed Papa to the door, trailing her inimitable scent of lilacs. When I was little, I used to climb in her bed after she had left and squash my face against the softness of her pillow. It felt like rolling on a warm spring day into a valley of lavender lilacs, still slightly moist from the fresh touch of the rain.

How much I wanted to put my arms around her and feel—even for a moment—that she was right here with me and not in surgery or at her parties.

"And don't wait for us. We'll be late." Mama closed the door.

I warmed Papa's *chykhyrtma*—a chunk of lamb stewed with zesty bouillon—and filled my bowl to the brim. Careful not to spill any on our sparkling ebony floor, I carried it to the balcony.

Clouds had cleared from the sky. The half-moon swayed in its cradle. The deserted part of our building loomed before me, its limestone turrets resembling the bows of a fairy-tale ship sailing across the starlit sky.

How many evenings had Almaz and I spent here alone with our dreams, imagining the invisible, magical world of Peri-faced princesses and lion-skinned knights?

In the sanctuary of the night, we practiced our witchcraft, spinning a piece of broken carafe to hear the voices of the dead and drinking a magical *sehrli* potion to read our destiny in the quicksilver of the stars. And as the city below lay drunk with sleep, we flew to the Desert of the Blind Dervish to swirl in the flames of the earth and receive our mystic powers from the Zoroastrian fire.

"Hey, I'm back," I greeted the headless gargoyle sitting on my balcony. The stone creature with wings spread wide had given our building its name: Gargoyle Castle. And it did look like a real castle. Soaring horseshoe arches draped its facade. Limestone *muqarnas* decorations hung like stalactites from the vaulted ceiling in the atrium. And marble cherubs danced atop the remains of a Baroque fountain in the middle of our courtyard.

One summer night when Almaz and I were nine years old, we cleaned up the fountain and carried bucket after bucket to fill it with water. Then we lounged on the marble balustrade, soaking our feet, gliding the soles back and forth across the smooth Moorish tile of the sky blue, sea green mosaic. Staring at the object of our infinite fascination: the faded fresco image of a fair-haired princess in an azure gown with a gazelle resting at her feet and a vermilion-colored bird perched in her lap. The Snow Princess.

Rumor had it that she was the daughter of the oil baron who had built our Gargoyle Castle to win the heart of his beloved from a faraway land. I still had a Snow Princess dress hanging in my wardrobe, one of two that Aunty Zeinab had made for Almaz and me for the New Year's Eve masquerade of 1973. Blue satin cloth with short, puffed sleeves and a flared skirt with a hem of sparkling tulle. She even crafted stuffed animals—a gazelle for Almaz and a bird for me.

I gobbled my dinner, listening to the noise of the city as it gradually surrendered to the harmony of the night and peeking into a brightly lit window across the street where a family was having dinner together. I felt the usual sting of loneliness.

"Time for piano practice." I patted the broken wing of my gargoyle. "The more I practice, the better pianist I become. And soon…"

I closed my eyes, visualizing myself in a shimmering dress on the stage of Franz Liszt Academy of Music, gliding to the piano, waiting for the orchestra conductor's call to action. Oh, how I loved the thrill of the stage!

"If I win in the Budapest piano competition—right after that I'll be playing in the Chopin piano competition in Warsaw. And then the most important of them all—the International Tchaikovsky Competition in Moscow. To win! Always win!"

The glorious maestoso of ascending chords in the main theme of Pyotr Tchaikovsky's *Piano Concerto no. 1* resonated inside my soul, igniting the cascade of fireworks across the sky of my future. The sky within my reach.

"Thanks for keeping me company." I gave a slight bow to my gargoyle, went inside, and closed the balcony door.

By now my music room was completely dark, its stillness assaulted only by a ticking clock. *Ticktock…ticktock…* Tiny arrows were flying out of the old gilded timepiece that hung over my baby grand Bösendorfer.

I had to focus on the "Rondo," the third movement of Beethoven's *Sonata Pathétique*, the piece I was going to play at Saturday's recital.

But first, I needed to try something. I lifted the lid of my piano, settled on the bench, and closed my eyes, evoking the nostalgic mood of Chopin's "Ballade no. 1" in Vladimir Horowitz's rendition.

The opening Neapolitan A-flat major chord set the majestic aura for the first theme, a song of the wind sweeping over the nocturnal sea. A shy moon peered through smoked glass, the pearl of her face in a blur. Agate clouds sailed solemnly across the sky, chasing a lone seagull. The wind picked up the tempo, blowing at the sea, raising the waves all the way to the sky, building up to a thundering *presto con fuoco*. A breath of silence—until the storm erupted into a fiery double-octave scale plummeting all the way down my keyboard.

Immersed in Chopin's melancholy, I played the "Ballade" along with the traitor Vladimir Horowitz, again and again, pouring my loneliness into the music. Knowing even then, in my very young, fifteen-year-old heart, that it wasn't Comrade Farhad's assignment that had brought me to the green room.

It was destiny.

CHAPTER 4

The next day I returned to Ashuglar Street. Nothing had changed. The same cast of grungy characters. A few *tztztz* followed me as I passed the *chaikhana*, and the fat grocer saluted me with his lewd three-fingered proposition. I went straight to the green door, pressed forward, and stepped inside.

Before my eyes could adjust to the darkness, I heard, "*Salam eleykum*, peace be upon you, sunshine. Which of the winds should I praise for bringing you to my temple of music?"

I peered through the dim light, trying to locate the source of the high, melodious voice. And there he was.

Aladdin, wearing a dervish turban and a white tunic, seated cross-legged on a dark burgundy Afghani rug that seemed to float between clouds of smoke. The same boy I had seen the day before. But he didn't look like a carefree Aladdin today. More like an Aladdin who had lost his magic lamp and didn't even care. His face looked ghostly in the amber glow of an oil lamp. A cigarette dangled from the lower lip of his mouth. And his almond-shaped eyes could hardly accommodate two terribly dilated pupils.

So that's what it was—that sweet scent of black currant. Hashish.

The boy-man in front of me was a hash head. A junkie. I turned to leave.

"Oh no. Don't go." Rising from the rug, he leaped across his grotto like a gazelle, planting himself next to me, blocking my escape with his arm across the threshold. "Don't leave. I'm not going to bite you."

He chewed on a cigarette, his eyes wide open, struggling to keep me in their focus. The task seemed to exhaust him. He removed his arm from the threshold and sagged back against the wall, tapping his fingers on his thighs. Rhythmically.

"Camille Saint-Saëns—*Danse Macabre*," he said. "The xylophone plays the dance of rattling bones. And here's the devil's interval." He made a loop with his hand in the air as if conducting the orchestra. "Fun, ha? I dig music, not little girls. You're totally safe with me here. The real monsters"—he squinted and jerked his head toward the door—"the real monsters are out there. So what's your name, sunshine?"

I hesitated. "Leila."

"'A dark-haired beauty bathing in moonlight, her olive skin as smooth as the touch of the sea, a thousand silver stars reflecting in her smile.'"

An ancient verse depicting the meaning of my name.

"How do you know this?"

"I know everything. I've got four eyes in the back of my head, and I know that you were spying on me the other day."

"No, I wasn't. I was just walking by. And then I heard music."

"I didn't know my music was blasting all over the street."

"No, it wasn't really. It's just that piece."

"Chopin?"

"Yes."

"Hmm. I guess you loved it so much you needed to take the sleeve with you as a memento." He paused. "Or as evidence?"

"Evidence of what?"

"Of my anti-Soviet activities."

His face reverted to its ghostly appearance. His eyes—now iron gray—scrutinized me openly. The air grew heavy, thick as molasses. Every breath sounded like a cello sawing away against the bouncing-bow contrabasses of my heartbeat.

Aladdin took the cigarette out of his mouth, rubbed it against the sole of his sandal, and aimed for the sink. Missed. His hands flew up in resignation. "Oh well. At least today it's pretty close. Don't they say a good guest brings good luck with him? With *her*." His mouth curled into what could pass for a smirk. "Would you like some tea, Leila? Then we can sit and talk in detail about my anti-Soviet scheme."

His offer made my throat dry. The room spun around me, the slow *ceyrani* dance picking up speed. Why did he reveal himself? Why?

Unless he was planning to recruit me for his spy operation. Should I play along, win his trust, and then expose the plot?

"I'd love some tea," I said. "Just not too strong."

"I'll make it to your liking."

Aladdin bolted to a small, dilapidated stove plunked in the corner of the room. He struggled to light a fire, striking one match after another, failing to turn the gas on in time. His movements seemed awkward, his motor coordination disorderly. What kind of spy was this?

"Do you have many customers?" I asked.

"Not really. I might even say you are my first one. With Allah's help, others will follow."

"With what you just said and with the rumors going around town, I don't think even Allah can help you."

"This town brews gossip as much as it brews tea. Which rumor have you heard? The one that I am an American spy? Or the one that I'm a villain straight from Jafar's cave, selling venomous music?"

I giggled before I could fight it off.

"What's so funny?"

"Nothing really. It's just…'venomous music' sounds like a flock of poisonous frogs singing in the swamp, all at the same time."

"Poisonous frogs, you said." He tilted his head, gaping sideways, as if visualizing the image, then grinned, displaying a mouthful of teeth. "Nice. I should write that down somewhere. Now let's make that tea happen."

He struck another match, managing to turn the gas on in time. Next he placed an iron pot on the fire that danced happily on top of the stove. Then, retrieving two *armuds*, pear-shaped glasses, from the shelf, he set them on a small tray with sugar and mint. The air of hostility melted away. The magic lamp returned to Aladdin's hands.

A barely dressed woman in a bowler hat smiled devilishly at me from the wall, her black bodice and satin shorts, fishnet stockings and shiny boots obviously aimed at exposing rather than concealing her voluptuous body.

Pornography? Did I break a law by looking at this indignity?

"Do you know who this lady is?" Aladdin asked.

"No."

"But you think she is fascinating, don't you?"

I shrugged.

"It's a poster for a movie titled *Cabaret*, in which she acts and sings. Her name is Liza Minnelli. I have a few of her songs. Would you like to hear?"

If you listen to his recordings, your skin will turn into fish scales.

"No, I really have to get going."

Aladdin swept to the alcove, drew an album, and placed it on the turntable.

A lazy clarinet zigzagged a melody, its timbre trailing raspy echoes as if a performer had chosen a worn-out reed or accidentally dropped one inside the instrument's bore. Then a pause, followed by the sound of a strenuous breath. A brazen, haunting female voice poured out of the gramophone. A voice of dark velvet. A voice like no other, carrying nostalgia from some mysterious, fantastic world. A world I had known before. Somewhere. A long time ago. Maybe in a different life? Or a dream?

I couldn't understand the words. Instead, I contemplated them like the images in old black-and-white movies: ripples of rain sliding down a window; the lights of the city fading into the night; sea waves breaking across a deserted beach; two silhouettes against the moonlit path, their hands entwined, their first kiss.

I closed my eyes, embarrassed. Exposed. The passion of the music stripped me of my usual common sense and left my heart vulnerable to secret desires. Now I knew for sure that I was in a sorcerer's lair. That I should run from this place as fast and as far as possible.

But I couldn't leave. I yearned for more as if I had fallen under the spell of Aladdin's music. The music had awakened in me something thrilling, forbidden, and so powerful that I felt wings—not fish scales—growing out of my skin.

CHAPTER 5

Azerbaijan had always played an important role in world affairs due to its unique geographical position at the crossroads of Iran, Turkey, and Russia. In the past, Islamic Azerbaijan served as the gate between the mysterious faraway East and prosperous Europe. By the 1970s, Soviet Azerbaijan had become a faithful, staunch outpost of European Communism as it made its way farther into Asia.

Our ally, Hafez al-Assad, became the president of Syria, and a Stalin disciple, Saddam Hussein, took the presidency of Iraq. The Iranian Revolution, with its Communist roots, sent the Shah and his family packing and out of the country. And the Marxist Party of Afghanistan appealed to the Kremlin for military support in its fight against the Islamic Mujahideen.

May 1979 was the month that would reshape the entire world. It was then, behind closed doors, that members of the Politburo of the Central Committee of the Communist Party of the Soviet Union signed a top-secret document ordering the invasion of Afghanistan. That single decree was the irrevocable beginning of the end of the great Soviet Empire, which had been crumbling since its inception in 1922. Of course we, the people of the Empire, had no idea at the time. Communism—the only order of life we knew—kept its mighty grip on our hearts and minds.

On Friday afternoon, I left college early to attend the Assembly of the 26 Baku Commissars District Committee of Komsomol for the first time as its junior member. Afraid to be late, I ran all the way there—along busy Communist Street, past the white colonnade of the Azerbaijan State Philharmonic Concert Hall, past a beehive of people moving in and out of the Baksoviet Metro station, past the pointed arches and ornate facade of the Academy of Sciences, and all the way to Nizami Square with the magnificent bronze sculpture of the medieval poet Nizami Ganjavi.

The sun patted me on the back. The wind sprayed me with salty mist. A shortcut through the alley, down Uzeyir Hajibeyov Street with its row of blooming magnolia trees, and I arrived at the steps of the District Komsomol Committee Headquarters, joining the motley crowd of delegates.

At exactly twelve thirty, the heavy doors opened, and we poured into the auditorium. Red satin covered its walls. A crimson banner hung over the stage with the slogan: "Long live Azerbaijan, the younger brother of the Soviet Union." At center stage, a placard depicted our founding fathers—Karl Marx, Friedrich Engels, and Vladimir Lenin—their names painted in gold on the red streamer of the Revolution.

I took my seat next to a young woman from some rural *aul* who wore a long, purple dress with multiple skirts, her head scarf tied in a knot so the ends stuck out like ears. On my other side sat a Russian sailor with the frame of a bear and the face of a Siberian husky, his watered-down blue eyes heavy with exhaustion.

The auditorium boiled in anticipation, but the sound of the drums silenced the crowd instantly. Comrade Farhad, poised and stately in a formal black suit, came onstage from the left side carrying the flag of Soviet Azerbaijan. Another man emerged from the right. Short but sturdy, with a pale face, thin blond hair, and a military bearing, he gripped the wooden pole of a notably larger flag of the Soviet Union, the Red Banner.

Meeting in the middle of the stage, they descended the stairs together and marched through the auditorium accompanied by the beat of the drums. Circling the rear, they returned to the stage, placed both flags next to the bronze bust of the leader of our country, Comrade Brezhnev, and gave him a military salute. The crowd rose and, on Comrade Farhad's signal, began singing the State Anthem of the Azerbaijan SSR.

"Azerbaijan, the splendorous flower of the Republic...
The astute leadership of the Party of Lenin set us on course..."

The young woman next to me reached into her sack, dug up a handkerchief, and wiped away the tears sliding down her cheeks.

"Attention!" Comrade Farhad knocked on the microphone, ordering silence. Leaning with both hands against the red of the podium, he announced, "Comrades, the thirty-seventh Assembly of the 26 Baku Commissars District Committee of Komsomol is officially opened. Long live Soviet Komsomol!"

Springing to our feet, we applauded enthusiastically until Comrade Farhad gestured for us to stop. The ovation gradually subsided, and we settled in our seats.

"Long live the next generation of the Communist Party!" Comrade Farhad shouted.

In a flash we were back on our feet with another round of applause. This time the front row seemed to be leading the chaotic ovation into a steady beat. After a while, Comrade Farhad knocked on the microphone. We returned to our seats.

"Long live the Communist Party of the Soviet Union!"

Another standing ovation. Another signal to stop. Down... up...down.

"Long live the Soviet people, the builders of Communism!"

That ovation was the loudest by far. I thought the ceiling was going to come down. Finally, Comrade Farhad raised his right hand and ordered the people to take their seats. This time for good.

"Comrades," he said, "today, as never before, we stand united against the vicious incursions of American imperialism. I have received an urgent memo from Moscow about the American military machine waving its muscle at our ally, the free people of Afghanistan. The people who have deposed their dictator and decided to choose the only right path of life"—Comrade Farhad struck his fist against the podium—"the path of Communism."

The room broke into a hurricane again. The peasant woman next to me shouted her support in the highest trumpet decibels.

"I'll tell you this." Comrade Farhad's powerful voice cut through the noise. "We will say to corrupt America—NO! We'll say to gluttonous America—NO!"

The crowd joined him: "We'll say NO! We'll say NO!"

"Let the enemy beware," Comrade Farhad continued, "that we, the Komsomol of Soviet Azerbaijan, the fearless future generation of the Communist Party, stand shoulder to shoulder with the freedom-choosing people of Afghanistan. And we are ready to spill our blood under our red banners!"

Tall and commanding, his eyes shining with determination, successfully restraining his stutter by carefully articulating every word, Comrade Farhad was a drummer of the Communist faith. He delivered his message clearly, logically, and directly, his charisma and fervor echoing in the hearts of his audience. Leaders like Comrade Farhad stood on the front lines of our lives, capable—I believed—of changing history.

But something didn't feel right. Was it the pounding of his fist against the podium that kept distracting me? It seemed disconnected from his body or his words and reminded me of the orchestra at the Baku opera house accompanying the "Sabre Dance" by Aram Khachaturian. A poorly rehearsed orchestra, with the xylophone and strings struggling to find a common pace with timpani in the opening ostinato. Then the dancers poured onstage, whirling in their war dance, waving their papier-mâché swords, and clashing with the low brass.

Comrade Farhad concluded his speech and gestured toward the blond man who'd carried the flag of the Soviet Union. "I'm privileged to introduce Comrade Popov, our honored guest from Moscow, the First Secretary of the Novokuznetsky Committee of Komsomol." He started clapping enthusiastically, conducting the crowd to follow.

Comrade Popov marched to the podium and cleared his throat. "I will focus on two issues: the People's Revolution in Iran, and the role of Marxism–Leninism in our successful annihilation of religion. As we all know, Free Iran abolished its American surveillance bases near the Azerbaijani border. Comrade Leonid Brezhnev sent his congratulations to Ayatollah Khomeini, promising to stand shoulder to shoulder with our new friend and neighbor, the People's Republic of Iran. And soon we will witness the final stage of the Iranian revolution—the victory of Iranian Communism…"

I listened to Comrade Popov in total confusion. Just a few days earlier, I'd overheard a conversation Papa had with his friend Parviz—a member of the Tudeh Party of Iran. Parviz said that the Communist revolution in Iran was lost to ayatollahs, and soon the entire country would be transformed into a single, giant mosque.

Was Comrade Popov misleading us? But why?

"Now I will focus on the role of Marxism–Leninism in our fight against a two-headed hydra, religious fervor coming from the East and toxic hedonism coming from the West," he continued. "As Karl Marx stated: 'Religion is the sigh of the oppressed creature, the heart of a heartless world, and the soul of soulless condition. It is the opium of the people.' The same applies to the so-called Western democracy, which is nothing more than a poisonous materialistic ideology used by the ruling classes to deceive and enslave their people.

"The only difference between those two ideologies lies in their methods—the venom of religious zeal is God, while the weapon of Western corruption is money. And Communism is the only alternative to these decaying, evil dogmas. We've been successful in annihilating the religious hydra on our soil, but we must continue to root it out, one head at a time…"

Comrade Popov spoke for a long time, slamming the podium in the same disconnected manner Comrade Farhad had done but with seemingly less conviction. I sank, melting into my chair, terrified by my state of mind. What was going on with me? Why was I doubtful about my leaders' sincerity? I had never had thoughts like this before. Seditious thoughts. Had I been contaminated? Had Aladdin slipped something into my tea?

Or could it have been his music?

Whatever it was, I had to clean myself up. To tell Comrade Farhad my findings about Aladdin. Something dangerous existed behind that green door. Something that had easily intercepted my rational thinking. And that's why Comrade Farhad had sent me there in the first place—to test my Communist perseverance.

I didn't like the idea of getting Aladdin in trouble. But I couldn't shirk my duty. The duty of a Komsomol member. I had to report him.

After the end of the assembly, I rushed to Comrade Farhad's office. The waiting room was empty so I peeked through the glass partition. Inside, Comrade Popov sprawled like a sultan in Comrade Farhad's big brown chair, smoking a cigarette, dropping ashes on the floor, and bossing Comrade Farhad around. To my surprise, Comrade Farhad, who I had never seen take a command from anyone, bustled about, swearing into a phone and trying to arrange a special tour for Comrade Popov at the major oil-refinery plant.

The moment he noticed me, his dark highlander's face turned carnation red, and he hastily waved me off. I reached into my bag, found the invitation to my recital on Saturday, placed it on his secretary's desk, and left.

CHAPTER 6

On the evening before my recital, I rehearsed Beethoven's *Sonata Pathétique*, carefully following Professor Sultan-zade's "list of final touches." Outside, from the top of the minaret of a nearby mosque, Muezzin Rashid called the faithful to *Maghrib*, the evening prayer. I stopped in the middle of my octave arpeggios and listened. His voice, smooth and ornamental, drifted in and out of my room, weaving melodies as intricate as the *Boteh Jegheh* paisley motif on a Persian rug.

Muezzin Rashid was a man of religion, so old that he looked less like a man and more like a sea turtle. Papa told me that he had resided in our castle since the Revolution. As a kid, Papa used to bring shoes for repair to his tiny shop two blocks away from our building—before Muezzin Rashid was appointed to sing the *Adhan*, the call to prayer at the mosque. Five times a day, stooping his shoulders and dragging his feet, Muezzin Rashid inched his way down the street toward the mosque and then up the spiral stairs of the minaret. From there, he recited his *Adhans*.

I thought of Comrade Popov's words about the dangers of the religion hydra that still remained on our soil and how we had to root it out, one head at a time. But why would we want to root out these beautiful, melodious *Adhans*? Could they be as poisonous as Aladdin's music?

I returned to Beethoven, practicing to sustain and resolve my chords in the first movement, "Grave: Allegro di molto e con brio." Then I skipped straight to the "Rondo," indulging myself in its perpetual motion until the ringing phone sliced through my arpeggio.

Almaz. "Are you coming or not?"

Six o'clock. I'd lost track of time. I was supposed to go downstairs to try on a dress Aunty Zeinab had made for my recital.

Almaz waited for me at the door, her pin-thin eyebrows raised to her hairline. "Why do you always have to make us wait for you?"

"Leave her alone, you featherheaded fool." Aunty Zeinab shoved her away and led me inside. "Come in, sweet Leila, and have supper with us first."

Their apartment was tiny. "Our dollhouse," Aunty Zeinab called it. A room with a kitchen and a bird-sized chamber where Almaz had built her cozy nest. There was a terrible shortage of apartments in Baku, and four years ago, Papa had used his connections to acquire a large two-bedroom apartment for them in one of the newer neighborhoods, half an hour away by bus. But Aunty Zeinab chose to stay in their dollhouse so Almaz and I could grow up together.

We sat on the rug-covered couch that was converted nightly into a bed. And we ate at the table that served during the day as their worktable, where Uncle Zohrab crafted his bisque dolls and Aunty Zeinab spun the wheel of her prehistoric Singer, sewing miniature dresses for the dolls.

As always, we shared lots of laughter, devouring Aunty Zeinab's signature dish, *plov*, made out of saffron-covered rice and layered, according to her own unique recipe, with thirty different kinds of herbs and greens. And we listened—for the hundredth time—to Uncle Zohrab's funny story about their betrothal.

"It was in the Sharg Bazaar where I met my Zeinab *Khanum* for the first time." He always referred to his wife in the most reverent way, adding *Khanum*—queen—to her name.

"When I saw her, I thought the sun had come down from the sky. She pierced my heart with a single glance of her gazelle eyes, with her sweet pomegranate smile. When I learned she was a relation, I sent a matchmaker to go see her parents and arrange our marriage. When she heard that 'pitiable, insipid Cousin Zohrab' had asked for her hand, she just threw the matchmaker out of the house. She has always had a tigress's temper, my *Khanum*."

Uncle Zohrab shook his head. "I lost appetite. I lost sleep. I walked like a madman calling her name. Then my mama, her soul be blessed, offered to send her most valuable possession, her own wedding mirror, as a dowry. My *Khanum*, let Allah keep her heart young and her face fair, loved the mirror so much she agreed to marry me."

"Allah knows how I wish I didn't." Aunty Zeinab threw her arms up in the air. "Every morning when I wake up and every evening when I go to sleep, I want to smash that mirror to pieces."

She mopped up the fat spilled on the tablecloth with a slice of bread, stuffed it in her mouth, and carried the dirty dishes to the kitchen.

"Oi-yoi-yoi." Uncle Zohrab laughed in a high quivering voice after her, pieces of rice falling off his mustache.

Aunty Zeinab returned with my new dress. A silver satin dress with long see-through sleeves and an emerald brooch on the collar. She carried it carefully by the shoulders with two fingers on each hand. Her crumpled, sweaty face shone with pride.

"Tomorrow, daughter, when you play, your arms will fly like wings," she said. "But first, I have to check the hemline. Put it on."

We did the fitting in front of their infamous mirror. Large, framed with flowers and silver calligraphy from the Koran written over blue enamel, it was permanently fogged, slightly distorting my reflection. To add to the effect, I squinted and imagined a pretty maiden strolling through the clouds, pressed my hands against my heart, and curtsied to the imaginary audience, the way Professor Sultan-zade had taught me.

"It's beautiful. Thank you, Aunty."

"For you and your mama—anything, a thousand times over."

Aunty Zeinab helped me to take the dress off, then carefully folded and placed it inside a muslin pillowcase. "Let it bring you good luck tomorrow, daughter."

I felt guilty. I knew how much she wanted to be at my recital, but when I asked if I could invite her, Papa had said, "No. They are like family but not of our class."

What class? Our Soviet Union was a class-free society. I should have stood up to Papa and invited her.

But I didn't. Was I uncomfortable with Aunty Zeinab, worrying that she wouldn't fit in with the refined music audience in the Baku philharmonic hall? Was I infected with Papa's innate sense of superiority, seeing Aunty Zeinab's family as commoners and my own as elite? Whatever it was, I felt ashamed of my feelings.

Aunty Zeinab brought out her traditional dessert—a large copper tray with rose sherbet, persimmons, dried fruit, and nuts. "Finish up, daughters, then you can have your girl time."

Almaz downed sherbet and grabbed a handful of nuts. "Let's go. I'll style you. You don't want to go onstage tomorrow with that hair sprouting like spring crabgrass."

I followed her to the kitchen, where she washed my hair in the basin.

"You'll look like a star after I'm done with you," she said, massaging saffron oil into my wet hair. "It will be shiny and soft with a tinge of red. Your Comrade *Aži Dahāka* will swallow his tongue when he sees you like this. Trust me."

"Why do you hate him so much?"

"Why do you like him so much?"

"I don't just *like* him. I admire his character. He's a self-made strong leader capable of inspiring and commanding the crowds. And he is sincere in his beliefs and actions."

"He's a brute—"

"He's not. It's his leadership style. Remember—'a true revolutionary is supposed to show no emotions, no attachments. He must be fully absorbed by his single passion—his fervent belief in the cause of the revolution,'" I quoted from our history book. "But I'm sure there is a softer side behind Comrade Farhad's tough exterior."

"Softer side?" Almaz shrugged. "Good luck finding it."

She finished washing my hair, dried it with a soft waffle towel, and mounted rollers all over my head in a valiant effort to smooth my feral curls into silky waves. "That's it. Sleep on it, and tomorrow morning I'll style you before the recital. Want to stay here tonight?"

It had been a while since Almaz invited me to stay overnight.

I loved sleeping in her bed. It was always warm. Unlike my bed, which felt like late autumn, even though Aunty Zeinab had made both our blankets from the wool of the same camel.

"I'd love to," I said.

I went home to get my pajamas and leave a note for my parents. When I returned downstairs, Almaz was already in bed. I turned off the lights and crawled under the covers.

"I miss you, Almaz," I whispered, kissing her forearm. "I truly do." My best friend, the closest I had to a sister.

"I miss you too. A thousand times over." She threw her arms around me, squeezing me tightly against her body, saying into the back of my neck, "You are my sister, for life and beyond. And it will never change. Promise me?"

"Of course I promise. But it's you who hasn't been sisterly lately. Why have you been avoiding me?"

"Because all you care about is either your Komsomol or your music competitions."

"But this is my calling. To represent our Azerbaijan all over the world. You can't imagine the challenge of playing the piano in front of an audience and holding them on the tips of my fingers."

"How could I?" Almaz asked wryly. "I wasn't born with sweet *halva* in my mouth, like you. Allah hasn't given me well-connected parents and the gift of music. All I've received is the curse of beauty."

"Why a curse?"

Almaz was strikingly beautiful. Papa said once that she fully epitomized the meaning of her name—a priceless, flawless diamond.

"Because beauty is like a blossom," she said in a sad voice. "Tonight it's here; tomorrow it's gone. Withered. Sapped. Like Princess Shirin."

One night, fair Princess Shirin fell asleep in the garden of blooming blue roses. The next morning as she opened her eyes, the red petals fell like droplets of blood from the roses' barren stems. And with them, gone was her beauty.

"It's just a fairy tale," I said. "And you're not Princess Shirin. She sacrificed her best friend, Nightingale, for the Blue Rose Garden of Beauty. You'd never do that, would you?"

Almaz didn't respond. We lay close in darkness-filled silence, our heartbeats resonating in unison.

"Leila."

"What?"

Almaz gazed at me, her eyes intense, the irises shimmering out of their ivory whites.

"What if you and I were really not who we are?" she whispered in the shadows. "What if you were me and I were you? After all, it was only a beauty mark that defined our destinies. But what if your mama was wrong? What if she made a mistake? It's possible, isn't it? Then it would be me living upstairs in your fancy quarters, and you'd be right here—in my place—under the stairs."

I felt the taste of tears inside my throat and an overwhelming rush of loneliness in my heart. Nothing I could say would bring Almaz back to me.

Jealousy had deaf ears.

CHAPTER 7

The audience at the Azerbaijan State Philharmonic Concert Hall seemed to hold its breath as a dimmed chandelier sprinkled the silence with golden dust. At center stage, a black Fazioli piano awaited me in the spotlight. Overhead, two muses soared protectively, their bodies draped in stucco tulle, lyres in their hands, surrounded by a panoply of rococo decorations—leaves, shells, waterfalls. All in white.

My family occupied the second-tier box reserved for the parents of the contestants: Mama, dressed in my favorite fawn suit, and Papa, his hair sticking out wildly. He whispered something in Mama's ear, and she smiled radiantly.

The auditorium was full except for the first three rows, always kept empty so as not to disturb the performers. In the middle of the fourth row sat the two-person jury: Comrade Sharipov, the First Minister of Culture, an imposing man with short gray hair and a thick black mustache resembling two Turkish swords crossed above his upper lip, and Professor Mira Levina from the Moscow Conservatory of Music, a petite, elderly woman wearing a wide-brimmed yellow hat that made her look like a chanterelle mushroom.

Professor Sultan-zade waited with me at the side of the stage, gently rubbing my fingers and blowing at them to keep them warm and agile. Tough during schooling, she showered her students with maternal affection at recitals and competitions. "Stay confident throughout the performance," she whispered to me, "and don't forget that delicate right hand in the 'Adagio cantabile.'"

"Leila Badalbeili. Beethoven. *Sonata Pathétique.*" The announcer introduced me.

Professor Sultan-zade slightly pushed me forward. "Let the world fall at your feet"—the words of her blessing followed me as I almost sprinted across the stage to the Fazioli, gulping the exhilarating air of anticipation. The notes of the sonata bounced around me, spinning like paper planes, calling me on a ride. I raised my eyes to the muses, asking for permission to join them in their sacred space, and swept my hands up high.

Before I could bring them down—what was that noise? Loud and blatant. Who's playing timpani?

Comrade Popov trudged across the hall to the front, the plush carpet powerless against the heavy, percussive stamping of his feet. Comrade Farhad followed him. They settled in the center of the first row barely a breath away from me. So close that I could see Comrade Popov's bright red socks as he took off his shoes, crossed his legs, and squeezed his toes.

I took a deep breath, trying to shake off the distraction and mentally return to the serenity of my beginning. To the silence before the opening chords.

Another noise. Comrade Popov was whispering in Comrade Farhad's ear. His seat crackled, reverberating through my body, jabbing a thousand needles into my arms and legs.

I raised my hands and brought them down with all my might onto the keyboard. What followed wasn't an explosion, but more like a whimper. My wooden fingers struggled to feel the touch of the keys. I paused, lifted my hands away from the keyboard, and hid them in my lap.

"Can I please start over?" I said without looking into the auditorium, rubbing my hands nervously against my skirt, warming them up, trying to bring them back to life.

A long pause.

"You may." I heard the thin and clearly annoyed voice of Professor Levina.

I closed my eyes, desperately trying to disassociate myself from everything but the music. I visualized the notes of the introductory "Grave" theme on the opening page and the syncopated chords building up to a vigorous passage in the right hand. I was almost there, when another bout of whispering pierced my ear like the sting of an angry bee. The notes I had finally positioned in the right places on the staff were now jumping off the page, swirling around me, pushing me off the bench into the dark, hostile audience. Frantic, I raised my eyes to the muses, begging for help. They soared away, high and unreachable, leaving me alone in the blinding spotlight. Exposed and humiliated.

I stopped playing and rose, ready to retreat from the spotlight into the merciful darkness. And then I saw him. No. First, I perceived the flow of his energy coming at me from the upper-left tier. *Then* I took him in. Aladdin, leaning forward against the railing. His smile, intended only for me, guided me away from the stage. Back to the magical world hidden behind his green door, spinning in slow reverie, drawing me into its wistful harmony.

My hands reached for the keyboard. The daunting silence of the black-and-white ocean exploded into the opening chords of the "Grave"—haunting and somber—slowly dissolving into the air like the summits of mountains adrift in the clouds. The sun was rising, spilling its peach hue across the drowsy skies. I passed through a tunnel of century-old poplar trees swaying in the morning breeze, whispering their century-old secrets. The tunnel opened into a vast valley of sunflowers swelling all the way to the mountains. I ran across the valley, caressed by the warm breath of the "Adagio cantabile," until I reached the edge of a cliff. A step forward—and I soared into the sun-streaked skies of Beethoven's "Rondo: Allegro."

I sprang to my feet as the last note still hovered in the air. The audience was silent. Eerily silent. Did they hate it?

Oh, I'd forgotten. The rules of the recital restricted the audience from applauding. I heard a single person clapping and strained to see where it was coming from. Through the blur and to my utter astonishment, I spotted a wide-brimmed yellow hat. Professor Levina had broken her own rule and rose to her feet, applauding me.

Thank you, Aladdin. I bowed.

CHAPTER 8

The next night, I lay in the dark, sleepless, replaying in my mind obsessively—over and over—my performance of Beethoven's *Pathétique* at the recital. A major disaster in the beginning. A bold—too bold?—approach to the "Grave" theme. Did I slow down a bit in the middle of the "Adagio cantabile"? Did they notice that I missed an A-flat in the left-hand arpeggio of the "Rondo: Allegro"? It just slipped from under my finger…

Professor Levina certainly liked my performance; otherwise she wouldn't have given me a standing ovation. But would the jury overlook my almost-meltdown and vote me the winner? If not, then good-bye, Budapest. After all the months of practice. Oh, how I would have let my parents down… Professor Sultan-zade didn't say a word about my performance, only that the decision would be announced sometime tomorrow afternoon. How could I last until then?

At dawn, I left Gargoyle Castle. From the minaret of Gevharaga Mosque, Muezzin Rashid chanted the first *Fajr Adhan*: "*Allahu akbar… Hayya alal-falah as-Salaatu khairun minan-naum… as-Salaatu khairun minan-naum…*" The yodeling of the prayer drifted through the air, bouncing between the walls of the buildings before disappearing into the pink dome of the sky.

I turned into the labyrinth of Old Town—Icheri Sheher—with its narrow cobblestone alleys twisting between old, shabby, crammed-together houses. Icheri Sheher was awakening, slowly, lethargically, the air hot and creamy, moistened by the sea and sprinkled with the aroma of black gold. The one-of-a-kind concoction called Baku air.

I passed by the ruins of the ancient baths and Caravanserai—the last frontier stop before Europe for the Silk Road caravans that carried sandalwood, saffron, and myrrh from China, India, Persia, and Egypt all the way to the Roman Empire. Here, a few centuries ago, merchants tied their fatigued camels to iron hooks still sticking out of the walls and rested for the night.

Lore had it that the merchants of the Silk Road believed in the magical powers of Maiden Tower. They called her Shrine of Wishes. Before daybreak, they rushed to the tower, eager to reach her walls before the other merchants so they could place their hands on her cold stone and make a wish as the first ray of the sun struck her crown: "Turn everything my hands touch into gold. And turn everything my rival's hands touch into stone."

Before I knew it, her silhouette loomed in front of me. Closer than I had ever before dared to go. Maiden Tower. Just a stone's throw away. The old, obese, decaying, and surprisingly majestic Maiden Tower, bathed in the soft pastels of the rising sun. A witness to glorious conquests, bloody defeats, hearts broken, and lips sealed. A stubbornly silent monument that refused to reveal its past.

More mystery surrounded Maiden Tower than the amount of stone and limestone used to build it. Of which, according to the archaeologists, there was enough to encircle the entire city ten times over.

No one knew how and when Maiden Tower came to be. The historians claimed that it had been built as a fortress in the twelfth century to defend the Khan of Baku from invaders, a hypothesis based on the age of an inscription found on one of the walls.

The archaeologists argued that the inscription was at least a millennium younger than the stone on which it was written. Excavations at the beginning of the century revealed that it was built between the fourth and sixth centuries on a large rock sloping toward the Caspian

Sea. The combination of its anti-earthquake wooden girders, its cylindrical shape with five-meter-thick walls, and a massive beak-like buttress helped it survive the years.

The astronomers believed that the tower served as an observatory. They detected thirty hewed stone protrusions on the tower's lower section and thirty-one protrusions on its upper section, linked with a belt that correlated the days of the month.

The anthropologists dismissed the views of the historians, archaeologists, and astronomers. They insisted that Maiden Tower was once a *dakhma*, a tower of silence, dedicated to the disposal of the dead. They seemed to win the debate because an illustration of the tower in our history textbook showed a corpse wrapped in a rug being lifted to the top of the tower, where ravenous birds were waiting to feast.

While learned men argued about the tower's origins over the centuries, ordinary people sought their own explanation of its name, passing their accounts from mouth to mouth, creating a fusion of Arabic-, Persian-, and Ottoman-influenced legends. Some of them referred to the tower as a fortress never taken by force, metaphorically explaining its name as Maiden's Tower.

Some believed in the goddess of water, Anahita, who once visited the tower and ordered priests to worship her with the fire gushing from the bowels of the earth. The Legend of Love told about a Byzantine princess whose father, the king, fell in love with her and wanted to marry her. The girl's heart belonged to a young knight so she tried to delay her father's advances by begging him to build the tallest tower in the kingdom. When the tower was completed, she leaped from its crown into the sea.

But the most popular was the Legend of Haunted Castle about the evil Shah of Darkness who conquered Azerbaijan and pronounced himself its supreme ruler.

The Shah of Darkness called upon his loyal minions and ordered them to erect an impregnable castle from the bottom of the Caspian Sea.

Caravan after caravan arrived, carrying stones for the tower. Enough stone to enclose the whole town with walls ten times and over. Endless columns of savages, from every corner of the world, were marched through desert sand dunes and snow-peaked mountains. Many died torturous deaths. Those who survived the journey and reached the Land of Fire were forced into brutal labor.

Seven years later, when the tower finally touched the sky, every maiden was taken from her family and imprisoned inside the tower, waiting for her wedding night to the Shah of Darkness. One maiden each night for the Shah's pleasure. The next morning, their maimed bodies were washed up on the shores of the Caspian Sea, all bearing the same expression of horror on what were once their lovely faces.

It continued until one morning when the Firebird soared over Maiden Tower, awakening the people of Azerbaijan, leading the sun to its rightful place in the firmament of the sky.

Once, a few years ago, two students from the nearby Civil Engineering Institute arrived to dig underneath the tower, sleeves rolled up, power drills and shovels in hand, eager to get to the bottom of the shrouded past. Witnesses saw them smoking cigarettes, drinking Armenian cognac, and shouting at each other before putting their gear on and disappearing inside the tower. They were never seen again. The efforts of a military rescue squad amounted to nothing besides discovering a bottomless well underneath the tower. No bodies. Did the students unleash the menacing spirit of evil Shah of Darkness, or were they pulled down by the souls of his dead maidens?

"Hey, old hag, show me your kefir smile, so I can barf on your face."

A shout came from a grapevine terrace, snuggled up against a sidewalk of Old Town where a dozen highlanders basked in the sun playing *shesh besh*, drinking tea as dark as their parched faces and harassing an old woman in a shabby gray coat and an old-fashioned straw hat. She hobbled around the plaza swinging her long broom, punishing the littered pavement and ignoring the insult, her face frozen in a mask of squeamishness as if she had just swallowed a dead rat.

"Look at the witch," barked one of the highlanders. "Isn't she juicy?"

"Look how she walks like she's got a broom shoved into her ass."

They broke into raucous laughter, hitting each other on the shoulders in camaraderie.

"Shame on you for insulting an old woman," I yelled at them. "Would you want someone to insult your mothers like this?"

"No, no, no. *Iraq olcun!* God forbid!" One of the men, his head wrapped in a checkered kaffiyeh, raised himself slightly and pressed his arms across his chest in a mocking apology. "She's no old woman. And she's not somebody's mother. She's the Immortal. The blood-sucking ghost of a dead maiden. So you better be on your way, *qiz,* before she spits her curse in your pretty face."

The Immortal? The old woman was the Immortal? I took a few more steps but stopped, fighting a temptation to sneak a closer look at her. She was nothing like what I'd expected her to be—a gorgon with rooster-like yellow eyes emitting mortal fires.

I thought of the night around a campfire we once had in summer camp when we told scary stories about the Immortal. "Go away or burn in fire!" we shouted into the darkness to scare her off before she could stick her teeth into our necks and inject us with her dead maiden soul. For years, those yellow eyes continued to follow me into every dark alley.

If this was her, she was an old, withered Thumbelina. With her head down, her elbows pushed outward, she reminded me of a wounded sparrow ruffling her feathers at the sight of one more stone flying in her direction.

63

Ashuglar Street was still asleep, the shops closed. A *chaikhana* owner fired charcoal under a gigantic silver samovar. It would take a while for the water to boil. His wife sat on the steps, a bowl with cardamom pods next to her. She bruised them slightly with a pestle and removed the seeds.

I slipped inside the green door and into the familiar sweet-and-tangy aroma of hashish. But today something else hovered in the air, something as intense and bitter as the odor of tree sap.

The smell of paint. Aladdin, his white tunic stained and crumpled, stared into emptiness from behind a large easel. Next to him, a wooden palette with a rainbow of oils.

"Good morning," I said. "I hope I'm not too early."

He raised his bloodshot eyes, gazing at me as if I were some sort of apparition. "Ahhh…it's you again."

Not the greeting I had expected. Especially after yesterday's recital.

"I had a minute. And I was just passing by—"

"No, princess. You weren't just *passing by*. You stopped to check on me."

"Check on you?"

"Yes, check on me. Because people like you just *love* checking on people like me."

"You don't make any sense."

"I don't, ha?" His mouth twisted in a sneer.

Aladdin picked up his palette, went to the basin, and started washing the brushes gently, one at a time, lining them up in orderly rows on the table. Ignoring me. Why?

Rejected and humiliated, I remained standing in the middle of his room, refusing to leave, feeling a strange sense of loss. I knew intuitively that if I responded to his rudeness and left, I would never come back and would miss something very important. I would never know who this odd person really was—a spy, a painter, a sorcerer? All of that? And I would never have a chance to ask him why he came to my recital and saved me from total fiasco.

"I saw you yesterday," I said in a small voice.

Aladdin washed the last brush, shook it in the air, and wiped his hands with his tunic. He gave no indication he had heard me.

"I had a difficult time with my performance. The noise threw me off. Your presence there helped me."

"Really?" Aladdin muttered from the corner. "I thought you did pretty well on your own."

Pause.

"I enjoyed your 'Adagio' the most. It brought tears to my eyes. If I had died right then, I'd have been the happiest man on earth."

"How did you know I would be performing?"

"It's natural for a spy to know everything, isn't it?"

"So you *are* a spy?" I looked straight into his dilated pupils, ready to detect the slightest sign of lying, not wanting to believe it. "And you *have* been working for the Americans?"

Aladdin stared at me point-blank, his expression unreadable, slowly blowing his cheeks out until they popped like a balloon. His mouth buckled into a zigzag, and he exploded with hysterical laughter. The room bounced as if struck by an earthquake. Was he trying to deceive me? If so, he was overdoing it. I waited patiently until the last aftershocks died out.

"Who sent you here?" he asked, wiping his watery eyes with the stained sleeve of his tunic.

"No one did."

"Witch hunt in progress. All right, let's put an end to the 'American spy' rumor. You can tell your handlers that no, I haven't been working for the Americans. Even though I'd do it in the blink of an eye. I just have never been asked."

"Then how did you know that I was performing on Saturday?"

"I didn't."

"Then why were you there?"

"I'm afraid it had nothing to do with you. I love music. And I rarely miss a good performance at the Philharmonic."

Aladdin pulled his tunic off and tossed it in the corner, tightening the belt on his jeans but leaving his thin upper body exposed.

So thin, his smooth, golden-brown skin seemed wrapped tightly around his spine with nothing between. Slowly, lazily, he stretched his arms—an uncoiled spring celebrating its release, a millimeter at a time—then he glanced at me. My eyes flew away from his chest. Not soon enough. His lips suppressed a smile, but the sound of a snort escaped through his nose. He bent over, picked up a shirt from the rug, and put it on.

His taunt intensified my timidity. My toes felt stuck in icy water while my underarms were taking a Turkish bath. How could I open up to this smug boy about what happened at the recital yesterday? How I'd walked through his green door and into the haunting valley of Beethoven's *Pathétique*, captivated by the reflections of the Chopin recording by Vladimir Horowitz, translating, reinterpreting the music into my own style. Would he laugh at me?

Aladdin went to the sink and turned the water on. The faucet gurgled, dredged up, and spit a funnel of brown water. He waited a bit, rinsed a glass, filled it, took a sip. "Quite an esteemed Communist retinue you had yesterday," he said over his shoulder. "If only I had known that such a fancy butterfly had flown into my humble abode."

It might have sounded like a joke, but it wasn't meant to be that harmless. Not with the air of hostility Aladdin projected.

So that was the reason for his resentment. He had seen me after the recital with my family, Comrade Farhad, and Comrade Popov. I represented the *other side* of life, the side he obviously detested. The same dark glow shimmered in his eyes that I'd seen in Almaz the other night when she had her attack of jealousy. But my mission was far from being over. I had to do something before he kicked me out. To get on his better side, to cast a line with bait he couldn't refuse.

"Can I ask you a question?" I said.

"What is it?"

"Who is Vladimir Horowitz?"

"The greatest pianist of the twentieth century."

"Then why did my piano teacher call him the enemy of the Soviet people? What did he do?"

"He left the Soviet Union in 1925 to study in the West and never returned."

"So he *did* betray our Motherland," I said.

"That's the Communist Party line."

"Why do you have him in your collection?"

"So someone like you could sneak into my shop and hear him play and learn from him."

He had programmed the whole thing—lured me into his lair and left Vladimir Horowitz playing on the turntable so I would hear his music and become contaminated. But how could he know about Comrade Farhad's assignment?

Oblivious to my inner turmoil, Aladdin leaned against the wall, carving a grape stalk with a pocketknife, trimming off its broken end. A sorcerer? No way. Even the idea of it seemed ridiculous. More like old wives' tales. Too irrational for someone as rational as me. So I had to admit the fact. Yes, Vladimir Horowitz was a traitor, but Aladdin's words made sense. As a student of piano, I admired Horowitz's phenomenal musicianship, and if I could, I would listen to and study every nuance of his playing, enemy of the people or not.

"Is he still alive, that Horowitz?"

"Yes, the maestro lives in America, while his recordings are banned in his own country. Any more questions?" He yawned and rubbed his eyes with the heels of his hands.

Oh, yes. I had more questions than there was air in the room.

Aladdin reached for a small ceramic jug with painted birds, poured some powder out of it onto a torn piece of newspaper, rolled it into a cigarette, and after a few attempts, lit it up. Blue smoke swirled around his face. He yawned again and tapped his toes, signaling his boredom and underscoring my irrelevance to him, but I had a feeling that he was trying too hard.

"It seems you know a lot about me," I said in a cheery voice, "while I know nothing about you. Not even your name."

"It's Tahir. Tahir Mukhtarov."

So Aladdin had a real name, after all. *Tahir*—meaning "pure." I liked it.

"Anything else you want to know?" He threw the grape stalk on the floor, folded his knife, put it inside the pocket of his jeans, and headed to his Afghani rug.

"I want to know everything, Tahir," I said, enjoying the sound of his name.

"Everything?" He lay back on the rug, hands laced behind his head, and closed his eyes, inhaling hungrily on his cigarette.

"Everything," I said, decibels louder.

"It's a long story."

"I'm not in a rush."

"I thought you said you had only a minute." He lifted his puffy eyelids, took a deep drag on his cigarette, and blew slow smoke rings through the lopsided triangle at the corner of his mouth.

We stared at each other as two opponents deciding their strategies for the next round. I knew he wanted me to stay. I heard it in his voice, in the vulnerable, warm undertone slipping through the crust of ice. He could grimace, blow his arrogance together with smoke in my face, but if he really wanted me out, I would have been out a long time ago. The boy in front of me didn't stand on ceremony.

As if sensing my rush of confidence, he pushed harder. Without taking his squinting eyes off me, he patted the rug next to him. Challenging me to a difficult task—getting down on the floor in the tight skirt of my school uniform.

I approached the rug, kneeled, lowered myself to the side, struggled to free my legs from underneath my bottom, then finally stretched them out, awkwardly, one at a time, and perched alongside him. "So what is this long story?"

He smirked. "I didn't expect to be taken *that* literally. You could have sat on a chair, you know."

After all the gymnastics. "No, I'm comfortable here." I pulled the skirt over my knees.

He rolled over to the other end of the rug, allowing an ample space between us. "Is that better?"

I nodded.

He reclined, kicked off his sandals, and curled his toes in and out. They were as long and tapered as his fingers. "All right, Leila," he said. "I assume you know what the word 'Azerbaijan' means."

Was he playing with me? "Of course I do. The Land of Fire."

"Almost. Translated from Avestan, it is 'Protected by Holy Fire.'"

"What is Avestan?"

"The language of Zoroastrian scripture. My family traces its roots to a group of Zoroastrian priests who arrived in Azerbaijan more than two thousand years ago. They came here to worship eternal fires erupting out of the earth and to become the guardians of truth."

"'Fire is truth,'" I recited, "'pure as love, it burns the pollution...'"

"You've read Khatai?"

"I love old poetry."

"'Azerbaijan—you are a fire gem—stolen, looted, violated—but your beauty is a forever maiden,'" he finished the verse. "A Persian gem stolen by Arabs, looted by Turks, lost in the Mongolian Empire, tossed between the khanates, and finally picked up by the Tsar's Russia. Our Azerbaijan—a constant vassal of different changing powers. A poor vestige of the rich, long-forgotten past. But it all changed with the oil boom. When Baku began producing more than half of the world's supply of oil."

"That's when the rich oil barons came and stole from the poor," I said.

Tahir glances at me distastefully as if I had just slobbered all over myself. "You're so brainwashed by your comrades, Leila, repeating after them this total nonsense. Just like a parrot. Think—why would wealthy oil barons steal from the poor?"

"Because they were greedy capitalists who appropriated our oil fields, sold the oil to the West, and made fortunes, while the proletariat continued dwelling in their mud huts, their children dying from starvation." I quoted our history textbook.

"You've committed that garbage to memory well. But what no one has probably taught you is that the oil barons—before they became rich—were very poor."

"What do you mean?"

"What I mean is that starting at the end of the nineteenth century, many poor adventurers rushed here to our homeland to try their luck. They hoped to place their empty pockets under the gushing fountains of oil and quickly fill them up with black gold. Most of them ended up scooping dirt out of the oil wells with their bare hands. Earning just enough to pay for a chunk of bread, a piece of *pendir*, cheese, and a moldy cot in a crowded fleabag. Only a few succeeded.

"One of them was my great-grandfather, Akbar Mukhtarov. Quite a character, according to my grandmother, Miriam. He started at the oil fields at the age of nine when his father, a poor shepherd from a mountain village, sold him to a local lord. Fifteen years later—and with a patent on the first-ever mechanical oil derricks—he emerged as one of the foremost Baku oil barons. Illiterate, despite his huge wealth, and apparently good looking, he sailed for Europe to get a proper schooling and find himself a wife."

Tahir paused to take another smoke, while I closed my eyes and imagined a boat gliding through the sea with its sails fluttering before the wind, a handsome young man, resembling Tahir, standing at the bow, looking down pensively at the blue waters. So romantic.

"He met her in Paris," Tahir continued. "A Dutch princess, Anneliese, who studied drama at the Sorbonne. He fell madly in love with her and, in accordance with Azerbaijani tradition, he sent a matchmaker to her parents the next day.

"'Their laughter could be heard all the way to the Caucasus Mountains,' Baba Miriam used to joke. You see, he had no relatives in Paris, so he went to the Oriental Bazaar, chose the most presentable looking old Turkish woman he could find, dressed her in brocade and sable, gave her gifts of gold and diamonds, and sent her to the Dutch princess's family castle to request permission for him to marry Anneliese.

"While the old woman went about her task, he waited outside, allowing the parents to take a look at their potential son-in-law. It was a hot summer day, and he was wearing a traditional frock coat and a large cylindrical lamb's wool *papaq*, hat. An elegant presentation in Baku. A true savage on the banks of the Seine. But their laughter changed to wholehearted acceptance when they learned how rich he was."

A broad smile spread across Tahir's face, reaching even its farthest corners. "I saw their wedding photo. He is short, wiry, with a bushy mustache curled up at the ends like a snail's shell, while she is a statuesque snow queen.

"As a wedding gift worthy of his noblewoman, my great-grandfather built a four-story, Mauritanian-style 'Villa Anneliese.' Right in the center of Baku. Light, ornate, carved out of limestone. Its gardens filled with Spanish roses and myrtles. With splashing fountains and shadowed marble arcades to shield his beloved one's fair skin from the burning Baku sun."

I watched Tahir, mesmerized. He spoke in a stirring pianissimo with his eyes closed, his face reflecting its own chromaticism of feelings. His hands came to his aid whenever he couldn't find the right word, swaying in the air as if conducting Robert Schumann's Romantic piano concerto. Yes, he was an absolutely compelling storyteller. But how could I trust that this fairy tale was the truth?

"Anneliese died," he continued, "shortly after giving birth to their only daughter, Miriam. Akbar never remarried. Instead, he poured all his energy into shaping the modern oil industry and rebuilding decrepit Baku into the Paris of the East. Working with other oil barons, they replaced the clay huts of workers with up-to-date urban flats, planted the first-ever Baku city park. The palaces grew around the city like mushrooms after the rain, housing the newly opened Opera, Philharmonic, and Theatrical College. They also created a new project that would later develop into the Nobel Prize Foundation."

"The Nobel Prize?" I asked. "But it's in Sweden, isn't it? How could it be connected with Baku and your family?"

"The idea was born here at the Villa Anneliese, when Alfred Nobel—also an oil baron—visited my great-grandfather. They talked about designing a progressive international cultural institution for the future that would honor their names, and they agreed that there was no better emblem for that institution than the image of Maiden Tower. So they decided to restore Maiden Tower to its ancient beauty as the symbol of free Azerbaijan."

"But Maiden Tower's never been restored. What happened?"

"Your Great October Socialist Revolution." Tahir spat with disdain. "It set a killing machine in motion. Akbar Mukhtarov died at the doorway to Villa Anneliese when a revolutionary mob on horseback attempted to storm the grand stairway of the building, smashing the sculptures and relieving themselves in the fountain. He stood alone at the entrance with a gun. Guarding his home. Guarding a past that was being mocked and desecrated. Then he turned the gun on himself."

"What about his daughter? Miriam?"

"My grandmother was abroad studying at the Conservatorio Santa Cecilia in Rome. That year, she had just received her first commission—to sing Despina in Mozart's *Così fan tutte* at the recently reopened Verona Arena. The great Maestro Feodor Chaliapin called her a phenomenon, the youngest and most intense mezzo-soprano he had ever had the honor to share a stage with."

I crossed my legs, moving furtively from side to side to relieve my itchy bottom from the coarse fibers of the rug digging into my skin. My eyes floated across the ceiling while I tried to decide if Tahir's tale was truth. Or had I been fed the fruit of his inebriated imagination? By now, his hashish smoke swathed the room in patches of white and blue.

"Unwisely, Miriam came back to the Soviet Union in the midthirties hoping to use her international celebrity and save my grandfather," Tahir continued, "but she underestimated the evil. Her Dutch passport was taken away. And, after two weeks of standing in line at the Foreign Ministry trying to obtain an exit visa, she was quietly picked up by a Black Raven and taken to a Siberian gulag."

"A Black Raven? What is that?" I asked.

"Stalin's secret police car."

"I didn't know there were secret police in our country, ever."

"Still are. They're called KGB."

Another slander. "And the Siberian gulag?"

"Not a very pleasant place. Overcrowded barracks, kilometers and kilometers of God-forsaken no-man's-land, and sixty million innocent deaths."

"You're talking about Nazi concentration camps."

"As bad as that, yes. But the gulag is our own national phenomenon with its own distinctly national flavor."

"So you're saying that there were actual concentration camps in our country—that they still exist?"

"What I'm saying is that your beloved Soviet Union is just one big gulag."

Enough. Time to leave. The sooner, the better. He had hypnotized me with his story, made me hang on every word. But now his smearing propaganda reminded me of the reason I came here in the first place. To expose an attack on Communist values, to prevent these lies from spreading around and contaminating our youth.

"Miriam spent sixteen years there," Tahir continued his saga. "Until Stalin's death in 1953. By then, everyone assumed that Miriam Mukhtarov had perished like millions of others. But she came back. From Siberian exile where the temperature rarely rose above freezing, where catlike rats shared her cell and ratlike wardens assaulted her repeatedly. She came back with her daughter—my mother. The new Soviet Azerbaijani government extended its apologies for the 'unfortunate excesses' of Stalin's regime and offered Miriam an apartment in the center of the city and employment at the Baku Opera House."

"So what did she say?" I held my breath rooting for a happy ending, startled by my emotional involvement.

"She said nothing. Just laughed in their faces and demanded to be released from the evil Kingdom of Darkness. It landed her in a mental hospital in Maştağa, outside Baku, along with many other dissidents. She was detained there until 1964 when the building she lived in was burned to the ground, and the patients wandered off in different directions.

"That's when Miriam returned to Baku. I was three. My mother died from tuberculosis. Miriam raised me. And to do so, she took a job, working as a guard of Maiden Tower and living in its basement."

"The Immortal?" slipped off my tongue.

"Her name is Miriam Mukhtarov. Miriam—Mukhtarov," Tahir uttered, a word at a time. "Miriam Mukhtarov—one of the greatest dramatic mezzo-sopranos of our century."

Silence settled between us like a dense fog. I had achieved my primary goal by making Tahir expose himself. All I had to do now was to report my findings to Comrade Farhad and forget about this whole encounter. But the very thought of leaving this place, this strange boy, and never coming back stung me with the same sense of inevitability that I had experienced when I first faced the notion of mortality. And once again, I wanted to slow down the time, to hold back the seconds that seemed to gallop onward like wild horses.

Tahir stretched out on the rug, his eyes closed, his body rocking to the rhythm of some silent chant, his face reflecting its shifting emotions. Radiant one moment, withdrawn the next. A strange boy, indeed. Had he been manipulating my feelings from the moment I stepped inside his green door, twisting the truth, turning my head upside down?

Secret police? Concentration camps in the Soviet Union? Nonsense. Lies. I had been pulled into murky waters. Maybe the smoke from his hashish, after all, was carefully planned to intercept my rational thinking. Every minute I stayed here, I was betraying my family, my Communist values. I was putting in jeopardy my music career, my entire life.

Like Comrade Farhad said: "Disloyalty starts with the small things." He had warned me, but I had failed.

"Why did you tell me all this?" I asked Tahir, more harshly than I intended, fighting off my inner shame, seeking his eyes.

They were changing a shade at a time from dark indigo all the way to lavender blue, warm and bottomless. And for a moment—a fleeting moment—I drowned inside them. All of me.

Embarrassed, I turned away.

"I told you because you are the girl who played Beethoven's 'Adagio' the other day. You are brainwashed and confused, but you've got a soul. You've got a free-roaming soul."

If I had died right then, I'd have been the happiest man on earth.

I rose to my feet, prickly after sitting in the same position for a long time. "I am going to keep everything you've told me a secret, but I want you to know that I do not believe you. Not a word," I fired off in one quick round and staggered—on porcupine needles—toward the door.

"By the way, it's not Gargoyle Castle," Tahir said after me. "It's Villa Anneliese."

"What?" I stopped. "How do you know where I live?"

Tahir didn't bother answering. Just took a long drag from his hashish cigarette and departed into his own dimension.

And that was the beginning. The beginning of the end of my cloudless Soviet childhood. My first glimpse into the tragic history of Tahir's family and into the horrors and lies of Communism. Into darkness I had never known before. Darkness that someday would enter my soul.

CHAPTER 9

I left Tahir's shop and roved the streets, the same mantra playing like a rondo in my head: *Lies... Lies... Nothing but lies...*

The city had awakened by now. Vendors had turned their shops inside out, blocking the sidewalks with baskets overflowing with fabrics, shoes, copper vases. Cars and noisy motorcycles zoomed by, their exhaust choking the air. A jet plane shot through the sky, then another, their milky contrails crossing, sweeping across the boundless blue. A flock of kids dashed past me trying to catch up with the rockets, almost knocking me off my feet. I used to do that too—run fast, exuberantly cheering the greatness of our country. Now I felt nothing. An empty swing dangling in the wind. An alien in my own city.

What a mistake it had been to go there, to nurture a fantasy of a magical world hidden behind the green door. There was nothing there but a treacherous scheme to lure and corrupt foolish innocents like me. And I—*I* who had been given the honor of exposing the treachery—had almost succumbed to it. To Tahir's music. To his absurd stories. *Open your ear to a mullah's preaching, and a bee gets in*—just like a *kəlam* says.

Why did I give him my word to keep it a secret? How had he pulled me so far off my senses and captured my empathy? Burdened my soul with a promise I couldn't keep?

My free-roaming soul.

More like my free-roaming *gullible* soul. Lost in a maze of sophisticated anti-Soviet conspiracy. No. I had to expose it. I had to fulfill my duty and report Tahir as a traitor, as someone who distributed awful, dishonest propaganda about our political and social system.

And he lied about going to the Philharmonic too—*I rarely miss a good performance.* Then why hadn't I ever seen him there any time before the day he showed up accidentally—*accidentally?*—at my recital? Nonsense. And his hashish smoking, his Western behavior, the pornography on his wall. All American, all probably bought or stolen from the black market or supplied by his handlers in the West.

But, no matter how I tried, I couldn't get the images out of my head—Tahir, a quirky teenager, walking barefoot on a busy street. Tahir, in a white tunic, standing alongside his painting. Tahir, seated cross-legged on the burgundy rug in his cozy lair, surrounded by music albums and ancient books, his deep, intelligent eyes following me.

Enough!

"Out of my sight—out of my heart," I muttered, pushing my weight against the heavy oak door of Gargoyle Castle.

Villa Anneliese?

I glanced down at the granite floor of the entryway. Was it here where Tahir's great-grandfather had turned his gun on himself? And then a hurricane of the riddle's pieces swirled through my mind— the Snow Princess on the fresco in our courtyard…the rumor that she was the daughter of the oil baron who built our castle…the world's greatest mezzo…Tahir's grandmother…the Immortal?

"*Salam eleykum*, Leila."

Chingiz's warped smile flashed at me from beyond the curvy balustrade girdling the third-floor balcony, followed by the piercing sound of an ivory piece slammed heartily against a game board. Chingiz was playing *shesh besh* with his uncle Ali Khan—his only positive contribution to the old man's life.

"*Salam eleykum*, Ali Khan. Are you killing Chingiz again?" I shouted. Ali Khan had lost most of his hearing after a bomb explosion during the war.

"*Eleykum salam*, Leila. Of course I am. As the old man looks for a bridge, the young man rushes to wade across the river." He slammed the checker and chuckled harmlessly. "And the young fool always drowns."

The door to our flat was open, the scent of oranges drifting in and out of the vanilla-saturated air, which meant Papa had baked my favorite sweet bread, *şəkər çörək*. A chorus of clanging dishes came from the kitchen, accompanied by the happy chatter of sparrows outside the window.

I was back to my life. My wonderful, real life. But along with the reality, the anxiety over my piano performance also returned. Had the decision been made by now? What if I didn't win?

"At last. The wandering star has returned."

Professor Sultan-zade?

She sat on the couch next to Mama, her revolutionary maroon dress defying the serene pastel greens of our living room, but today she wore something else that I had rarely seen on her—a rosy, gap-toothed smile.

"Good morning, Professor," I said, impatient to hear the verdict.

Papa entered from the kitchen, Mama's red-and-white polka-dot apron on top of his trousers. He carried a steaming potbellied samovar.

"There is nothing better than a good stroll in the morning," he said, pecking me on the top of my head. "That's what we all should be doing."

"What's the occasion?" I asked.

"Sunday family breakfast. What can be a better occasion to celebrate?"

"Stop teasing her." Mama got up, fresh and elegant in a pleated skirt and a blouse with gem buttons, her golden locks falling on her shoulders, framing her freckle-peppered face. "Professor Sultan-zade stopped by to make an informal announcement prior to the official one."

"Yes, indeed." Professor Sultan-zade stubbed out her cigarette in the ashtray. "What can I say other than that you were absolutely outstanding? And fully deserving of the win." She rose to her feet, her face radiating pride, the crow's-feet at the sides of her eyes cracking the foundation layer of her makeup. "You won, Leila. You won a big A-plus. Both jurors loved you. Especially Professor Levina. She just couldn't stop praising you, and this is not something that comes easily to her. Starting right now, you are an official ambassador of Azerbaijan at the International Piano Competition in Budapest. Congratulations. I am extremely pleased."

"I won! I won!" I shouted, jumping up and down, laughing and crying at the same time, releasing the nervousness that had been mounting inside me since the recital. I was thrilled. Yes. But deep inside I wasn't surprised. I expected to win. I knew that my performance in the competition, despite its shaky start, deserved the win. I played my Beethoven; I pushed the keys. I always did, but in the past, only as a messenger of Professor Sultan-zade's emotions and visions, never having experienced my own so intensely before.

I stopped, trying to catch my breath. "Professor, do you believe in the divine presence in music?" I asked.

"Divine presence?" Professor Sultan-zade's green eyes examined me closely for a few moments before looking away thoughtfully. "No, Leila. Music is about the notes, the technique, and the precise execution of the dynamics. Done well, that combination creates a performance that can become a strong emotional weapon. But to attribute it to anything mystical? No."

"But where does music come from? How does it inspire us? Or make us lose ourselves in those irresistible musical phrases composed by, for example, Chopin more than a hundred years ago?"

"I would say that's the humanity of music," Professor Sultan-zade said. "But definitely not its divinity."

We celebrated by having breakfast, sitting around our large table, a set of fine china with pink roses in full display on the snow-white tablecloth. The conversation ran as fluidly as the tea out of the samovar's crooked nose.

"There will be big changes at the Conservatory," Professor Sultan-zade said. "Our rector is being moved to the Azerbaijani State Institute of Arts—our longtime rival. The years under his leadership had been the most victorious in the history of our institution. Of course it didn't hurt that the Minister of Culture was married to his sister and provided the Conservatory with unlimited funding.

"Now the situation is on the verge of changing. The choice for whoever will be appointed in the rector's place is a big secret. Everybody's been on tiptoes. Especially a recently hired Professor Kulik. She says that she graduated from the Leningrad Conservatory of Music, but I don't believe it. I heard her playing a recital with her students—amateur level."

Professor Sultan-zade shook her head, her heavy, Egyptian, gold-chandelier earrings jangling, pulling the earlobes down and threatening to tear them loose.

She looked a bit like Nefertiti. The same long aquiline nose, high sunken cheeks, slanted eyes, extended neck. Even the yellowish color of her skin, the result of her intense smoking, was the same as the tinting on Nefertiti's bronze bust. I asked Papa once why she never married. He laughed, said she had a stinger instead of a tongue, and that men didn't like bees that couldn't make honey. That's what he called her behind her back—Old Stinger.

I put three cubes of sugar in my cup with boiling hot tea, mixed it with the spoon, and let it stand for a while.

"I don't understand how you can drink it warm," Papa said. "For me to enjoy the flavor of tea, it has to burn my lips."

"You're a man of extremes." Mama smiled.

"Being with the two smartest girls, I have to find some excuse to stand out."

"All you have to do to stand out, honorable Mekhti Rashidovich, is to stand up," Professor Sultan-zade interjected, the corner of her mouth curling up.

Oh yes, Papa's height was quite striking, especially measured against the Lilliputian sizes of Mama and myself.

Papa slowly blew air through his mustache. "I'm in bad shape if my height is my *highest* achievement. I definitely need to do something to improve my reputation, don't I?"

Retrieving a small, dark blue box from his pocket, he placed it ceremoniously on the table in front of me. "Let's see if this helps."

"What is this, Papa?"

"Open it."

I did. Inside, a dazzling ring sat on a blue velvet pillow.

"It's braided platinum with sapphire—a gift for you, Leila," Papa said, his brow glistening with a sheen of sweat. "I ordered it from a very special jewelry maker in Şamaxı. Cost me a fortune. But for you, my precious *brilyant*, I'd give up my last breath. Try it on."

Carefully lifting the ring out of the box, I slid it down my second finger. The oblong sapphire immediately captured a sunbeam and swelled into a huge orange sphere of light.

"Perfect fit! The same size as your finger, Sonia." Papa smiled, took both Mama's and my hands and kissed them, then turned to Professor Sultan-zade. "How am I doing?"

She clapped her hands theatrically. "You've done very well, Mekhti Rashidovich. A very lavish gift, indeed, and in such exquisite taste. Beethoven's *Pathétique* is definitely deserving of such splendor. As for Leila, she still has a long way to go, and a reward of such magnitude might spoil her sense of humility, which is vital for a student of piano."

"Don't worry, Professor," Papa said. "My Leila has Badalbeili ambitions, and a major interruption, even one the size of this sapphire, won't slow her down." He winked at me and burst into roaring laughter.

"Oh, well." Professor Sultan-zade smiled courteously. "I have a different kind of gift for you, Leila." She reached for her bag and retrieved a brand-new copy of the score for Wolfgang Amadeus Mozart's *Piano Concerto no. 20*. "This is the piece you'll be playing in Budapest—your best friend for the next nine months."

I reverently touched the smooth, satined cover of the score—an entry into Mozart's delicate, romantic, eloquent soul. And, hopefully, the passport to my first international success.

The front doorbell rang.

Probably Almaz. We had made a tentative plan to go to the movies. I jumped up to open the door.

Comrade Farhad's black eyes shone from behind a large bouquet of bloodred roses.

"Good morning, L-l-leila, I'd like to speak to your father if I m-m-may."

"Oh, Farhad, how nice to see you." Mama came to the door. "Would you like to join us for breakfast? We're having a small celebration here. Leila has won the competition."

"Congratulations!" Comrade Farhad placed his right hand across his chest and bowed his head briefly. "I'm very proud of your daughter. But no thank you, Sonia *Khanum*, I don't intend to intrude on your f-f-family time." A henna-red blush ran across his cheek.

"This is for you, Sonia *Khanum*." He held out the bouquet to Mama. "Is Mekhti Rashidovich available for a second? I'm here to ask if he would kindly agree to be our point speaker at a conference I am planning for June."

"I'd be honored." Papa joined us at the door and shook hands with Farhad. "I've heard a lot of good things about your dedicated, hard work on behalf of our Young Communists League. And we, Sonia and I, have been most pleased to have you as an excellent role model and mentor for our dear Leila."

"Thank you, Mekhti Rashidovich, for your kind words." Comrade Farhad pressed his hands to his chest, tilting his head sideways to convey humility. "We strive to continue the legacy of illustrious leaders such as yourself and your distinguished family. Again, I apologize for the intrusion, Sonia *Khanum*." He turned toward me. "You played exceptionally well, Leila. You've made us all very proud. I'll see you—"

"Leila dear." Mama gently moved a curl off my eyes. "Why don't you walk Farhad out?"

"Of course, just a moment."

I zipped to my room, kicked off slippers in favor of my heeled shoes, and joined Farhad outside the door. We went downstairs in total silence except for the *clack-clack* of my heels slapping the granite. I could feel his presence, strong and manly. And suddenly I became very much aware of the four-year difference in our ages. He was a man, unlike my immature schoolmates who *talked* about all these *things*. How would it feel if Farhad took my hand in his, brought it to his face, and touched my fingers with his lips? The way Papa had just kissed Mama's hand? How would it feel to hear a beating heart inside Farhad's steel armor?

We crossed our courtyard and stopped in the niche with no one around. Just Farhad and me. I kept my eyes down, fighting off the tremolo in my stomach.

"Where is your Komsomol badge?" he asked out of the blue.

My hand flew to my collar. The badge wasn't there. I took it off to go visit Tahir and forgot to pin it back on. I closed my eyes in embarrassment, expecting to be reprimanded.

"Don't worry, Leila," I heard Farhad saying in an unusually mellow voice. "I have this special badge given to me by Comrade Popov himself."

He pulled a large badge out of the pocket of his trousers and began to pin it to the collar of my blouse.

I wanted to put my foolish head on Farhad's shoulder and cry and confess my treasonous behavior and my confusion and my fears. He would understand and forgive because he really cared about me. How could I have been so foolish as to think that Comrade Farhad had wrecked my recital? It was stage fright. That's all. The rest I invented myself.

Farhad's pinkie seemed to slowly move down to my breast… poking…probing…reaching the nipple…all while attaching the Komsomol badge. Then he furtively looked around, grabbed my hand, and brushed it against his bulging crotch.

"That's what you've done to me," he whispered in my ear

accusingly, breathing flames. "You are mine now. Do you hear me? You belong to me, Leila. To me and no one else. I think about you all the time. All the things I'm going to do to you." He grinned, yellow snakes dancing in his eyes. "And remember, I'm watching you. Watching your every step. So you better never—*never*—let me down."

He turned and hastily walked away, leaving me standing in the shadowy niche. Staring absently at a faded fresco of the Snow Maiden in an azure gown, a gazelle at her feet, petting the bird in her lap.

Was it my fault? Had I done something to cause it? I stood numb, confused, shaken, wishing the last few minutes had never happened.

CHAPTER 10

That night I couldn't sleep.

Why? Why did Farhad treat me so disrespectfully? Had I given him any reason? Had I somehow unconsciously prompted him to become rough with me?

Since childhood, we had been taught that girls would always be blamed for enticing men. That was engraved in our Azeri mentality. But how did I entice him? All I ever showed him was my respect and admiration. Maybe I showed it too much, giving him the wrong idea? I did dream that someday Farhad would choose me as his girl. And I did want Farhad to touch me. But not in the rude way he did, as if I was some unscrupulous, cheap, dirty street girl.

I had to talk to him. On Thursday, after the Komsomol meeting. To explain that what had transpired was wrong. That he had scared me, diminished my sense of self, and that his behavior reflected negatively on my relationship with him.

Would I dare to say all this to his face?

I pulled the blanket over my head and began counting camels: *One, two, three…seven…* Aunty Zeinab's recipe for sleep that had always worked. Even on the night before the chemistry exam, when all one hundred seventeen elements of Mendeleev's periodic table bounced around my brain like a horde of restless moths. *Twelve, thirteen…* Arabian camels began moving across the walls, slowly, one after another. *Eighteen, nineteen, twenty…thirty…fifty-nine…*

Hayya alal-falah as-salaatu khairun minan-naum...

The morning prayer, *Fajr Adhan*, lifted me out of my dream. I opened my eyes to the lazy sunrise. To Muezzin Rashid's tranquil modulations suspended in the air.

I had an idea.

On my way to school, careful not to be seen, I snuck downstairs and knocked on the door of Muezzin Rashid's apartment that he had inhabited, as Papa told me, since the Revolution. He lived by himself, and he kept to himself, a hermit dwelling in basement rooms in the rear of our castle. No one ever visited him or talked to him. A pariah. A man of religion. An atavism of the old world. At the same time, though, a silent aura of respect for him—or maybe fear—reigned across the neighborhood. *A fear of God?*

Muezzin Rashid opened the door, the thick shrubbery of his eyebrows raised in surprise over faded eyes drooping inside hammocks of crumpled flesh.

"I need to ask you something," I whispered.

"Come in, come in, *qız*." He took my hand and led me inside his apartment. "Anything you ask for."

The place was tiny and dark, its linoleum floor filthy gray, mirroring a ceiling infested with moldy smudges and fissures. A decrepit television was set on top of a broken stove. An old rug, in need of soapy water, hung on the wall. Across its surface, two lovebirds flew on a magic carpet through dusty gray clouds instead of soaring into blue skies.

"Sit down, *qız*. Let me bring you an *armud* of tea."

"Thank you, Muezzin Rashid. I don't want to be late for school, but I need to ask you..." I stumbled. "It's about the Immortal. I mean, Miriam Mukhtarov. Did you know her? And is it true that our castle is not really Gargoyle Castle but—"

"Villa Anneliese," Muezzin Rashid finished for me, a thin, nostalgic smile lighting up his creased face, baring his toothless mouth. "Villa Anneliese," he repeated as if enjoying the sound of it. "The gardens were filled with roses. They bloomed all year

88

around, each season a different fragrance. A lot of revelry we had here. In the Oriental Hall, all in azure tile, it looked like the tent of a Mauritanian princess."

Was it in the forsaken part of our building, the black gap in the sky I stared at every evening?

"Let me show you something, *qız*." Leaning his wrinkled, blue-veined hands against the table, Muezzin Rashid lifted his feeble body. He shuffled to a wardrobe with a missing door, pushed aside a pile of ragged clothes, and rummaged around until he found a packet swathed in a piece of olive-green flannel. Unwrapping it as gently as though a rare rose had bloomed inside, he retrieved an old photograph.

"This is me." He pointed at a young, flamboyant man, wearing traditional Azeri dress—a glossy satin *rubakha*—and a tall lambskin hat. "In Uzeyir Hajibeyov's production of *Arshin Mal Alan*. In 1921."

"You sang Arshin Mal Alan?" I said, startled. Arshin Mal Alan? The swanky main tenor in the first Azerbaijani national comic opera—a wealthy bachelor who disguises himself as a cloth peddler and travels around to see women at their houses without chadors to choose his bride. I couldn't believe it.

Muezzin Rashid stared at the photograph, a reflective shadow across his face, slipping back to the distant rooms of his memory. "And here is Miriam."

A young woman next to him, in a white gown, a garland of flowers in her long, blond hair, her eyes gleaming through the layer of tarnish on the aged paper.

"This is her?" I asked, astounded.

"Yes, irresistible Miriam Mukhtarov. The glowing mezzo. And oh, her magnetism… With a flicker of her eyelashes she could capture the audience and set their hearts aflame. A real diva." Muezzin Rashid swallowed strenuously as if a pebble had gotten stuck in his throat.

Had she set his heart aflame as well?

"And who is this?" I indicated a young man in a beret and checkered breeches sitting in front of Miriam.

"Caspar the Poet. *Xəyalpərəst*, a dreamer with his head in the clouds. What did Miriam see in him? Ech." Muezzin Rashid shook his head. "It is because of him that Miriam came back to the Soviet Union. To save him."

"From what?"

"He was accused of intellectual and religious sabotage."

"And did she save him?"

"No, they executed Caspar."

"But why?" I exclaimed.

"Shhh." Muezzin Rashid's finger flew to his lips.

I could sense his fear.

"Muezzin Rashid," I whispered, "have you heard of the gulag?"

He didn't answer, just sat with his head in his hands, shaking back and forth, a little old man alone with the ghosts of his past.

"I didn't have Miriam's courage," he said. "No one did. She was a steel maiden who never compromised even the least of her principles. She used to say: 'An egg thief becomes a camel thief.' Who would have expected such spirit in a delicate, raised-in-gold-and-feathers princess?"

"I don't understand. If they executed that man, Caspar, because of the *religious sabotage*, how can you be allowed to sing in the mosque?"

"Oyi, *qız*." Muezzin Rashid sighed. "Times have changed since then, and now they have to be clever with the Islamic revolution in Iran and Ruhollah Khomeini just across the Kura River from us. As the old *hikmət* says, to stay alive, a wolf will put on a fox's tail. So *they* play games—keep a few mosques around to show off their tolerance and respect for our national Islamic culture. But it's only a facade supervised by the KGB. And me? I'm just another puppet, wagging my lamb's tail to butter my rotting bones before they burn in Allah's fire."

"This is not true," I said firmly. "I can't even imagine the sun mounting the sky without your *Adhans*. They are so beautiful. And meaningful too. An inseparable part of our lives." I paused before adding an old adage, "'Even a blind man can hear the nightingale sing.'"

A slight wave of a hand. The faint, barely suppressed flush of a former operatic star. He walked me to the door.

"Muezzin Rashid, do other people know what you just told me?"

He hesitated for a moment, his breathing rapid and shallow, his head sinking lower, his eyes locked on the wall. "What did I tell you? I don't remember what I told you. I'm so old, I've outlived my own mind. Go to school, *qız*, and have a sunny day, with Allah's help."

The door closed behind me with a moaning rustle.

Even a blind man can hear the nightingale sing. It was the least I could say to thank Muezzin Rashid for what he had given me. Now I knew—Tahir's story wasn't the fruit of his hashish imagination or political propaganda. He had told me the truth.

CHAPTER 11

A shiny black Chaika waited outside the green door with the engine running. It was the type of car usually reserved for very important Communist Party members like Papa and a few of his friends in the government. When he wasn't traveling to the oil fields, he—and sometimes me and Mama—were driven around town in a car just like this. What was it doing here in this part of town? At the green door?

The back window rolled down, and a girl my age, maybe a year older, leaned out, showering her face with the sunlight. A doll-like face with perfect kohl lines around her eyes and iridescent, bright pink mousse drawing attention to her full lips and high cheekbones. Just the way Almaz liked to apply her makeup and unsuccessfully tried to teach me to do.

I snuck inside the fabric store across the street and took my post by the row of silks, happy that a wearisome customer was rambling nonstop and keeping the grumpy saleswoman busy and away from me. The clock on the wall showed two thirty. An eternity later, the minute hand still hadn't reached the thirty-five mark.

The boys kept running up and down the street, throwing stones at sparrows. One of them, delayed by his short, bowed legs, had a difficult time catching up with the rest. He was the son of the shoe-shop owner. Tahir's neighbor.

Finally, a short, stocky man in a gray suit emerged briskly from Tahir's shop carrying a painting of Mona Lisa, her face looking downward, peeking through the torn newspaper wrapping. The chauffeur leaped out of the car and threw the door open. The gray-suited man disappeared behind the tinted windows, and the Chaika roared away. I waited for a few minutes, crossed the street, and stepped inside the green door.

Tahir stood in the corner, counting a stack of cash.

"So you're running a lucrative business here," I said, unable to suppress the chirping overtones in my voice.

"Hmm. It's you." He scratched an eyebrow, trying to tone down his own apparent excitement. It didn't help. Not with the grin. Was it because of the money? Or me?

"I'm here, but don't you think for a moment that I'm here because I agree with your accusations about Communism and my beliefs." I muttered a phrase I had been rehearsing tirelessly. It didn't come out in the strong, assertive way I had planned.

"Patience is the key to paradise." Tahir smiled, his eyebrows arched like the wings of a soaring swallow.

"What do you mean?"

"What I mean is that an illness comes by the pound and goes away by the ounce."

I'd heard that old saying before but couldn't quite understand what he referred to as *an illness*. I chose to sway away from his interpretation. "Did you just sell stolen art?" I asked instead.

"Oh yes, straight from the Louvre. Haven't you read in the paper that *Mona Lisa* has fallen in value recently? So I thought—ah, first, Picasso, now me."

"I don't understand."

"It's a long story."

"I've got time."

"Aren't you supposed to practice piano all day long?" he said, failing to keep his face straight.

"Oh, thanks for reminding me. I better go, then."

He shrugged. "You can stay if you want."

"Then what about Picasso?"

"Picasso? Well, when *Mona Lisa* was stolen from the Louvre in 1911, the magazines accused Picasso of the theft."

"Did he do it?"

"No, some Italian nationalist did it. He wanted Leonardo da Vinci to hang in the Uffizi Gallery. But Picasso's name attached to the story gave the painting instant attention. And the value of *Mona Lisa* rose astronomically." He stopped, biting his paint-stained thumbnail. His nails had been chewed down almost to the quick.

"Very interesting," I said, "but what about *your* Mona Lisa? And the black Chaika I saw outside with a man and his daughter."

"She's not his daughter. She's a *kəniz*, one of the many concubines he's picked up at the Turkish baths. That's where your glorious Communist deities hold their bacchanalias, you know." He clicked his tongue in loud judgment. "Back to your inquiry. It's very simple. One has to do a lot of different things to survive in this Kingdom of Darkness."

Kingdom of Darkness? "So you paint for important Party members while you actually loathe them?"

"That's quite perceptive for a girl of your age."

For a girl of my age?

How old was Tahir? Not that much older than me. Seventeen maybe? Judging by his self-assurance, his stories, and his knowledge, he had lived a few lives already, but his eccentric manners reminded me of the hyperactive five-year-old son of one of Mama's nurses.

Tahir put the money on the stool and slapped his hands against each other as if washing away the dirt. "At the moment," he said, "Leonardo da Vinci is in fashion among the Baku Communist elite. I paint the phony replicas, good enough for Comrade This or Comrade That to impress their cohorts with their fine arts patronage and bring me more business. And the buffoon who was just here, I'm sort of his *court painter*. And, on top of that, I run some not-quite-legal errands for him from time to time.

"In exchange, he provides me with flimsy but, nonetheless, vital protection. He's my safeguard—my *krysha*. I make him good money; he pays me the crumbs. For the time being, I'm safe from the KGB's Iron Maiden, so I can buy music records on the black market and lure foolish girls into my temple of music."

He narrowed his lilac eyes, a sly smile hopping all over his face. "Would you like to have some tea and hear some music, Leila?"

Was he mocking me? "I think I'm going to leave now."

"Oh no." Tahir sucked in his lower lip and raised his eyebrows, looking like an apologetic child. "I'm sorry, that didn't come out right. What I said. Ignore that last part. The 'foolish girls' part. The 'tea' part stands though. So?"

I took my time. "I guess I can stay, but just for a few minutes."

"Perfect. Give me a few minutes, and I'll change your world," he crooned in his high voice, heading toward the alcove with the recordings. He sorted through the stacks and pulled an album from the shelf. "I'd like to play something very special for you. I think you're going to like her."

"Who is this?"

"Nina Simone. No one can strip life down to a bare emotion the way she does."

The blue light of the Rapsodija languorously illuminated the room as he placed the disc on the turntable.

The sweeping sound of an orchestral opening followed by a rough voice singing in English. The song defied every rule of classical music—the odd resolutions of the chords in the accompaniment, the distorted pitch of the singer, the almost unintended hint of light in the chromatic piano lines conflicting with the gloom in the vocal intonations—yet all together it had an emotional impact that I could only compare to the music of Richard Wagner with its poignant romanticism emerging out of symphonic mayhem.

"You said 'she,' but it sounds like 'he,'" I said after the song was finished.

"Many of the female jazz vocalists are black. Their voices are very guttural and feral, yet they carry the relentless power to reach deep inside your soul."

"Isn't it prohibited to play or even listen to jazz music?"

"Of course it is. Just as prohibited as it is to breathe, to think, and to know. You see—" he started, then broke off. A naughty grimace broadened his face, twisting his mouth and revealing slightly crowded lower teeth. Mimicking a soldier's pace, he strutted theatrically across the room, stopped at the hearth, and swiftly turned to face me.

"Comrades," he said in a low oratorical tone of voice, heartily hitting the air with the fist of his right hand. "Jazz is a hydra of Imperialist propaganda. Today you are listening to an American saxophone—tomorrow you'll sell your Motherland." He hit the air. "Exterminate!" Another hit. "Wipe out!" Hit. "Burn to ashes!"

Feeling annoyed and amused at the same time, I watched as he quite accurately impersonated both Comrade Farhad and Comrade Popov in their addresses to the Komsomol Assembly, complete with a simulation of them banging their fists against the podium. Tahir's timing, though, was definitely better.

"We, the generation of selfless builders of Communism, we won't stop until we behead the hydra monster of Western Decadence one head at a time…"

I glanced at my watch. Five minutes to four. I could still make it in time for the Komsomol meeting. But I dreaded facing—and even more so, confronting—Comrade Farhad. So I decided to just call his office later and report that I was not feeling well.

"We, the mercenaries of Communism—"

"Stop it." I cut Tahir off, even though part of me rejoiced. Carefree Tahir, with his bizarre performance, was so different from rigid, grim-faced Comrade Farhad. "You are ridiculing my beliefs. Do you want me to leave?"

At once, Tahir cast off the orator's image. "I'm sorry. I didn't mean to upset your ideological sensitivities. And if I did so—unintentionally—I hope the distress hasn't spread its claws to your stomach and we still can share a pleasant feast together. Will you join me for *kutabs*? I'm famished."

We ate on his Afghani rug, a pile of steaming *kutabs*—traditional Azeri crepes filled with meat and herbs—on a newspaper in front of us. Plunging one after the other into a glass bowl with coriander kefir, we stuffed them into our insatiable mouths. How weird. Here I was, alone in a room with a total stranger—a definitely odd stranger—sitting on the floor, inhaling the sweet scent of hashish, and feeling more comfortable than I had ever felt with anyone.

"*I put a spell on you... I put a spell on you,*" wailed Nina Simone in her deep manly voice from the corner in a language that I, then, could not understand.

"Why do you smoke hashish?" I asked.

"Because it takes me back to places I'll never see again in this life—Paris, Rome, Barcelona. Beautiful cities. Beautiful people."

"What do you mean by *again*?"

"I had the good fortune to see them. To be there."

"What? You have been in the West?"

"A year ago, when I turned seventeen, I was sent to study art in the Hochschule für Bildende Künste Dresden, the Dresden Academy of Fine Arts. By mistake, of course. A typical Soviet screw-up. When the right hand didn't know what the left hand was doing. Someone misspelled my name, missing a letter. So when I won a national art competition in high school, the KGB somehow didn't connect me to the Mukhtarovs, *the dangerous enemy of the Soviet people*, and gave me a visa.

"After a month there, I ran away. You see, even though Dresden is a part of East Germany, the atmosphere there is much looser than in the Soviet Union. I traveled all over Europe." He sighed. "But I failed. Stupidly failed. Gorged myself on freedom. Choked on it. And ended up walking into their trap. They brought me back and threw me into a correctional institute."

A convicted defector? Had I gone another stroke away from the shore into even more troubled waters? I remembered one morning at the Pioneer camp, two summers earlier, when my group went for a swim, I ended up going so far that when I looked back, the shoreline seemed more distant than the horizon. But I didn't feel scared, not at all. If anything, I had to fight the temptation to keep going farther toward the vast, thrilling unknown. Like now. With Tahir.

He leaned back on his elbows, inhaled from his cigarette, and closed his eyes, immersed in the music.

"Tell me about the places you've been to," I said.

"You're hearing them. They're like the jazz music. Different. Tantalizing. Stimulating. An instant splash of color across a canvas." Tahir reached for the shelf and pulled another album, holding it protectively against his chest with both hands. "Wait till you hear this one. My favorite artist of them all. She is like no one else. Her name is Billie Holiday, but the world called her Lady Day."

The recording sounded to me as if it was playing at 20 instead of 33 rpms, slurring, hiccupping. Trying to follow Lady Day's vocal lines felt like stumbling into the unforeseen dead ends in the labyrinth of Icheri Sheher. She juggled her phrases tirelessly up and down her ample tessitura. At the same time, I felt her sitting next to me, speaking into my ear, saying something soothing and promising, drops of sunshine sifting through her dark, smoky voice.

"This music doesn't sound very happy, does it?" I said, unsure of my reaction.

"How could it? Jazz is a soundtrack of real life. And life isn't a very happy phenomenon."

"Why do you think it's better there in the West than it is here at home?"

"You can be free there. You can choose how to dress, where to live, what music to listen to, which God to believe in. You can be *you*."

Tahir looked ethereal amid the hashish rings hovering in the air. His body moved in rhythm with the music—slowly, in a trance—as if performing some ancient ritual.

"Jazz is good for you." His voice drifted through the haze. "That's why they forbid it. Because it's so emotionally rudimental that the music finds its way straight to your soul and cleanses it from fifteen years of Soviet pollution."

Soviet pollution?

Another one of his attacks on my Communist ethics. Then why did I sit here like a stone? Why didn't I try to defend what I believed was right? The real question though—what was *right*?

Comrade Farhad with the yellow snakes in his eyes? Touching me, intimidating me, diminishing me to just a garnished piece of meat sitting on his plate, waiting to be devoured?

No. There had to be a reason why I landed on Tahir's magic carpet, on the other side—the *wrong* side—of the green door. Why I enjoyed sitting cross-legged next to him, listening to the crackling fire dragon, sipping pungent *mekhmeri* tea as strong and smooth as an Armenian cognac. There had to be a reason why I was so persuaded by his confusing, esoteric perspectives, perspectives that had taken me far beyond my own horizon. Drifting away in clouds of hashish, surrendering to his forbidden LPs with their bewitching musical potions, there had to be a reason why I was beginning to take it all in, making it part of me.

Cleansing my soul?

CHAPTER 12

That evening, Almaz and I went to see the Russian movie *Moscow Does Not Believe in Tears* at our favorite open-air cinema in Seaside Park. Surrounded by walls of vines, caressed by the warm, jasmine-scented sea breeze, we sat, tearful, holding hands, rooting for the young heroine on the screen to win her lover.

"She did nothing wrong," Almaz said, wiping her eyes, as we were leaving the cinema. "She was young and vulnerable, and the man took advantage of her fantasies. They always do. It's a man's world."

"All I know is that Papa would kill me if he knew I went to see this movie."

"Don't tell him."

"Of course, I won't. It's just strange that a movie like this was allowed in Baku, with our norms of modesty, don't you think?"

"Norms of modesty?" Almaz grunted sarcastically. "Where are they, other than in your Communist manual?"

I didn't respond.

We turned into an arcade of acacia trees, dimly lit and empty. I instinctively looked over my shoulder. A dark figure behind seemed to flit to the side, blending with the trees. Did someone follow us? Or was it my imagination? I sped up, dragging Almaz, until we exited Seaside Park onto crowded Neftchilar Avenue.

When Almaz and I were kids, we had a Saturday evening ritual. First, Papa took us to his office to play Ping-Pong, then to the open-air cinema for a movie, and to conclude the evening, on the way home, we usually stopped for supper at restaurant Baran. The owner always gave us the best table, separated from the rest of the room, and treated us as family, cooking lamb shashlik to Papa's taste.

Since then, the restaurant had been closed, and the owner, we heard, was in jail for stealing. But every time I passed by the sign, I salivated, recalling those skewers with the succulent chunks of lamb, marinated in fig vinegar, onions, and tomatoes.

What a surprise it was when we turned into Djaparidze Street, and instead of the aged facade of Baran, a new neon sign read "Little Star."

"What is this?" I asked Almaz.

"A new café. It's only been open for a few weeks. Let's have a quick supper."

In Baku, decent women were not supposed to be in a restaurant by themselves. Especially at nine in the evening.

"Leila, please. Just for a few minutes," Almaz pleaded. "No one will know."

I hesitated. Never before would I have agreed. But now, following the afternoon spent with Tahir and his music and the movie with its stirring emotional message, I felt like doing something different, daring. Shaking up the rules a bit.

We entered. The café was packed. Mostly young men and a handful of girls with heavy makeup, loudly dressed. Columns of blue smoke rose to the ceiling.

A fidgety young waiter approached us, sizing up Almaz and me openly.

"Two of you?" he asked with a cheeky smirk.

"Yes," Almaz said before I had a chance to say no. "That table by the window." She pointed toward the area we used to occupy with Papa. Still looking the same, separated by a hanging rug from the rest of the room.

The waiter led us through the café, past the sneers and muffled derisive *tztztz* of the male guests.

"Are you sure we're fine here?" I whispered to Almaz.

"Don't worry. The owner knows me."

We ordered kebabs and, waiting for food, drank a sweet rose tea with honey. Everyone in the room smoked, a subtle trace of black currant scent making me think of Tahir. Putting me at ease. Relaxing me.

Almaz retrieved a small green package out of her purse. Foreign cigarettes.

"You smoke?" I asked in disbelief.

"Want to try?" She winked, pulling a long, thin cigarette out of the pack. "They are Dunhills. With menthol, very light, specially for women."

"Where did you buy them?"

"I have my sources."

Almaz lit her cigarette with a miniature golden lighter and leaned back against her chair, closing her eyes. Blue smoke swirled around her beautiful face. I had a sudden impulse to open up, tell her about Tahir. But something stopped me. No, it wasn't worry that she would tell anyone. I knew I could trust Almaz with my life. It was fear of her quick, negative judgment.

Indian music rippled through the room, the seductive sounds of sitar and tabla slipping in and out of the crowd's noise. I sipped my tea, feeling happy. Free.

"I thought you weren't feeling well."

I jumped at the sound of the voice. Comrade Farhad stood over our table. His slightly misty black eyes held me captive.

"Not well enough to attend the Komsomol meeting," he said sternly. "But well enough to have a good time in a restaurant at night."

A dark figure behind us in the alley. Was it him following us?

"But, Comrade Farhad, how did you know—"

"You called in sick today, didn't you? So, after the meeting, I phoned your home to inquire about your health, and honorable Mekhti Rashidovich told me that you went to the cinema. You should be ashamed of yourself, Leila."

He grasped my hand, forcing me to get up. "Let's go. This is not a proper place for a decent girl. Even less so for a young Komsomol leader."

Almaz stared at me in shock. "You're not going to listen to him, are you?"

Comrade Farhad responded by aggressively sticking his finger in Almaz's face. "You stay out of it." Then, to me, "I'm taking you home," and he led me out of the café.

Almaz followed, muttering, "Why are you listening to him? Who is he to dictate how you should behave? He is not your master."

We walked home in the custody of dark, heavy silence. Three of us. Almaz and I, and Farhad a few steps behind, escorting us as if we were captured fugitives.

When we reached our building, Farhad caught up with us. "You go." He waved a dismissive hand at Almaz.

"I'm not going anyway without Leila," she replied, grasping my forearm.

I faltered, torn by a gush of emotions. After all, I had lied and missed the Komsomol meeting for no reason other than that I wanted to stay with Tahir and listen to his jazz. And the café with hashish smoking and women of low virtue wasn't the place for me. What if Farhad would tell Papa about it? I could only imagine Papa's fury.

Farhad waited for my decision, anxious, a drop of sweat sliding down his forehead. The same Comrade Farhad I had always trusted. Feelings of guilt and confusion overwhelmed me. What if I was wrong? What if I had somehow elicited his male instincts and caused that shameful episode to happen? Maybe he felt terrible about it and had come to apologize.

I freed my arm from Almaz's grip. "Don't worry. I need to speak to Comrade Farhad."

She looked at me, uncertain. "You sure?"

"I am."

I waited for Almaz's steps to fade into the night.

"Comrade Farhad, I need to explain—"

But before I could finish, his lips sealed mine, and pushing me into the dark corner, he squeezed me with his whole body against the wall, harder and harder, his tongue fighting its way inside my mouth through my tightly locked lips, his hands burning my flesh like hot coals.

How long did it last?

Long enough to break the spell of his magnetism. Long enough to know that I could never trust him again. Long enough to see him for whom he really was—*Aži Dahāka*—a mighty fire dragon with a serpent's bite. How blind my eyes had to be to miss something that Almaz saw right away. Yes, he bit me hard. Reduced me to nothing more than a powerless thing, his possession.

"Someday, you'll be my wife, Leila," Farhad whispered into my ear. "I've chosen you. Remember this."

The sound of the steps. Farhad quickly looked behind and stepped back, taking on his usual aura of formality. A couple of passersby came near.

"How's the Ashuglar Street assignment going?" he asked out of the blue.

I panicked, almost choked on air. What if he knew that I'd been spending time with Tahir?

"I've been working on it—"

"I expect your report the following Tuesday. At four in the afternoon in my office," Farhad said. "Now go home. And please send my regards to your papa. Tell him that I safely delivered you home, as promised."

CHAPTER 13

The following Monday, I had my final history exam.

"Long live the Party of Lenin, the Communist Party of the Soviet Union, the shining star that guides us toward peace on our planet and a fruitful cooperation between people." I wrote a mandatory conclusion, placed my essay on the teacher's desk, and left the classroom.

Craving a well-deserved pastry, I headed toward the bakery located across the street from Karl Marx Park.

"Hey, Tchaikovsky. Wait."

Malik the Weasel. My former classmate and the architect of both my outsider reputation and standoffish nickname "Tchaikovsky." He first threw them at me when we were in third grade, and they had stuck as irrevocably as a hump on a hunchback.

"Where are you going?" he called, catching up with me while licking the leftovers of lula kebab from his greasy fingers.

"Why would you care?"

"I need to talk to you. Listen, my father is the director of the Shusha Museum of Rugs. He asked me to ask you to give a message to your father. It's like from my home to your home. You see, my father has been trying to get permission to build a vacation home on the beach in Zağulba."

"What does your father's vacation home have to do with my papa?"

"He needs a signature, that's all, from City Hall. We all know your father can help to get it because he already got one for our cousin who designs the fancy Şamaxı sapphire jewelry. And our cousin paid him back well. Tell your father my father will give the most expensive rug for your dowry. It's antique, costs a fortune... from the fourteenth century."

"What? You're implying that my papa has taken a bribe? You're disgusting, and I'm going to tell Papa what you said."

"*Yaxşı!* Good! That's exactly what I asked for." A sneer prowled beneath his obsequious smile. "See you around."

He hopped aboard a passing bus.

That evening, I told Papa about Malik's outlandish request. He just laughed and brushed it off. "He's a real weasel, your friend Malik."

A week later on Sunday evening the doorbell rang. I rushed to look through the peephole to see who was at the door. Two delivery-men. The tall one had a cleft lip appallingly turned inside out.

"Delivery for Badalbeili," said the shorter of the two in a grating voice.

"Open the door, Leila," Papa shouted. "And bring them here."

I led the way to the smoking room. Two men and their burden—a large rolled-up rug.

Papa lounged on his throne, his bare feet comfortably poised atop its carved lions' feet. His boyhood friend Uncle Anatoly—a gentle giant with blue eyes, silver hair, and muscles on his arms the size of pomegranates—sank into the plush pillows of an overstuffed red armchair. They had first met more than thirty years ago when they were both just short of twelve years of age.

On his way home from a training session in a boxing gym, Papa passed a group of hooligans harassing a small, pale, fair-haired boy who, as it turned out, had just recently moved to Baku from a small Belarusian village. Without a second thought, Papa put his boxing skills to work defending the boy, earning a broken nose, a scar behind his left ear, and a friend for life.

Papa and Uncle Anatoly had obviously been drinking. And the

empty cognac bottle, the half-full *flakon* of vodka, and the close air redolent with alcohol fumes meant they had drunk more than usual. Both had their shirts unbuttoned, exposing Papa's black, hairy chest and Uncle Anatoly's pinkish, shiny upper body.

"Where should we hang it?" the short, chubby deliveryman asked as he retrieved carpet hooks from his small toolbox.

"Right here," Papa slurred, waving his hand toward the wall behind him. Then, turning to Uncle Anatoly, he said with a sly grin, "My girl will have a big enough dowry to marry a sheik."

Uncle Anatoly smiled. "But if you continue piling it up, you might have a hard time finding a sheik worthy of her dowry."

The comment was whimsical enough to trigger a gale of laughter from both Papa and Uncle Anatoly.

"Here's the certificate." The cleft-lipped deliveryman looked around for a vacant surface to leave the document.

"Give it to me." I took the certificate and read the serial number and the authentication of the priceless value of the ancient fourteenth-century Ardabil carpet confirmed with the stamp of the Shusha Museum of Rugs.

Shusha Museum of Rugs?

I read the words again and again as if hoping my eyes would erase them. The words became blurry, yes, but only because of the tears breaking loose from my eyes. The shame remained crystal clear in black calligraphic lettering, framed by a pattern of lotuses and the sweeping signature of the museum's director—Algazarov. Malik the Weasel's father.

Papa, how could you do this? How could you shatter my faith in you? I wanted to shout, but shame seized me so tightly that my shouts had no sound. Sobs stuck in my throat. *Or did you wish to add this ugly Ardabil carpet to your collection so badly that you didn't even care? What about all the ancient swords hanging on the walls of your study, the lion-legged, ivory-inlaid furniture pieces, the silver jars you claimed had come from some Egyptian pharaoh's tomb? Are they all bribes you've taken in exchange for your favors?*

"Leila, bring us some fresh tea." Papa leaned over and kissed me on the top of my head, oblivious to my misery.

I turned away and wiped my tears with the cuff of my blouse. A shaft of light from a sconce got caught in the ring on my finger, and shimmering serpents crawled out of its one-of-a-kind Şamaxı sapphire. My gift for winning the piano competition.

Another bribe.

I swallowed and cleared my throat. "I'll be right back with tea."

I stumbled out of Papa's smoking room, went to my room, removed the platinum ring with the sapphire from my finger, and stuffed it away under a pile of old dresses in the bottom drawer of my wardrobe.

On Tuesday at exactly four in the afternoon, I marched into Farhad's office. He was seated in his brown chair under a large portrait of Leonid Brezhnev. I saluted him and took my place a safe distance away, next to a glass partition where people could see me.

"Comrade Farhad," I said loudly, quite a few decibels higher than my usual voice. "I came to report my findings on the assignment you gave me."

Farhad examined me closely. If I was hoping to find any sign of remorse or discomfort on his face, I was fooling myself. There was none.

"Go ahead." He waved his hand.

"I was able to enter the shop located at the address 33 Ashuglar Street and meet the suspicious element. As I engaged him in a conversation trying to detect any wrong thinking or wrongdoing, a customer arrived. A very important member of the Party. I've had the pleasure of meeting him at a few events hosted by my parents. I believe he is the Second or Third Minister of Education of Azerbaijan. The said customer paid the suspicious element a sum of money for a work of art—"

"Good work, Leila. I'll write the report." Farhad jumped up from his chair and stepped toward me. Every muscle in my body tensed. "Not a word to anyone," he commanded in a whisper. "The assignment is closed."

"But I thought you wanted me to collect more information. I'm fully aware that I have just implicated an important Party member in illegal activity."

"Shhh." Farhad shot an icy stare at me as if trying to detect whether I was *that* stupid. For the first time ever, I had actually dared to mock him. To scare him with his own weapon. It felt good.

I left to the victorious tarantella drumbeat of my heart.

CHAPTER 14

The last school bell of the year rang in my ears like the finale of Gustav Mahler's *Symphony no. 9*, the most tedious, long-winded symphonic climax ever written. Free at last.

By now spring had swayed into summer, keeping its clouds and cool mountain breezes with us longer than usual. The sun fox-trotted in and out of the sky, warming rather than roasting the air, promising rather than granting the irresistible bliss of Baku summertime—the blue-green waves of the Caspian Sea washing over Zağulba Beach with its soft-as-down sand dunes.

The delay suited me well since I had no time for pleasure. Professor Sultan-zade put me on an Olympic rehearsal schedule: every day counting down to March 17 and my performance at the Budapest piano competition, every hour devoted to Mozart's *Piano Concerto no. 20*.

At exactly five minutes before my scheduled lesson, I warmed up in the Conservatory practice room, playing Carl Czerny's études.

"How is our 'Romanze' today?"

Professor Sultan-zade entered the practice room carrying a tray with a steaming teapot, a glass *armud*, and a mound of sugar cubes on a saucer. "Have you been working on fingering? Last time you were terrible with the middle section."

"Yes, I spent two hours last night."

"We'll see."

"Should I start from the beginning?"

"Do you want to start from the end?"

"No, I just thought—"

"You thought? No, I'm here to think. You are here to play. Go."

She settled in her plush chair, drinking tea and tapping her foot to keep me at a dainty tempo.

I closed my eyes and played the B-flat major theme of the rondo, imagining myself on the stage at the Grand Hall of Franz Liszt Academy of Music. As I glided through Mozart's hidden musical inflections, Tahir glided invisibly beside me. Opening for me an entirely unfamiliar dimension of emotions, teaching me to feel first and comprehend second, to weave harmonic tenderness around rhythmic consistency, to blend Baroque's reserve into Romanticism's expressiveness. The faint, white whispers of "Romanze" spun hypnotically in the air like snowflakes.

Oh, how I missed Tahir. If I could only sneak inside his refuge even just one more time. But how? I didn't dare. After reporting my discoveries about the green door, I had no official reason to be near the place. It would get me into trouble. Farhad's raven eyes followed me ubiquitously.

"Stop it already. It's dreadful," Professor Sultan-zade shouted. "If I listen to another measure of this anarchy, sewage will pour out of my ears. Mediocrity meets Mozart. You are killing me, Leila. You are killing me alive. You sound like someone who has lost her footing on the slope of Mount Everest."

I rubbed my sweaty palms against my skirt. Maybe Professor Sultan-zade was right. Maybe I was lost in the capricious waters of creativity, experimenting with a new, freer approach to phrasing, moods, dynamics—a scary musical challenge, a risk of losing what I had known and accomplished before I could fully grasp my new self.

Professor Sultan-zade swept to the piano and leafed through the pages of my Mozart score. "These are the instructions for you. Can you read?" She pointed her finger at a slur.

"Legato."

"And this?"

"Pedal."

She moved her face close, so close I could see bits of her scalp shining through her thinning hair. "Then why are you disregarding what Mozart himself has written here? The instructions are all over the place, and each has a precise meaning. All you have to do is to follow every one of them. It is so simple, isn't it?"

"Yes, it is. All I was doing was trying to reveal Mozart's emotional intentions through my own feelings."

"Your own feelings?"

Professor Sultan-zade dramatically closed the lid of the piano, stroking it protectively with her fingers. "I'm afraid Mozart doesn't need your own feelings. And if you have such an urgent need to express them, find a different outlet. Go take polka lessons. Or buy yourself a chador and go pray at the mosque with crones."

Chador.

Chador!

Why hadn't I thought of this before?

A black, body-length silk veil would make me invisible. A lot of old women still wore them, scurrying like crows around the town. No one paid any attention to them—they were a fading relic of the past. The Soviets even spread a mockery that the women wore chadors to hide their old, ugly faces.

"Thank you. Thank you, dear Professor," I exclaimed.

"Thank you for what?" Professor Sultan-zade tilted her head sideways, staring at me in bewilderment.

Silver bullets of rain pounded the ground, threatening to blast the flimsy roofs of Icheri Sheher houses to pieces. A typical Baku summer rain—short-lived and tempestuous as a mountain river. Within a blink, the streets were flooded and deserted. What more could I have asked for? I ran through the puddles slashing and clowning, free as a monkey that had just escaped from the circus. I slowed down by the ruins of the ancient bathhouse and turned into its trashed yard—most likely a rat kingdom at night—and there, in the seclusion of a large, leafy oak tree, I wrapped the chador around my face, leaving a slit for my eyes. For extra security, I pinned the fabric to my blouse beneath the chador.

"You have a ghost for a visitor," I said as I entered Tahir's shop, waving my arms underneath fluid silk.

"Nice." Tahir sucked a long toke of hookah, exhaling lazy smoke rings and staring through me as if I was made of glass.

"Oh well. I guess you're used to ghosts." I unfolded the fabric from my face.

"Wait. Don't move." Tahir grabbed a brush from the table. His gaze caressing me, he traced the brush through the air, sketching invisible lines, then disappeared behind the easel. Occasionally, his eyes peered around the canvas to take me in. His bare feet fidgeted, doing a happy tap dance.

I stood still like a statue, soaked, chilled, but afraid to make the slightest move. The water from my chador dripped all over the floor. I didn't care. All I knew—I was being painted. What if my image stayed around long after I was gone? Like the image of Cleopatra on a two-thousand-year-old coin?

After what felt like a millennium, Tahir finally acknowledged the living, breathing me. "Want to check it out?"

"Yes." I threw the chador off my face and gasped for air. Instead, hashish fumes tickled my lungs.

The painting looked nothing like what I had expected. No Cleopatra immortalization for my image, not even close. I saw a cluster of grotesque items thrown all over the canvas, fighting for attention. A rat with a long, hairy tail won my notice at once—a fat black rat sprawled across a crimson couch. Behind the rat was the silhouette of Maiden Tower, the jagged edges of its crown stabbing the sky. In a pale mauve sky, an ashen moon dueled with a carroty sun, and a red-orange bird helplessly flapped her wings, trying to escape from the rat.

Where was *I* in that chaos? I looked closer. The couch had two legs—one was shaped like a hammer, the other like a sickle. The rat's only eye was ablaze just like the red star on top of the Kremlin. In the upper-right corner stood an elongated female figure veiled in sheer black silk that illuminated and traced every hollow of her body. Tiny breasts, curvy hips, with a barely visible triangle between her legs. I felt embarrassed. And, at the same time, I couldn't take my eyes off the sensual creature.

"I wish you had come earlier," Tahir said, wiping his hands with the wet towel. "Then I wouldn't have had to stick you in the corner. Oh well, we'll do another one. What do you think?"

My palms went sweaty. "I don't really know. So much is happening here, the rat and the sky and the moon. All jarring. And then the message—the negative message. No, I'm afraid it's not Mozart."

"That's for sure. What else?"

"Maybe I'm wrong…but the figure wrapped in a veil… She is so lyrical in the middle of the dissonance, and all these evil creatures don't seem to overcome her even though she's pretty flimsy… And another thing, why did you paint me so thin? So stretched out?"

"For dramatic Amedeo Modigliani effect. To bring out the sensuality and—" Tahir stopped. "I'm sorry, sunshine. Sometimes I forget that you're just a little girl."

"I'm not a little girl. I'm fifteen," I said, staring into Tahir's eyes, struck by the same sensation I'd felt once before when our eyes had met—an irresistible connection. As if an electric glissando coursed through my body, joining Tahir and me into the same circuit, sparks flying off each other. Did he feel the same? Or was it just my imagination?

"I like the way you painted my hand," I said, breaking the magical moment. "It seems to almost come out of the painting as if you gave it a third dimension."

"That's the idea." Stepping back, he examined his work from different angles. "I used a technique called 'tenebrism'—dramatic illumination—created by Michelangelo da Caravaggio, the greatest painter of the seventeenth century. His light is starkly luminous against the darkness."

"Like in a black-and-white photograph?"

"No. Not even close." Tahir twisted his mouth from side to side, his habit when he was short of an explanation. "Think Bach. A few independent voices are interwoven into a polyphonic relationship. All of a sudden, one voice steps into the light while the rest become dimmed to create the dramatic disparity. Do you understand?"

"I think so."

"You see, when you entered, light from there"—Tahir pointed toward a small hexagon-shaped window in the ceiling—"splashed onto your figure and gave me the idea. Now let me try something else."

He reached for his brush and began to darken the silk of the chador on the painting until almost all the outlines of my body had disappeared. The hand, though, seemed to come to life, moving the fabric away from my stretched—but now quite animated—face.

"The effect has changed drastically," I said.

"Maybe." He skewed his head to the side, tapping his teeth, deep in thought. "Or maybe not. Not sure."

"Why?"

"Because it has as much life as a week-old corpse."

Gripping his brush, Tahir smeared thick, black strokes across the painting, destroying it. Then he threw the brush on the floor, zoomed back to his rug and his hookah, and soon disappeared behind a cloud of smoke.

But I didn't feel abandoned. Not at all. If anything, I felt jealous. Tahir, like all true artists, was impetuous, riding freely on his head-spinning carousel of emotions. Unlike me, who could never rise above the boring sameness of a dedicated, hard-working student of piano.

"I've been having a difficult time too," I said, trying to win his attention, "with Mozart's *Piano Concerto no. 20*. It's the piece I'll be playing at the International Franz Liszt Piano Competition in Budapest. My professor is in panic. She says that I'll never win the first prize if I continue to experiment. With just eight months left before the competition, I still can't settle on a particular voice, one that balances structure with color. Technique with emotion."

"Neither could Mozart himself."

"What do you mean?"

"What do I mean," Tahir repeated slowly, trying to catch the stream of his thoughts. "You see, the pleasing, *melodic* Mozart we know today is actually the outcome of *tragic* Mozart who tried to break away from the rigidity of the dying Baroque. As a court composer, he had to create in accordance with what was expected of him; as a performer, he had the liberty to reinterpret—even reinvent—his own scores. He rarely composed cadenzas, as you know, improvising them on the spot, moving closer and closer to the oncoming Romantic period."

"Then there is nothing wrong with me playing it differently every time, the way the Romantics did, depending on my current state of mind?"

"Your state of heart, actually. That's the power you possess as an artist. To find and express your own unique message."

"Have you found it?"

"Found what?"

"Your own unique message?"

"I've been able to formulate it internally through listening to music. But no, I haven't yet found the right tools to communicate it."

"You mean to communicate the music in your painting?"

"Yes. For me, painting *is* music. Inseparable. To paint, I have to hear music."

"And for me, to feel my music, I have to see images and colors."

"The relationship between color and music is an old phenomenon," Tahir said. "The spectrum of colors is arranged in scales, similar to the language of musical notation. Beethoven called B minor the black key. Schubert described the E minor key as a maiden in white with a red rose. And Kandinsky used musical polyphony to paint his works."

"Then tell me, what would be the perfect score for your artistic message?" I asked.

"Rachmaninoff. *Piano Concerto no. 3.*"

Of course. How could Tahir have chosen anything less gripping than Rachmaninoff's *Piano Concerto no. 3*, the most challenging piano masterpiece ever written?

"Why this piece in particular?" I asked.

"It opens me to higher powers. It bridges Caravaggio and Renoir. Caravaggio—spectacularly bold, real, and imposing, demanding immediate attention. Renoir—dreamy, soft, suspended in time. The challenge for me is to bring those two languages together."

Silence. Time to leave.

"I better get going," I said.

"I'll see you soon?"

My heart skipped. Tahir wanted me to come back.

"I can stop by tomorrow at two."

"I'll be here."

Outside, not a trace of rain other than an occasional silver thread of moisture trapped in the salty air. I headed to the music store a half an hour away by bus—enough time to replay over and over again every word and every glance Tahir and I had exchanged, to scrutinize each one for possibly missed, unspoken messages.

At the music store, I bought a secondhand copy, published in 1957, of the score for Rachmaninoff's *Piano Concerto no. 3*.

CHAPTER 15

"Let's go to Taza Bazaar," Tahir suggested the next day when I came to his shop.

"Why Taza Bazaar?"

"Because there's no better place to get inspired. And to get deliciously stimulated too. Remember what Rumi said—'Thirst drove me down to the water where I drank the moon's reflection.'"

It was reckless enough to come to his shop. To go out into the city with him would be suicidal.

A few minutes later, wrapped in my chador, I strolled through Taza Bazaar next to Tahir. I'd never seen him gleeful like this, bouncing between the vegetable rows like a violin bow playing "Flight of the Bumblebee."

Behind the nearest stand, a hairy midget juggled fat, juicy tomatoes, slicing them in half in midair, then holding them out on the end of his bejeweled dagger.

Outside the bread store, three old women, Turkish triplets, sat cross-legged on the ground, overstuffed burlap bags filled with all kinds of nuts and dried fruit in front of them. Each triplet had to be at least a hundred years old.

"Sunny day with Allah's help," a woman with the face of a Caspian tiger and the voice of a Persian gazelle greeted us, baring her toothless mouth, her hair—whatever was left of it—henna-dyed into blinding flames. She sold greens and herbs, stashing cash inside the kilim purse hanging from her neck on a rope thick enough to moor a ship.

"Wait," Tahir said to me. "I need to sketch her."

And he was gone—into his creative process. Sitting on a wooden box filled with rotten potatoes, chewing on his pencil, he devoured the woman and her greens with his eyes. Nearby, someone was singing *muğam*—a traditional Azeri art form that wedded classical poetry and musical improvisation—its lamenting, throaty calls untamed for a thousand years, zigzagging through the air like calligraphic lines, embroidered with the pearls of ancient verse.

I'm a poet, no ridicule touches me.
I'm a king, no arrow touches me,
Only her sweet smile bites into my heart.
I'm a man, only beauty touches me...

I rambled by stands overloaded with ready-to-burst peppers and eggplants from Lankaran, sweet-smelling apples and pears from Guba, pinkie-long grapes from Fuzuli, squashy, mouthwatering persimmons from Khachmaz.

The wide-screen panorama through the slit of my chador resembled a worn and tattered Azeri rug woven centuries ago in a swirling paisley motif—a cacophony of conflicting figures and colors that somehow managed to coexist and even benefit from each other.

Tahir waved at me.

"What do you think?" He showed me his drawing—total chaos. Half-human, half-animal figures shifted across the page, all on top of each other.

"I don't know. Everything is happening so close together," I said, careful not to offend him.

"That's the idea. The breathing, living, hiccupping real world. I'm trying to capture its spontaneity."

Spontaneity. Maybe that's exactly what I'd been missing in my

Mozart, getting more and more predictable, polishing, cleaning, stripping it of any *spontaneity*.

The Rose Garden Fairy—a short, stout woman in a tattered rabbit-fur vest—guarded the Rose Garden stand with its honey-saturated desserts, seducing passersby. "Try my *halva*. It will melt in your mouth like rose sherbet. If you don't like my *halva*, smell my *pakhlava*. Oh, it will take your soul to Allah's rose garden."

Tahir did a fast sketch for her—a flattering one—with the face and wings of an angel. She loved it and gave Tahir a huge, juicy chunk of *pakhlava*.

"You just compromised your artistic integrity," I teased him.

"It was all worth it. Want some? Would be fun to see you eating through your chador. Like a mouse." He pulled his shirt over his head and stuck the *pakhlava* underneath, making squeaky, munching sounds.

"Don't make fun of me." I slapped him playfully on the shoulder.

We turned into Tea Alley. A tall, dark young man guarded a tea shop, his bloodshot eyes trailing every passing woman with a filthy stare.

Why did he make me think of Farhad?

I couldn't get past him soon enough. Tea Alley opened into Fish Row, the most privileged section of the bazaar. Here, the members of the Caspian Sea's royal family of sturgeons—belugas, osetras, sevrugas—lay in barrels, twisting their tails in a last agony. Next to the barrels stood large jars filled with beluga caviar.

"Phew…I hate fish." I pinched my nostrils closed with my fingers. "And I can't stand the taste of caviar. When I was little, my mama used to force it down my throat. Literally."

Tahir bit on his lower lip, started to say something, chose not to, then changed his mind. "Let me show you some people who'd kill to taste a single roe of caviar, even if they had to lick it off the ground. Follow me."

It was the first time I'd ever stepped foot into Beggars Corner, the far section of Taza Bazaar. I felt both appalled and guilty. How could such poverty and destitution exist in Baku? Beggars Corner was mobbed with invalids, some of them still dressed in World War II uniforms decorated with medals. They begged for money and food, pleaded for sympathy by parading their stumps.

Their "elder"—his legs amputated just below the knees, his left arm missing below the elbow—sat on a soiled rag at the exit of Taza Bazaar, waving a bunch of dried plants with the little white bulbs, *uzarlik*. In front of him lay a service cap with a few coins. He wailed: "Burn my *uzarlik* and inhale the scent, then spread the ash on your forehead and neck. No evil will ever harm you. Buy my *uzarlik*, one portion—25 kopeks."

Tahir bent over and placed a ruble in the invalid's gnarled palm.

We left Taza Bazaar and wandered through the city, winding our way down to the ancient burial grounds. We ambled among the remains of tombstones dating back to the twelfth century, deciphering the inscriptions and snacking on sunflower seeds and halva. I found a place to sit in the shade of an apple tree, and Tahir climbed on top of a moss-covered stone fence and recited an eight-hundred-year-old ghazel by Nizami Ganjavi.

> *Oh my friend, to lose my soul in the garden of your love is a*
> *blessing.*
> *To saddle a horse of misfortune that would take me to you is*
> *a blessing.*
> *To thaw like a candle in the silver of your smile against the*
> *night sky,*
> *To empty your cup of tears and overflow it with happiness is a*
> *blessing…*

How different Tahir looked in the light of day. No longer a sage. Just an eccentric eighteen-year-old teenager in black slacks and white shirt, a wicker basket filled with pink-headed radishes at his feet. He smiled at me, his eyes catching a shaft of sunlight darting through a cocoon of climbing vines.

"You know, I bought the score of Rachmaninoff's *Piano Concerto no. 3*," I said.

"Bravo!" Tahir clapped. He jumped down from the fence and dropped next to me, rubbing his hands in delight. "I'm proud of you. To take on Rach 3—it requires guts. But you can do it. There's enough power in your hands, and at the same time, you make piano sound like a human voice. Now we can really work in sync with each other."

His brushstroke—my musical note.

"Look at the Immortal's bastard."

A hissing voice came from a group of lowlifes congregating outside a tobacco shop.

"Now the little shit's got his own whore to himself. Why is he hiding her under a chador? Maybe she's got balls instead of a cunt just like the Immortal."

The gang broke into dirty laughter, punching each other, stirring themselves to move from insults to action. A scrawny hashish freak with a fresh pink scar across his forehead separated from the crowd and wobbled toward us, obscenely sticking his thumb in and out of the curled fingers of his other hand. "Come here, slut, I'll do you better than the old witch's fairy," he shouted, waving at the rest to join him.

Tahir sat frozen, blinking nervously, his face ablaze, eyes spilling hot lava, teeth clenched tightly. Embarrassed or frightened? I couldn't tell, but deep inside I rooted for him to act as my hero.

He didn't.

"Let's go." He grasped my arm tightly and pulled, his hand so hot I thought it would burn me to the bone. I tripped, almost tumbling to the ground, Tahir keeping me on two feet until we turned a corner.

We kept the pace for a few more blocks, both of us breathing hard, neither saying a word, until we reached the busy intersection of Kirov and Torgovaya streets and stopped.

"Please listen... I mean, *don't* listen to those dirty, filthy lies,"

Tahir said, his voice cracking almost into a sob, his pleading eyes seeking mine. "Don't listen to what they're saying. She is an incredible woman…my grandmother. You wouldn't even believe whom she knew in her previous life—Rachmaninoff, Horowitz. She's like no one else." He squeezed his hands into fists, banging the air, at a loss for words.

"I'd like to meet her," I said, a bee buzzing inside my stomach. "After all, I grew up in her home. She's been a part of my life since long ago, since I was a little girl who dreamed of being like her. Like the Snow Princess."

"Don't tell her that."

"What do you mean?"

Tahir cleared his throat. "Don't tell her that you live in her Villa Anneliese."

The gray bastion of Maiden Tower obscured the sun. The streets of Icheri Sheher, drenched in light just a minute ago, were now dark, as though they had suddenly dropped to the bottom of a well. A brown mound surrounded the tower. All dirt, with patches of burned grass and trampled dandelions.

Gingerly, I followed Tahir through the rusty gate and along the crumbled stone-laid walkway. Four steps down, a door with loose shreds of paint, fortified by an iron belt, led into a small gallery. Across the gallery, another door. This one arched, with intricate metal carving along the edges. Tahir pushed the door with his shoulder. It opened with a low rasp. He held it for me to enter.

Thin Mudéjar columns, bearing the weight of the ornate arcade on their shoulders, surrounded a small octahedral courtyard with moss creeping up its walls, with the soggy smell of *once upon a time*, with the echoes of dripping dew and rain. The sun peeped through an Islamic window grill in the towering cupola.

A dark silhouette separated from one of the columns and stepped into a red cone of sunlight.

"You have a guest?" the Immortal said in a deep, slightly croaky mezzo.

"Yes. This is my friend Leila." Tahir turned to me. "Leila, meet my grandmother, Miriam Mukhtarov."

CHAPTER 16

The sun skewed through boards nailed across the frame of a window, casting strips of light onto neatly stacked rows of books. Nizami Ganjavi. Jalāl ad-Dīn Muhammad Rūmī. Anna Akhmatova. Honoré de Balzac. All in different languages. Francisco de Goya's cartoonish *majas* and *caballeros* flew a kite across the woven surface of a small tapestry on the wall.

We were inside Miriam Mukhtarov's chamber.

The Snow Princess—sixty years older than her portrait in the courtyard of our Gargoyle Castle—sat at the head of the table. Her face resembled a dried-out tree stump with scars, knots, and warped lesions. Her eyes revealed irises almost fully buried beneath snowy sclera. Her spine curved so badly that she had to heave her neck up—like a turtle peering out of her shell—to see anything above the floor. A wispy silver braid slid down her shoulder from underneath a worn-to-threads straw hat.

But her black woolen dress with a white batiste collar and cuffs was starched and ironed as if she was waiting to go to an opera. And a figurine of the bird from the fresco in our courtyard sat proudly on top of her gramophone. The same swan-like neck with a frilled emerald necklace, folded wings of faded gold and scarlet, two curled ears. The bird had been beaten by life as much as her mistress, her beak broken, her tail gone, but her tiny claws were still in place holding tightly to the lid of the gramophone.

Tahir poured us tea from a green copper samovar.

"Baba," he said, placing his hand on top of Miriam's, "Leila is a serious student of piano. She has recently been studying Rachmaninoff's *Concerto*."

"Which one?" Miriam asked, her deep, chesty mezzo defying her withered body.

"Number three."

Miriam smiled and sipped her tea, elegantly holding the handle of her tin cup between her thumb and index finger. "Do you come from a musical family, Leila?" she asked.

"No. My mama is a doctor, and my papa is an engineer." I downplayed my heritage.

"Well. Then how and when did you discover your love of music?"

"On my sixth birthday. My mama took me to the Philharmonic hall to hear Sviatoslav Richter. On my way home, I told Mama I wanted to be a pianist. A week later, a baby grand Bösendorfer moved into my room."

"That's a bit too impressive an instrument for starting to learn piano, but I'm sure it fully complements your talent."

"Baba," Tahir said, "I told Leila that you knew Rachmaninoff. Please tell us about him."

"In a minute." Miriam rose heavily from her chair and shuffled to the corner. Her feet—the same feet depicted on the fresco, thin and delicate, peeking through the clasp of her golden sandals—were now twisted and troublesome, failing to hide their puffiness inside black felt boots. She took an angora shawl from the couch and wrapped it tightly around her shoulders. By now the daylight had vanished; the room had succumbed to brown haze. How had she survived in this wintry, damp stone chamber?

Miriam returned, an oil lamp flickering in her hands. She placed it in the middle of the table and eased into the chair.

"Sergei Rachmaninoff was a tall man, and with such a tendency to melancholy," she said in her slightly hoarse voice. "Stravinsky called him a 'six-and-a-half-foot scowl.' Out of jealousy, of course.

There was a lot of it between us émigrés. But there were close friendships too. Like between Sergei and Volodya—Vladimir Horowitz. Sometimes they would come over and play piano pieces for four hands. *Bellissimo!*"

Miriam smiled nostalgically, the light from the oil lamp illuminating her clouded eyes and accentuating every crevice in her wrinkled face. "The musical giants' duo. But after the first time Sergei heard his *Piano Concerto no. 3* performed by Vladimir, he never played it himself again. It had nothing to do with envy. He just simply explained that he might have composed the piece, but Horowitz absolutely *owned* it."

"He definitely does." Tahir turned to Miriam. "Can I play it for Leila?"

"The *Concerto*?" I asked, excited.

"Yes, the legendary Number 3. Recorded by Horowitz in 1930."

"And Tahir's favorite," Miriam added. "I should blame both Rachmaninoff and Horowitz for Tahir's love of art. The first time he heard the *Concerto*—he had just turned twelve—he told me: 'Baba, I see this music. And I want to paint it.' I went to the store, bought the aquarelles. He tried the color and said, 'No, it's too pretty. I need something thick and dark that sticks.'"

"Shall we hear the music?" Tahir interjected, bringing the gramophone to life.

The music began, passages of immense technical complexity fluidly bridging Caravaggio's chiaroscuro with Renoir's impressionism. The gloom and shadows of claustrophobic chambers contrasting with the vibrant radiance of a wide-open landscape. The realism of humanity down to its dirty nails and rotten wounds combined with the fleeting sanguinity of the moment. Vladimir Horowitz played piano along that fine line, crossing back and forth effortlessly as only a genius could have done.

Miriam listened with her eyes half closed, the exposed ashen slits making her look blind, the musical notes traveling along her lips, contorting them into a ghostly smile. But I could see that through

her desecrated, crippled facade shone the indomitable spirit of the
Snow Princess from my childhood. That through every crack in her
face and voice spilled charisma of a magnitude reserved only for the
world's greatest opera divas.

"Have any of your performances been recorded?" I asked Miriam
after the recording finished playing.

"I never thought I was good enough. Maestro Arturo
Toscanini—oh, he had a quick temper—once stormed out of our
dress rehearsal when I stopped in the middle of 'Habanera' for the
third time. But what could I do? I had to make it right. Once, my
impresario decided to record my *Carmen* at the Palais Garnier, and
I said not yet. The tone of my upper register sounded too thin,
lacking in overtones. I needed more *meat* to my voice, and I thought
that it would come with age. That's why I never stopped rehearsing.
Even in the labor camps."

Her white arched eyebrows collapsed. "And then it came—the
right tone. When I was forty. The new warden had given me a
privileged assignment. While everyone else was sent to the forest to
cut trees—in terrible blizzards—I was left alone in the barracks to
rid the prisoners' clothing of lice using a piece of broken glass. I sang
'Habanera' to myself. I knew right away that my voice had reached
that prime I had strived for. And that it was too late."

I imagined the young woman from Muezzin Rashid's old photograph, with her blond hair cut off sitting in her cell, killing lice, and
humming *Carmen's* aria.

"But how can it be," I said, "that if...when...all those horrible
things you're saying happened, with millions of people disappearing
in the gulags, how can it be possible that no one ever talks about
it? I asked my papa about Stalin, and he said that Stalin was a great
Communist leader with titanic vision and that his wisdom had saved
the world from fascism."

"Your papa is part of the generation of blind innocence, indoc-
trinated with lies from early childhood. Lies presented as truth.
Darkness portrayed as light. Slavery labeled freedom."

She leaned against the column, her mouth twisting nervously from side to side. How strange, sixty years apart, Tahir and Miriam shared the same verbal and facial expressions. Like this one, which indicated that she was deciding whether to respond to my question.

She finally did.

"I'll tell you a little story. More like a fairy tale but without a happy ending." She clasped her small hands against her chest. "It goes like this."

Once upon a time, there lived a maiden called Truth. She was fair and sweet. And innocent. As only truth can be. Her voice, pure and powerful, reigned across the meadows and the seas until it reached both Heaven and Hell, but before Heaven could respond, Hell snatched Truth into the dark forest of Lies.

"Give up your voice," he demanded of the chained and shackled Truth.

"Never," she replied. "I'd rather die."

Hell kept her without food or water. But Truth didn't bend.

"Why don't we just kill her and bury her so deep that nobody can ever find out?" the head of the Ministry of Lies asked Hell.

"If we do that, the enemies of the Soviet people will turn dead Truth into a martyr," he answered with strong conviction.

"What if we buy her out and send her away?"

"Where? To the West? So the Imperialists can use her in their propaganda against us? No. Useless idea. I need her around. She will give credibility to Lies if she is alive but silent. We will pass her into the hands of the KGB. They have their methods."

They did. They beat her until all her bones were broken. They burned her skin and blinded her eyes. They carved out her tongue. Then they dressed her in a jester's costume and took her through the streets of their cities, greeted by the cheers of the happy Soviet people. And they kept a vigilant account of those who refused to cheer or didn't cheer enough. For them, they built concentration camps throughout Siberia. Sixty million deaths later, nobody dared to question the truth of the lies of Communism.

Miriam pushed her hands against the table and lifted her weight with effort. "I'd like for you to see something, Leila," she said, putting on a heavy coat and taking an oil lamp from the table.

Tahir and I followed her through a dark corridor to a rusty metal door. Rummaging in a pocket of her coat, she retrieved a key and, after a few failed efforts, finally fitted it into the keyhole. The door opened begrudgingly.

"Welcome to Coronation Hall," Miriam said.

We entered a large room, the light from Miriam's lamp making its ornamented stone walls shimmer like silk tapestries.

"It used to be a Zoroastrian sanctuary," she continued, "with eternal fire burning in the middle. There is a large reserve of oil underneath. Priests used to sit here around the fire searching for the essence of existence, worshipping the good, burning evil. Later, in the times of Shirvan rulers, Shah Ismail turned it into his royal assembly hall, Divankhana. And it was right here where he held his sumptuous feasts and entertained guests with the most enlightened ideas and poetry of the time, sitting on his throne." She pointed toward a raised stone pedestal interlaced with fig and vine leaves, then led me to an object in the corner covered with a woolen blanket.

"What is this?" I asked.

"One of a kind, the Mukhtarovs' two-hundred-year-old clavichord. A very special instrument. The tone is so minimalist, no place to hide. It leaves you with nothing but the reflection of your own soul. Would you like to try it, Leila?"

I removed the blanket and carefully lifted the lid, revealing, on the inside panel, a lacquered pastoral scene with a sleeping shepherd boy and happily grazing sheep. I stroked the keys, their touch so sensitive, giving me the illusion of tapping the strings with my fingers. The sound soared to the cupola, rich and immensely powerful for such a small instrument, yet tender and pure as the voice of a child.

I played the rondo from the "Allegro assai" of my Mozart *Piano Concerto no. 20*, rippling upward, trying to impress—no, blow away—both Tahir and Miriam. But somehow the clavichord's discolored but proudly elevated keys, the pink-cheeked boy shepherd sleeping peacefully on its grassy lid and, even more so, the surrealism of Coronation Hall steeped in dusk, called for something with less bravura. Maybe Bach's *French Suite in D Minor*?

I switched to the fugue without even stopping, weaving three independent voices into a contrapuntal exchange of ideas, making the polyphony flawless, the dynamics precise, the emotions sustained.

But my fingers seemed to handle the musical notes on their own, merging Bach's modulations into the first theme of Rachmaninoff's *Concerto no. 3*, forcing my mind to release its claws from the steering wheel of my performance. I slipped into an emotional free fall—past the *Cabaret* poster with Liza Minnelli, past Billie Holiday's heart-wrenching *Body and Soul*, past Goya's grotesque *majas* and *caballeros* flying their kite, past Farhad's intimidating glare, past Beggars Corner and Papa with his Ardabil carpet.

But before I hit the ground, a powerful Khazri lifted me into the air, carrying me over the ocean, farther and farther toward the horizon. To an island with the sand sparkling like gold coins, where the ocean meets the sky and the sky is as blue as Tahir's eyes. Weightless, I drifted away, lost between the blue of the sky and the blue of the ocean, trailing Vladimir Horowitz's smooth crescendo, listening to the distant echoes of approaching thunder.

I couldn't have lived more vividly through my music if, dressed in a concert gown, I had been performing in front of hundreds of music aficionados. No, I was touching the heavens as I played Rachmaninoff on a dusty clavichord in Coronation Hall, buried within the catacombs of Maiden Tower, for two odd people standing in the corner: Tahir, his arm wrapped protectively around Miriam's frail frame, and the old woman who, in the pearly moonlike glow of the lamp, had reverted to her youthful self—the Snow Princess from the fresco of her Villa Anneliese.

I didn't come home till after nine in the evening. The living room was dark, but a sliver of light slipped beneath the door of Papa's smoking room, along with the sound of his laughter. Papa had guests.

As I walked through the hallway to my room, I heard another voice—a familiar one—its sound making my knees tremble. I tiptoed to the smoking room. Pressed my ear against the door.

"—will worship and guard her till my last breath," Farhad was saying.

"Leila is my only child, and she is the sunlight of my eyes. I'll do anything—anything—to see her well protected and happy."

"Mekhti Rashidovich, the honor you are giving me is beyond any words of indebtedness. Only my future actions as your faithful and dutiful son will give me the opportunity to prove myself worthy of your noble kindness and acceptance. You have been my role model since I first heard you speak at a Komsomol meeting in September of my junior year. Since then, I have been determined to succeed in my academic and social activities, to achieve a position of esteem and power in our society. Something I could put at the feet of your flawless jewel, your Leila."

"My precious girl… Time goes too fast. Just yesterday, she was a baby, sitting here in my lap. And today, look at her—a young, blossoming woman with a prosperous piano career and a man seeking her hand. It's hard for a father to see his daughter grow into a woman, you know. But that's the way life goes. Parents get older, and kids take their place. And some day, when the time comes, I will close my eyes in peace, knowing that I have left Leila in good hands."

I stood, stunned, gasping for air. Hearing something that just couldn't be true. Or was it?

"Mekhti Rashidovich, with all my life I will strive to rise to your expectations," Farhad exclaimed.

"I know you will! And remember—there are no limits to how much I can help you."

I heard the floor creaking. The sounds of the footsteps approaching the door.

I darted into my room, my heart hammering in the hollow of my chest. Closing my door quietly, I threw myself on my bed, crying.

"Leila," Papa called from the hallway. "Come here. Farhad wants to say good-bye."

I wiped my tears and slowly entered the living room.

Papa, in his casual slacks and sleeveless shirt, holding a glass of cognac, stood next to Farhad, formal and impressive in his black suit and tie.

"Where have you been so late?" Papa asked.

"Practicing piano at the Conservatory," I lied.

"Why couldn't you practice at home? Why did I pay a fortune for your grand piano? So you could practice at the Conservatory?" Papa laughed heartily.

"It's not the same, Papa. The acoustics of the concert hall are different."

"All right. All right. You know better." Papa put his arm around my shoulders and kissed me on the forehead.

"Good evening, Leila," Farhad said, bowing his head in a respectful manner.

"Good evening," I replied, hating the way my voice trembled.

"Farhad came to talk to me. Man to man." Papa took a sip of his cognac. "He asked for your hand, daughter, and I gave him my wholehearted consent. Now Farhad can leave town knowing that you've been promised to him."

"Leave town? Where are you going?" I asked eagerly.

"I have been called to Moscow to take a summer course at the Dzerzhinsky Higher School of the KGB," Farhad said, his eyes flicking between Papa and me. "A major honor for me, as well as for our 26 Baku Commissars Komsomol District Committee. If I distinguish myself and excel on the exam, then I will have a shot at staying at the Higher School and joining the ranks of the KGB."

"I hope you will," I blurted out, silently praying for the KGB to keep Farhad in Moscow and away from me forever.

"Thank you, Leila, for your faith in me. Thank you, Mekhti Rashidovich, for the honor of your acceptance of my marriage proposal. I will wait for as long as it pleases you and Sonia *Khanum* before we can proceed with the formal betrothal."

They shook hands, and Papa slapped Farhad's arm heartily. "I'm proud of you, Farhad, and I've always felt close to you, like family."

"We *are* family now, Mekhti Rashidovich. Knowing that Leila and I are promised to each other lessens the pain of having to leave her while I'm in Moscow." Farhad turned to me, burning me with the intensity of his gaze. "Leila, I want you to know. I'm going to be far away geographically, but I'm never far from you. You will always be with me, right here." He pressed his hand to his heart, turned swiftly, and left.

I slammed the door behind him.

"He is a great fellow, your Farhad." Papa smiled, raising his glass in salute.

"He is not mine."

"As of today, he is. I have given him my blessing—gladly."

"There is no way I'm going to marry him," I cried, stamping my foot.

"I don't understand. I thought you liked him." Papa frowned in bewilderment.

"I used to. But not anymore."

"You young girls." Papa laughed. "With your 'I like' yesterday and 'I don't like' today and who knows what tomorrow. Your frivolous emotions are as capricious as a spring breeze. That's why you need someone steady and reliable. A man like Farhad. I'm not going to be around forever. But I've amassed a nice fortune for you, Leila. And with Farhad at your side, you will always be protected. He will be there for you—for the everyday demands of your life as well as your career as a famous concert pianist."

"But, Papa, he is not an honest person. He's a hypocrite—"

"So what? Even the best of us have our hypocritical moments. What unsuccessful fools never realize is that to achieve high status in our society, you have to know how to maneuver the hearts and minds of people. And Farhad is a natural in that respect. Even with his humble upbringing, and especially with my help, he's going to rise higher than anyone in his generation. And someday, fairly soon, I'll have my son-in-law in one of the highest offices in the Azeri government. Maybe even in the Kremlin. Trust me."

"But Papa! He mistreated me," I shouted, trying my last weapon.

"Mistreated you? How?" Papa's brow furrowed in anger, giving me some hope.

"He kissed me. Against my will." I uttered, embarrassed.

Papa rubbed his chin, a doubtful look in his eyes. "But what did *you* do? How did *you* behave? I can't believe he would have done that without you enticing him. That's the wicked power that you women have over men. But I'll tell you this: the fact that Farhad came to me asking for your hand—especially after he'd kissed you—only increases my respect for him."

"I'll never marry him, no matter what you say." I anxiously squeezed the bitter words through my teeth. "And Mama will understand me when—"

"What?" Papa's face turned pale, his eyes flashing fury. Angrily clutching his cognac glass, he hurled it to the floor, shattering the glass into pieces. "No one will ever overrule me! No one! You *will* marry Farhad," he roared in the loudest voice I'd ever heard from him. "I have given my word. The day you turn eighteen, *you… will…marry…Farhad!*"

CHAPTER 17

Pushing the boundaries of my golden cage, searching for new ways of expression and freedom, unveiling the ambiguities between music and art, friendship and love—that was my summer of 1979. My Farhad-free summer that I swore to live to the fullest.

I couldn't sleep anymore. I lay in bed counting the hours until Muezzin Rashid's morning *Adhan*, afraid that if I fell asleep I might wake up and lose my real-life dream. Every hour unclaimed by Professor Sultan-zade I spent either behind Tahir's green door or inside Maiden Tower. He painted; I listened to his jazz recordings or played the Mukhtarovs' clavichord. Sometimes we talked; often we didn't. We didn't have to—our art shared the same creative palette.

I had been studying Rachmaninoff's *Concerto no. 3*, both terrified and fascinated by its unfathomable soul, its vertigo of sweeping texture, rhythm, and dynamics. Playing Rachmaninoff was like walking on a rope bridge across a gorge with dreamy skies above and a raging, muddy river below. Sometimes I switched from Rachmaninoff to my Mozart's *Concerto* in the middle of the piece without even thinking. Because I had followed in Tahir's steps and reached the most unique place of inspiration—my own island. The place where Mozart and Rachmaninoff and Billie Holliday and every single expression of joy or misery suddenly become one. The inner reflection of me.

The sun passed across the Islamic window in the cupola, spreading its garnet rings throughout Coronation Hall.

I stopped playing the clavichord and held out my hands, and a few rings melted into my open palms.

"Look. I caught the sun," I said.

Tahir didn't respond. He was busy fighting his battle with a canvas, striking it metrically with a brush. Staccato in color. I couldn't see his face from behind the easel, only the smoke from his cigarette curling around the canvas like a restless sea horse. He was so unpredictable. Blissful one moment, withdrawn the next. His mood shifted like sands in the desert, his eyes mirroring every passing emotion. The most lasting shade was lavender, the lustrous lavender of the Caspian Sea during a summer sunset. That's why looking into Tahir's eyes felt like drifting in warm tranquil waters farther and farther from the shores of reality.

Had I complicated my life by tying my music—my whole being—to him, constantly seeking his approval? Never before had I cared about the way my hair looked or if my skirt matched my blouse. Not anymore. Every morning, I smoothed my curls with saffron oil and slipped into my silk *sarafan*, sundress. I even asked Almaz to put pink polish on my toenails so they would look fancy in my red gladiator sandals peeking from underneath the chador. Tahir never noticed.

But the connection between us was in the air, growing stronger with each stroke of his brush and with every cadenza of my piano performance as we struggled to find our unique voices. He by bringing musical tonality to his painting; me by unlocking my inner sluices, letting the palette of emotions spill freely into the art of my music.

Miriam came in quietly, a book in her hands. Guy de Maupassant. In French.

By now, I knew where Tahir received his gifts—his plentiful intellect, his knowledge of music and art and history. He was raised by Miriam as the only remaining Mukhtarov. As the glory of the vanished clan. And its last hope.

I played the opening theme of "Finale: Alla breve" slowly, the way

Professor Sultan-zade taught me to approach difficult new material. Why did Rachmaninoff have to flood this piece with so many notes? An insane quantity of notes. I felt dizzy looking at the pages. My hands were too small to reach for the wide intervals he catered to his own long fingers. I couldn't do it. I stopped, embarrassed that Miriam witnessed my surrender.

"Don't think about the notes," she said as if reading my thoughts. "Search for silence. Music is not in the notes but in what is between them. That's what makes it powerful, so powerful it can overcome evil."

"Oh no. Not again," Tahir muttered from behind his easel. "The jaunty illusion of an idealist. Music can provide an escape from evil, not fight it. Music is for the sake of music, nourishment for the soul. Evil is inevitable and incessant, at least in our lifetime."

"Our lifetime is less than a square on a chess board," Miriam said, "and we never know on which one—dark or light—we are going to land."

"That's exactly my point. Why even bother trying?"

"Why? Because you might never have another chance to experience the joys of living."

"I don't need 'the joys of living.' All I need is to be left alone and paint. And hopefully, when the time moves to the light square on your chessboard of life, my works will be the one true statement of this miserable era."

"What you're saying is escapism in its most debilitating form. No wonder you prefer to drift away into the world of hashish."

"What do you expect from me? To be a hero like you? To fight? Fight whom? Evil? You of all people should know that he's a dragon with many heads. You cut one, two grow in its place."

"I'm not saying you should fight evil, but I don't want you to fold your wings, either. You must keep a sense of perspective. The external evils are nothing compared to the evils that we harbor in our souls. This is our true enemy, not the temporary darkness." Miriam turned to me. "What do you think?"

"Me?" While Tahir and Miriam debated notions of evil and light in the catacombs of Maiden Tower, I lived in their Villa Anneliese, a lucky recipient of both evil *and* light. "I think we need to discover goodness inside ourselves and hold on to it," I said, avoiding Tahir's gaze.

"Beautifully said. The eternal goodness of humanity." Miriam patted the stone wall as if finding confirmation in its thousand-year-old solidity. "Accumulated goodness will eventually break through the gates of evil, but we first have to find forgiveness in our hearts so we can recognize and welcome the light when it returns to our country."

"Bravo." Tahir sprang to his feet, applauding theatrically. "Now you've got yourself a follower. But the truth is, if your generation wasn't so naive, then *my* generation wouldn't be paying the price. And the price is our future. A future we don't have. So I guess I'd better leave you two to generate the goodness. Pardon me— *accumulate* goodness—while I have work to do."

He packed his easel and brushes and stormed out of Coronation Hall.

"He's like a porcupine, my grandson. Sharp needles outside and a fragile soul inside." Miriam sighed sadly. "When I learned I was pregnant with my daughter Ziya, Tahir's mama, I kept it a secret, working on lumberjacking in the Siberian taiga, afraid to be discovered and sterilized. My daughter spent her formative years in the gulag and returned to Baku with me in 1953. But her lungs were never strong. And eventually, she died." Miriam paused, rocking her body. "Tahir is the reward we have been given for suffering. A miracle. What an abundant intellect he possesses. Just like his grandfather."

I thought of the young man in breeches in Muezzin Rashid's photograph. *Caspar the Poet.*

"Who was he, Tahir's grandfather?" I asked.

"My best friend, Caspar. And the love of my life." Miriam locked her eyes on the wall, smiling wistfully. "I had known him since childhood. A shy boy with big, dreamy eyes. We never spoke until the annual ball at the Lyceum when I invited him for a dance. After that, we became inseparable. The Troika Society."

"What is this?"

"Caspar had a friend, Halil, and the three of us created the Society, wishing to bring the arts to the poor. I sang; Caspar recited his poetry; Halil impersonated famous people. When I turned sixteen, I left for Europe to study opera, and Caspar joined me in Paris just before the October Revolution. There he became deeply involved with the intellectual libertarian movement. He believed his place was not among cranky Azeri émigrés but in his beloved homeland where real history was being made."

"So what happened?"

"He returned to Baku. But once he was home, he realized that his ideas of democracy had nothing to do with the reality of Communism. He published his 'Fairy Tale about a Maiden Called Truth' in a small Azeri publication."

"The story you told me?"

"Yes. And right after that, no more letters from him. I wrote Halil, asking for help. By then, he had a position of power in the Communist regime. He replied that the Azerbaijani government would welcome me back as their 'national singing treasure,' and in exchange they would close their eyes on Caspar's treason. On November 3, 1937, I arrived in Baku. Caspar and I were blessed to spend three days together before they came for him in the middle of the night."

Miriam traced her silver braid with her trembling hand, twirling the end of her lace collar between her fingers. The lace was as starkly white as her face etched against the impending darkness. The Caravaggio face, screaming out its silent heartache.

"But why didn't Halil help?"

"Jealousy knows neither morality nor empathy. I had chosen Caspar over him, and Halil was an ambitious young man who didn't like to lose. Even as a boy, he used to climb on the ledge of my balcony, and standing high up above the city, he would impersonate Napoleon. He did it very well. Maybe too well." She sighed, shaking her head. "He didn't become the twentieth-century Napoleon, but he did get a city street named after him. Together with my balcony."

"What—" I didn't have to ask. I knew. But maybe there was still a chance. "What was his name?"

"Halil Abbas Badalbeili."

If I could have scraped off my skin together with my name, I would have done it.

I found Tahir in the courtyard outside Coronation Hall. Hunkered down in a recess, his back against the wall, he smoked, the light of his cigarette trembling in the shadows.

"You've known it from the beginning, haven't you?" I said.

He nodded.

I slid down next to him and hid my face between my knees. "I don't know what to say."

"It's not your fault. Has nothing to do with you. We're all married to our destinies."

"But we have the power to change our destiny, don't we?"

"Destiny is a stubborn maiden," Tahir said. "She likes herself just the way she is. I can fool her though."

"How?"

Tahir cupped his hands around his mouth and whispered eerily, "The sooner I burn myself into the ground this time around, the sooner I'll have a better stake in the next life. Hopefully as a human. And with Allah's help, somewhere far, far away from here."

He pushed against the wall and got to his feet. "Let's go make peace with Miriam."

In the evening, Tahir and I waited for Miriam to fall asleep before we snatched a cluster of keys from her sheepskin pocket and tiptoed to the inner gate leading to Maiden Tower. Matching one after the other with the gate's battered old lock, Tahir finally found the right key. The cast-iron portal growled in protest and opened reluctantly into sheer darkness.

"Don't be afraid. I'm here." Tahir tapped softly on my shoulder. "Hold on to the railing. Some of the stairs are broken."

It was a long way up—round and round—along a spiral stairway that kept getting steeper, sending my head into a spin. We reached the top of Maiden Tower and mounted its rocky peak, standing so high in the sky that the rondo of shimmering stars around us seemed closer than the city lights below.

"I used to come here all the time when I was young," Tahir said, his face tilted to the sky, his long eyelashes flickering like a butterfly's wings. "At dawn, I hid behind the staircase, waiting for the Firebird to return and take on her human appearance. I imagined her—half princess, half bird—standing on the crown of the tower, her wings reaching into the sky. Once Miriam caught me here, and I confessed my fantasy. She sat next to me, right there on the *pebble of dreams*"— he pointed toward a fallen fragment of the stone crown—"and told me the *real* Legend of Maiden Tower and Princess Zümrüd."

"I've heard so many variations."

"But not this one." Tahir reached for my hand and helped me to climb atop the pebble of dreams. There, aboard the vessel of the night, traveling from one rim of the sky to another, he told me the legend.

The Legend of Maiden Tower and Princess Zümrüd

A long, long time ago:
    When the evil Shah of Darkness reigned over the Land of Fire, hiding the sun inside his underground caves;
    When the orphan sky peered at the Caucasus Mountains from the black dome of sorrow;

When the rain shed its tears of ice upon the barren earth—
The old Shah Samir and his most favorite wife, Queen Mehriban, welcomed to darkness their only child, Princess Zümrüd.

No celebration took place in the Land of Fire. The court heralds didn't blow the plangent sounds of their powerful nays. The ashiks *didn't pluck the harmonious strings of their golden sazes. And the sad troubadours recited in silence the admiring verses they had composed for a long-awaited royal heir. For it wasn't a daughter whom Shah Samir needed so desperately, but a son. A strong young man, a great warrior to stand up to the Shah of Darkness. To free the sun from the dungeons. To bring harvest to the fruitless soil. To return life and prosperity to the people of the shattered kingdom.*

But the first time Shah Samir laid his gaze on the baby princess, he loved her with all his aging heart. Her olive skin was as clear as the spring air, and the sun had found its way into the brilliance of her deep brown eyes. With beauty like hers, the princess could only be a gift from heaven.

Shah Samir dressed in his finest white robes and rode his horse for twenty-seven moons to the heart of the desert, the Desert of the Blind Dervish. There he lay on the cold sand, turned his face to the sky, and waited. At the onset of the seventh moon, the Blind Dervish emerged out of the dim horizon.

"Oh, worthy son of Moon—"

"Say no more," interrupted the Blind Dervish, penetrating into the Shah's mind with his hollow sockets. "I see your Land of Fire submerged in darkness. There is more hardship and suffering ahead, but light will prevail over the darkness. The roots of joy grow out of the seeds of despair."

The sage moved apart the clouds blocking the moonlight. "The Fire and the Sea will carve a castle out of a rock. With a tower—a Maiden Tower—high enough to scrape the dome of the sky. So high that one day in the future your beloved

148

daughter, Princess Zümrüd, will leap from its crown, reach the sun, and lead it back to its blue cradle."

"Then Princess Zümrüd is destined to save my kingdom?" the Shah cried out in euphoria.

"She may…or may not… It all depends on the choices she makes…"

With these words, the Blind Dervish disappeared behind Shah Samir's stone-heavy eyelids. The Shah exhaled his last breath, lay down once again upon the sand, and locked his eyes with eternity.

As the Blind Dervish foretold, a splendid castle grew out of the Caspian Sea with a tower ascending into the sky. Princess Zümrüd, unaware of the reign of darkness outside, lived merrily in the castle surrounded by the riches of the world. Lavish carpets of dazzling colors covered the austere stone walls. Exotic birds from faraway forests sang cheerfully, evoking the sounds of never-ending spring. Musicians and poets fashioned glorious verses in different tongues, praising their princess's youth and beauty. And fire torches, placed in every niche, illuminated the castle like a thousand suns, preventing the gloom from sneaking into Princess Zümrüd's life.

All this continued until her fifteenth birthday. On that day, the princess was playing hide-and-seek with her friends when she ran upstairs to conceal herself behind a rug, the most beautiful rug in the castle. It was there, while standing quietly and admiring the picture of two lovers floating on a magic carpet across the turquoise sea and into the blue sky, that she discovered a secret door.

"Where does this door lead?" she asked her nanny.

"Oh, light of my eyes," wailed the nanny. "Promise me you'll never come near that door again. There is a cursed world outside that door, and the evil Shah of Darkness is waiting there to take you away from us."

The joy left Princess Zümrüd's heart. From that time on,

she sat alone in her stone chamber, clad in a shimmering white and silver gown adorned with the finest emerald jewels, but she felt neither love nor lament, buried in the monotony of lasting darkness.

Until, finally, she made up her mind. That evening, after everyone in the castle had fallen asleep, she tiptoed up the stairs, pulled aside the beautiful rug, opened the secret door, and stepped into the pitch black outside. The night blinded her eyes. The mysterious smells of the sea and the unfamiliar touch of the air against her skin clouded her senses. Overwhelmed, she stood at the crown of Maiden Tower, taking in the majesty of the night with tears of joy rushing down her cheeks. So beautiful was the sight of the maiden—her black silken hair blowing in the wind, the flawless curves of her body draped in a fluid satin gown, fine emeralds sparkling around her long neck, her slender wrists and ankles—that the stars began to break through the clouds, one after the other, greeting Princess Zümrüd with their silver smiles.

And then she saw him. A Knight in Lion's Skin. Riding the waves of the Caspian Sea, looking up at the princess of his dreams showered in brilliant starlight. The moment they laid eyes on each other, love struck the hearts of the Knight in Lion's Skin and Princess Zümrüd with a double-edged arrow of fire, lighting the knight's path to Maiden Tower.

But it also awakened the evil Shah of Darkness in his cave of sleep. A fierce fight broke out. The clashing sound of steel against steel and steel against stone. A deadly battle for every step leading to the beautiful princess.

Princess Zümrüd stood at the top of the tower, helpless and frightened, begging the Sun and the Moon and the Sea to spare the life of her beloved. Offering her own life instead.

Then silence came. Deafening silence. Followed by the sound of heavy footsteps echoing like thunder throughout the stone tower. Shah of Darkness, thought Princess Zümrüd in anguish. The monster has defeated my beloved and is coming for me.

*"Death is more dear to me than life without my beloved,"
she whispered to the stars, waved her arms like wings, and
threw herself into the roaring waves of the Caspian Sea. But
the sky and the sea traded places, and the beautiful Firebird—
Zümrüd Quşu—was born.*

*By the time the Knight in Lion's Skin reached the top of
the tower—for it was he, not the Shah of Darkness, who had
won the battle—his beloved Zümrüd had soared over Maiden
Tower, burying the Shah and his Kingdom of Darkness under
pillars of smoke, carrying the infant sun in her powerful wings
to the dawning dome of the sky.*

Tahir finished his story and lit a cigarette.

We sat silent for a long time at the very edge of the tower with
our feet dangling over the faraway city. Just Tahir and me, alone in
the infinite space where nothing else mattered, where everything
was possible.

"If you could make one wish now, what would it be?" I said, both
fearful and hopeful that Tahir would ask for permission to kiss me.
I had dreamed of it for a long time. To be so close that I'd recognize
my love in the mirror of his face, feel his black currant breath closing
around my lips, possessing them. Like in my book *Legends from the
Land of Fire*—Knight and his Princess sharing their first kiss on the
magic carpet floating between the stars and the crescent moon.

I closed my eyes and waited, the breeze stroking my face, caressing my hair. Then I felt Tahir's fingers touching my skin, tracing
invisible lines from my eyes all the way to my lips. Slowly, tenderly.
Tossing a trillion tiny fireflies in my direction. I could feel the first
one landing somewhere around my neck and then the next one on
my shoulder, then more and more and more. Until I was completely
wrapped in the invisible veil of seduction.

"I desire to know you," Tahir whispered. "Every breath of your
heart, every fleeting look on your face, the rhythm of your joys, and
the melancholy of your sorrows."

Suddenly, the touch was no more. My eyes blinked open.

"But you're still very young and vulnerable." Tahir shook his head, his intensely violet-blue eyes reaching deep inside my soul, making me shiver. "And I don't want to complicate your life any more than I've done already. Maybe in a different place and different time it would be a different story. But we are here and we are now. I have no future. While you're at the launching point, with your life ahead of you—a career, the whole world at your feet.

"I can't give you what you need. All I've got is my art...and my inner freedom. That's what keeps me afloat. Feelings...love...those are luxuries I can't allow myself. They will enslave me, suffocate my creativity, make me miserable, and, ultimately, will hurt you."

"I don't understand... Why? Why are you saying this to me now?" I sought his eyes like a beggar, hoping to stir him into changing his mind.

He looked away.

"It's not just now. I've been thinking about it for quite a while. And tonight we have come to the point of no return. We should probably stop seeing each other."

"But why?" I almost shouted.

"I explained why. Let's go."

Tahir got up and helped me to my feet. We descended the long staircase in silence, a sob stuck in my throat. A dark abyss opened inside me. What had I done to make Tahir turn into this stranger? Why had he smashed my heart against the stones of Maiden Tower? Of all places.

I knew he cared about me. Of course he did. I could see it in his face even as he spoke those painful words. Then why? Why? How could I wake up tomorrow knowing that he was no longer a part of my life? The center of my life? That his green door had closed, shutting me out forever. How could he do this to me? And how could he say my love would suffocate him?

We stopped at the foot of Maiden Tower. Tahir took my hand,

my skin against his—warm and slightly moist—brought it to his chest, and pressed it firmly against his heart.

"You will always be here," he said. "No matter what. You are my Princess Zümrüd. You asked me if I had only one wish to make what it would be. I will tell you. It would be to ask for a pair of wings to carry you away from darkness, all the way up to your dreams."

Silence. A long, hopeful silence before he let go of my hand.

"But we still can be friends. Just good friends, the way we've been," I pleaded, swallowing my pride, tears gushing down my face.

"It won't work like that, Leila. It's better to cut down the tree with one quick stroke than to keep chopping away at its branches."

Why do we have to cut the tree at all?

Tahir walked me to my bus stop. Not a word exchanged. The soft rustle of an olive tree. The lights of the approaching bus. Too soon. Before the bus door even closed, Tahir turned away and headed back toward Maiden Tower. I watched him through a blurry window. The slender figure, the gait with a bounce, rushing back to his solitude, shouldering the heavy burden of our flawed world. I waited for him to change his mind, turn around, catch up with the bus, pull me out of here, and tell me he was wrong. Or at least to look back and wave good-bye.

He did neither, just kept to his strenuous pace before fleeing into the first alley.

CHAPTER 18

Autumn came. First inside me, then everywhere. Trees rushed to shake off their leaves like last year's fashions and stood half naked, bowing to the advances of the northern wind. The Caspian Sea abandoned its good disposition and released its demons, spewing out bursts of white foam.

"No jasmine growing this year," complained Aunty Zeinab. "A bad sign. The last time we had an autumn like this I got married. With Allah's help, make the skies sunny for Sonia *Khanum*'s birthday."

Aunty Zeinab's wish came true. On the morning of Mama's birthday, the sun burst out of the clouds, filled with late-summer ambitions, and the winds, exhausted from last night's race through Baku's streets and beaten down by blind alleys, finally died out.

As always, we celebrated Mama's birthday in our courtyard: four long tables set for eighty persons around the perimeter; baskets with irises, lilacs, wild gladiolus brightening every surface; the lemon tree raised in the center bearing its golden fruit, the symbol of happiness and health; seven bulging leather sacks with wine from Tabriz and a dozen bottles of sweet Kurdamir waiting in the corner.

Uncle Kerim raised his goblet with wine and began one of his famous long-winded toasts: "Once upon a time a Caliph invited an Artist to entertain him by playing his *tār*…" Mama's oldest friend and second to her in command at the pediatric department, Uncle Kerim acted as *tamada,* the master of ceremonies. I had known him since his hair was still ink-black and he could squeeze underneath my bed when we played hide-and-seek.

By now, his hair had turned aluminum-silver and his figure had grown amorphous, but his elegant ways and tailored suit did magic, concealing his advancing age. The joke around the hospital had it that Uncle Kerim, with his golden tongue of Scheherazade, could talk his patients to sleep during surgery without any anesthesia.

"…and the Caliph promised the silver of the stars…" Uncle Kerim continued.

Everybody at the table remained so quiet that I could hear the crackling of the coal in the corner where the lamb, skewered on ramrods, was slowly turning into a mouth-watering *shashlik*.

Finally, Uncle Kerim waved his goblet in circles above his head and bellowed the conclusion: "Let you, our beloved Sonia *Khanum*, continue to light up our lives like the silver stars, the golden sun, and the platinum moon, shining through all our days and nights."

A storm of cheering swept throughout the tables, followed by the long and hearty clinking of glasses.

"Clean up your plates for hot *kutabs*, just off the fire." Aunty Zeinab lumbered down the stairs with a gigantic tray, a cloud of steam hovering over it. Uncle Zohrab followed right behind, running his fingers over the strings of a long-necked *tār*.

"*Kutab* is not *kutab* without singing a *muğam*," cried a voice from the opposite corner of the courtyard. Bülbül, a celebrated Azeri singer and Papa's childhood friend, made a dramatic appearance wearing a traditional tall hat, *papaq*, and carrying a lacquered frame drum, *ghaval*. He danced his way through the crowd to the fountain in the center, sat down cross-legged under the lemon tree, and stroked the *ghaval* with all ten fingers. The rhythm meshing with the plangent sounds from Uncle Zohrab's *tār*, he closed his eyes and sang:

"*A woman's beauty is the crown of this world…*"

The rhythm changed into a six-beat pulse of the *lazgi*, and Mama's surgical nurse, Margo, slid to the center. Nimble, her black hair waving around her face like ravens' wings, she slithered around Bülbül, Uncle Zohrab, and the lemon tree, seeming to float on a current of air beneath her feet. Her arms undulating, she followed the *ghaval*'s rhythm in a manner that was coy and teasing at the same time—faster and faster—until she was dancing hypnotically around the courtyard like a whirling dervish.

Almaz and I ran back and forth collecting the dirty dishes from the table and transporting them to Aunty Zeinab's kitchen where a few women worked together like a well-functioning mechanism, washing and drying and stacking the plates for us to carry them back to the table. Together with dozens of the most imaginative desserts.

Uncle Zohrab carried out a giant bronze samovar and placed it at the head of the table, opening the tea ceremony, accompanied by the sounds of Mama's favorite song "White Acacia," composed by the legendary Soviet composer Mark Slavkin—a song she had chosen for her wedding dance sixteen years ago.

Papa led Mama through the crowd, twirling her into the steps of the waltz, his hand wrapped around her slender waist. Her hair flying, she turned and spun, throwing her head back in enchanting laughter. *The generation of blind innocence. The generation of blind innocence.* Miriam's words rang in my mind.

And with those words came a sudden sense of estrangement from the crowd of people I had known and loved since my childhood, from the celebration around me I had grown up with and always looked forward to. This celebration had no right to be here, with the empty wine bottles piling up in front of the Snow Princess's fresco. Not when the true owners of our Gargoyle Castle...no!—Villa Anneliese—dwelled in a dark, damp basement.

And suddenly more than anything else I wanted to be there. To play my Rachmaninoff on the Mukhtarovs' old clavichord in the rings of twilight. To hear their stories of people and places long gone. To be part of their world with its complex, demanding beauty. Because their world had become mine too, and being back in my old life—my real life—felt claustrophobic.

As for Tahir's rejection, I would convince him that I could love him without suffocating his creativity, that I could be a friend who inspired and stimulated his work. And I would tell him to stop treating me like a child and protecting me from the inevitable. Too late. Like Princess Zümrüd, I had made my choice. No way back for me.

I couldn't wait. I had to do it right now. Make a quick trip to Maiden Tower and talk to him. It would take an hour at most, and I'd be back before Mama's party slowed down.

Unnoticed, I slipped out of the festive courtyard and into the back alley. By now, it had plunged into darkness and looked rather hostile, most of the lights broken and the remaining few only highlighting the eeriness of the street.

A long silhouette came into view. Probably one of the local boys, hiding in a niche and smoking hashish in the sanctuary of the all-forgiving night.

Except that something in that silhouette seemed familiar. I stopped, holding my breath, listening to the muted sound of panting and something else. The cadenced rasp of brand-new leather shoes. I glanced at the ground and let my eyes gather in the color first—lime-yellow. Large shoes with pointed toes and a signature silver strap.

"Papa?"

The figure turned around. At first, I didn't recognize him—a mad, sweaty face with eyes glistening in the darkness, flashing chilling fires.

"What are you doing here?" he muttered in an angry, croaky, unfamiliar voice.

"I…just…"

There was someone else in the niche, hiding behind Papa. I strained my eyes to see. But I didn't really need to. Not with the presence of the one smell I would recognize in a million. The smell of my childhood. Oud oil mixed with jasmine, amber, and saffron. *Sevgi iksir*—the potion of love Almaz and I had created a long time ago.

"Go back right now," Papa commanded in a muted harsh tone.

Now I could clearly see Almaz, her bright red lipstick smeared around her mouth. Her fingers fidgeting around the pearl buttons of her undone blue blouse. I had an identical one, only in pink. Aunty Zeinab made them for our fifteenth birthdays.

"Leila, please..." Papa tried to put his arm around my shoulder, but I pushed him away. I didn't want him near me. I couldn't let him touch me.

I ran. I ran as far as possible. Down the dark alleys with their rank odors and their menacing silence...away...away...from lies and betrayal and Papa and that witch Almaz...

Until I saw the lights. Dots of light at first, appearing out of nowhere, getting bigger and brighter, coming closer. Blinding me. The headlights of a car. I stopped in the middle of the empty street, paralyzed by fear, my eyes transfixed on a taxicab speeding toward me.

"Leila... Daughter... No!"

Some powerful force threw me to the side, my head hitting the sidewalk with a painful crunch. For a brief moment I thought I saw Papa's face—affectionate, remorseful. Then I heard the deafening screech of tires. A cry. A curse.

Then nothing. Only darkness.

CHAPTER 19

The wind outside was loud, beating against my window like a trapped bird. And fog. Everywhere. Hanging in thick bundles, pushing me into the downy abyss of my bed.

And then, far away, the sound of a harp, its strings plucked in sobbing arpeggios seeming to come out of the wind, followed by a slow procession of strings. The music grew louder, swelling into the full orchestral despondency of Gustav Mahler's "Adagietto." I lay listening as the first violins painted a summer sunset; the violas sang the last autumn song of a skylark; the cellos drifted away with the spinning snow; then all the voices joined in spring's bittersweet harmonies—eternal and ephemeral. I cried and smiled at the same time. The music passed on, its echoes fading away. I slept.

I woke to silence, the ghostly silence when you feel like you're the last living soul left on earth. My head felt heavy as lead, while the rest of my body was weightless, floating on the smooth waves of my bed. Both windows in my room were draped, leaving me a prisoner of darkness. And of smell. A repulsive smell clogged the air. Where did it come from? I had to get away.

I stole out of bed. Too fast. The room spun around me. I held on to the wall, waiting for the spin to die out. The mirror next to my wardrobe was covered with white fabric. And so was the other mirror, hung over my piano. I thought of a custom to cover mirrors in the house of mourning. Did someone die?

I started toward the hallway, unsteady, clutching the wall, sliding my bare feet in short thrusts across the floor. My skin was numb; my bones crunched and ached. A light loomed ahead, scattering yellow spiders across the hallway. I pushed myself forward.

The living room was mobbed. People everywhere, lumped in groups, their lips moving but making no sound. At the sight of me, as if by command, everyone stepped aside, clearing my way to the center of the room.

There, on the dinner table, lay Papa. Asleep, dressed in his only formal black suit—the one he always refused to wear.

You have my permission to bury me in this suit. That'll be the only time I wear it—for my funeral. I could hear Papa cracking his joke, right in my ear, the familiar tobacco breath brushing against my nostrils.

Then why was he wearing it now? And why was he sleeping on the table, enclosed in ice and flowers? Surrounded by the fumes of that terrible odor. And watched by an audience all dressed in black?

"Papa!" I screamed, throwing myself toward him, anxious to reach him before this dark crowd could stop me from waking him up. But a single step was all I could manage before plunging to the floor.

"Papa," I muttered, "I'm sorry. Please forgive me. Papa…"

Someone lifted me. Uncle Kerim, his lips clenched tight. I had never seen him before without a smile. I leaned my head on his shoulder.

"Give her another Demerol," I heard him say.

Nurse Margo's face came close, her red, puffed-up eyes blinking rapidly. A bee sting on my arm.

"Papa, I'm sorry. Please forgive me, Papa."

Could he hear me?

Mama sat alongside him, a small porcelain figure buried in the folds of a mourning dress, a scarf tied so tightly around her face and neck that it seemed to drain any vitality from her cheeks. They were as ashen as the wall behind her. Eyes closed, she was rocking slowly

from side to side, her hand stroking the black silk on the table, back
and forth, as if ousting wrinkles from Papa's resting sheet.

Did she hate me? Did she blame me for Papa's death? Of course
she did. Just like everyone else must. Blame hovered in the air as
strongly as the odor of formaldehyde. It was my life Papa had saved
by sacrificing his own.

"Papa, I'm sorry. Please forgive me, Papa," I kept saying, over and
over, the words that would be carved into my heart for the rest of
my life.

By the time we reached the cemetery, the sky had cowered behind the
angry face of a rainstorm. What started as a drizzle quickly intensified
into a relentless shower.

Mama walked on my right, her shoulders squared, her
face withdrawn.

"It's good the rain waited until Mekhti Rashidovich was inside
the coffin," sobbed Nurse Margo, squeezing my hand.

That's what I thought too. How horrible it would have been if it
had poured while Papa was carried a few blocks in an open coffin,
followed by a large crowd to the waiting catafalque. Getting wet
before being buried under the ground. Did Papa feel anything?

A gust of wind slapped me in the face and continued whipping
through the Alley of Honor memorial park, lifting into the air
anything that wasn't rooted in the ground—batches of loose soil,
broken twigs. Someone's purple shawl quivered against the gray sky.
How much grayer could the sky even get?

A group of drunken gravediggers in high rubber boots lingered
in the distance, leaning against their weapons, smoking, impatient
to wrap up their job. If I had only stayed at the party instead of
wandering the dark streets, they wouldn't be burying Papa with their
rusty shovels.

And I wouldn't have known.

Almaz, that witch, pretending to look innocent, joined a group of female mourners performing a traditional mourning ritual—tearing her hair, beating her chest with her fists, lamenting loudly. Miserable, wicked *ifrita*. How dare she come here? Had she no shame left at all? She had always been jealous of me, of my family. And that's why she stole my papa—to take my place, to become more important to him than me.

"What if you were me and I were you? Then it would be me living upstairs in your fancy quarters, and you'd be right here—in my place—under the stairs."

A cobra who spit her malignant venom into Papa's heart. A traitor who dropped me as a sister so she could spend time with Papa and put a curse on him. The curse of her beauty. Oh, how I wanted to scratch out those heinous hyena eyes, to see her bleed to death, twisting her whoring body in her epileptic convulsions. *She* should have been inside that coffin. Eaten by worms. Instead of Papa.

When did it all start? When? Was it two years ago when we went to the Black Sea? Mama couldn't go, and Papa offered to take Almaz with us so I would have a friend to play with. One morning we were supposed to tour the Swallow's Nest Castle. Almaz said that she wasn't feeling well, and Papa sent me alone with the tourist group. When I came back, Papa seemed annoyed and edgy, even snapped at me for buying two blue shells for fifty kopeks. He made me so mad that I threw the shells out the window. Was it then and there that it started?

But why did Papa yield to her spell? Did she really make him love her more than he loved me?

Excruciating pain stabbed through my head. I touched the bandage. No, it wasn't physical pain. It was the realization that, ever since that doomed evening of Mama's birthday, Almaz and I had been knotted together again. This time as the keepers of a dirty secret protecting Mama's heart and Papa's reputation. With me alone absorbing the blame. And it made me hate *her* even more.

"Very well-attended funeral," I heard Farhad's voice behind me.

"Honorable Mekhti Rashidovich would be proud to know that the love, encouragement, and inspiration he gave to all of us would carry his good name beyond his tragic death."

Farhad had arrived yesterday morning, on a short leave from the KGB Higher School in Moscow, where he had been accepted into a three-year program. Along with my parents' closest friends— Uncle Kerim, Uncle Anatoly, and Uncle Zohrab—Farhad worked tirelessly: dealing with the bureaucracy of the morgue and with the proceedings at the cemetery; ordering and picking up flower wreaths; organizing and welcoming crowds of visitors. His presence disturbed me, and his active participation in the arduous business of arranging a funeral made me feel cornered. He hovered over Mama like a doting son-in-law, trying to fill in the missing male presence in our Papa-less family. And Mama, who hadn't shown much delight at the prospects of our betrothal, now seemed to succumb to Farhad's efforts.

The whole upper crust of the Azerbaijani Communist oligarchy was in attendance at the Alley of Honor, grouped around the plot for Papa's burial located next to the tall, granite monument with the portraits of his parents.

A sudden buzz in the crowd. Headlights turned on the brightest high beams, a black ZIL limousine—the official carriage of the *Nomenklatura*—traveled toward us along a path too narrow to accommodate its obese body, causing the chauffeur to drive over graves bordering the path.

"Is this the First Secretary of the Party himself?" A wave of awe spread through the crowd.

The Chairman of the Council of Ministers emerged from the car, a young member of his entourage holding an umbrella over his head. The Chairman made his way toward us, his face somber, his lips pressed tightly. He vigorously shook Mama's hand, patted me playfully on the cheek, turned to the crowd, and said loudly: "It's your turn—the young Soviet generation's turn—to carry on the torch of Communism."

He walked to the podium and began his eulogy, the wind and rain restraining his voice, only brief snatches of his monologue reaching my ears: "…Soviet Azerbaijan…under the guidance of our government…many sacrifices…beloved country…dedication to the morals of Communism…My hard work on behalf…"

Why was he giving propaganda rhetoric at Papa's funeral? Why did he turn our tragedy into a self-promoting spectacle? And why did Mama gaze at the speaker with admiration, nodding her head in agreement with his empty words? Just like everyone else in the crowd.

Except for Tahir. He hid at the very end of the burial plot, leaning against a white poplar tree that fearlessly held its skinny branches up against the blasts of the roaring wind. *I am here for you*, I felt him say.

Upon returning from the cemetery, our family and our closest friends gathered in the courtyard at the same tables where—just two days earlier—we'd celebrated Mama's birthday. Nothing seemed to have changed. These were the same faces, except for Almaz—she wasn't there. The same dishes cooked and served by Aunty Zeinab. The same flowers spread around the courtyard, their fragrance futile against the odor of formaldehyde.

"My condolences, worthy Sonia *Khanum*, on the passing of your asshole husband." The insult sliced through our gathering like a dagger.

Everyone stopped talking, chewing, breathing. A deadly silence took over the courtyard, all heads tilted up, all eyes glued to Chingiz.

He leaned over the balustrade of the third-floor balcony, his cow eyes glistening, his gold-tooth mouth twisted in a drunken sneer, slurring and weeping at the same time. "Look at you. You're all there, sitting there, speaking there. All respectful. Saying all these nice things—he did this and he did that. But no one says that he was a dirty *haramzadə*. A pedophile. And a thief."

Uncle Ali appeared behind Chingiz, hitting him, trying to pull him back inside their apartment. "Don't listen to him," he cried. "You good people all know that the boy is not well in his head. Just like his mother. You all remember her, my poor niece, how sick she was, don't you? Please! Good, worthy people! Don't listen to his jabber. He's not only cuckoo and *beyinsiz*, but he's had too much vodka and opium. He's drunk and weak in the head. Forgive him good people."

"*Sikdir!*" Chingiz swore and pushed his uncle off. "I know what I'm saying. I saw it with my own two—" He forked his eyes with his fingers, then turned the fingers on the crowd. "You." He pointed toward Papa's friends assembled in the right side of the courtyard. "I saw all of you. I gave my buddy *anaşa* to smoke; he let me watch. My buddy works at the Turkish baths on Dzerzhinsky Street.

"Don't you good people know it's not just baths but *fahişəxana*, a whorehouse for important men like Mekhti Rashidovich? I watched how they *atdirmaq* my Almaz. Her and other girls. They would *atdirmaq* them, then use them as their urinals. Perverts." Chingiz bent over the railing and spat down at our gathering.

"Let's get him, the lying son of a bitch." Farhad threw his chair aside and rushed upstairs followed by several other men.

Everyone tried to sneak a glance at Mama, to see her reaction. There was none. She kept digging her fork into *dushbara*, dumplings, her eyes downcast.

"And you, my future mother-in-law Zeinab," Chingiz howled. "How much did you pay my uncle so I would marry your dishonored daughter?"

The sound of a blast shook the courtyard.

Aunty Zeinab's copper tray had crashed onto the stone floor, her *plov* spilling around. She didn't move, her mighty arms hanging helplessly, her crimson face frozen in pain.

"I loved your Almaz," Chingiz whimpered. "I loved her before he made her a whore. *Allahu Akbar*, the bastard got what he deserved, smashed like a pea."

The men reached the third floor and grabbed Chingiz, beating him fiercely and dragging him inside Uncle Ali's apartment. He didn't resist, just cursed, wailed, and cried his drunken tears. Soon the police arrived, and Chingiz was heaved away, his face bloated beyond recognition, his torn lower lip hanging like a crab leg.

Papa's wake resumed with everyone trying to act as if nothing had happened, shedding tears, hugging Mama and me, offering long praising toasts in Papa's remembrance. Uncle Kerim even made a clumsy attempt to tailor one of his toasts to the incident when he said, "The best memory is that which forgets nothing but injuries. Write goodness in marble and write injuries in the dust."

But nothing could change what had happened. *A knife wound heals, but a tongue wound festers.*

Ayib was out. The shame had been revealed.

The next morning I woke to the screeching of car brakes followed by the slam of the doors. A gray GAZ-2424 Volga van was parked beneath my balcony. Two men in white aprons rolled out a stretcher. I grabbed my shawl and ran downstairs.

Uncle Zohrab stood at the entrance to his apartment, his feeble body swaying, banging his head mercilessly against the wall, wailing: "*Al-laa-hum-magh-fir li-hay-yi-naa wa may-yiti-naa wa shaa-hi-di-naa...*"

"What happened?" I asked, terrified.

"She took her own life." Uncle Zohrab sobbed, covering his face with his hands. "My sweet *gül*, my Zeinab... She hung herself... quietly...while we were asleep... She hung herself in the kitchen. My beloved Zeinab. Allah, give wings to her soul..."

Then I saw Almaz. She lay huddled on the floor in the corner, shaking as violently as if a thousand volts of lightning poured through her body. The pallid irises burst out of her eyes. Her mouth salivated, chewing on air. An epileptic seizure.

"Uncle Zohrab," I shouted. "Help!"

"Let her die. Let the *fahişə* die." He hit his head with his fists. "Oh, my Zeinab, my sweet *gül*, why did you do this to yourself? Why did you leave me in shame?"

Almaz struggled to breathe, foam forming at her mouth. Her clenched fingers pulled at the collar of her nightgown. A rasping sound rattled through her throat. Her head bounced against the hard floor.

I dithered, torn between the wish for Almaz to die an agonizing death and a fear of losing my only sister.

Fear won.

I knelt beside her, placed the palm of my hand between her head and the floor, pushed her body to one side with my free hand, and positioned my knee firmly against her back. She continued to tremble but not as violently as before. I took off my shawl, wrapped it around her shoulders, and dropped on the floor next to her.

How long had it been since we were like this together? How long had it been since I saw her face without coats of makeup? Her baby skin, a tiny mole above the bow of her upper lip, her eyes fringed with her own black lashes. How long had it been since a sanguine girl ran up and down our castle's stairway, her red ponytail flying, her crystalline laughter echoing throughout the courtyard, bringing sunshine to my childhood?

A pair of jorabs, two petals of a rose, Aunty Zeinab used to call us, holding us to her breasts, nursing us at the same time.

Aunty Zeinab, my sweet Aunty Zeinab.

Two men in aprons struggled to roll the heavily weighted stretcher out of the apartment. The gray plastic sheet slipped down at the threshold bump, cruelly exposing Aunty Zeinab's body. Uncle Zohrab rushed to adjust the sheet. Then he hobbled next to the stretcher, weeping, holding Aunty Zeinab's bloated hand in his.

In the niche of the courtyard, next to the Snow Princess, Muezzin Rashid recited a prayer, the fingers of his hands entwined, his eyes closed: *"Al-laa-hum-magh-fir li-hay-yi-naa wa may-yiti-naa wa shaa-hi-di-naa…"*

How can I keep living, keep breathing, putting one foot in front of the other, when the people I love the most are no more? Cold flesh wrapped in white shroud, stuck in the ground for the worms to feast on.

How can I continue when I am the one who killed them, even if by nothing more than accidentally pulling on the loose end of a knot? A knot of perversion and betrayal the people I love the most had been entangled in.

How can I grieve for them when anger flashes through my heart and burns up my tears? When my head is like a desert with rising sand dunes of questions and not a speck of an answer?

I flipped open the seat of my piano bench. Tchaikovsky's *Seasons*. I'd bought it a few years earlier but never got around to playing it. I turned over pages: *January, February…June.* One note after another, I wove a spell of remembrance, grieving my lost childhood and the people who had taken it away.

June: Barcarolle

Almaz and I lay under the limbs of an old weeping willow in Governor's Park. We're here to become sisters at last—blood sisters.

We dig the hole and line the colorful splinters of glass in the shape of a heart, carefully pressing them into the dirt at the bottom. We keep redoing it until the heart is perfect.

"Time for the surgery." I reach for a package weighing down the pocket of my blouse.

"Always a doctor's daughter." Almaz laughs.

I unfold the cloth that holds Mama's scalpel, cottons, and a roll of sanitary bandage. Just in case.

We poke each other's index finger and squeeze two drops of blood inside the small glass saucer, turn it over, and place it atop the heart.

The burial looks magical—the heart glitters from under the glass saucer—clear except for the two snakelike rosy paths of our blood coming together, connecting at the pinnacle.

As the sun reaches its zenith, we take our vows of sisterhood.

"With the Sun, Moon, and Earth as my witnesses, I swear to be your eternal sister…"

Why did Tchaikovsky name it "June: Barcarolle"? More suitable would be "Autumn Song." A musical eulogy.

As the broken chords of the song's coda melted into the air, I heard Almaz's words:

"What if you were me and I were you? After all, it was only a beauty mark on your tummy that defined our destinies. What if your Mama was wrong? What if she made a mistake? It's possible, isn't it?"

What *would* have happened if my parents had raised Almaz, and I was Aunty Zeinab's daughter? What then? Would it have been me, instead of Almaz, taken to the Turkish baths' whorehouse by my own papa? Would it be me, dishonored and shamed? Offered to a retarded Chingiz out of desperation to save my stolen honor?

An egg thief becomes a camel thief.

First, fancy rugs, rings, swords from the museums, and then my only sister—*a priceless, flawless diamond*, he called her.

Oh, how I wanted Papa to walk in the room, poised and dependable, so I could fall again under the spell of his laughter. So I could erase, scrape, tear out of my mind those unbearable thoughts.

But the only image of Papa that seemed to survive in my soul was that of a beast with his eyes glittering in a dark alley, spitting flames of lust.

Enough. I needed an escape from death and misery. I tucked Tchaikovsky back inside the bench, closed the lid of my piano, and grabbed my chador.

Bus Number 51 passed by crammed with people hanging from the doors. I ran to catch up with it at the next stop and arrived just as it was starting to pull away. Friendly passengers' hands lifted me off the ground, and with one foot on the lower stair and the other hanging in the air, I traveled up Niyazi Street.

The Caspian Sea lazily rolled its turquoise waters. On the hillsides, mottled grape vines bathed in the slanting rays of autumn sun. I jumped off the bus at the entrance to Icheri Sheher and ran through its labyrinth toward Ashuglar Street. Energized. Feeling alive again.

"*Salam eleykum, qız*," Tahir's next-door shoe-shop merchant greeted me. He sat in the threshold of his shop, playing *shesh besh* with his bowlegged son.

I reached for the knob and tried to turn it. Locked.

"Take off that chador!" I heard a commanding halt.

I turned around. Two young men in leather coats approached me. The one with a pale face took a paper out of his pocket and read: "By the District Committee in Charge of Communist Ideology and Ethics, you, Leila Badalbeili, are charged with moral debauchery and criminal association."

CHAPTER 20

I woke to Muezzin Rashid's morning prayer *Fajr Adhan*. It had been four weeks since Papa died—an eternity. With my eyes closed, I saw a lark flying in the blue sky between the sea and a rainbow, fluttering her wings in rhythm with Muezzin Rashid's vocal trills. If I could only stay like this forever in the haven of my bed. No comrades wagging their accusing fingers in my face. No college peers making nasty grimaces behind my back. None of Mama's muffled sobs nibbling at my heart from across the hallway. Nothing but my little blue universe.

I pulled the blanket over my face.

A mistake. The blanket's camel hair muted the chant. Darkness swallowed the blue. Silence trapped me in its cave, with tritones of shame and regret creeping inside my ears.

I threw the blanket to the side. A cold draft brushed against my body, seeping into my skin. The balcony door was ajar; the rain pattered against the glass. Droplets streamed down, filling a puddle underneath the door and continuing along the gaps in the parquet floor. The curtain was soaking wet like the sail of a boat flapping in a crosswind. Outside, nothing but dull skies and Muezzin Rashid's last inflections fading away like autumn leaves.

A knock on the front door. I wrapped a scarf around my shoulders and ran barefoot through the hallway.

"Who's there?"

"It's me."

Almaz. Shrunken to bare bones and skin since I last saw her at the Seventh Day ceremony after Aunty Zeinab's suicide.

"Can I come in?" she said, looking down at her feet, blinking.

Her face was pale, her lips as shredded as if she'd been chewing on broken glass. In her arms she held a large bundle wrapped in a yellow tablecloth. She knew Mama had left for work. Otherwise she wouldn't have dared to show up.

I hesitated. She slipped in anyway, closing the door behind her.

"We need to talk," she said.

"I have nothing to say to you."

"But I have something to say to you. Something I *have* to say… before I leave. Because we might never see each other again."

Never see each other again?

"Why? Where are you going?" I said in a flat voice, holding back anxiety.

"Papa is taking me to Kishlak Gadzhi later today to marry me off to a cousin. A widower. To wash his hands of my shame."

I thought of a small, desolate village high in the Caucasus Mountains where Almaz and I once spent a few days in the summer. Even then it was cold, in a rocky cavity surrounded by glaciers, with toilets outside and no plumbing. My heart shrank with sorrow.

"I know you hate me," Almaz said somberly, looking down, "and there is nothing I can do to make up for what happened. All I can say is that I am sorry…so sorry…that I wish I had never been born. I wish your mama had never saved me."

"What do you expect me to do? To forgive you?" I choked back tears. "I always knew that you were jealous of my family. But never did I imagine you would sneak behind my back, bewitching, destroying Papa. Making him love you so *madly* that he completely lost his sense of judgment."

"You're wrong, Leila. He never loved me. And I did nothing— *nothing*—to entice him. Yes, Mekhti Rashidovich was my idol. Yes, I was jealous that you had your papa and I had mine. Because I always wanted my papa to be like yours—important and powerful.

And yes, I wanted to get approval from Mekhti Rashidovich, to impress him—"

"Well," I uttered bitterly, "you obviously succeeded—"

"He made me do it," Almaz cried. "Right here, in his smoking room…the first time… It happened three years ago, when you went with Mama to Swallow Nest in the summer. He called on the phone and asked me to bring him some coriander for his tea. I came over… and he asked me to kiss him, the way we did when we were kids, when you and I climbed in his lap and kissed him on both cheeks. I felt embarrassed, but I was afraid to disappoint him.

"And then everything happened so quickly…fear…pain…feeling both special and dirty…" Almaz paused, staring into space, her face shadowed by hurt and shame. "Afterward, he blamed me for provoking him, for unleashing his male instincts. He threatened to send me away for spreading malicious lies and ruining his reputation if I ever opened my mouth to anyone about what had happened. I started crying, and suddenly he became his old self, kindhearted and caring, telling me that I was his beautiful little girl. Which made me feel guilty, as if I had caused injury to an invincible man. I thought he regretted what happened and would never do it again… Only I was wrong."

I stood still, with my head down, afraid to look at Almaz, feeling the intensity of her eyes on me. I knew that Almaz had told the truth. I remembered how Papa blamed me for provoking Farhad. *That's the wicked power that you women have over men*, he had said.

What *wicked power* could a twelve-year-old girl have?

But what could I say? I was trapped, torn emotionally. If I accepted Almaz's truth, then I would be disloyal to Papa, betraying his memory.

"It's easy to blame someone who can't defend himself," I finally said sheepishly, avoiding Almaz's gaze.

She took a deep, exasperated breath. "All right, Leila. Then I'd better go. But at least let me give you some advice before I leave."

"Advice? About what?"

"About your situation. Please don't be stubborn. Just hear me. There are plenty of people around who'd be happy to see you fall, take Allah as my witness." Almaz pinched her fingers together and raised her arms in the air, the way Aunty Zeinab used to do. "I wouldn't be surprised if someone staged this whole investigation about you and the Mukhtarovs."

"What do you mean?"

"You see, your papa... He had a generous heart and liked to live in grand style. Many people ate and drank at his table and were willing to cut off their right hands if he had asked. He had many friends then. But now he has a hundred times more enemies."

"But why? Why would they turn on Papa...on me now?"

"An exposed red apple invites a stone," Almaz quoted an old *məsəl*. "And you are exposed now. Every vulture around has been eyeing a piece for himself: your papa's collection, your apartment, your mama's position, the Badalbeili name."

"You're ridiculous. Who can take my name away?"

"Your Papa's cousin."

"Uncle Mahmoud?"

Eşşək—donkey—Papa called him.

"Even a donkey dreams of a fancy saddle," Almaz said. "If your reputation is smeared, he's the one to wear the Badalbeili crown. And so it goes."

Maybe there was some truth in Almaz's words. Since Papa's funeral, it seemed Mama and I had been living in a lonely desert, as if a forceful Khazri had blown Papa's high-placed Party-member friends away. Everyone who had something to lose tried to disassociate himself from Papa's disgrace. Only his boyhood friend, Uncle Anatoly, visited us every day, bringing fresh fruit and roses from his garden, along with his openhearted smile. But he had no connections within the Party and could do nothing to help my situation.

"Even if what you're saying is true," I said defensively, "Mama still has many people who love her, who owe her their lives."

"They might love her with all their hearts, but no one seems to be rushing to attend to a fallen mare. Don't forget, Leila. We women are mares—to be paraded around grandly so long as there's a powerful rider on top."

"Enough. I think you should go." I turned to leave the room. "I've got enough gloom without your—"

"I didn't come to upset you. I want to help."

"How? By telling me how awful everyone is? Not much help there. They've turned me into a *şortu*. They're accusing me of debauchery, immoral conduct, hiding under a chador in order to prostitute myself—"

"I have a plan," Almaz cut me off. "I'm going today to the Baku Central Komsomol Committee to write a report that there has been a mistake. That they've unjustly accused you of *my* wrongdoing. That it was *me*—not you—wearing the chador and going to Ashuglar Street. And that when they caught you outside the shop, it was my fault because I begged you to go there and return some money I owed to the Mukhtarovs."

Tears clogged my eyes. "You'd do this for me?"

"Of course. You're my sister, for life and beyond," she said.

Oh, how I wanted to put my arms around Almaz and cry together so our tears could wash the past away, even if only for a brief moment.

"Thank you for wanting to help me," I said instead. "But your plan won't work."

"Why not?"

"Because I've already admitted my relationship with the Mukhtarovs."

Almaz frowned, biting her lips. "That's not good. Now you have to take action."

"How?"

"Blame the Mukhtarovs. Write a letter to the First Secretary. Beg for forgiveness. Claim that they poisoned you with their hex, threatened you or something like that. Show yourself as a victim corrupted by the Mukhtarovs."

"I can't."

"Why?"

"Because it's all lies. And I'll prove them wrong."

"*Pərvərdigara!* Oh my God!" Almaz threw up her hands. "They don't need your proof. They're foxes. And foxes use their tails as their witnesses."

"I can't purge the Mukhtarovs. They have done nothing but good for me."

"No one cares about the Mukhtarovs. It's you they're after. It's you they're using as a *qapazalti*, a scapegoat, to teach a lesson in obedience to others. To show that when it comes to their Communist justice, your privileged background and all your accomplishments don't matter. As for your Mukhtarovs—they might spend a few days in jail, but I've heard Miriam's kid has a nice *krysha* dealing hashish and other things for comrades. They'll keep him out of trouble for as long as he's useful. So you better worry about yourself. And your mama."

Almaz sniffled, a sad smile pulling the inside corners of her eyes down. She shut them tight, then opened them, using the eyelids as blotters to dry the tears.

"I better get going," she said. "And this is for you to remember me." She laid her package on the table and left in haste.

I unfolded the package. Inside lay Almaz the Doll in an Islamic dress with the red Pioneer tie around her neck, her jade eyes pure, her hair hidden modestly under a scarf. Almaz's most treasured possession and the source of her great vanity. She had left her with me.

I pressed Almaz the Doll against my chest, carried her to my room, and placed her lovingly on top of my piano between the photograph of Mama, Papa, and me, and the marble bust of Sergei Rachmaninoff.

Like a mouse, I scurried through the back entrance of the Conservatory and up the oval staircase to the second floor, my face buried inside the

THE ORPHAN SKY

loop of my scarf. I chose the shadowy corner behind Lenin's sculpture and hid there, imprinting myself into the wall. Waiting—*dreading*—the approach of four o'clock. My first piano lesson in four weeks. And the first time I would face Professor Sultan-zade since Papa's funeral.

Had the rumors of my *indecent behavior* reached her? And if so, would she scream at me—loud enough for the entire Conservatory and ten blocks around it to hear—before throwing me out of her practice room? It was the worst thing that could happen now, just five and a half months before the Budapest piano competition. I needed this win more than ever—my only real opportunity to redeem myself and make the horror and humiliation of the past few weeks go away.

The light flickered in one of the sconces down the long, dim corridor. *One, two, three…one, two, three…one, two, three…* How fitting was the pulse of a waltz. Robert Schumann's *Papillons* was playing behind the door of Professor Sultan-zade's rehearsal studio. I listened to the legato passages, smooth and silky, like the wings of a butterfly touching the keys. Who was playing? I didn't remember any of her students working on this piece. Besides, the performance had something of a Vladimir Horowitz emotional carelessness that could never come from any of her apprentices.

The "Waltz in F-sharp Minor" modulated into the "E-flat Major Polonaise," the melodies as intertwined as the vines on the frieze running along the vaulted ceiling. I recalled Professor Sultan-zade saying once that Schumann's *Papillons* was her cure for melancholy, a masquerade of moods and masks, whirling her into a dance, making her careless.

I squinted, my eyelids trembling. A thousand yellow butterflies dispersed in the air—one for every staccato flying out of the rehearsal studio. In pairs, they twirled in the dance steps of the *Papillon's* "D Major Waltz," leaping across the corridor, luring me to follow, drawing me into a fantasy.

"I didn't expect you."

Professor Sultan-zade stood at the threshold of her studio, dressed

179

in a coat and clearly ready to leave. Instinctively, I peeped behind her to see who was playing the Schumann. But no one was at the piano. So it had been my professor herself giving that airy, stirring performance of Schumann's *Papillons*. The best I'd ever heard.

"I came for my lesson," I said.

Without saying a word, Professor Sultan-zade led me inside the practice room and closed the door behind us. Then, still wearing her coat, she lit a cigarette and walked to the window, the pervasive marcato of her heels crashing against the floor. Each step a rejection. Each step a drumbeat of remorse.

I waited near the door, terrified, tears pouring down my cheeks, while she stood at the window in smoke-filled silence.

"Animals," she muttered angrily. "Absolute animals. To strike you at the time you're grieving." Her hand clutched the collar of her coat, tightening it into a fist as if trying to block the air, to restrain her throat from speaking. "Why? Why did you give an excuse to your enemy to destroy you?"

"What enemy?" I asked, confused.

She released the collar, cleared her throat. "You're so naive, Leila. Don't you understand that there is a whole world of politics behind every success? Consider this: our new rector doesn't have any significant connections within the Ministry of Culture. Meanwhile, our former rector—with all his relations in the Party—now heads the rival Azerbaijani State Institute of Arts. And he's determined to put his institution on the map. To do so, he will stop at nothing.

"I'm almost convinced that he's behind the hounding to purge you from participation in the Budapest competition. Then they can have their student, that talentless Sharipov boy—or whatever his name—the one who took second place at the regional competition—to represent Azerbaijan in Budapest."

"But, Professor, I haven't done anything—"

"You've done enough and more to destroy your entire life, Leila. Didn't I warn you months ago when you showed me the Vladimir Horowitz album? What did I say to you? Stay on course and away from murky waters. Dedicate yourself to building your career and future. Because the only altar for you to worship at should be the altar of music. The rest is mere garbage. But you didn't listen to me. Do you know why?"

I shook my head.

"Because everything came too easy to you. When I was your age, I dreamed of becoming a concert pianist. My parents couldn't afford a piano, so I befriended a janitor at my school, and she allowed me to practice on a broken, out-of-tune piano in the evenings. But no matter how hard I tried, I just wasn't good enough.

"While you had the perfect hands, musicality, and charisma right from the start. You didn't have to work hard—you're a natural. And unfortunately, you are also spoiled and reckless. You wanted to play the piano—your parents bought you an exclusive Bösendorfer. You won the competition—you received costly jewelry. All of which distorted your sense of reality, making you feel impervious to its dangers."

Professor Sultan-zade threw her cigarette out the window, came over to me, and took my hands between hers, rubbing them softly as she always did before recitals.

"This system can be brutal," she said in a low voice. "Very brutal. And now you've gotten yourself trapped between its grindstones."

"Professor, please trust me," I whispered in fast presto, touched by her compassion and desperate to prove my innocence to her. "The rumors, whatever you've heard about my indecent behavior—they are lies. Yes, I did spend a lot of time with the Mukhtarovs, but they are incredible people. They are cultural and intellectual and artistic. Tahir is a painter, and his grandmother, Miriam Mukhtarova, used to be a famous mezzo long time ago, before the Revolution. She sang with Feodor Chaliapin. She told me stories about Sergei Rachmaninoff. They were friends. Please believe me. I'm not a *şortu*. I haven't dishonored myself. Please believe me—"

"I do. I know who you are, Leila. I know you very well. I've known you for six years, since you were a little girl—always inquisitive, adventurous, and oh, so unique. Nothing will ever make me doubt your integrity."

Professor Sultan-zade hesitated, then put her arm around me—something she had never done before. "I will help as much as I can. Meanwhile, let Mozart heal your broken heart. The way Schumann keeps mine together. Remember—the hurt is the place where the music enters you."

"I'm sorry, Professor. I'm so sorry." I wept, her empathy breaking down all my defenses.

"I know you are."

Professor Sultan-zade hastily removed her arm, as if feeling uncomfortable for revealing her softness, and marched back to the window.

"Why are you waiting there by the door?" she said, assuming her usual pedagogical articulation. "We've already wasted ten minutes of your lesson."

Like Schumann's *Papillons*, I took my wings to the piano.

"Czerny, *The Art of Finger Dexterity*," Professor Sultan-zade announced. She lit a cigarette and turned away toward the darkening sky, as if losing interest in me.

But she couldn't fool me anymore. Despite her gruff exterior, I knew Professor Sultan-zade cared deeply about me, vowing me her support while compromising her own position.

On my way home, I took a shortcut through Mercury Plaza—an old fountain where the Greek god Mercury once stood beneath a large rotunda surrounded by mulberry trees. On a hot summer day, there was no better place in town to hide from the scorching rays of the Baku sun.

But no more. The mulberry trees had been cut, the rotunda turned into a mound of eroded bricks. Mercury lay next to it deposed, still holding on to his wand with two serpents entwined in mortal combat. When Almaz and I were young, we believed that at night, when no one was around, Mercury waved his magic wand, stepped off the pedestal, and flew into the star-studded sky to carry his messages.

Chechen workers sat cross-legged on a rug decorated with peacocks under the only surviving mulberry tree, drinking tea and counting prayer beads. Bulldozers circled the area like hungry hyenas, their teeth bared, juices flowing, eager to finish devouring Mercury Plaza.

One more page of my cloudless past had been torn off. I kicked a pile of dead leaves. The wind followed through, snatching and lifting them high into the air—a pageant of purples, dark reds, flame reds, browns, and yellows flitting in their last autumn dance.

I sped up. I knew what I had to do. To see Almaz before she left. To hold her close, as I used to, to hide my face inside her hair and to tell her how much I needed her. Even now. *Especially* now.

The rug at the entrance to Almaz's apartment was in place. I pushed it out of the way. The door behind was wide open. Inside, nothing but bare walls and the scent of Aunty Zeinab's saffron *plov*. And in the corner, propped against the iron-cast stove, was their wedding mirror with its Koran inscription. Shattered, with lightning bolts flying across its cracked surface.

I came closer and traced carefully one of the protruding slivers with the tip of my finger. Papa's eyes followed me, night black, their cradles overflowing with tears.

I closed my hand into a fist and pressed it against the broken mirror, grinding it in, hard, hypnotized by the streaks of red running down the sliced reflection of my face. Papa's face.

"Why? Why did you do it? Why? And why did you save me? Why didn't you just let me die?"

CHAPTER 21

The condemnation hearing took place on November 4, 1979.

A bloody ocean closed in, eager to swallow me. Red banners, red podium, small red flags in the hands of the audience. Each member had received one to wave in support of my condemnation. The tribunal of three took their places at the table at stage center with their head in the middle—the Secretary of the Baku Komsomol Committee in Charge of Communist Ideology and Ethics, Comrade Guseinov. A veteran of internal cleansing. Tall, thin, soft-spoken, and neatly dressed, a crimson handkerchief peeking out of the breast pocket of his gray suit. He conducted the proceedings as flawlessly as a well-staged show. Raising his right hand, stilling the rumbling noises from the audience, he invited an orderly, morbid silence.

I felt my body scrunch up. Something icy crept up my spine.

Fear.

"Comrades, we're here today with a burdensome task," Comrade Guseinov said. "We're here today to determine the future of one of our own. Yes, it's easy to point an accusing finger. We have all the facts all the *raw* facts. They don't just *prove* Leila Badalbeili's guilt; they *scream* of her despicable, degrading conduct. But no. This is not what we do here. This is not what's written in our Communist codex of honor.

"What do we do? We give the benefit of the doubt. We paint a moral portrait of one of us who has slipped. Who knows? Maybe there is still hope. Maybe we can still give a hand to one who has fallen victim to her own bad choices. We shall see. And to do so, I'm going to invite you, her classmates and friends, to come forward and tell us who this young woman really is."

I knew that no one would speak in my favor. And I knew that my fate had been decided before the hearing. But I still gasped and held my breath, waiting for a single word—or just the slightest sign of kindness—to bandage my tarnished honor.

Malik the Weasel was first, taking his time and enjoying every minute in the spotlight as he listed all my transgressions since kindergarten. What a memory he had. He even remembered how I had whooping cough in third grade and kept coughing and falling out of step with the others while marching in a school column at the Great October Revolution parade.

Then Vera, a girl with a stubby pigtail and mouse ears, who desperately tried—unsuccessfully—to become my best friend after Almaz dropped out of school, eagerly cooed her suspicions about my *elevated* interest in Western music, total lack of enthusiasm for our contemporary Soviet songs, and my questionable morals.

Others followed. A continuous stream of my schoolmates flowing to the podium. All singing the same tune with the same detached mask of condemnation, their inescapable slanders tearing down what was left of my spirit.

My headmistress testified last. She was my only hope. Just three weeks ago, Mama operated on her younger grandson. A bad case of neglected appendicitis. After the successful surgery, my headmistress swore in the presence of the whole hospital that she'd see her family burn in fire before she'd let a speck of coal fall on Mama's clan.

"As you can imagine, I am shocked," she said, panting, pressing her small hand against her sumptuous bosom. "Shocked and dismayed at Leila's behavior. Who would have thought that a girl from such a distinguished family would get involved with a person of the lowest moral standing? Shame on you, Leila, for soiling the honor of a Young Communist, for bringing misery and embarrassment to your illustrious family. My heart goes out to your mama. Such a distinguished woman who's experienced so much sadness."

She shook her head in distress and withdrew like a royal barge. With her departure, my tepid hope drowned in the enthusiastic applause of the crowd.

Comrade Guseinov rose from the tribunal table, straightened the pleats in his trousers, and took a few steps toward me. A spider on long, skinny legs.

"You are a stain on the reputation of our valorous Komsomol Organization," Comrade Guseinov announced, sticking his finger in my face. "You are a stain that must be wiped out."

High-spirited, continuous applause.

I kept licking and biting my parched lips, tasting blood.

Satisfied with his remark and even more so with the audience's reaction, Comrade Guseinov marched to the podium, placed his hands on the stand, gazed confidently at the audience, and began his closing speech:

"Comrades, I know how difficult it must have been for you to testify against someone you have known for a long time. But speaking the truth requires fortitude and an exceptional moral clarity. The tribunal has demonstrated both those qualities. And after hearing your honest, heartfelt statements, I have come to the conclusion that the previous life of this confused young woman has all led up to this dreadful moment.

"And after scrupulous deliberation, I am ready to proceed to the final indictment. Leila Badalbeili, standing here in front of you, spent day after day alone in the company of a certain criminal. A criminal who had a history of incarceration for the most abominable of all crimes—for attempting to betray our Motherland and desert to the decadent West. And how did she try to cover up her immoral conduct? By hiding beneath a chador."

Almaz was right. Throughout the trial, Tahir's name had never been mentioned other than as a *certain criminal element*. No one cared about him. The pack of wolves was after me.

Comrade Guseinov paused to allow the angry murmurs of the crowd to surface before continuing.

"So this is my recommendation," he said, rising to his fullest height, taking on the gravity of a grand inquisitor. "For immoral, degenerative behavior, I propose to expel this Leila Badalbeili from the Komsomol. And I recommend further measures, as well. I personally will submit a request to the Central Committee of the Azerbaijan Communist Party to revoke her participation in the Budapest music competition. She does not deserve the honor of representing our country abroad. Never! Now let's vote. Who is for the expulsion?"

A forest of hands flew up. The reaction was unanimous.

My world came to an end. Dark, grim hopelessness crashed into my heart.

"Comrades, now, for the conclusion, let me ask you a question," Comrade Guseinov said, slowly challenging the audience with his daunting eyes. "What is the lesson each and all of you have just learned?"

I felt a brief moment of satisfaction at seeing the audience in panic. This was the only impromptu part of the proceedings, unlike the rest, which had been honed and rehearsed for weeks. Everyone dedicated their full absorption to the task, knitting brows, biting nails, tapping finger against forehead. Comrade Guseinov took it even further with his own dramatic pose—head rested on his fist, deep in inner reflection—a self-conscious portrayal of Rodin's *The Thinker.*

"I'll tell you what the lesson is," he said finally, releasing a spasm of relief in the audience. "And the lesson is—those who sleep with dogs will rise with fleas."

Like a well-rehearsed choir, one row after another, the audience members got to their feet. Waving their red flags, they repeated Comrade Guseinov's slogan again and again:

"Those who sleep with dogs will rise with fleas! Those who sleep with dogs will rise with fleas!"

I stood at center stage, disgraced and terrified, alone against a crowd unleashing its inner beasts. Against a crowd swelling with more and more hatred toward me. If they'd had stones in their hands, would they have hurled them at me? Purposely missing my head, prolonging my humiliation, my suffering.

"Enough of it!"

A loud, commanding voice echoed from the rear of the auditorium instantly ending the Symphony of Odium.

Farhad, in a blue military uniform, made his way through the middle of the hall, strong and confident, fully aware of the effect his appearance had on the crowd. He wore his sense of self-entitlement as comfortably as he wore the brand-new azure badge of Alpha Group, the elite counter-terrorist unit of KGB.

"Oh, Comrade Farhad, what a pleasant surprise," Comrade Guseinov said stiffly, not at all pleased by an unexpected appearance that seemed to steal his thunder. "Congratulations on your promotion. What could have made you interrupt your security training in Moscow to honor us with your presence?"

"I am here to straighten out the situation and to clear Comrade Leila Badalbeili from this unjust indictment."

Farhad ascended the stage in one broad step and stopped next to me, shielding me from the crowd of people who had been keen, just a few minutes earlier, to throw me into a fire pit.

"Comrade Leila, please acc c cept my apologies," he said solemnly, his dark eyes looking at me with deep empathy. "This investigation should have never taken place. I can only imagine the heartache you and your dear mother have endured, while still mourning the untimely death of your father, honorable Mekhti Rashidovich."

I broke down, wailing hysterically. Crying out the shame, the guilt, and the losses. Pouring out all the tears that had been hoarded inside me in the past weeks. As if the realization of what happened had finally caught up with me, ignited by compassion from the most unlikely source.

Farhad retrieved a handkerchief from his pocket and held it out to me, waiting for me to wipe my tears. Then he turned to the audience and raised his hand. "Comrades!" he said. "I have arrived here at your gathering to correct a mistake. A terrible mistake." He made a subtly dismissive gesture in Comrade Guseinov's direction. "With all due respect."

He spoke without a microphone, and he didn't need it. His voice, full of powerful conviction, would have broken through a stone wall.

"Comrades, as you all well know, I have been away for the last few months going through vigorous training at the KGB Higher School in Moscow. In my absence and without my consent"—he shot a fiery look at Comrade Guseinov—"a special operation that I personally initiated was intercepted. Intercepted by the ego of one of our leaders."

The audience held their breath in unison.

"Now, since the operation has been unfortunately disclosed, I can speak about its details. A while ago, I received a directive to investigate an establishment with possible links to Western intelligence services. I called upon this young woman standing in front of you—my trusted colleague and protégé, Leila Badalbeili, the granddaughter of one of the greatest heroes of our Communist Azerbaijan, Comrade Halil Badalbeili. Why did I choose her? Because there couldn't have been a more natural choice for an assignment of this magnitude. Especially considering the fact that Leila is a talented pianist and the suspicious establishment masked itself as a music shop.

"Using her intelligence and strong perseverance, she developed a plan of her own, and using a disguise—a chador—she was able to win the confidence of the suspected element. Gathering vital information, she reported to me just in time to expose a sophisticated Western plan to instigate a dangerous, catastrophic act. Need I say more?"

Farhad turned to me, a vague smile playing on his lips. I couldn't read it. But I felt even more lost in his words.

"Thank you, Comrade Leila, for your selfless service to your Motherland," he said. "On behalf of our Komsomol Party, I wish you victory at the Budapest music competition where you, the ambassador of our Soviet Azerbaijan, will continue to carry the torch of success for your country and your people."

He gave me a salute—a military salute—with his right hand flying briskly to his temple, the heels of his combat boots striking together. Then he began clapping, gesturing for the audience to join him. After a moment of confusion, the crowd sprang to their feet, stomping, applauding, shouting happy cheers, waving their red flags. At the side of the stage, Comrade Guseinov observed the spectacle. Fidgeting nervously, biting his lips, he stormed out of the auditorium.

Part of me felt vindicated, the other part petrified. What was all this about? Why would Farhad come to my rescue, sacrificing his principles and risking his own reputation? Why did he say that he knew of my communication with Tahir? And what was all that about me successfully exposing a dangerous Western operation?

"Comrades," Farhad shouted, silencing the crowd, pulling a sheet of paper out of his briefcase and handing it to me. "Comrade Leila is going to sign an official report of her recent courageous activities, and with that, the case will be considered closed."

I cautiously took the document. It spelled out how Tahir tried to use my innocence for American propaganda. There was an empty space left for my signature right next to my printed name. I kept reading it, again and again, trying to swallow the dryness in my throat, blinking nervously, as if hoping to clear my sight and find an entirely different connotation in the document.

Or was I simply stalling for time? Because I had to make a decision. Fast.

A decision? What decision? I'd made it a while ago when I stepped inside Tahir's world—only to discover my own. When the veil of ignorance fell away from my eyes. When I began to see the pain and the beauty of truth. No, there was no way I would betray Tahir. Not for the world. Even if I had to face another tribunal. A much scarier tribunal with Farhad as my main inquisitor.

I gave him back the report, my hand trembling. He wasn't smiling. Not anymore. His eyes stared at me like the two barrels of a gun.

The tension in the air reached its climax, blatant and contemptuous like the finale of Shostakovich's *Symphony no. 7*, the timpanis echoing the sound of my departing footsteps.

CHAPTER 22

I came home.

Mama stood by the window, the silhouette of her small, wrapped-in-black body against the darkening sky. A snake of smoke crawled out of her mouth. I had never seen Mama with a cigarette before. Papa hated when women smoked. He used to say that he would rather kiss a donkey than a woman smoker.

"Farhad phoned," Mama said without turning her head to me. "He promised me he would do anything to save you from the disaster you've gotten yourself into."

"I have done nothing wrong, Mama."

"Nothing wrong? Befriending that pervert…a criminal with a dangerous past. Degrading yourself, sneaking around town wearing a chador. Spending day in and day out alone with him in his filthy nest. And you have done nothing wrong?" Mama shook her head. "Oh, how you have changed, Leila. How you have changed."

"He is a gifted artist, Mama," I said, trying to sound calm, looking for the most persuasive words to explain, to make her understand how unjustly she and everyone else had condemned Tahir and me. "He introduced me to the beauty of music that helped me to open up. I have never played piano better in my life. Please trust me. He and his grandmother—they are very special people."

"They are enemies of the people, Leila. They are outcasts of our society who prey on fools like you to lure into their decadence, their drugs, their pornography."

"That's not true. There was no pornography there. And nobody preyed on me. It was my own choice. It was my destiny."

Mama turned to face me—livid, sarcastic. "Destiny? What *destiny* are you talking about? You—the clever girl I thought I had raised. *Destiny*. Yours was to go to Budapest and win the piano competition. So you would rise to a position of power. So you wouldn't have to get down on all fours and kiss asses and act as if you're enjoying it."

She laughed, or wheezed, rather, almost in a deranged way. Then, surrounded by swarming shadows, she staggered across the room and plunged onto the couch, disappearing inside the thickening darkness, trailing the smell of alcohol. My mama was drunk.

I heard hushed sniffles. Was she crying? I tiptoed to the couch and perched next to her.

"You used to be so different," Mama said in a somber voice. "A serious and responsible girl with everything going for you—career, success, excellent marriage prospects. Now look at you. Cast off by your friends. A step away from being expelled from Komsomol, ejected from the piano competition. And what about your reputation? *Our* reputation as a family? What shame you've brought upon all of us."

The volume of Mama's whisper began to rise, and so did its fury. "All because of your catastrophic choices. You've brought shame and a curse on our family. If you hadn't snuck around, hiding, going to places you shouldn't have gone near, our life would have been the way it used to be. We would have been just fine."

So that's what it was all about. Mama blamed me for exposing the rot. The rot that had been concealed inside fine wrapping until I accidentally tore open the cover. The suppressed pain of the last few weeks exploded out of me.

"Just fine? Living with lies?" I cried out. "Just fine while Papa was sleeping with Almaz?"

"Don't you ever…"

"What? Don't I ever what? Speak the truth? Then why, Mama, did you teach me to be honest, to keep my integrity no matter what? Why did you tell me that bad truths were better than good lies? Why? The lies we've been living with weren't just bad. They were vicious. They hurt people. People I loved."

Mama didn't respond, just kept nervously rubbing the arm of the couch with the skirt of her dress, wiping away invisible dust.

A devastating thought crossed my mind.

"You knew, didn't you, Mama? Everything. About the bribes and Almaz and everything. You just chose to keep your eyes closed so we could continue with our '*just fine life the way it used to be.*'"

"How could you?" Mama's hand flew across my face. Hard. Hurting me. Cutting my lip with the lock of her watch. I could feel the salty taste of blood. Tears burst out of my eyes.

"I hate you," I shouted. "I hate you. You are just like all of them."

I ran to my room and slammed the door behind me, shielding myself from the eerie ghosts prowling the hallways. I curled up on my bed. Alone. More alone than I had ever been in my entire life.

Who could I go to? I had no one.

Tahir? I had no idea what had happened to him. Was he in danger? Or were his *krysha*—his powerful clientele of Communist oligarchs—able to protect him?

Almaz? She was gone, taking our childhood away with her.

I opened my baby Bösendorfer. Its shiny silhouette felt foreign, almost hostile. The sound of its keys only added to the grief devouring me from inside. Mozart's *Piano Concerto no. 20* rested against the music stand as the gravestone to my career. I had spent months and months polishing this passage…this trill…getting just the right pianissimo here…stretching my hands for this octave arpeggio… practicing and practicing and practicing every day.

All for nothing. The end of what was supposed to be the beginning of my *brilliant music career*. How many times had I imagined myself in a sparkling dress on the stage at the Franz Liszt Academy of Music in Budapest? Giving a slight bow to the jurors and the audience, gliding to the piano, waiting for the sweep of the conductor's baton—a signal for the restless strings to invade the silence of the concert hall and begin their dramatic rise to a full forte.

My fingers reached for the keyboard, drawing out the first melody of my doomed *Concerto*. One line at a time. In the dark tonic key of D minor. Challenging Mozart, pushing my performance to new heights of passion. Spinning a pinwheel of imagination.

White as far as the eye can see. Shrubs and midget birch trees all buried beneath a blizzard. A gust of arctic wind sweeps across, swirling into a snow blur. Dogs howl in the distance. Dogs or wolves? A large owl lands on barbwire, its yellow eyes like two frozen moons. A cluster of barracks. A watchtower with armed guards.

Snow Princess. *She is slim in a black lace gown and mantilla, her red heels boldly dancing across the icy desert.* Luring and teasing, seducing and daring, she sings the "Habanera." Her deep, almost visceral mezzo silences the owl and the wolves and the drunken guards. The crystals of her upper register slide effortlessly into the notes of her purring low range.

I knew right away that my voice had reached that prime I had strived for…and that it was too late.

Miriam's face, aged and worn. Sitting at a table, she cleans the prisoners' striped coats, hunting lice with a shard of glass. In a stinking barrack of the gulag. In the middle of the Siberian tundra. Singing the "Habanera." Knowing she had arrived at the pinnacle of her artistry.

And that it was too late.

The same with me. Now, when I had finally reached my own island of creative freedom where I could reflect my inmost emotions through my music, it was too late.

I cried out in frustration, hurling the book with Mozart's *Concerto* across the room, its pages flying in every direction. I slammed my fist all over the keyboard, a cacophony spreading through the room.

I stopped. Guilty. Listening to the dissonant assault hanging in the air.

Quietly, I closed the piano lid and laid my head on its polished surface.

Wishing to die.

It was still dark when I opened my eyes. But morning was in the air, flooding my room with the chirping of sparrows and the polyphony of an awakening city.

Where is Mama? What if she's done something to herself? What if I've lost her too?

I sprinted to the door and threw it open.

Mama sat on the edge of the couch. Frail. Tiny. *Alive!* Her bare feet hung helplessly above the floor. She was shrouded in that awful smell so much like the chamber in the Museum of History with the Egyptian sarcophagi and embalmed mummies. Was she asleep? I carefully came closer so as not to wake her up, but seeing her face etched by the first gleam of light, drained and ethereal, I knew she hadn't slept at all.

My fault. It was all my fault—my reckless actions and my hurtful words—that had reduced my mama to this pitiable state. How could I have left her like this, alone, surrounded by the ghosts of death? What if she never comes back to me? To her own normal self?

I crouched on the floor next to Mama and put my head on her lap. At first she didn't respond. Then—hesitantly, slowly—she combed her fingers through my hair just the way she used to a long time ago when I was little and couldn't fall asleep. She would sit next to me, stroking my hair, singing her bedtime song:

Long night—little island of peace,
Long night—endless ride in the moonlight,
Long night—magic party for two,
Bring us closer—me and you.

"I didn't have a happy childhood, Leila," Mama said in a shaky, thin voice and brought her hand to her throat as if to help get the words out. "I grew up the only girl among a dozen boys in an orphanage. Outside Baku in Suraxanı, a small village. We were *un*supervised by a childless couple: a monster named Mohammed and his wife, sweet Aunty Habiba. He beat her mercilessly for not giving him a son. He beat her, and she cried her eyes out. Just like the old saying: 'Man's power is in his fists; woman's defense is in her tears.'"

Mama paused as if contemplating the harsh absurdity of the aphorism.

"The boys in the orphanage took after him, torturing me endlessly, exercising their unrestricted, emerging powers on me no matter how much Aunty Habiba tried to protect me from their disgusting tricks. They wanted to see my tears, but I never gave them the pleasure."

A lump rose inside my throat. Mama had never told me that before, about the boys and about being ridiculed and harassed. The stories from her childhood always had been happy ones, about the summer sports camps and campfires, with the photographs showing her as a tomboy, a red Pioneer tie around her neck, always smiling, always cheerful. Another lie? Another false facade? Heart pounding in my temples, I pressed and rubbed them, trying to put off the fire.

"Mohammed ran a business," Mama continued. "He bought the catches from village fishermen for close to nothing and then sold them at Taza Bazaar at his regular stand in the fish sellers' row. When I turned seven, he began taking me with him to the Bazaar. All day long, I would sit on top of a freezing barrel filled with fish, learning the craft of cheating and haggling."

What? Mama—my refined, my sophisticated Mama—sold fish at Taza Bazaar?

"Yes, at the spot where the Rose Garden Fairy now sells her pastries. Of course the smell was quite different then, nothing like a rose garden. It continued until one autumn morning, a particularly nasty morning with a wind gushing through empty stalls and scattering hailstones the size of quail eggs. I sat in my usual place wrapped in Aunty Habiba's aged woolen scarf. Freezing. Scared. I had been left by Mohammed to keep an eye on his goods while he lingered in a nearby *chaikhana*, drinking hot tea with other men. And that's when I saw him—the prince of my dreams. A boy with long, curly hair in a fancy coat, gloves, and shiny boots. Running toward me.

"'What is your name?' he asked. I couldn't answer. I just kept looking at him helplessly as if I was utterly deaf. My tongue, usually quite loose, now felt stiff as lead and the size of an apple. 'Are you a girl or an icicle?' the boy asked playfully, taking my frozen hands in his, rubbing them between his soft, furry gloves and blowing on them with his warm breath. Then he said something to a well-dressed woman in black who accompanied him. She looked at me with revulsion, turned, and pulled the boy with her.

"After they left, I saw his gloves lying on the ground. I picked them up and ran after the boy. I waited for his mother to enter the building, then I held out his gloves. 'I left them for you,' he whispered. That day, I escaped from Mohammed and the orphanage and swore in my mind to the boy that I would turn my life around. Ever since that day I have had a strong drive to become successful and important and worthy of him."

"Did you meet him again, that boy?" I asked, captivated.

Mama's eyes wandered around. Getting that far down the road of confession, it seemed as if she suddenly felt hesitant—scared?—to go on.

"Did you?" I pressed for an answer.

"That boy, Leila…" Mama buried her face in her hands, sobbing quietly. "It was your papa, Leila. That little prince was your papa."

A taut string inside me snapped. I cried. Cried hysterically, besieged by grief. Mama put her arm around me, stroking my hair, bringing the palm of my hand to her lips and kissing it softly as if thanking me for understanding.

"I thought you and Papa met at the hospital when he had his accident," I wailed through tears.

"No, that was our second time. But I never told him."

"You never told him? Why not?"

"His mother—that *Black Widow*. She would never have allowed her boy to marry me if she'd known I once sold fish at the Bazaar. Even without knowing, she rarely acknowledged me. With all my achievements, I still wasn't of her class.

"You see, Leila, your Papa, with all his *flaws*, wanted to be good. He just didn't know the difference between right and wrong. Between ethical and corrupt. The only thing he knew was 'I want because I can.' That's how *she* raised him. That's how society allowed him to be. He was the successor to a highly decorated hero of Soviet Azerbaijan, a lifelong member of the Communist oligarchy, a club of powerful and spoiled men who never acquired any sense of reality. Except for their own."

"But what about you? You've become a part of the same elite."

"Yes, while I was married to your Papa. He was my *krysha*."

Krysha? Like Tahir's *krysha?* Why would my celebrity surgeon Mama need protection? And from whom?

"Without his connections," Mama said, "I would have been dispatched—after Medical Academy—to work at a clinic in some remote mountain *aul*. The only reason I was given a surgery department at the central hospital was because the First Minister of Health—Papa's third cousin—made a call."

"But that's degrading. You're too good for that. You're the best in the city. This whole thing is crooked."

"Yes indeed. The kingdom of crooked mirrors. Nothing is as it looks. That's how I felt at the beginning when I was young and naive like you. But, with time, we learn that this crooked-mirror reality is the only reality we've got in our lifetime. And we have to make the best of it."

"But not at the price of other people's misery, especially people we care about."

"Please, Leila, hear me." Mama leaned against the back of the couch, sapped, her voice trembling. "That boy from the music shop—he might be everything you believe he is. But in the eyes of our society, he is a convicted criminal. He has nothing to lose. He is stuck where he is. On the bottom. While *you* are walking away from the greatest opportunity a girl can have. To win. To become independent. To achieve international fame and choose the life you desire.

"Music is the key to your freedom. Please, I beg you. Take Farhad's help. He has risked everything—his honor, his career—to save you. He cares about you, Leila. Cares greatly. And he is the only one who can help you. The other one—that *boy*—he is pathetic. He can do nothing for you but hurt you more."

There was truth in Mama's words, even if I didn't want to admit it. I thought of the afternoon when the gang of lowlifes insulted Tahir and me, and how Tahir, scared, had run away as fast as he could. Would Farhad have ever done this? No, he would have fought for my honor. He'd have killed those thugs. The same with the tribunal. No doubt, Tahir knew about it. Then why didn't he come and shout that I was innocent, that all those "prostitution charges" were nothing but despicable lies? Not as if it would have changed anything for the better—probably would have made it worse—but still. He didn't even try.

"And it's not only your music that's at stake." Mama gulped air nervously. "There's something else. Without Papa—and with the many jealous powerful enemies he amassed—it is also my job that is at stake."

I got up to fetch her some water. She reached for my hand, took it in hers, and squeezed gently, initiating a special bond. A friendship I had always dreamed of sharing with her.

In the rays of daylight seeping through the closed drapes, her hair had an unusual copper color. I looked closer. Threads of silver dominated her natural gold hue. My mama had become gray over the past few weeks.

A flood of regret crashed over me. If I had never set foot inside the green door, everything would have been fine. I wouldn't have awakened the bad *lənət*, and the curse wouldn't have fallen upon all of us. The curse had taken away Papa and Aunty Zeinab and now threatened to turn my Mama into a dismal, old woman.

"*Mamochka*," I cried, throwing my arms around her. "Please forgive me. Forgive me for everything. I love you. Love you more than anything else in the world."

Mama smiled at me through tears, placed her calloused palms against my burning cheeks, and said in a gentle but indisputable manner, "You have to do it, Leila. You don't have a choice. What is brought by the wind will be carried away by the wind. And what's gone is just memories. Hold on to them, but move forward. Your life is just beginning. And so is your music."

Later that day, Mama and I arrived at Comrade Guseinov's office, and witnessed by Comrade Farhad, I signed the fraudulent confession that cleared my name. And sacrificed Tahir's.

CHAPTER 23

On March 17, 1980, at few minutes past seven, I came onto the stage of the magnificent Great Concert Hall of the Budapest Franz Liszt Academy of Music. Almost fourteen hundred music aficionados were crammed into three auditorium tiers and the chorus seats at the back of the stage, little more than an arm's length away from the orchestra.

As I passed Professor Sultan-zade behind the stage curtain, she whispered her blessing: "Go and show your greatness. And let the world fall at your feet."

An imposing Bösendorfer—a 290 Imperial model—waited for me in the spotlight, the great-grandfather of my baby Bösendorfer at home, with eight full octaves and a fully resonating, almost orchestral sound. A sound suited for the performances of convoluted, contrapuntal compositions by Bartók, Debussy, Ravel, and Busoni. Even Edvard Grieg's *Piano Concerto in A Minor*, played before me by a girl from Warsaw with spiky, straw-like hair, benefited from its grandioso tone.

But my Mozart? With his delicate lyricism and pleasing harmonic resolutions? With his melodic mélange and touching emotions? Could I tame the imperious Bösendorfer before he overwhelmed gentle Mozart? It would be a challenge. Sweat erupted on my palms. I wiped them furtively against my skirt.

The conductor of the Hungarian State Symphony, Maestro István Lukács, waited to escort me onstage. Tall and thin, his forehead remarkably high, making up almost half of his pale face, his long, lank hair spilling over his shoulders, he looked like Franz Liszt himself. I wondered if that factor had helped him get the job with the Liszt competition. A silly thought, of course, but I welcomed it as a distraction from my anxiety.

The maestro took my hand and led me to center stage, his mouth curled in a suave portamento smile. He clapped, inviting the audience to join, waved his hand toward me, then briskly mounted the rostrum and signaled for the orchestra to rise.

I bowed, first to the jurors' box, then to the rest of the audience. A deep breath. I turned toward the piano. Now I had to make four steps on my own, four steps that would set me on the right emotional path and cue the audience to love me or hate me.

Wearing my brand-new concert dress, a mermaid confection made by Baku's premier tailor—its jade scales sparkling, its tail flipping from side to side—I proceeded to the piano. Just the way my steps had been rehearsed—day after day—with Professor Sultan-zade. She had also conceived the concept of my mermaid dress. And I fully appreciated it now, standing in the malachite spotlight of the ornate Art Nouveau auditorium.

I could see the wowed eyes of the audience. I could hear the accelerando of their heartbeats. No, just one. One heartbeat. My own. The audience had become *my* audience, tuning to *my* heartbeat.

Unhurriedly, I seated myself on the bench, adjusted the folds of my dress, and rubbed my perfectly dry hands against my thighs. This time for stage effect only—to give my audience a sneak view inside the intimate world of a performer. Finished with that little bit of theater, I closed my eyes. Shutting everything out. Everything. Except what I needed to win.

To win!

Because I had sacrificed my soul for it. Because *to win* was the only justification for the betrayal I had committed. And because only the win could possibly give me the power to repair the damage.

"Mozart. Piano Concerto Number Twenty." The voice of a presenter hushed the audience.

Maestro Lukács stamped his foot for a count, waved his long arms in the air, and the orchestral tutti came crashing down on me. The strings swept through dark, threatening skies, hammered by wild staccato winds of the east. Too loud. Too fast. Totally different from the way the orchestra played during the rehearsal. I stared at the maestro in panic as he coiled his boneless body in perpetual motion, his hair falling across his face, leaving nothing visible except his hawk nose.

Why did he want to kill my performance? To help a local participant? That Hungarian boy who played Beethoven? But he was so weak. No chance he could place anywhere even close to the top.

The skies cleared. A sweet, almost idyllic theme in F major brought me relief. But not for long. The fragmented, chromatic angst returned as the momentum built toward my piano entrance.

Think Rachmaninoff—sweeping lyricism, contrasting textures. Caravaggio—bold, real, imposing. Renoir—dreamy, soft, suspended in time. Kandinsky—

"No, Tahir. No!" I shouted to myself. "No! Not now. Not here. I have to win."

And to win, I had to deliver a conventionally beautiful and burnished performance of my Mozart *Piano Concerto no. 20*. The way it had been interpreted and rehearsed with Professor Sultan-zade. The way the jury and the audience expected to hear it. I couldn't take any chances. Professor Sultan-zade had warned me that any emotional deviation from the pages of my *Concerto* would result in a fiasco. The head of the jury and my former idol, Sviatoslav Richter, believed in carrying out the composer's intentions to the letter.

Then think about Mozart. The real Mozart. How did he feel—detested by the audiences in Salzburg—writing this piece in an urgent rush, eager to pay off his huge debts? Composing it in just a few days. Rehearsing the first movement while the last one was still in manuscript form. Humiliated by the obnoxious critique of his patron, Emperor Joseph II: "Too beautiful for our ears and far too many notes."

Too beautiful? How could music be *too* beautiful?

I raised my hands over the keyboard's fearsome ocean of black and white keys. And—one key after another—I began to tame them, weaving a melody of pain and longing. A bare voice against a large anonymous orchestral force in D minor.

Not just D minor. For Mozart, it was the demonic D minor, the same key he used to write his own Requiem.

The timpani announced a forthcoming storm. The nocturnal sea was no more. The waves were dashing against the rocks, grudgingly sliding down. I turned my face to the blistering wind. I was ready.

I clashed with the orchestra in the tempestuous climax of the cadenza. A brilliant, dramatic cadenza composed by Ludwig van Beethoven for his beloved Mozart's *Concerto.*

Then—trouble in paradise—the tranquil second-movement "Romanze" in B-flat major. I painted the melody with a soft brushstroke—the lush legato of Edgar Degas's *Blue Dancers* and the mezzo-staccatos of Georges Seurat's *Morning Walk.* The G-minor middle section threw me back to the battlefield to exchange a few agitated passages with the orchestra. Just a few. Then, back to Billie Holiday and her white gardenia and to the original B-flat major.

The last movement, "Allegro assai," came as a dream. A cascade of Kandinsky's colors splashed on a canvas. Not the palette Professor Sultan-zade had envisioned for Mozart's music. Not a pretty fusion of pink and more pink. Instead, high-pitched yellow screams, sonorous blue stabs, silent voids of black, and shades of gray. Like the sky over the cemetery during Papa's funeral. Like the plastic cover over Aunty Zeinab's body on the stretcher. Like the silver threads in Mama's golden hair.

Only at the very end did I allow the beautiful—too beautiful?—Impressionistic violet-blue tones to prevail. The rhythmic mantra of the crashing waves. A lavender sunset spilled into the Caspian Sea. Tahir and I sailing away into the purple glow of the horizon.

"Young and innocent, they savored the violet-scented wine of first love and became deeply intoxicated... Her eyes shone for him in place of the

sun; his desire for her lit up the night sky… She was his rose, and he was her nightingale… Their hearts became one…"

I ended the *Concerto* with the jubilant passages in D major surging up and down the keyboard.

The last chord of my finale drowned in the ovations that shook the Grand Hall like the temblors of an earthquake. I glanced anxiously at Professor Sultan-zade, waiting for me backstage, staring from behind the curtains on stage right. She waved at me, applauding, her face dripping with tears. Maestro Lukács abandoned his rostrum, his orchestra, and his urbane style. He rushed to me, grabbed my hands and kissed them. Even the jurors released their guarded smiles, applauding me, joining the rhythm of the audience.

I did it. I had the win! The win that would secure both Mama's and my positions. The win that would propel me to the highest elite of the Soviet music intelligentsia en route to international celebrity. To recognition. To fame and freedom. To power.

But no matter how many rosy scenarios I spelled out in my head, it didn't help. Inside I felt nothing. No joy. No satisfaction. Nothing.

Nothing but emptiness.

CHAPTER 24

I came back home a national hero. A crowd of my new music fans greeted me at the airport with flowers, and I had to sign a few dozen copies of *Komsomolskaya Pravda*—a newspaper from Moscow that had printed my photograph on the first page. It showed me in my mermaid dress accepting the Grand Prix from the head of the jury, Sviatoslav Richter. My icon—before I heard Vladimir Horowitz, of course. Underneath the picture, his accolade: "One of the most uninhibited and dramatically succulent interpretations of Mozart I have ever heard."

A fancy Mercedes with dark windows picked us up at the Baku airport.

"Why?" I asked Professor Sultan-zade when we were alone inside the car. "Why did the jurors unanimously choose my performance over all the others, despite the fact that I didn't give them their conventional Mozart? Instead, I played Mozart in my own way."

Professor Sultan-zade smiled knowingly. "Why do you think that the Mozart you played yesterday wasn't the real Mozart?"

"Because I abandoned quite a few of the written dynamics in the 'Allegro,' took my time in the middle of the 'Romanze,' and played the 'Allegro assai' as if it had been composed by Beethoven, or even Rachmaninoff."

"What a nice cocktail that would be." She opened the car window, lit a cigarette, and blew the smoke outside. "I'm afraid, Leila, that what you're saying is too cerebral. Just think—how many times has your Mozart *Concerto* been performed by every acclaimed pianist, not to mention every mediocrity? Thousands and thousands in the past two hundred years, every performer trying to reflect the real genius of Wolfgang Amadeus Mozart through his or her own talent or the lack of it. So by now, we've fashioned a Mozart canon—as well as Beethoven and Rachmaninoff canons and everyone else who can't rise from the dead, put their foot down, and scream: 'Leave me alone. I didn't mean it. Not at all.'"

Professor Sultan-zade smiled and turned toward the sun, allowing the sunbeams to hop all over her face.

"Anyway," she continued, "there are two schools of music pedagogy, or, rather, two egos—the more powerful one sees its mission as locking their performances into those canons; the other will do anything to break them, usually at the cost of the music itself. And poor music—as the most illusive and subjective of all forms of art—ends up being a bouncing ball between the egos and politics. What happened yesterday was a phenomenon. Your performance was so visceral it reached into the souls of your listeners, completely bypassing their reason. You brought emotions that can be felt but can't be described."

The Mercedes drove us to City Hall, where Mama was waiting for us. The Secretary of the Baku City Communist Party presented Professor Sultan-zade with the title of "Public Teacher of Soviet Azerbaijan" and rewarded Mama and me with a trip to a government resort on the Black Sea.

A telegram from Farhad waited for me at home: "You Made Me Proud!"

I had made everybody proud. Everybody but myself. Guilt—voracious guilt—devoured me from inside. I had kept it at bay through the weeks of relentless piano practice, rehearsals, and more piano practice before my travel and performance in Budapest. But now, after returning home, greeted by praise and festivities, I knew that only Tahir's forgiveness would free me from the pointy barbs of guilt.

I needed to see him. To explain that I had no choice but to go ahead with the competition. To let him know that his artistic guidance had led me to victory. To confess that I had been in love with him from that very first moment I saw a boy with lavender eyes walk barefoot down a busy street, lost in his own world. Since then, *his world* had become mine. The only place where I really belonged. My heart knew it always, but the mind had wicked ways of dealing with feelings. It pushed them into the corner with the whip of doubts and jailed them behind the bars of common sense.

But the bars had come down. They crashed to the ground when I took the spotlight on the stage of the Grand Concert Hall of the Budapest Music Academy. The winner. Adored by the crowd, bouquets of flowers landing at my feet. Whispering under my breath, "I dedicate my victory to my love. To my only love. To you, Tahir."

I waited for evening to fall, watched the sun sink slowly toward the west. The sky finally darkened, unlit by an anemic sickle moon. Even better. Swiftly, I made my way across the heavy-eyed city, slipped inside Icheri Sheher, and zipped through its web of alleyways toward Ashuglar Street. To my great relief—and even greater surprise—the green door was still there. I reached it in a heartbeat, grabbed the brass knob, pushed the door open, and stepped inside.

Into a blinding cascade of fluorescent light illuminating—in all its grotesqueness—a corps de ballet of dancing cows. All dead. All hanging from a rack. Suspended in the midst of their fatal grand jeté.

Promenading between the corpses was the maestro himself—a Robespierre. A tall, emaciated butcher dressed in white coveralls and a blood-spattered apron swinging at the slaughtered herd with his ax of terror. Slicing off ribs, loins, chucks, and thighs.

"*Salam eleykum, qız,*" he greeted me with a syrupy smile.

"*Eleykum salam,*" I said in a state of shock, my eyes searching for any sign of Tahir's shop inside this butchery. "This place. It used to be a music—"

A loud thumping cut me off in mid-sentence. A huge, industrial-size blower yawned and began to spin, faster and faster, generating a steady roar, setting the dead cows in motion, splashing me with a burst of air saturated with the odor of death. The blower was mounted on the wall, right on top of Liza Minnelli's poster, a slice of her fishnet stocking peeking from behind the gray metal.

"It used to be a music shop," I screamed over the fan's noise. "Do you know where the owner is?"

"Ahhh, the outlaw. He's gone."

"Where?"

Robespierre sized me up, a licentious grin shriveling his face into a rotten fig. "Why would a nice girl like you be walking around inquiring about a felon?"

"Oh, it's my elderly neighbor Ali Khan who sent me," I lied, my stomach turning. "The music shop owner owes him some money."

"Ohhh. Too bad. Tell your neighbor the kid's gone."

"Where?"

"How do I know? Back to prison or dead." And he threw a freshly hacked bloody tongue on the scale right next to me.

I vomited before I could struggle to the door.

The butcher rushed to help me, wiping his bloody hands on his apron, causing me more sickness. I pushed the door open and darted away, stumbling down the dark, deserted street.

I had to find out what happened to Tahir. Now. Right now. But where? Could I face Miriam after what I had done?

I stopped, leaned my head against a cold metal lamppost.

The sound of a whistle. Was it for me? My stomach tightened. Another whistle. Then a nasal voice, "Hey. I have something for you."

I turned around. A boy waddled toward me like a bowlegged duck. The son of the shoe-shop owner, Tahir's neighbor. I'd seen him a dozen times, sitting on the threshold of their shop playing *shesh besh* with his father or running with other boys, throwing stones at sparrows.

"What is it?" I asked.

The boy huddled in a shaded corner a few meters away. "It's about your artist. Come here. I'll show you."

I approached him cautiously. He glowered at me, making a *tztz* sound with his tongue, trying to get rid of something stuck between his teeth. "I'll show it to you if you show me your tits," he said.

"What?" I raised my hand to smack him. Hard. Then stopped. The kid couldn't be older than twelve. And he was even small for that age.

"You did more than that with the artist," he whined. A child who was just refused a treat.

"How about if I give you ten rubles instead?"

"Ten rubles," he repeated, confused, not believing his luck. "Show me."

I retrieved a wad of cash from my coat pocket, let him see it, then slid it back. "So what do you have for me?"

"It's just this thing. This man stopped by a while ago. He's really tall and important. He told my father and me to spy on you. And we did. And I followed you home and told him who you were. And he gave me a pocketknife. That was after I called him and they came and caught you here in your chador."

Something sounded rotten. "Do you have it with you?"

"What?" He looked suspiciously from one side to the other.

"The pocketknife."

"Give me my money first."

"No. Show me the pocketknife."

He fidgeted, then pulled the knife out of his trousers. A Finnish Army pocket knife with the large letters KGB imprinted on its handle. A small engraving underneath. I took the knife to a shaft of light from a nearby window and read the engraving: *To Comrade Farhad for his dedicated service.*

The kid snatched the knife out of my hands. "Now give me my money."

I did. And he left. But not before sliding his hand against my breast and sticking an obscene *dulya* in my face—a hand with fingers curled, a thumb thrust between the index and middle fingers.

I deserved worse than that. How could I have not figured it out from the beginning? Farhad had staged the whole spectacle, with my exposure and humiliation.

He brilliantly executed his own motto: "Let your rival throw a stone that kills two rabbits at the same time." The first—to teach me a lesson that when Farhad said I belonged to him, he meant it. And the second? To use the situation for the advancement of his own career.

He had set up Comrade Guseinov—his former superior—to prosecute my immoral conduct and then showed up to embarrass him and to blackmail me into signing the fabricated report against Tahir. And he ended up as a hero who rescued my honor and my music career, while exposing and preventing a terrorist attack against our country. How could I have been so stupid?

The door to Miriam's chamber was ajar. What if she was gone too?

Anxious, I pushed the door open. It was so dark I couldn't see a thing. Then familiar objects began to materialize, their silhouettes indented on the walls by the glow of a kerosene lamp. Glimmers of light parachuted like dandelions around the room, spread by the lamp's etched glass. A nippy draft across my feet. Only midautumn. How had she survived winters here?

Miriam sat on the sofa, wrapped in a woolen blanket, drowsing to the recording of Bach's *Goldberg Variations*.

The best sleeping pill, she called that haunting opus.

The serpentine saraband glided across the chamber along with its counter lines, speeding up the steps, spiraling into a polyphonic euphoria. I remembered a conversation we had at the table here when Tahir and Miriam crossed swords. Tahir called Bach's polyphony abstract and mind-bending and compared it to Wassily Kandinsky's paintings. Miriam shook her head, insisting that Bach's counterpoint was the most logical artistic technique ever created. I just sat there, my eyes flying from one to the other, having no idea what the quarrel was about. How I missed those times.

Miriam looked up, saw me, and gestured toward a hassock between her sofa and the coal stove. "You'll be warmer here," she said. The tone of her voice indicated no anger, just heartbreaking grief. Could it be that she wasn't aware of the truth, that she didn't know who had betrayed her Tahir?

I landed on the hassock, and together we listened to the twenty-fourth Goldberg variation until a barking cough rocked Miriam's body. She leaned forward, trying to reach a mug on the table. I leaped up from the hassock to help. No—she waved her hand. She repositioned herself closer to the table, lifted the mug, and shaking, brought it to her lips for a hungry sip. Then she replayed the same painful effort in reverse, returning the mug to the table without ever lowering her aristocratic pinkie finger.

"You know, the type of cough you have can be a dangerous one," I said. "It sounds wet. There might be some viral infection in your lungs. You need to see a doctor."

"Don't ever trust those who tell you that old age comes with dignity." Miriam sighed, ignoring my insight. "No. It comes with disgrace. Youth is a blessing; old age is a nuisance."

Another bout of coughing traveled through her body. This time I dismissed her attempt at self-sufficiency and helped her with the tea.

As I came close, she grasped my forearm. "They sent Tahir to Afghanistan," she wheezed, painfully suppressing her cough. "They sentenced him to three years in punitive battalion. Some terribly lost soul accused him of serving the Americans and instigating some terrorist activities."

Terribly—lost—soul. Every word branded across my forehead. How could she not see it?

Miriam released my arm, but I couldn't move. Couldn't speak. My whole being seemed to melt into a puddle. One big, dirty puddle.

"I had the pleasure of watching him grow up," she said, her voice hoarse after the coughing spell. "He was a shy boy. Was bullied a lot. But I taught him to be careful about choosing which battles to fight. Some just weren't worthy. I took him to his first art class. I knew that the Mukhtarovs' charisma would shine through in him in one way or another."

She smiled through tears. "He liked you, Leila. I could see it in his eyes. And when we Mukhtarovs take someone into our hearts, they stay there forever and beyond."

"Aria da Capo." The *Goldberg Variations* returned to the opening saraband, wistful and resigned like something coming to an end.

Miriam seemed to be slipping into a doze, her eyes disappearing beneath the hoods of their lids, a tiny stream of mucus seeping down the side of her open mouth. The face of the burned, scorched, beaten, humiliated Truth. I carefully took her limp, cold hands in mine and brought them to my face. Small and delicate, the skin as rough as sandpaper.

"I'll find him. I'll find Tahir," I whispered, kissing the tips of her fingers, placing her hands back in her lap. "I promise." Quietly, I turned to leave.

"It's always about choice." Miriam's husky, now sedate voice reached me at the door. "It's one choice we make that determines the rest of our lives. I always go back to that moment when I made my choice—to return to Baku to save the love of my life. I didn't save Caspar. And I ruined myself. So I had many—too many—days and nights behind barbed wire to examine my decision. Was it worthy?"

I held my breath, waiting to hear the verdict on my own choices.

"Yes, Leila. It was all worthy. Choosing light over darkness is in our human nature. And at the end, there is always a reward. Mine was my grandson," she said with such tenderness that I had to clasp my mouth with my hand to mute my sobbing.

"Come here and take *her*. And keep *her* always by your side."

The figurine of the vermilion bird from the fresco. Miriam held it out between her shaking hands, tears streaming down her hollow cheeks. "Take good care of *her*. She kept me alive throughout my life. A life that often envied death. She is Zümrüd Quşu, the magical Firebird. She was born on the night Princess Zümrüd leaped into the sky from the top of Maiden Tower and burned away the darkness with the fire of her wings. She is yours now."

Miriam gently placed Zümrüd Quşu onto the palm of my hand. "Now go and do whatever you can to save my grandson."

A short pause. A dizzying polyphony of thoughts.

"And save your own soul," she added resolutely. "Good-bye, Leila."

PART 2

CHAPTER 25

1982

The world of classical music was a dark, lonesome place, ruled by rampant egos and Party connections, ruthlessly purging artists who failed to consistently deliver first prizes.

Professor Sultan-zade tirelessly navigated those treacherous waters on my behalf. My win in the Liszt International Piano Competition in Budapest had elevated me to the ranks of the Azerbaijani music elite, but there were fifteen republics in the Soviet Union, and each had its own stable of young and talented champions eager to race, while Moscow had the final word.

As a result, in the two years since my Budapest win, I hadn't been invited to a single competition. My applications to play at both the International Chopin Piano Competition in Poland in 1980 and the Van Cliburn International Piano Competition in Texas in 1981 never left my file at the Ministry of Culture in Moscow.

Not much more luck with concerts. The first year after Budapest, I went on a national concert tour playing my Mozart's *Piano Concerto no. 20* with major symphony orchestras in the philharmonic halls of Moscow, Leningrad, Kiev, and Minsk, being stamped by the music critics with the label of a "Mozart girl"—something that quite limited my musical versatility. Gradually the stages, as well as the orchestras, became less prestigious, and Professor Sultan-zade pulled me out of the concert tour and back into the practice room, while she continued chasing engagements for me with key orchestras and international competitions.

At the end of 1981, my mentor's assiduous work and her wide-reaching connections finally paid off. I received an invitation from the Tchaikovsky International Piano Competition where I was supposed to play Rachmaninoff's *Piano Concerto no. 3*, the same piece and on the same stage that catapulted Van Cliburn in 1958 into stardom and one of the most unsurpassed piano careers of our time.

I practiced endlessly. Almost eight hours every day, until I could execute the technical demands of the *Concerto* flawlessly, sweeping through the passages with my eyes closed. And the subtlety of the sweet Russian lyricism in the midst of the composer's torn, chaotic, lonely soul—something I'd struggled with for a long time—had finally been mastered. But still the piece wasn't happening. How could it? My heart was out of tune.

If I could only tune up my heart. If I could hear Vladimir Horowitz's recording of my *Concerto*. If I could sneak into the Coronation Hall of Maiden Tower and play it—just once—on the Mukhtarovs' clavichord. That would make the difference. But how could I? I didn't dare to step my foot inside the walls of Icheri Sheher out of fear of meeting Miriam.

It had been over two years since she gave me her Zümrüd Quşu along with a chance to save Tahir and my own soul. And what had I done? Nothing. Just kept her Zümrüd Quşu on top of my piano. At first, she offered me a soothing sense of hope, a connection with Tahir and Miriam. After a while, staring at me angrily from under her faded vermilion feathers, she had become a painful keepsake of my guilt.

A month before the Tchaikovsky piano competition, Professor Sultan-zade withdrew my participation.

"You still need to define your relationship with Rachmaninoff better," she said. "If you lose this competition, you will lose your entire career. Trust me. Meanwhile, I'll start working on the Queen

Elisabeth Music Competition in Belgium in 1983. A year from now, so it will give us more time."

I felt crushed, but I knew Professor Sultan-zade was right. After almost three years of practice, my performance of Rachmaninoff's *Piano Concerto no. 3* didn't stand a chance to win. Virtuosic and skillful, yes. But the original romantic palette—Tahir's palette of Impressionistic pastels—I had used while learning the *Concerto* on Mukhtarovs' keyboard in the twilight of the Coronation Hall had been replaced. Replaced by aggressive primary colors, edgy pauses, and jarring chords—the reflections of my miserable, guilt-torn soul.

If I could only fly to Afghanistan, find Tahir, and through him, seek my way back to the beauty of music. The simple and coherent beauty that would stitch my soul back together.

The first casualties of the Soviet war in Afghanistan began arriving home. People called them zinc boys. They came quietly, inside zinc lined coffins covered with red silk. Their families held funerals in secret at the instruction of the KGB so the growing numbers of fatalities wouldn't lower the morale of the Soviet people.

Brezhnev's Golden Era—the "Period of Developed Socialism"—reigned over Soviet Azerbaijan, the last phase leading to the long-promised Communist paradise where one and all would share the superabundant riches of a class-, religion-, and corruption-free society.

So it said in our history books. In reality, the USSR continued as a feudal state ruled by a hierarchy of mafia with Brezhnev's Kremlin on top.

Leonid Brezhnev had been General Secretary of the Communist Party for the last eighteen years, longer than any other Soviet leader, except for Stalin's three decades of bloody terror. Through all those years, our country produced absolutely nothing. We lived off our natural resources, supporting a black market. The Kremlin

Communist oligarchy, in full control of Azerbaijani national staples—black gold petroleum and black caviar—traded and sold them on the international markets, amassing a fortune that would have given a jealous heart attack to the richest of the Shirvan shahs— the mighty Muslim rulers of ancient Azerbaijan. But recently, three republics in the Caucasus—Azerbaijan, Georgia, and Armenia—had been displaying some alarming tendencies toward autonomy.

To reinforce Moscow's supremacy and to wave his fists toward the Kremlin's naughty vassals, Leonid Brezhnev officially announced that he would visit Azerbaijan in September 1982.

And Baku burst into madness. What used to be a laid-back, too-far-from-Moscow-to-care town made plans for a major makeover.

Azerbaijanis were known for their remarkable hospitality. Even the smaller gods from Moscow usually received the most ostentatious gifts. But this time Baku outdid itself, erecting a concert hall—Gülistan—on the city's highest hill. It looked like a Fabergé egg floating in the sky, washed in sun dust, draped in the tulle of waterfalls. A marble stairway framed with cypress trees and tea roses led to its golden atrium and to the more extravagant interior: a colosseum-shaped nightclub with floors made of handwoven Turkish rugs, chandeliers with garlands of crystal lights, and the fragrance of exotic Arabic oils mixed with the hypnotic sounds of *muğam*.

A show of never-before-seen magnitude would take place on its stage. As the appetizer, belly dancers straight out of Scheherazade's *Arabian Nights*—seven voluptuous women, their hair, fingers, and toes stained with henna. Like snakes, they would glide and twist between the guests to the beat of *ghavals*, enticing, provoking. A whole army of Chinese acrobats would follow, juggling, rolling on fireballs, twisting their elastic bodies in fantastic, seemingly impossible ways. Then, the Oilmen Choir would sing traditional Shamakha songs. And for dessert—me, the national treasure, playing Tikhon Khrennikov's *Five Pieces for Piano*, a composition as tedious as the slogans pouring nonstop out of the loudspeakers set along Baku's major streets.

The moment I finish with my performance, before the curtain goes down, I will rush to the edge of the stage, take a bow toward Brezhnev's box, place my hand on my heart, and say fervently: "Comrade Brezhnev, on behalf of the Komsomol of my beloved Azerbaijan, I humbly ask for the honor to be named a music ambassador of my republic and sent to Kabul so I can share the joy of music with our heroic army."

So I can find and rescue Tahir.

I had been studying the map of Afghanistan, with its gorges, mountains, and deserts, day and night. I listened to every scrap of news I could tune my ear to, and I had worked out an itinerary through the Khyber Pass and the Afghan mountains. These were the relatively quiet areas spared of guerilla warfare. There we would find a nice, old Pashtun who, for the price of my sapphire ring, would lead Tahir and me across the Pakistani border. After then, we are free. Free to climb the Eiffel Tower. Ride in a Venetian gondola. Dance to the rhythms of jazz in a New York nightclub.

Foolish? Immoral? Devious?

What about Mama? Would I be able to live the rest of my life far away, knowing that I had betrayed her and left her behind?

My mind had turned into a battlefield. Missiles of doubts, fears, and guilt fired from one side intercepted by the justifying anger from the other.

My heart? It was suspended in dreamy rubato, longing for Tahir. For his presence. His touch.

His forgiveness.

On September 29, before dawn, thousands and thousands of us gathered in Lenin Square. Columns and columns of factory workers, collective farmers, students, athletes, cultural intelligentsia. The girls from the State Ensemble of Dance, wearing traditional Azeri dresses, encircled the newly constructed podium, holding large silver bowls filled with rose petals. Ready to be laid at the feet of Comrade Leonid Brezhnev.

At midafternoon, a seemingly endless cavalcade of black government cars and police motorcycles arrived at the Square. The door of a tank-size ZIL flew open. And Brezhnev, aided by a dozen gray suits, stepped out onto the rose petals, looking like an effigy of the impressive leader who watched us from thousands of billboards. An effigy on strings, his movements jerky and unnatural, wearing a death mask. Only his bushy eyebrows seemed alive, moving up and down over his half-closed eyes.

He slowly approached the podium and waited at the bottom, staring helplessly at the stairs, as if deciding whether he should take the challenge of mounting the stairs himself or wait for his cluster of assistants to aid him. A wave of suppressed giggles swept across a crowd appearing less restrained and more impatient than any I had ever seen at an official Communist gathering. Like me, they were all anticipating how the spectacle would end. Little did they know.

At last Comrade Brezhnev made the decision. Shaking his pasty face from side to side, he canceled his speech and signaled his entourage to lead him back to his ZIL. As they did so, the "Hymn of the Soviet Union" broke out of the loudspeakers at a deafening volume, accompanied by the patriotic words of the anthem and the barely concealed chuckles in the audience.

The next day, he gave an incoherent speech in the Marble Hall, pinned the Order of Lenin to the flag of Soviet Azerbaijan, and was gone, skipping all prepared festivities, including my concert. Back to Moscow for recuperation.

Back to the drawing board.

Or maybe not.

"The show goes on." Professor Najafov entered the practice room, rubbing his hands in delight. He was a small, round man with an even rounder face and a belly so perfectly round that it looked as if he'd swallowed a soccer ball. An outsider, from a provincial music college with no connections, he was recently appointed the rector of the Baku Conservatory of Music.

"I just heard from the Ministry of Culture," he said, giving Professor Sultan-zade an ambiguously intimate smile. "The government airplane departed in a hurry, but Comrade Brezhnev's entourage has been left behind. I had to push a few buttons so we—and not the State Institute of Arts—could host a concert. Guess for whom?"

Professor Sultan-zade smoothed her brand-new beehive. "I have no idea," she said with a coy smile illuminating the striking green eyes in her thin Nefertiti face. Today she wore a new black suit and soft ballet flats instead of her usual loud stilettos. Could Professor Najafov be the reason?

"Mark Slavkin. Our Conservatory will host a concert for Mark Slavkin." Professor Najafov knocked his knuckles on the wood of my piano. Winked. "Not to spoil it."

Mark Slavkin—Mama's favorite, the composer of her wedding song "White Acacia." He was the patriarch of Soviet popular music, the composer whose songs had created the soundtrack for the Soviet Union's last forty years: war songs, wedding songs, songs for every possible occasion. Their lyrics, crafted by the most distinguished Soviet poets, extolled Communist values. But Mark Slavkin's melodies had something that bypassed the phony words and hit you straight in the heart. So hard, you could never chase them away. Just like Mozart or Verdi. Or Billie Holiday. The sign of a true genius.

On top of that, Mark Slavkin had long been the Kremlin's favorite. Someone who probably had more real power and influence than most of its current inhabitants. Maybe, after all, if I played it right, I still had a chance to carry out my Afghanistan plan.

The concert took place later that day, in a small, intimate auditorium of the Baku Conservatory of Music. Without Chinese acrobats or belly dancers. And with no extravaganza at all. Just a few local classical musicians performing patriotic pieces by Soviet composers.

Scheduled last on the program, I waited my turn, watching Mark Slavkin from behind the side curtain. He sat in the VIP box surrounded by sycophants—local Party members, other Moscow guests, reporters—hovering over him like obtrusive mosquitoes. Well into his sixties, in a white sweater with a colorful scarf, he carried both his celebrity and his age with disarming candor. After saluting artists with an amiable smile, he promptly fell asleep a few minutes into their performances.

When my turn came, I bowed and proceeded to the piano. I knew in my heart that Tikhon Khrennikov's *Five Pieces for Piano* with its revolutionary passages and avalanche of chords would not be Mark Slavkin's chosen way to wrap up his boring evening. How could I spare him the musical mayhem of Khrennikov's over-the-top patriotism?

I struggled through the first movement, keeping the volume down, sneaking glances into the audience. Sleep had once again claimed Mark Slavkin, and seven more minutes of my dreadful piece still remained. I had to do something. I desperately wanted to impress this man. But what could I do?

My heart is sad and lonely—Billie Holiday whispered in my ear in her stirring, daring voice, dimming the obnoxious cacophony of Khrennikov, bringing in the aura of Tahir's room with its timeless, unbroken harmony.

Without even resolving Khrennikov's dissonant chord, I switched into "Body and Soul." At first just accompanying Billie Holiday. Unobtrusively. Giving her vocal lines a subtle harmonic support. I gradually picked up the emotion, elaborating her melody with passages and intervals of my own, building it up to the point where I couldn't even tell where Tahir's favorite jazz song ended and mine began.

After the concert, Mark Slavkin came up to me, bent over, and kissed my hand. "Bravo, *bravissimo*," he said, avoiding the microphone. "If you could breathe life—*body and soul*"—he winked—"into that Khrennikov opus, then let the skies be your limits. Your range of emotions and that inimitable quiet intensity...well, it touched my heart."

What a revelation. Mark Slavkin knew Billie Holiday. Mark Slavkin loved jazz music. Mark Slavkin—my clandestine partner in crime. I felt terrible taking advantage of this great man's kindness, but I didn't have a choice.

"Comrade Slavkin," I spurted out, right into the microphone, "on behalf of the Komsomol of my beloved Azerbaijan, I humbly ask for the honor to be named a music ambassador of my republic and sent to Kabul. So I can share the joy of music with our heroic army."

He stared at me as if questioning whether I had been bitten by a mad dog, then shrugged in bewilderment. "As you wish. I'll pass on your request."

The next morning, as I walked out of our building, I saw a car parked a block away. A very unusual car—silver and squat. I'd never seen a car like it before. The yellow license plate beneath the snow contained English letters.

"Leila."

Almaz? Behind the car's tinted window, her face peeked out of a shimmering silk *kelegayi*.

She rolled her window down and stuck out her head. She had changed so much. Everything about her seemed to sparkle—her emerald eyes beneath the kohl arrows, her ruby hair, gold earrings with diamonds, her lips painted cherry-red beyond their contours, overwhelming the rest of her face.

"Get in," she said.

I thought of the possible repercussions of me entering a foreign car. No, I shook my head. I couldn't take a risk. Not now.

"Then meet me at Governor's Park. By our tree."

She waved to the driver. The car took off.

I stood, uncertain, my mind in a tumult of emotions. No doubt, I was thrilled to see Almaz, but her sudden appearance ripped off the bandage from my wound that had never healed, testing my loyalties again.

I decided to go. And to keep it a secret from Mama.

By the time I reached Governor's Park by tram, Almaz was pacing underneath a weeping willow where years ago we took our vows of everlasting sisterhood. She rushed toward me. "I missed you so much. And a thousand times over." She threw her arms around me.

I missed you too, I wanted to say but the words refused to come out.

"I've been following all your successes, you know. Your win at Budapest, your performance at the Tchaikovsky Concert Hall, the interview you gave to *Pravda*. I clip every single newspaper story about you and keep them in my jewelry box. I'm so proud of you. But..." She stumbled, the look of uncertainty in her eyes. "I've heard about your performance yesterday. And it got me worried... I know why you want to fly to Afghanistan. But you don't realize how dangerous it is there. Not all hymns and flowers they show on TV. It's a really nasty war there."

"How do you know all this?"

"From Bulut."

"Who is Bulut?"

"I met him a year ago in Kishlak Gadzhi, of all places. *Allah akbar*." Almaz rolled her eyes to the sky. "What a mafia there, you wouldn't believe it. They live like in feudal times. No electricity. No water. But my cousin had a million rubles buried underneath his barn. Crazy, ha? He forged the numbers of the cotton crop, bribed everyone all the way to the Ministry, received government rewards, and then sold all of the crop to the Turks through my..." She paused. "Through Bulut. He works at the Turkish consulate."

"How long since you've been back?"

"Almost three months. Have my own apartment. Here it is." Almaz scribbled her address and phone number in her little blue book, tore the page, and held it out. "Come visit me anytime."

I took it. "I will."

"Please don't go to Afghanistan," Almaz pleaded, her eyes welling up. "If you don't care about yourself, then at least think of Sonia *Khanum*. After everything she had been through…"

Her words hit me hard, raising an instant wall of ice between us.

"I have to go now," I said.

"I understand." Almaz hugged me and kissed on both cheeks. "Just please be careful."

CHAPTER 26

The following night, I lay in bed, counting camels.

One hundred sixty-seven, one hundred sixty-eight...sixty-nine...seventy... Hoping Arabian camels would start moving against the maroon damask of the casement, across the foliage of the wallpaper...*one hundred eighty-five...* Into the silence of the nocturnal sky...*one hundred ninety-eight...* Into the glow of a virgin crescent... Into the Desert of Sleep.

Not tonight. The camels refuse to leave my room. Instead, they walk in a circle, gazing at me with their unblinking doe eyes, breathing out hot vapor. Multiplying. Crowding my room. Crowding my mind, out of control—dusky, beige, taupe, fulvous...eyes, tails, humps...one hump...two humps...

I threw off my blanket. Sat up. Aunty Zeinab's remedy for insomnia didn't work. I was too restless. Too excited.

I switched on the lights. The camels were gone, and with them went any possibility of falling asleep.

Drip...drip...drip... I listened to the sound of droplets slamming against the basin. What started as a random drizzle gradually metamorphosed into a pelting rain.

I rushed to the bathroom and twisted the faucet handle with all my might.

Silence.

Interrupted by the howl of the wind. By the rustle of the cypress trees. By my heartbeat.

A face stared at me from inside the mirror, shadows moving across her skin like the fragments in a revolving kaleidoscope. Her eyes were quite expressive, just like Papa's used to be. And the black curls that once spread wildly in every direction finally reached down to her shoulders, framing her oval Modigliani face.

Mirror, mirror on the door; I'm not an ugly duckling anymore.

But not yet a swan, either. A fresh pimple bloomed on the bridge of my nose. And my teeth were as crowded as Taza Bazaar.

I tiptoed back to my room, climbed onto my cozy yellow chair, and turned on the radio. The Voice of America broadcast from Washington came through the speakers. I had discovered this station by accident while browsing through the radio waves, fighting insomnia.

With my ear to the radio, through the avalanche of noises, I listened to snippets of information that never appeared in the Soviet press:

"…The Helsinki Committee for Human Rights demands the release of the dissident Andrei Sakharov, a Soviet nuclear physicist… had been exiled… Soviet Union and Maoist China resumed their tepid relationship… And now, *Voice of America Jazz Hour.*"

I turned the sound up a bit and closed my eyes, letting Duke Ellington's "Take the A Train" carry me to my dream.

Tahir and I—our faces, our skin all covered with oozing bubbles and blisters—are crossing the desert, a barren desert with no beginning or end. The lights flash ahead. Oasis or mirage? We run toward the lights, the sand dunes scorching our feet, pulling us down. The lights are getting closer and closer, until a curved triangle of Eiffel Tower appears against the night sky. Not a mirage. Not at all. The real Eiffel Tower is waiting for us, so real I can touch it with my hands.

The next morning, I lingered in bed, replaying the images from the night on the insides of my eyelids. It was Sunday, and I didn't have to go anywhere.

The doorbell rang.

"Mama, can you open the door?" I shouted. "I'm going to take a shower."

A few moments later, I heard a voice that made my body break into a cold sweat. A frightening sense of entrapment returned from the past.

Why? Why now? I hadn't heard from him for over a year. Not since his last letter, when he informed me that the Higher School of KGB was sending him to study in Germany. I never responded to any of his letters, hopeful he would vanish from my life, along with his obsession to control me.

I stayed in the shower for a long time hiding in the steam. Then I dressed slowly—as if going to my own execution. Waiting for a miracle that would take Farhad away. Then, having no alternative, I finally entered the living room.

Sprawled out on our living room couch, Farhad slurped tea, his mouth disappearing into and out of a teacup with pink roses. Mama hadn't taken this special-occasion set of china out of the cupboard since her birthday. Her doomed birthday. An older woman sat across the table from him. His mother?

Mama came out of the kitchen, carrying a tray with fruit and nuts.

"What a beautiful daughter you have, Sonia *Khanum*," the woman said, pursing her heavily painted lips and knitting her brows. Actually, a single brow that traveled—nonstop—across the complete span of her eyes and nose. Undivided. A visage stamped with the perpetual "bandit's mask" of a raccoon.

I gasped for air.

The Raccoon. Baku's premier matchmaker. Her skills were legendary, her reputation repulsive. She matched vulnerable sheep with hungry wolves for a sweet commission.

"Thank you, Tamara *Khanum*, for your kind word," Mama replied with a courteous smile, placing the tray in the middle of the table.

"With Allah's help, let all your grandchildren, Sonia *Khanum*, be as beautiful as Leila. Don't you think, Farhad *jan*?" Raccoon patted the cluster of fur tails attached to her stole. Dozens of them. Lives cut short for the sole purpose of giving her an aura of importance.

Farhad bowed slightly to Mama. I couldn't deny his good looks— athletic, dark-skinned, with spiky black hair, wearing a parade KGB uniform with two shiny stars. But I knew too well how those stars had landed on his broad shoulders. After all, there weren't many heroes aged twenty-one walking around Baku, rewarded with the rank of a lieutenant in the KGB for saving his country from Tahir's *imperialist act of terrorism.*

How could he show his face to me?

Then it hit me—the timing. Farhad saw me on TV appealing to Mark Slavkin to be sent to Afghanistan. That brief exchange had been shown all over the news. That's why he was sitting in my living room accompanied by the Raccoon.

I had to play it safe. Maybe even give him some hope. Anything to put to sleep his suspicion of my enthusiasm to fly to the war zone because of Tahir.

"It's so nice to see you, Farhad. Back home from Germany," I chirped.

He nodded. An ignition of pleasure in his eyes. A curl of satisfaction on one side of his mouth. "It does my heart good to see you, Leila," he said, pressing his hand against his heart.

As we settled at the table, Raccoon began a nuptial talk:

"I will say this—there is one most important thing in Leila's favor: having such a distinguished family. Honorable Mekhti Rashidovich"—she wiped an invisible tear and pointed her finger at Papa's photograph on the wall—"let Allah bless his generous soul. And you, Sonia *Khanum.* What an enviable example of a long-suffering, tolerant wife and mother."

Raccoon caressed her single eyebrow and stroked her dead animals' tails.

"But let's face it," she said, "Leila has had an involvement with a person of perversion. A dangerous element from a family of enemies of the Soviet people."

236

She paused for dramatic impact. "If not for the timely intervention of Farhad *jan*, Leila's innocence would have been compromised, taken away by that filthy element. She would have been expelled from the Komsomol, and she would have had no chance at a piano-playing profession. Even now, there are plenty of rumors around town about Leila's indecent behavior. You can close the city gates, but you can't close the people's mouths. Farhad *jan* has come for a rose, but the rose has some *qüsur* on it. Farhad *jan* is willing to brush the dust from the rose so it can bloom again.

"And what is even more shameful"—Raccoon rolled her eyes before delivering the final blow—"Leila's best friend is a *fahişa*. A whore."

The room plunged into iron silence. Mama sat motionless, as pale as the wall behind her, gazing at the bottom of her teacup. Farhad tried his best to display his shock, a titanic slice of baklava stuck in the gap between his front teeth.

"Farhad *jan* is like a son to me," Raccoon continued plaintively, her voice a poisoned arrow dripping with honey. "Look at him. An honor graduate of the Higher School of the KGB in Moscow, he has a highly regarded, bright future and will provide plentifully for his wife and children. His former professor, General Tamerlan Jabrailov—our compatriot—has been appointed to launch a new department at the Azerbaijani KGB head office, and he has recruited Farhad *jan* as his assistant."

Taking the cue like a character in a well-scripted play, Farhad rose from the couch. With great pomp and circumstance, he unwrapped and displayed an engagement ring with an ostentatious, boulder-size diamond.

"Dear Sonia *Khanum*," he said, displaying as much humility and sincerity as he could generate, "I've been in love with your daughter since the first day I laid my eyes upon her pure face. I have loved her through thick and thin. I have loved her despite her troubles and her impetuous actions, and I helped her to learn a life lesson."

A *life lesson*? By humiliating me and using me for his own advancement? That was his gift of love. I could only imagine what other gifts of love would await me if I agreed to marry him. A rehabilitation program, perhaps? A labor camp? My own personal gulag?

How I wanted to roar in anger at this insult, to kick both Farhad and the Raccoon out the door. Or, better yet, out the window.

"Thank you for your kind words, Farhad," Mama said, in her official, indisputable, head-of-the-surgery-department voice. "And the ring is absolutely lovely. I'm sure you have gone to great effort in choosing it. But I'm afraid Leila is too young for a marriage proposal, even such a praiseworthy one."

The Raccoon, unwilling to lose the commission, swiftly placed herself between Farhad and Mama. "Sonia *Khanum*," she moaned, "we can agree on a betrothal now and plan the wedding in a year."

"I'm sorry." Mama got up, bringing the negotiations to a halt.

Farhad lowered his head, not knowing what to do.

"Leila has been promised to me, Sonia *Khanum*," he said at last, his voice cold, his resentment barely contained behind a mask of politeness. "And I will not allow anyone to disregard the consent given to me by honorable Mekhti Rashidovich. I had sworn to him to marry Leila and to take care of her. And that's what I intend to do. This is my word!"

Crumpling the package with the ring and shoving it into the pocket of his coat, Farhad marched to the door and closed it behind him. Quietly. Ominously.

CHAPTER 27

I had never seen such a filthy gray sky—sagging, worn out, with scattered stains and fissures like the linoleum in Muezzin Rashid's apartment.

The sky of Kabul.

Sixteen hours in the air on a dilapidated TU-134, an hour and a half of circling over the airport defrosting the landing gear, hoping for the wheels to lower before the plane ran out of fuel.

And before the Mujahideen could shoot us down with their American missiles. How ironic it would be to come here and be blown up by missiles from Tahir's jazz mecca. Do they listen to Billie Holiday as they melt and mold lead into bullets to make them as flawless and penetrating as her voice? If so, we are doomed.

The TU-134 plunged onto the runway, raising a dust cloud the size of a nuclear mushroom.

"Welcome to Kabul International," screamed a large poster in Russian, garnished with a hammer and sickle, a hammer so massive it threatened to squash visitors into the ground.

The Kabul International terminal reminded me of Taza Bazaar's Beggars Corner. It was a busy beehive of human misery. Men, only men, everywhere, cursing, haggling, begging, praying, waving their stumps—fresh relics of the war.

Outside, two wrecked buses waited—a fat yellow cylinder with shattered windows and a small, windowless tin canister punctured with bullet holes.

"I'm splitting you into two groups," yelled Lieutenant Medvedev. He had collected us from the terminal and now counted us like sheep.

Twenty-eight of us, mostly dancers from the Belarusian folk group, Zabava, and singers from the Georgian Rustavi Choir. The rest, like me: *outsiders*—classical musicians. The man in charge, Captain Vassil Popovich, a Siberian force of nature, a polar bear with a shiny, bold head and a thick, walrus mustache, got drunk before the plane took off in Moscow and slept peacefully throughout the duration of our rocky flight. He also didn't take orders from anyone.

"Fuck off, Medvedev," Captain Popovich shouted back. "My artists are delicate people. They go by bus. Their gear—suitcases, instruments—ride in that fucking tin canister."

"I'm in charge here, and this is my order." The much younger and lower-ranked Lieutenant Medvedev attempted to stand his ground.

"Wipe your soiled *zhopa* with your order." Captain Popovich pushed the lieutenant aside and gestured to us. "*Gospoda* artists, what are you waiting for, a special invitation? You got it. Board the yellow bus."

"But I have orders," Lieutenant Medvedev almost whimpered. "And orders are orders. In case one bus blows up, the other goes on. And so does the show tonight."

"Ai-yi-yi." Captain Popovich stuck his sausage finger in Medvedev's sullen face. "Where did you grow up, *mudak*, to become so callous-hearted? These artists are our national pride. Our majesty, I can even say. They interrupted their valuable artistic schedules and risked their lives to come here and entertain assholes such as yourself, and all you worry about is your damn order." He heartily spat on the ground and rubbed it into the cement with his boot. "Let's get moving, *gospoda* artists. It's dinnertime."

A platoon of heavily armed troops escorted us through the city of Kabul. A city? A long time ago, maybe. Now it was just one big pile of rubble rising like a fatigued Mount Vesuvius in the aftermath of the eruption. And dark. Daytime dark, the sun buried alive in a thick shroud of smoke. A few passersby dashed away from our motorcade. Faceless women wrapped in heavy, opaque burkas pulled their barefoot kids inside, slamming doors and windows shut.

The motorcade passed by another larger-than-life Soviet placard. "Welcome to Kabul International!"—the same stern Russian letters and hemorrhaging Red Star.

"That's where you perform." Comrade Medvedev pointed behind the sign toward a large area filled with debris, where hundreds of Afghanis in turbans and tunics moved in slow processions, cleaning, raising stands and rows of seats, piling rocks and sandbags. "They're setting up for your show. Used to be their football stadium."

Our final destination was a partially demolished three-story villa with walls of muted olive-gray pebbledash, a tiled white ribbon beneath the cupolas, and arched Islamic windows, just like in our Gargoyle Castle but blocked with wood. Two ancient-looking marble columns guarded its entrance. Between them, another sign in Russian—"Hotel Kabul International."

While everyone rushed to their rooms, I lingered in the foyer—a windowless basement with cracked walls, shredded gold-leaf wallpaper, a dusty bronze chandelier, and a folding metal table encircled by a dozen chairs. Lieutenant Medvedev sat at the table, our documents piled in front of him. I needed to start a conversation with him. To get on his good side.

"You probably have been here for a while," I said, reverently, dropping into one of the chairs.

"My seventh month," he replied without lifting his head, so all I could see was the hay-tinted crown of his buzz-cut head.

"And where do you come from?"

"Ural."

"My best friend's brother has been here for almost sixteen months."

"Ohhh."

"She asked me to look for him."

"What division is he in?"

"She told me but I forgot."

"Then it's like looking for piss in a ditch."

"What if I give you his name? Could you find him?"

"I guess."

"I really—really—need to find him."

Lieutenant Medvedev sized me up, a twinkle in his eye. "Not just your girlfriend's brother, ah?"

I nodded, biting my lip.

"All right, give me his name. I'll ask around."

That evening, I played piano for ten thousand barely-out-of-their-teens boys who filled the Kabul stadium. Boys with pimples and crew cuts in oversized military uniforms, holding on to their toy guns. Toy guns that killed. I played as if there was no tomorrow. Because for many of them there wouldn't be, other than inside a coffin draped with a Soviet flag. Or on the Beggars Corner among the new veterans, showcasing their wooden limbs and glossy government medals.

But on this night, we celebrated life, surrounded by the snow-crowned summits of the soaring Kabul Mountains, safeguarded by dozens of helicopters hanging in the starless sky like luminous planets. With boisterous, patriotic Tikhon Khrennikov's *Five Pieces for Piano*, loud enough to drown out the dissonant sforzando of the not-so-distant artillery explosions.

I played with all my might, plunging into thunderous passages, my fingers striking the keys like falling rocks.

I stopped abruptly, hid my hands in the folds of my skirt, the aftershock of my chords still hovering in the air. The unaware audience of boys broke into a stormy ovation, shouting, stomping their feet, asking for more. I didn't deserve their admiration at all. I had given them nothing but a stream of musical slogans. I had cheated them. I had used them to come here and get what I wanted—redemption.

What had I been thinking? That I would just show up in Kabul, find Tahir in this very real, very brutal war, and together we would fly to the Eiffel Tower on his magic carpet? How poetic, how convenient it looked from a distance. But here and now, that fantasy sounded as disjointed and obtuse as Tikhon Khrennikov's opus.

I closed my eyes and stroked the keys up and down the keyboard again and again, chasing away the spirits of deceit. Then I dipped my fingers into the opening theme of Rachmaninoff's Third. My first public performance of this defiant piece with the ephemeral, bitonal revelations I had been rehearsing for the last two years and still couldn't grasp.

I played the piano part and sang the orchestral sections to myself. With my fears and muse taking turns, I spilled out my soul through my music.

The Legend of the Stone Heart

A thousand and thousand-times-over moons ago, a maiden with skin as dark as chocolate lived in a small village in the Caucasus Mountains. One day, Div—a wicked demon—came to the village. In his traveling bag he carried a shining piece of the moon.

"Sell me your goods," the maiden begged Div. "I want my skin to become as white as the moon."

"If you marry me, you'll receive not only the gift of the moon, but all the treasures in my Moon Cave," replied Div.

"I can't marry you, Div. My heart belongs to Ali the shepherd."

"The choice is yours—if you marry me you become Mistress of the Moon Cave; if you marry Ali you stay a shepherd's wife and clean up after the sheep."

The temptation blinded the maiden's soul, and together with Div she rode away to his Moon Cave and its treasures. There, as she anointed herself with shining pieces of the moon, her skin became moon-white, but the everlasting darkness of night devoured her soul.

"Take your moon treasure back," she pleaded with Div. "Take your Moon Cave. Let me go to Ali."

"As you please," he replied. "Go to Daş Səhra—Stone Desert—and there you will find your Ali."

The maiden traveled many moons before she reached Stone Desert and found her lost love.

"Ali, it's me," she cried. "I came back to beg your forgiveness."

Ali didn't move. He sat, silent, looking at the sky, counting the stars.

She came closer. "Ali, don't you recognize me?"

Ali lowered his eyes, his stone-cold eyes.

"You are a beautiful maiden," he said, "and your skin is as white as the moon, but I don't know any maidens with white skin."

In despair, the maiden reached to touch his heart, but all she felt was the chill of Stone Desert. Her love's heart had turned into stone.

What about Tahir's heart?

I lay on the crude, dark-stained backseat of a UAZ-469 military jeep, dressed in a long, blue Afghani dress with a gray shawl covering my hair. Under a pile of uniforms saturated with stagnant sweat and cigarette stench. The small opening I'd created for my nose kept closing with each of the car's jerks and shudders.

"You all right?" Medvedev's voice cut through the crusty layer of uniforms. "We're almost there. Another maybe fifteen minutes. Keep tight. And like I told you—if anybody talks to you, don't say a word. Act as if you don't understand Russian."

Medvedev had come to me after the concert as our artists' brigade waited for the convoy to be transported to President Babrak Karmal's palace for a lavish dinner. "I found your *friend's brother*," he whispered furtively. "He's with the 108th Motor Rifle Division stationed near Bagram, the air base where you arrived. I can take you there tonight after dinner. You just have to wear Afghani dress...you look dark, like them...I'll get one for you. But don't tell anyone. I'm risking my head, you know."

"Why? Why would you do this for me?" I asked, stunned.

Medvedev shrugged. "Your piano music touched me, you know. Really touched me. Like it pinched me all over my skin. You're a real talent. It's not every day that I meet real talent. Like my girl back home." A pale scar above his left eyebrow stood out as his face turned red. "She did it to me too, you know. With her voice...sweet, sexy, you know. She's also dark like you. The first time I brought her home, my grandma crossed herself against the devil."

"Is she waiting for you?"

Medvedev dropped his head. "I'll bring the dress," he said, avoiding my eyes. "And don't speak Russian under any circumstances or both of us will stand before a tribunal. Understood?"

Suddenly, the vehicle jerked to the side and came to a brusque, tire-screeching stop.

"Documents," I heard a high, nasal voice.

The door of the jeep opened, then slammed shut. Medvedev seemed to have gotten out. A few pairs of boots stomped on a gravel road.

"Hey, *mudak*, don't you see? It's Medved with his fucking whores," shouted another voice, grumpy and boorish, swearing and slurring the words. "Let's see what kind of meat he's got tonight."

I heard the sound of a tarpaulin being hurled up. Then someone shoved aside the uniform stack, and the bright, penetrating beam of a flashlight struck my eyes before assaulting the rest of my body. From behind the blinding shaft of light, a square, pimpled face with elephant ears peered in, grinning lasciviously, glazed eyes examining me closely, the breath of a rotten mouth turning my stomach.

"Medved, you're fucking God's gift. How much do you want for her?" The rough fingers of a probing, calloused hand thrust beneath my skirt and groped my thigh.

It was a trap.

Medvedev hadn't acted out of the kindness of his heart. He'd brought me here to sell. Tears of anger and despair burst out of my eyes. I wanted to scream, to scratch my way out of this horror. But the beefy hand bandaged my mouth while the other hand kept busy drilling a tunnel between my legs.

"No, Kolya, not this one," said Medvedev sheepishly, pulling the soldier away from me. "She's for Colonel Prokhorov himself. She's a virgin. You know how he is—a family man, always careful. He wants them clean."

The hand continued to try to separate my legs but with less conviction. "Virgin, you say." The thumb managed to squeeze and probe itself all the way. Then, suddenly, it was hastily pulled aside. Followed by the sound of something—of someone?—thumping into the gravel. I was free.

"What the fuck is wrong with you?" yelled the slurred voice. "Why didn't you tell me before? What am I gonna do now? Walk around with my dick on fire?"

"Go jerk off in a bucket," replied the first—the nasal voice—cackling. "What's the big deal? It's what you usually do, pederast."

"I'll show you the bucket. I'll stick it in your ass."

A fight broke out, accompanied by grunts and shouts, intercepted with the dull thuds of punches landing while I lay immobile as a lamb waiting to be slaughtered.

"Okay, that's enough, you assholes," shouted Medvedev.

"Not enough. That *blyad* broke my nose."

More scuffling, gradually subsiding beneath muttered curses and obscenities.

"What's the difference if I do her in the mouth?" the slurred one tried to reason. "Nobody's gonna know. I'll give you two bags of poppy."

Pause. Then the flick of a lighter. Another one. "I can't, pal. Prokhorov will hang me."

"He won't know."

"You've got a dick that smells like a dead horse—and you think he won't know?"

Coarse laughter. "I better get moving before fucking *churki* blow up the crossing."

"Be safe, *bratok*."

The door banged shut; the vehicle was heaved into gear and drove off. Shaking violently, I pulled myself into a sitting position and looked back. Two small figures in long overcoats—just like the boys in my audience at the Kabul stadium—stood with their guns in the middle of the dirt road wrapped in a cloud of dust, looking after our UAZ speeding away. Behind them nothing but a void-black sky.

I pushed the tarpaulin aside and quietly vomited over the side of the fast-moving jeep.

"I'm sorry," Medvedev said without taking his eyes off the road. "It's the war, you know. No promise of tomorrow. So you take what you can today."

We drove in silence as I tried to still jabs of sickness coursing through my abdomen. We drove along a too-narrow road edging a cliff: on the left, austere snow-peaked mountains fading into the sky; on the right, a deep gorge shrouded in darkness. In front of us, a blizzard of insects twirled in their final suicidal dance, smashing into blurred streaks across the windshield of our jeep.

I was alone in a vast foreign space with a very bad person who traded women for drugs. And who, tonight, had chosen to be my hero.

Air, crisp and cold, tasted heavenly. Just like the air in Swallow Nest, a resort in the Caucasus Mountains where Mama used to take me every summer to drink *narzan* from the mineral water stream and stock up on its magical, curative energy for another year. We used to wake at dawn and hike through the Valley of the Rising Sun and up the mountain trails to Swallow Grotto, carved out over the centuries by the stream's ancestor, the feral, fast-flowing mountain river, Baksan.

Once there, Mama placed her glass *armud* under the thin stream, filled it with cool, crystal clear water, and watched me drink it, a contented smile on her face. Then we sat on a rock coated with spongy moss and watched the birth of the sun. How it drew apart the sea and the sky and emerged bashfully from behind the regal snow fedora of Mount Elbrus, the highest mountain in all of Europe.

I remembered one morning. Mama, her golden hair spilled across her shoulders, wearing my favorite *sarafan* with daisies, stood against a backdrop of stern glaciers and deep green valleys. The toe of her sling shoe probed the edge of the cliff, sending a few small rocks on a tumbling journey downward. Fear seized my throat, buckled my knees. *What if she slips and falls down into the abyss? What if I never see my mama again?*

"Don't worry," she said, moving away from the precipice, her sky-blue eyes smiling. "I'll always be there for you."

A wave of guilt surged through me. What was I doing here in the middle of the night, hiding like a thief in the back of a military truck? How could I have planned this crazy mission? What if I never saw Mama again?

A few minutes later, as we descended to a level plain, a cascade of blasts shook the earth, killing the fragile stillness of the night, slicing the black canvas of the sky into red shreds of flames.

"Bad luck. *Churki* shooting their fireworks," Medvedev shouted against the wind, speeding up. "Might be a problem."

He was right. Our journey ended at the next checkpoint, a makeshift shed at the side of the road surrounded by a dozen busy soldiers. Erecting barricades, arguing with the drivers of trucks and jeeps, they directed every vehicle to reverse direction and head back the way they had come. A scraggy, gray-haired officer with the withered face of a retired accountant—so out of place amid the squad of young soldiers, most of whom seemed no older than me—approached our jeep.

"Ai-yi-yi." He waved a finger at Medvedev in a fatherly gesture.

"These recruits are fighting the war here, and you're still driving around in your mobile trading post."

Medvedev leaned out of the car holding a fresh pack of Belomorkanal cigarettes. "Listen, Ivan Anatolievich. The thing is, I gotta get through to Bagram. Very big deal."

"Can't let you through." The gray-haired officer hastily stuffed the cigarettes inside the pocket of his coat. "*Dushmans* blew up the bridge. As for your *very big deal*"—he waved mockingly in my direction—"it will have to wait."

We arrived back at the hotel long after midnight. Saying goodbye, nervously pacing from one foot to the other, Medvedev held out the day's edition of the military newspaper with my photo on the front page.

"Will you give me your autograph? Please? And would you write"—he hesitated for a moment—"'with love'? You know, we're not bad...not really...not in real life. The brute—Kolya—is from a village in Siberia, just like me. And he saved my life, you know...six months ago." Medvedev touched a scar on the side of his forehead. "A stray bullet grazed my head, you know. And he covered me, kept me going until we could find a safe place in a cave. With no food, no ammunition. Only three of us survived, out of twenty. So I owe him."

I took the pen, drew a heart, and wrote in big letters: "To my dear friend Lieutenant Medvedev—From Leila with Love!"

A single kerosene lamp dangled on a chain from the ceiling, dispersing murky shadows across the long, narrow corridor. I dragged my feet toward a room at the very end, a whirlwind of regrets spinning in my head. I had done the Zümrüd Quşu part—spread my wings and leaped into unknown. And the result? Never got to see Tahir. Instead, I could have been raped by a Siberian village boy with pimples, my fire wings chopped off and thrown into Panjshir Valley for the hyenas.

Stupid, childish me. Princess Zümrüd belonged in Tahir's legend, not in the middle of an ugly war. Oh, how I wanted it all to be a dream, to wake up from this nightmare in my own bed, to smell the fresh Baku morning air instead of the vapor of vomit and the stench of moldy uniforms. A spasm clenched my stomach. The back of my throat tasted bile.

I rushed to the room and started to use my key, but the door opened the moment I touched it. I surely remembered locking it when I left. No time to worry about that. The spasm overwhelming me, I groped my way in the darkness, found the sink and threw up, emptying my guts of the rest of Babrak Karmal's dinner. Then, a drip at a time from the rusty faucet, I rinsed my mouth. And the fear returned.

The door. Why was it open?

I turned around. A silhouette. Someone sitting on my bed.

"Princess Leila." The silhouette rose, stepped toward me.

Tahir?

In the million possible visions of our reunion, this was the one I'd missed. Tahir in my hotel room, waiting for me to come back from my expedition to find him. An absolutely irrelevant expedition as it turned out. Because there he was, standing in front of me. All I had to do was just reach out and hold him.

But I couldn't. In some bizarre way, I felt that by making it so easy he had minimized my heroic task, dismissed my daring efforts to find him. To save him. To redeem myself.

He had changed. Taller, broader in the shoulders than the lanky boy I remembered from almost three years ago. Almost an eternity. What if the war had changed him in other ways too? What if he'd become like the pimply-faced monsters on the road? They too had probably been nice, idealistic boys before life presented them with the miseries of Afghanistan.

Except Tahir had more reason to be angry than any of them. Angry at me. After all, I was the sole reason for him being here.

"It's so nice to see you," my mouth muttered, stupidly, just to say something. The words so banal and clumsy. And so out of place. My feet did no better, tripping over a Kalashnikov rifle leaning against the wall.

"I'm sorry." Tahir rushed to move the weapon aside and help me keep my balance.

Tahir. So close. His warm breath brushed against my neck, sending fireworks up my spine.

"I saw you in the concert," he said. "It brought back good memories."

Good memories?

"I…I played the Rachmaninoff…tonight. My first public performance. At first, I couldn't find any focus. Lots of different emotions, you know. The flight and the sense of danger." *No. The anticipation of seeing you. The thrill of finding you and the fear of being rejected.*

"I know what you're saying." Tahir paused. "It was the same with me. With my art here at the beginning. No matter how I mixed paints, the images kept coming out gray." He smiled wistfully, his eyes taking on a shape of a crescent. "I enjoyed your Rach 3, the way you blended conflicting reds and blues into harmonies…"

How sad. There we were, two strangers in a dark room, desperately trying to keep our disjointed, reserved conversation alive. One long pause after another, interrupted only by the buzz of a hungry fly spinning in circles. My eyes adjusted to the darkness, I studied the new Tahir. Head shaved, dressed in a neat uniform with a sailor shirt peeking out. I wouldn't have recognized him in a crowd with the other boy soldiers.

"So…I guess I better get going." Tahir reached for his Kalashnikov. "You had quite an eventful day. With the flight and the show and the fancy dinner at the Puppet's palace," he said, a touch of the old Tahir sarcasm in his voice.

I felt rejected. I knew I should stop him. Ask his forgiveness. Tell him that I had come to Afghanistan to make his wish for me come true. That I had grown wings, traveled with a stranger on a dangerous road in my quest to find him. That he had become my obsession, my destination.

"Good-bye, Princess Leila. Have sweet dreams," he said and hastily left the room.

I watched as he disappeared in the dark corridor. Tahir the stranger in heavy combat boots, their clumping hobnails echoing his footsteps.

How could I have come here to meet him, to save him, to share the rest of my life with him, and then let him go? What was it—fear? Pride?

He stopped for a brief moment, then the sound of his steps resumed. But now the echoes grew louder and louder. Tahir was walking—no, he was running—back to me.

"You know, I was thinking," he stammered, out of breath. "Would it be too rude if I asked you to sit for me? Now?"

"It would be more rude if you didn't," I said, my heart ripping through my chest.

"Oh, great. I brought really good paper with me. Traded it for poppy."

"Poppy? Do you still smoke hashish?"

"Not once in the past year. You know me, I don't like being part of a crowd."

Opening his bag, he retrieved a wood palette and a few sheets of paper. He obviously had come prepared. The same old Tahir, obsessed with his art.

"Touch it, doesn't it feel like canvas?" he said. "The best German paper for oil painting. It's saturated with a special chemical that will keep the texture and the vividness of color forever."

"How will you paint me in the dark?"

"In the dark? Look at this." He reached over and gently turned me toward the window. Outside, a half-moon with a misty halo fought its way through the dense clouds.

"I couldn't see it like this before," he said, "beauty in its rudimentary way. Remember how I used to be obsessed with creating my own *unique* formula? Too much ego gets in the way when you're young and stupid. Here, though, in this dreadful place, life reduces your most powerful ambitions to mere shades of gray, yet it frees you from your own self-imposed boundaries."

"'Who can say that today's key will not be tomorrow's lock, or today's lock not tomorrow's key?'" I recited an ancient verse.

"That's true. Nothing ever stays the same." Tahir carefully organized his brushes. "Life is a desert of shifting sand dunes. Unpredictable. Erratic. Harmony changes into dissonance, the immediate outlives the profound, esoteric becomes clichéd. And vice versa. Isn't it weird? All those experiments I did with colors and techniques. Looking for the perfect greens, blues, and violets that would express the transparent beauty of the Zoroastrian fire. And I found them here. Right here, in the middle of macabre fighting in this war-torn country. They have been here for a thousand years. Juno irises. Growing on the top of the Kabul Mountains. Waiting for me. The precise cocktail of hues breathing with life. You see, if I didn't come here, I wouldn't have found them. So it was all worth it."

He placed a chair next to the window and urged me to sit down, holding my shoulders for a brief moment, taking me back to the night at the top of Maiden Tower when I offered myself to him and he refused.

"Here you'll be bathed in a natural light—like Caravaggio's light, remember?" he said, walking around the dark room, considering the best spot for himself, checking the light and angles, moving the table to different positions before settling near the sink. Rubbing his hands in delight, he commanded, "Do not move."

Then he painted in total silence.

Was this the only reason he came to see me?

I sat motionless for a long time, my body itching, my head swarming with half thoughts, waves of sadness rising inside my heart until I wanted to scream it all out, to let this self-centered stranger know that I had gone through hell to find him and to be with him. Not to pose like a lifeless mannequin for his painting.

I moved slightly, just enough to let a lock of hair fall across my face. *Will he notice?*

He did. He leaped across the room and gently pushed the hair behind my ear. I wrapped my arms around him, stroking his porcupine head, bringing him close to me. To break the wall between us. To give us a chance. Now or never.

Tahir hesitated. He might have changed, but the taut energy of rejection coming from him felt the same as two years ago. I released my embrace. Tears clogged my throat. The pain concealed inside me had no remedy. His heart, after all, *was* made of stone.

He didn't move. Stayed next to me, uncertain. Torn. *Feeling sorry for me?* Then he kissed me on the back of my neck. Soft legato. Reached for my hands and pressed them against his burning face, his dry lips, his moist tongue.

Stop. Stop right now. I heard the voice of reason. *This is not the right time nor the right place. Look around. Look where you are.*

I did. I looked around Room Number 12 of the Kabul International Hotel. A dingy room with fatigued saffron flowers on the stained wallpaper, with washed-out gazelles dragging their feet across a bedspread spotted with cigarette burns.

And with a magical painting on the table. A half girl and half bird with chiffon wings at the crown of Maiden Tower, ready to soar into the sky. Against the misty moon—my face. The face of love.

"'Every passing breeze carries the rose fragrance of your breath to me,'" Tahir whispered an ancient ghazel. "*Every splendid sunrise reflects the golden glow in your eyes for me. Every rustling leaf and every fleeting rain whisper your name to me. My heaven is yours; your sorrow is mine, I am forever drunk with your love's wine…*"

It didn't happen the way I was told "the first time" would be. With pain and embarrassment. Giving in to a man's unleashed desire, submitting to his male dominance. Exercising the only power given to a girl by nature—the ability to keep her man just hungry enough so he would return for more. That was the axiom we Azerbaijani girls were raised to believe.

No, what happened between Tahir and me was the Dance of Love created by two partners equal in every way—tenderness, longing, vulnerability. Two souls who met in the dark to spark the glow. Two halves of a pomegranate that joined, kernel to kernel, to form one beautiful whole. Two dreamers—Princess Zümrüd and her Knight in Lion's Skin—who discovered a magical world of love hidden underneath a stinking Afghani bedspread.

"Will you remember me tomorrow?" Tahir whispered in my ear as we lay afterward, sweaty, naked, and shameless, his scrubby head rubbing against my neck.

"Of course not." I giggled. "What about you?"

"What about me?"

"Don't be silly."

"I'm not."

"Then tell me."

"Tell you what?"

"Will you remember me tomorrow?"

"Well, it's hard to remember every adolescent girl who falls for me," he said, failing to suppress a smile, a mischievous smile sweeping all the way beyond the margins of his thin face.

I made a half-playful gesture to tear myself from Tahir, but he tightened his arms around me and stroked my hair, hypnotizing me with the infinite luster of his lavender eyes.

"You are the only one, Leila," he whispered. "You are the love of my life. You are mine as I am yours. Forever."

And he kissed me feverishly, bringing the taste of arousal to my lips, making my every cell explode with new desire. A much stronger desire. Because now I had known the blossoming garden of lovers' oblivion—our private paradise. And I craved more.

With our eyes locked, caressing each other with words and sighs of love, we slowly danced our way back, following the accelerando rhythm of our hearts until there was no more *him* and *me*. Only *us*, the eternal *us*. Free like water rushing down an overflowing mountain stream. Weightless like a bird soaring in the air on her fire wings of love—higher and higher—over the barren deserts, snow peaks, and into the clear sapphire sky.

And, sadly, toward the new sun seeping from behind the Kabul Mountains. Night had slipped away so fast.

"I've come here to find you, Tahir," I whispered hurriedly before we were lost to sleep. "I've been planning this for a long time, since your grandmother gave me her Firebird, Zümrüd Quşu. I've never parted with her, and finally she led me to you. I have a plan. We'll defect. Together. It's not that difficult. We're less than three hundred kilometers from the Pakistan border. You speak Farsi, and with this"—I showed the platinum ring with a sapphire—"we can bribe some nice Pashtun—"

"Shhh." Tahir didn't let me finish, touching my lips with his finger. "Not now. We'll talk about it tomorrow."

I woke up alone to a biting grayness. The sun, after all, didn't make it through the clouds. The painting was gone—gone with the palette and paper sheets and every possible trace of Tahir's presence.

Except for his smell. Intoxicating. Evocative. Torturous.

I didn't see him throughout the day, and I didn't hear from him the next night or the morning after. Ashamed, I sat in my hotel room guarding the crime scene. Me and Miriam's washed-out vermilion bird.

Zümrüd Quşu? A Firebird?

Nonsense. More like an evil *lənət*. A curse. The sole reason Miriam ended up in the gulag. I threw the bird in the trash can. Then, struck by guilt, took it out and put it back inside my suitcase. At dawn, we were loaded into the buses and driven to the airport in a heavily shielded cortege. But not until the plane lifted into the sky and the city disappeared beneath a blanket of smoke did I accept the reality—Tahir had painted me, made love to me, and then walked away. Free and unattached as always. I'd been used and discarded.

And my heart shattered into a thousand tiny pieces scattered all over the Afghani wasteland.

CHAPTER 28

"Why did you abandon me? Why?"

"I'm sorry, Princess Leila. But to be fair, I warned you once before—feelings are a trap that suffocates creativity."

"What about love? You said you loved me."

"And I still do. But I sacrifice love for my art. You did the same when you had to choose between me and your music."

"It wasn't like this."

"However it was, I'm here now in this bloody millstone because of a report signed by this musical hand of yours."

"I thought you forgave me."

"There are things that are impossible to forget."

"So you punished me… But what about us?"

"Us? Well, let me teach you a lesson, Leila, so the next time you won't be fooled so easily. Don't let a naughty boy's words into your head and his sneaky fingers under your skirt."

A sharp pain skewers me, tearing my insides apart centimeter by centimeter, creeping up my chest, puncturing my lungs, leaving me to lie flat and helpless, choking on the thick, gooey black air.

If I can only reach—even just one more time—that closeness where I can hide from Tahir's callousness and from my own shame.

I move nearer, pressing my body against his.

"That's better," he says, his hand trailing up inside my thigh. "You're going to love it."

"Of course she's loving it. She's a whore, just like her best friend."
Raccoon? How did she get in here?

"Whore…whore…whore…" Raccoon hisses, climbing on the bed, hitting me with her dead squirrel tails. "Whore…whore…whore…"

I forced my eyes open. Light seeped through the door left ajar, illuminating a figure bent over me. The end of her soft angora shawl brushed against my cheek.

"Mama," I breathed out in relief, "it's you."

"You're shivering." Mama touched my forehead. "No fever, fortunately. You must break this vicious pattern of going to sleep at dawn and destroying your nervous system. I should probably give you something to calm you down."

"No. Just sit with me, please." I grasped her hand.

"I will, but let me cover you first. You're soaking wet."

Mama picked up my camel-hair blanket from the floor and, holding one side, threw it high up in the air, a shielding tent settling over me. Just the way she used to do when I was little, while reciting a verse of which only one line had stayed in my memory—"Let the lace of your dreams carry you up to the stars." The line now echoed with sheer ridicule. If Mama only knew where my pathetic dreams had taken me.

"Tell me what's going on with you," she said, settling on the edge of my bed, folding her legs up and under her shawl. "You haven't been yourself since that trip to Afghanistan. I wish I had put my foot down."

"It has nothing to do with Afghanistan," I said into my pillow.

"What does it have to do with, then?"

"Nothing. I'm fine."

"No, you're not, Leila. You think I'm blind? You think I don't see you wasting away like a ghost? You haven't touched your piano in days. Professor Sultan-zade called. You never showed up for your lessons. Why?"

"I had a headache."

"A headache over the last two weeks?"

Oh yes—a grave one, along with a heartache dragging me into the same continuous dialogue with Tahir. Attempting to explain how much his abandonment hurt me. Asking him for the thousandth time—*Why?*

My days spun like a broken record. Up and down the stairway to the mailbox, hanging next to the Snow Princess's fresco, on the lookout for Fatima the mailwoman.

Our exchanges didn't last long.

"*Sabahın xeyir,* Fatima."

"Good morning to you too, with Allah's help."

"Is there anything for me, Fatima?"

"What are you expecting, a diamond ring?"

And she was gone.

Afterward, I usually lingered a while by the Snow Princess, staring at her faded visage, seeking some magical sign, blaming her for my misfortunes. Then I rushed back home and—riding on a new wave of hope—began my countdown to the next day's mail delivery.

"I wanted to talk to you about something," Mama said in a strange—forced—manner. "I received a nice apology note from Farhad, full of remorse for his inappropriate behavior. He claimed his temper got the worst of him and he felt miserable afterward."

"It's not his temper but his ego. He's not a good person, Mama."

"People change, Leila. Especially men. With tolerance and your intelligent guidance, you'll be able to mold him into someone you can respect and rely on. That's what we women do."

"What are you talking about?" I examined Mama's face for any clues.

"What I'm saying is that maybe we should give it some time. After all, Farhad has great prospects, and with him on your side, every door will open up to you. You'll easily receive a visa that enables you to tour all over the world, to have an international career, freedom, financial means. And then—later—who knows? You'll still be young and in a position to make your own, independent decisions."

First Tahir and now Mama. Betraying me.

"How did he get to you to change your decision overnight? After you were so strong," I said.

"It's not overnight. I've been thinking, weighing pros and cons."

I felt the same anger and despair that I did in Afghanistan when I lay in a cold sweat, waiting to be sold as a sex slave for a bag of poppy. I hid my head under the blanket.

"Trust me, I understand you more than you think," Mama said. "You are the only one I care about. I'm not saying that you should marry him. Yet. A simple, private engagement ceremony would calm everything down."

Mama pulled herself up, tightened a shawl around her slim shoulders, and left the room, quietly closing the door. Leaving me in a womb of darkness.

The next morning, I called Professor Sultan-zade and asked if I could visit her at home.

She lived on the second floor of a four-story Democratic Republic-era building with large vaulted windows and soaring domed ceilings. Her living room served as a recital studio where we occasionally had our lessons. A few settees upholstered in red-wine damask sat along the perimeter of the walls.

In a position of honor in the center of the room—her cherished baby, a full-sized concert grand piano Blüthner from 1854 signed by Annette Essipoff-Leschetizky, a brilliant pianist from the second half of the nineteenth century for whom Tchaikovsky composed his *Concert Fantasia*. Lyre-shaped carvings ran along the piano's rosewood body, and its lid, when propped open, resembled the wing of a giant swallow.

The rest of her place—a closet-sized bedroom and kitchen— maintained the same stark quality, with sparse furnishings and a lack of any knickknackery. "Less dust to collect," Professor Sultan-zade liked to say.

"How are you feeling?" she asked, taking my coat. "Your mama told me that you came down with something after your return from Kabul."

"I'm fine, Professor."

I headed to the piano but stopped. "Would it be all right if we skipped today's lesson?"

Professor looked at me doubtfully, slightly squinting her eyes. "Maybe it's a good idea to take a break." She pointed at one of the settees. "Get comfortable. I'll make some tea for us."

I sat down, waiting, listening to the noises coming out of the kitchen, falling under the spell of the unique—formal, old-fashioned, and oh, so classical—music atmosphere of the room.

"You've done well. I received a glorious report from Moscow." Professor entered carrying a tray with teapot, *armuds*, and sugar cubes heaped on a saucer. "They said you were absolutely marvelous and inspiring in Kabul. And I'm glad that you went ahead and played Rachmaninoff. Bravo!"

"Professor, I have to ask you something."

"About what?"

"When can I start performing again? I miss the stage, deeply miss it. The Kabul performance reminded me of what I've been missing."

"You might be right." She placed the tray on a small rosewood table carved in the shape of an elephant. "As a matter of fact, Professor Najafov and I have been thinking of booking you on a tour."

"When?"

"Next fall. I'd love to see you with the Leningrad Philharmonic Orchestra, conducted by the great Yevgeny Mravinsky."

"But that's almost a year from now."

"I know. But it takes time to schedule performances with a major orchestra."

I took a long pause before letting it out. "Please…understand me. I need to go somewhere. Anywhere. I need to be away for a while. To be busy, to play a concert every day, to play and play and not think because…because my heart is broken." Tears began to spill out of my eyes. "I don't need a major orchestra or a fancy stage. I just want to be away. To disappear. Far, far away."

Professor Sultan-zade came over. Sitting affectionately next to me, patting my hair, wiping my tears, she kept repeating, "My poor girl, my poor Leila. How did it happen?"

We stayed like that for a while, watching the peach sunset disperse a thousand butterflies throughout the room. They embraced us with the gentle air of their soft staccatos, flying around, luring us into the oblivion of Schumann's carefree *Papillons*.

"Well, tears will not solve the broken-heart problem," Professor Sultan-zade finally said, "but a bit of activity might. You're right. You need to play. And maybe this is partially my fault. Maybe I've been keeping your wings clipped for too long, waiting for the one perfect spotlight that would lift you to the very top. So I'll call the Ministry of Culture as soon as their office is open tomorrow and ask them to book you for an extended national tour. An opportunity to experience different places, faces, nature. Get newly inspired. As for your heartache, remember what Franz Liszt once said: 'Mournful and yet grand is the destiny of the artist.'"

On November 10, 1982, Leonid Brezhnev died. After five days of national mourning, he was buried in the Kremlin Wall Necropolis.

The king is dead! Long live the king!

The Politburo of the Communist Party of the Soviet Union laid upon Yuri Andropov the duty of general secretary, along with the *crown* of the State.

A Gray Cardinal, as Andropov was called among people, had brought to the Kremlin's high office a long list of his glorious deeds: the key role in crashing the Hungarian Revolution in 1954, invading Czechoslovakia and halting the Prague Spring in 1968, the creation of an elaborate system of psychiatric hospitals for dissidents, the principal voice in the decision to send Soviet troops to Afghanistan in 1979, and at the top, the longest serving head of the KGB.

Yuri Andropov moved to Brezhnev's office on November 12, 1982. Coincidentally, on the same day, I flew to Vladivostok via Moscow to join a national Siberian Far East tour.

A rugged ellipse of light swept across the audience before settling a few centimeters away from my icy toes. Another sixty-four bars of orchestral anarchy before I would step into the spotlight and escape from my gloomy, chaotic, lonely life into a realm of illusion.

My thirteen-minute-long Chopin act was jammed between a potpourri of Soviet songs performed by the Tatarstan State Orchestra and a patriotic poem titled "Communism, You Are the Flame Burning in My Heart," recited by the author, Igor Yakut. A thin man with a pencil mustache and sunken cheeks, clad in a black dusted-off suit, he looked as if he had just stepped out of a coffin. His poem—lengthy at the start of the tour—grew a new verse with each performance. If not for Chopin, I would have lost my mind.

We had been on the road for two months, starting in the Far East—a vast area of more than six million square kilometers stretching from Lake Baikal in Eastern Siberia, the world's oldest and deepest body of fresh water, all the way to the Pacific Ocean. Strikingly scenic and inviting during its short, two-week autumn, the Far East turned into a deadly, vacant ice kingdom with the arrival of the first days of winter.

A recent directive from the Ministry of Culture extended the tour indefinitely, adding concerts located in geographically conflicting locations, making us fly and fly and fly, far enough and long enough to land on the moon. But no such luck. No matter how far we traveled, we always ended up on the wrong side of the Iron Curtain. The Soviet Union indeed was a great country—distance-wise.

Crimson banners pompously waved their hammers and sickles.

Long "bread" lines in front of empty stores wound like ravenous pythons throughout the cities' streets. Comrade Lenin, dressed in stone, wood, or marble, stared from every corner at the fruit of his experiment—a hungry, impoverished, and destitute Communist nation.

We played one, two, sometimes three shows per day, *bringing culture to the masses*—that was the official slogan of national concert music tours. A prince-and-a-pauper experience. In the mornings, it could be an all-granite-and-gold concert hall with an audience of five thousand. In the evenings, we entertained dozens of highlanders in an obscure mountain *kishlak*, where, equipped with a flashlight during intermissions, I raced on my high heels across the village, tripping over donkeys, on my way to a wooden toilet stall.

Oh, how tired I was of dilapidated planes, filthy trains, broken-down buses, cockroach-populated hotels. But more than anything else, I couldn't take any more of eating pig fat, the only available staple of the *great* Soviet Union. Pig fat with an egg for breakfast. Pig fat with potato for lunch. Pig fat with pig meat for dinner.

A bout of nausea hit my stomach. I squeezed my fists into my abdomen, trying to force the bout to die out. It worked.

One night we performed in a small town in the Kazakh oblast of Semipalatinsk, where more than four hundred nuclear tests, equal to twenty thousand Hiroshima bombs, had been carried out in the previous forty years. During those nuclear experiments, the residents of the site had been moved to safe homes. A few days later, they were delivered back to their farms with contaminated soil and irradiated livestock. A "heroic Communist act"—that's how the director of our hotel, Bright Future, proudly described their return.

All of a sudden, a scent of saffron touched my nostrils. I sniffed intently. No mistake—the smell of home. But why here, in the heart of the Siberian taiga?

I would do anything to taste a *plov*. With walnuts and cherries and the hint of lemon. And *kutabs*. Greasy and spicy. With yogurt and mint and lamb.

The audience applauded the poorly tuned Tatarstan State Orchestra, and the conductor, a petite butterball with greased-up hair in a golden brocade tuxedo, rushed back onstage, signaling his musicians to return for an encore before the clapping could expire. The trombonist, while marching to his place behind the orchestra, dumped the excessive spit from inside his instrument onto the floor directly next to me.

Another bout of nausea.

Finally, the orchestra cleared, and the local presenter wobbled to the microphone. I could smell his alcohol breath from behind the curtain.

"And now let's put our hands together and welcome a special talent. Leila Ba-d...Leila B-a-a-da-..."

Without waiting for him to announce me properly, I sprang toward the piano with a single wish—to get it over with as quickly and as painlessly as possible on this corroded, out-of-tune Rostov-on-Don upright piano missing the first octave F-sharp key. I thrust my right hand onto the keyboard with the opening chord of Chopin's *Revolutionary Étude*—the explosion of the artillery—enjoying its disturbing, obnoxious timbre and letting it ring out before throwing my left hand into the battle. The polyrhythm of the melody clashed with relentless arpeggios like a wounded soul trapped inside a dark maze of passion, loneliness, and fear. Running and running.

But no matter how far and deep into the Siberian taiga or the Kazakh Desert I tried to bury myself, no matter how many logical explanations for the spells of nausea I had mastered in my head, there was one devastating reality to face, accept, and deal with. As soon as possible.

I was almost three months pregnant.

CHAPTER 29

The Fable of Crane and Frog

Once Frog jumped out of the swamp and saw Crane flying in the azure sky.

"Let's be friends," said Frog.

"I'm afraid our friendship is not possible," replied Crane.

"But why?"

"Because you live in the marsh, and I fly in the clouds. I can't breathe under the water, and you don't have wings to fly."

"If you take me with you into the sky, I'll grow wings. I promise."

So, on a nice, clear day, Frog climbed on Crane's back, and together they took off, both enjoying the journey until Crane soared too high into the sky, and Frog fell back into the marsh, hurt and crippled.

The blast of a gale-force Khazri threw a cascade of rain in my face, but I didn't even bother putting on my hood. Why worry about getting wet when you're already drowning?

Old Town felt creepier than ever: on one side, the clusters of crumbling houses, their inhabitants asleep; on the other side, the ancient catacombs with dead from the thirteenth century. All was obscured in the shadows of the night, under skies vomiting rain and hailstones.

"The night hides a world, but reveals a universe," said an old adage. True. Alone on the nocturnal streets of Baku, I couldn't have seen my universe more clearly—shrunken to minuscule, an out-of-control elevator dropping with mind-blowing speed down a deserted shaft.

The music of *muğam* wove through the rustle of the vines disturbed by the wind. Faint light streamed through the window of a small teahouse. I peeked inside. An old man in a white robe and turban sat cross-legged on a rug next to a steaming teapot. His eyes closed, his hand held prayer beads, and his thin, agile upper body swayed in rhythm with music.

A whirling dervish performing his ritual *dhirk*? Oh, how I'd love to spin into his all-forgetting, all-forgiving trance and vanish into oblivion.

A bolt of lightning split the sky, illuminating the jagged edges of a stone crown. Then the rest of Maiden Tower, solemn and daunting, stared at me through the eyes of its hollow embrasures.

I entered the gate, ran along the walkway. Four steps down, the door opened into the courtyard. I tiptoed past Miriam's quarters. Not a sign of life; she was obviously asleep. Reaching between the bars, I examined the wall until my fingers came upon the bulky key. Carefully removing it, I crept to the iron gate of the tower.

It opened slowly, reluctantly, with a creaky yawn, freeing my way to the top.

Hesitantly, as if crawling into my own tomb, I mounted the spiral staircase, the steps becoming steeper and slipperier with each flight, making my head spin. Not into the peaceful trance of the twirling dervishes. No. Into the agonizing carousel of the same unanswered questions, jarred emotions, and disjointed solutions.

As I reached the top, I pushed the door open and stepped outside onto the crown of Maiden Tower. And into the starless sky. A powerful wind whipped through the darkness, threatening to knock me off my feet. Resisting, holding on to the railing, I stepped toward the edge. Then another step, slowly removing my hand from the safety of the railing. Giving myself to the calamitous, stormy, pitch-black night.

"When the orphan sky hid behind the black dome of sorrow,
When the rain shed its tears upon the barren earth,
Princess ran to the top of the tower, waved her arms like wings..."

Tahir had translated the legend into his painting so brilliantly that I could see it clearly now in the reflection on the black canvas of the sky. In the reflection of me standing on the lip of the tower, my arms like wings fluttered by the gusty wind. How easy to be free. How strong we are when we have nothing to lose. *Half girl and half bird.* The ultimate decision belonged to me. Tahir had just pushed me closer to the edge, toward black infinity.

All of a sudden I noticed a tiny gleaming firefly. Then another. No, not fireflies. Silver stars had broken through the bulging clouds, spilling one after another into the sky, moving toward me, lighting up my night.

And with them came an overwhelming desire to live. To be awakened in the morning by Muezzin Rashid's soulful *Adhan.* To play piano, to share the spotlight on the stage with Chopin, Rachmaninoff, Schumann in front of an adoring, spellbound audience. To stroll the streets of Baku, breathing thick and creamy Caspian Sea air rinsed in the autumn rain. To watch with Mama the peach sunrise over the snow summit of the Caucasus Mountains.

But I couldn't move. Fear had taken me hostage, numbing my body, twisting my equilibrium, leaving me at the mercy of the Khazri that wouldn't give up until it had pushed me into the abyss.

Suddenly, a powerful force hauled me back, away from the rim of the tower.

Miriam. She breathed like an overheated engine, her creased face with its ashy eye sockets in shocking proximity to mine. Without saying a word, she took me in her arms, as strong as if she had borrowed them from someone three times her size. I buried my face into her bony shoulder. She smelled the way I always thought a grandmother should smell.

"I'm with child," I whispered into her neck.

No reaction. Maybe she didn't hear me.

"I'm with child. Pregnant," I repeated louder, unable to keep the anger out of my voice.

"Then how could you even think about harming yourself when you're carrying a new life? A child is a gift. No matter what the circumstances are."

What right did she have to judge me? Who was she to preach the wisdoms? She, who herself had ended up in a dungeon. Hadn't she done enough damage to me already?

"I did what you asked me to do. I went to Afghanistan to find your grandson. And I did, despite all the danger and humiliation. Only to be taken advantage of and left." The tears blocked my throat. "He left me alone…all alone…with his baby. What am I going to do with it?"

"He loves you," Miriam said, wiping tears off my cheeks with her calloused hand. "He loves you with all his heart. And if a Mukhtarov loves someone, it stays with them to their grave."

"Mukhtarov, Mukhtarov. That's all you've ever cared about." I pushed her hand away from my face. "An obsession with your noble blood. That's what it is."

"You are the love of his life, Leila. That's what he said in his letter."

"Letter? In his letter? So he writes to you. Then why hasn't he written to me? Not even so much as a postcard. Not a word. Not a stroke of his brush. Nothing."

"He's at war, Leila."

"And so am I." I stepped back from Miriam. "It is my problem now, and I will deal with it. I don't need your lecturing anymore."

"Leila, it's normal for a pregnant woman to be emotionally distressed." She clasped my forearm. "Please let me help you. Please. I'll do anything to relieve your burden. I'll raise the baby."

"No." I pushed her away.

"I beg you." She slid to her knees, an apparition in the silver light of the stars, her white hair and her nightgown tormented by the storm, her hands folded in plea. "Keep the baby. He is our only hope for the future. The last of the Mukhtarovs…"

I shook my head vehemently and rushed down the stairs.

Miriam's voice followed me, echoing between the walls of Maiden Tower, tearing to pieces what had been left of my heart.

I had no one to go to except Almaz.

I found her easily. She lived in a large apartment building on Erevansky Street, half of its facade hidden behind a huge banner hung in preparation for the fifty-fourth Anniversary of the Great October Socialist Revolution. The wind kept thrashing the red silk with its stern faces of Lenin and Andropov against the concrete of the building, together with the assortment of underwear, socks, and sheets drying on the balconies.

What if she wasn't home? Or if she *was* home but not alone?

Almaz opened the door. Barefoot, wearing flannel pajamas with yellow flowers, her hair pulled high into a ponytail, the ends reaching all the way to her buttocks.

"You came!" she exclaimed, hugging me. "I'm so glad! Come in, but leave your shoes outside. I have new floors."

I left my shoes and coat outside and entered Almaz's abode of pure extravagance. A large crystal chandelier in the shape of a tulip hung from a tiled ceiling; off-white silk wallpaper complemented the Oriental redwood furniture inlaid with mosaic marquetry; plush Turkish rugs covered a sparkling-white marble floor.

"I'm so happy you came," she said, placing a pair of fuzzy, comfy slippers at my feet. "I'll make some hot tea, so you don't get sick. Or"—she winked—"I can give you something really incredible. Veuve Clicquot."

"What is it?"

"French champagne. All French aristocrats drink it. Want to try some?"

I had never tasted alcohol before. Maybe now was the time to try. To get drunk and hush all my troubles, even if just for tonight.

"All right. Sure. Why not?"

Almaz retrieved a large curved bottle from the refrigerator and filled a silver bucket with ice. "Go check my bedroom and my new bathroom," she said, decorating a tray with nuts and dried fruit, lining them up in perfect oval rows just the way Aunty Zeinab used to do.

Almaz's bedroom looked like a nineteenth-century boudoir—a white bed with lilac satin sheets and two matching chairs with gilded arms and legs; embroidered purple-and-gold velvet curtains; antique alabaster wall sconces. I opened the door to the bathroom. All in sky-blue—the sink, the bathtub, and the tile, from floor to ceiling. Even the handles of the glass cabinet over the sink had been painted blue.

"Don't you love it?" she called from the living room.

"Yes, it's really beautiful." I slightly opened the door of the cabinet. Sets and sets of makeup, Arabic perfumes, jewelry boxes. And behind everything, Papa's photo, framed and wrapped in plastic. A Papa I never stopped loving—tall, strong, and dependable, with a wild mane of black hair, his left eye slightly squinted, as he exhales the smoke from his cigarette through the corner of his mouth. I remembered the exact moment the picture was taken. On a hot summer afternoon, after the three of us visited Leo Tolstoy's house in Yasnaya Polyana where he wrote *Anna Karenina*. We hiked through the forest and came upon Tolstoy's grave in a small clearing next to a long ravine.

"This part of the forest is called 'Place of the Green Wand,'" Papa said, leaning against the sturdy trunk of an old tree and lighting his cigarette. "Do you know why, girls?"

We shook our heads.

"There is a belief that the person who finds the magic wand here will never die." Papa smiled, challenging mortality.

Click.

Why was she keeping Papa's picture? Wouldn't she want to erase any memory of him? As if he had never existed? But then she would wipe out her entire childhood, along with me.

Or maybe, despite everything, she still loved him? As I did? How twisted…

"Leila, come here. I'm ready," called Almaz.

I quietly closed the door of the cabinet.

She waited for me, veiled in yellow-gold candlelight, ceremoniously holding the champagne bottle wrapped in a towel. With no effort at all, she popped the cork, whisked away the towel, and poured fizzy liquid into a pair of tall crystal flutes. "For our eternal sisterhood!"

We drank—glass after glass, toast after toast—slouched on the red velvet sofa, listening to soft music flowing from Almaz's latest acquisition—a Pioneer music system made in America.

"What is it?"

Almaz shrugged. "Some French music, I don't really know. But it touches you, huh?"

Touches? It scraped me from inside, evoking, rather than burying, the memories of my night with Tahir. How he lifted me in his strong, masculine arms and twirled me around the room. How the dark shadows of the Kabul hotel room spun into fireworks of greens, blues, and violets, and our closeness became the only reason for living. How the flames of our hearts spread through our skin, reaching the tips of our fingers and the scarlet threads of our lips. "Forgive me." I whispered through tears what I meant to be *I love you.*

Tahir responded by stroking my eyes with his tongue. Laying me gently on the bed. Taking me in slowly, one brushstroke at a time.

> *Every passing breeze carries the rose fragrance of your breath to me.*
> *Every splendid sunrise reflects the golden glow in your eyes for me.*

Every rustling leaf and every fleeting rain whisper your name
  to me.
My heaven is yours; your sorrow is mine,
I am forever drunk with your love's wine…

Enough!

"Let's dance." I jumped off the couch and pulled a resistant Almaz
to the center of the room, placing her hands on the back of my neck
and wrapping mine around her waist. We shifted in a slow motion
from side to side.

"I need to move out of here. To change my address. To disappear
for a while," she said.

"Why?"

"In July, Chingiz is getting out of jail. He's gonna come after me,
I know it. I asked Bulut to find me another apartment."

"After he spent a fortune on this one?"

"It's a drop in the sea for him, trust me. Which reminds me. I
have to show you something."

Almaz darted to her bathroom and returned with something
sparkling in her hands.

"The Queen of Sheba used to wear it. Made of pure platinum."
She placed a necklace on top of the coffee table—twelve quail-egg-
sized white diamonds framing a pear-shaped blue boulder. "Don't
you love it?"

"So your attaché is a millionaire. He probably paid—"

"Paid? He never paid a dime for it. He never pays for anything.
He's a thief. No doubt in my mind, he stole it from his government's
treasury, leaving half of Turkey destitute."

Almaz put the necklace on and moved the collar of her pajamas
aside, allowing the diamonds to sparkle against her olive skin.

"He gave it to me after that time when his little member, you
know, finally did its little job. *That* little." She laughed, holding her
thumb and index finger an inch apart.

"Don't make fun of the old man."

"The very *filthy* old man, who sweats and grunts like a pig when he tries to do it, you know."

She jumped on top of me and began squealing and puffing and wheezing and squeezing my throat playfully, then rolled off me, laughing. "That's how it goes. And when he gets high on opium, he can be really, *really* nasty and sadistic. What can I say?" She shrugged. "By the way, do you still have that doll I left for you?"

"Almaz the Doll?"

"Yes."

She paused. "Would you mind if I took it back? You know, there's something I always wanted to do. As a tribute to my parents. To have her on exhibit at the Baku Museum of Fine Arts where she used to be."

"How could you do that?"

"Bulut can make it happen. He promised. He and the museum director get drunk and go to the Turkish baths on Tuesdays together."

"It will mean a lot for Aunty Zeinab and Uncle Zohrab."

We lay silent, cuddled by a warm cashmere spread, listening to the violins swirling in the dying candlelight, watching the wax metamorphose into lacy skirts adorning the bronze holders.

"Almaz, I need your help. I'm pregnant," I said.

Pause.

"I told you not to go to Afghanistan."

Did I hear disdain in her tone?

"It's late. I better get going." I dropped my feet to the floor, made an attempt to get up.

"Don't even think about it." Almaz grabbed my hand, pulling me back under the spread, close to her. "I know how you feel, Leila. And I'm sorry. It's no fun."

"Have you ever…"

"Remember that evening I snapped at you, when I was washing your hair before your recital, the time you played Beethoven? That was the first time for me."

"The first time? You mean—"

"Yes, that's exactly what I mean. I was pregnant then. For the first time."

"Why? Why didn't you tell me—"

"Tell you what? That your papa made me pregnant? That I didn't know what to do? That I wanted to kill myself? That I went to Samed Vurgun Park and kept jumping down from the tree—the same tree you and I used to climb and play the Cockle, Cockle Golden Comb game? That I jumped and jumped until it just came out?"

"But maybe if you told me then, we could have done something," I said defensively.

"Something what?"

"We could have stopped Papa and prevented the tragedy—his death, Aunty Zeinab's suicide, everything." I cried out harsher than I intended.

"No one, including you, would have believed me," Almaz replied sadly, wearily. "Besides, I didn't want to hurt Mekhti Rashidovich. Wouldn't you have done the same to protect him?"

I had no answer. All I could think of was that Papa had caused Almaz the same torture I was going through. And that my pain was the punishment for what he had done to her.

"How far along are you?" Almaz asked.

"It's over three months."

"What have you been waiting for?" She shook her head in disbelief.

"I've been on tour."

"Tour? What tour? You're crazy. You should have come to me instead of going on a stupid tour. Now, at this point, there's only one thing left outside of an abortion."

"What is it?"

"Can you stay overnight?" Almaz said, ignoring my question.

"Mama thinks I'm still touring."

"Good. Then get undressed. I'll make a bath for you."

I spent the night in the bathtub in near-boiling water, inhaling the vapors of the vinegar that Almaz kept adding. On top of that, she made me drink a half bottle of vodka with parsley, iodine, and arsenic. The torment resulted in projectile vomiting, a blazing throat, and an excruciating headache.

But no miscarriage.

The next day, as soon as the sun went down, Almaz and I wrapped ourselves in chadors and boarded a tram that took us to Black City.

CHAPTER 30

A Baku I had never seen before unfolded through the dusty window of the tram: deserted streets, broken lights, and decrepit apartment blocks with the leftovers from better times—beautiful ironwork railings on curved balconies and, here and there, colorful stained glass windows.

Black City. An industrial oil district of Baku that used to be a French Gothic quarter built by the oil barons for their overseas workers at the beginning of the twentieth century.

"Our stop." Almaz pulled me to the exit.

We got off and walked alongside the tracks. The smell of black oil, *neft*, was heavy in the air. Dark, slimy puddles spilled across the road.

Then, out of nowhere, a figure emerged through the shadows, head slouched inside his shoulders, eyes bloodshot, a leer on his face. He hobbled toward us on the narrow street unwavering, as though he could pass right through us. We split to make room, but at the last moment, he attempted to grope Almaz's breast.

"*Kiopek oghlu,*" she cursed, pushing him forcefully aside. He stumbled against a wall as Almaz grabbed my hand, and we ran toward an alley at the end of the block—our destination.

"Pay fifteen kopeks if you want to enter." A girl no older than six, with blond curls and small oblique eyes, a strawberry embroidered on her skirt, guarded the gate. Behind her lay a pile of decaying trash with something shifting around inside. Rats?

"Shameless! Leave them alone! Like mother, like daughter."

An old hag, her face a patchwork of hard, dark brown crust, sat on the pavement in the middle of the inner courtyard surrounded by heaps of sheep wool, spinning it skillfully with a long stick. Seeing us, she twisted her toothless mouth in disdain and followed us with a penetrating glare until we disappeared up a staircase. The splintered staircase squeaked beneath our feet, threatening to collapse before we could reach the third floor.

Renata waited by the door. Vasilisa the Beautiful, the heroine of a Russian fairy tale, I thought, looking at the tall woman in her midthirties with flawless, alabaster skin on her round face, her blond hair entwined in a thick braid, a touch of the Siberian steppes in her slightly slanted gray-and-green eyes. She was a Tatar and a midwife who moved to Baku after marrying an oilman. Or so she thought.

As soon as she arrived, she discovered that her "husband" had another family and not the slightest intention of accepting her and their newborn daughter. Trying, to no avail, to get a job as a nurse, she ended up providing "clandestine female services" to her quickly expanding clientele. To my total horror—and yet with some relief—I learned that Almaz had used those services on two occasions.

"You're late. I thought maybe your friend changed her mind." Renata smiled, inviting us inside, then snapping the door shut with two massive locks. "Happy to see you again." She hugged and kissed Almaz on both cheeks. I noticed that one portion of Renata's index finger was gone.

Almaz retrieved a small jewelry box from her purse and handed it to Renata, who opened the box and peered inside, eyes flashing with greed.

"Take good care of my sister," Almaz said, "and do it with opium so she doesn't feel a thing."

I felt ashamed that Almaz was paying for my abortion with her pricey emerald ring, but she had refused to listen to my protests. "I've got diamonds pouring out of my ears," she said, "while you make five rubles per concert."

Renata took my hand and led me into the kitchen. "Don't be afraid," she said, her voice motherly. "We women are like cats. Heal fast. Those *podonki* think they're strong. Ha! I'd like to put one of them through this, to see the scum drooling and shitting and begging for mercy while others watch."

Why was she telling me this? To scare me? Or to strengthen me with her Russian-style tough love?

"Trust me," Renata continued, "men would quickly learn to keep their dirty thing inside their pants instead of waving it around, having fun, and afterward expecting us women to pay. Not a big deal to them. Animals." She spat with repugnance.

The small kitchen had been transformed into a surgery. A seventeenth-century surgery. In the center, a gray towel covered a long table. More gray towels hung on a rope stretched from one wall to another. On the stove, a huge pail of boiling water and a stainless steel bowl for sterilization stood ready. I furtively peeked inside and my heart nearly stopped—what I saw wasn't just syringes and needles but large, scary pincers and pliers resembling medieval instruments of torture.

"They look worse than they are," Renata said lightheartedly, seeing my anxiety. "And if everything goes well, I might not even use most of them, but it's good to have everything just in case."

In case of what? I wanted to ask but didn't dare, shivering uncontrollably, sweat oozing all over my body.

Renata looked out the window and called, "Shushana *Khanum*, would you mind watching Sabina for an hour? I'll pay," then closed the curtains and turned to me. Gone was Vasilisa the Beautiful, the caramel smile replaced by a hard face without a trace of empathy.

"All right. Get on the table, take off that bottom, and pull your dress up. And listen carefully," she said in an indisputable, stern voice. "You don't move, or you get hurt. Hurt badly. And then, it's not just you who suffers but me too. So no matter what—Don't. You. Move."

Why? Petrified, I glanced at Almaz for help, but she just nodded her head.

I climbed on the table and, soaked with shame, brought my skirt up, exposing myself to the intense light of a single bulb hanging from the ceiling, swinging monotonously, dispersing rainbow rings. Renata shaved my pubic hair with a razor, splashing me with ice-cold water as if making sure it hit my body with the force of falling rocks.

From the corners of my eyes I watched Almaz take a small package out of her pocket and carefully empty its contents next to a kerosene lamp on the kitchen counter. Atilbatil seeds? Old women used to burn thirteen atilbatil seeds as a remedy for the evil eye. Picking out thirteen seeds, Almaz wrapped them in a piece of newspaper and gently lowered the package over the lamp flame. The seeds immediately began to crackle.

"*Atilbatilsan havasan.*" She intoned a traditional incantation, walking around the room, spreading the smoke, repeating again and again: "*Atilbatilsan havasan, Atilbatilsan havasan, Atilbatilsan havasan…*"

A familiar fragrance touched my nostrils—sweet and tangy black currant. I inhaled thirstily. Then more. Slowly inviting the dreamy musical nostalgia of the Rach 3 "Adagio."

Oboes played somewhere outside. Tenderly. The notes drifted through the rainbow rings like snowflakes, white and soft, pirouetting in the white air, clustering around me like busy white hens. Spinning an icy web across Aunty Zeinab's Orenburg downy shawl.

"It will keep you warm," Almaz whispered, wrapping the shawl around my body.

The strings began to take over, silencing the oboes, slowly moving their bows through the white snow.

Why so slow? I can't wait anymore. Soon the dusk will break through the window, splashing me with the garnet rings of the falling sun.

"Breathe! Breathe! Don't be lazy!"

I'm not lazy. I'm waiting for my solo. Only four more bars left.

And here it is—I strike the keyboard, my hands in full control of its obstinate, elevated keys. The keys of the Mukhtarovs' clavichord with a shepherd boy and his flock running across its lacquered cover. So that's what this Rach 3 is really about—unrestrained, wild, brazen lovemaking. A spatula instead of a brush. Immediate in place of constant. And no more legato. Just an agonizing staccatissimo of twilight pouring through the window in Maiden Tower's Coronation Hall, splashing, cutting me with its ruby shards of glass.

"Hold her hands tight!"

No! No one can stop the passion of my music that pierces through me like a fire arrow, its flaming tongues licking me from inside, spreading throughout my body, scorching my hands, my eyes.

"Ahhh!" I scream in pain. Let me first finish my cadenza.

"Hold on, Leila. Just keep breathing." Almaz's face hovers over me.

Why is she crying? Did someone just die? And where is the snow? If I can cool down my hands in the snow, then I'll finish the "Adagio."

I reach out for the snow. Instead, a sea is spilling around me, sucking me in, deeper and deeper, into its warm, cozy, gray nothingness.

I awoke in a hollow of darkness, in the grave, soundless serenity of a hospital room, as if the world outside had ceased to exist. Or had just shut the door on me in condemnation.

Mama sat on a chair in the corner, frighteningly fragile, hands pressed against her face, rocking from side to side. Mourning.

Gleams of fluorescent light crept in from under the door like the heads of coiled snakes. Slithering across the floor, they climbed onto my bed, stalking, probing what lay buried beneath the sterilized, iodine-smelling gauze bandages. Was I hallucinating?

I closed my eyes. Back to sleep. Sleep was my only sanctuary.

Almaz had brought me to the hospital in her arms—bleeding and half conscious. Mama couldn't give me an anesthetic, afraid to add more to a heart abused by the concoction of Renata's narcotics, so the pain played freely inside me, its obtrusive arpeggios followed by discordant triads, short pauses, and never-ending, recurring cadenzas.

I welcomed the music of pain. It made me a part of Mama's heart-hacking labor, not just its languorous observer. I felt every motion of her strong, sinewy hands. I followed every tear spilling out of her deeply focused, red-rimmed eyes as she operated on me. By herself. In the seclusion of her surgery. Without nurses and their keen eyes and gossipy tongues. She finished the abortion, removed the infected tissue, then sewed my slashed uterus with her tiniest golden needle so as to avoid a second infection and leave no scars.

But there was nothing she could do to prevent the gossip that spread like gangrene, its symptoms showing up even within our closest, most benign inner circle.

The first time I left the room and limped alone through the corridor, towing my IV, I saw Mama's surgical nurse, Margo, standing by the window, surrounded by a flock of nurses, smoking and discussing something ardently. At the sight of me, they shushed at once.

"Leila, daughter, you're on your feet," called Margo, breaking the tongue-tied silence. "Oh, I'm so glad… You're safe now…and looking healthy and pure like a rosebud…" She stumbled, with her arms stretched out toward me like cactus spines. Then she rushed to me, squeezing in her arms, wailing, "Sweetheart, what a nightmare… what a nightmare had fallen on your tiny, little shoulders and on your poor mama."

The next day, Uncle Kerim, Mama's lifelong friend and a colleague, stopped by the room to check on me. As always, he looked elegant and well groomed, emitting a musky oud cologne scent.

"Hi, şirin qız. My precious girl, how is our little body healing?"

He took my temperature and blood pressure and then perched on the edge of the bed.

"I want you to know," he said, gently patting my hand, "you've always been like a daughter to me. And what's happened will never change that."

He pulled a handkerchief out of his doctor's gown and wiped

the glossy, bald slope in the middle of his head. Winked. "Do you remember our little song? 'Do, Re, Mi'…"

How could I ever forget those cloudless, sun-filled days of my childhood? With Uncle Kerim and his wife, chatty Aunty Sultanat. She baked the best *heyva pirog* in town, and she taught Almaz, her three children, and me how to play the Do, Re, Mi game to keep us busy during Uncle Kerim's endless toasts. She would get us in a circle and dance with us, raising our arms, getting up on tiptoes, singing:

> *Little sparrow sings her song*
> *On the tree, Do, Re, Mi.*
> *Go round, go round,*
> *Do, Re, Mi, you and me.*

Uncle Kerim coughed and cleared his throat. "Your task now is to get back on your feet, and your positive attitude is the key. Don't you worry about anything else… You'll have other children…at the right time… With a nice boy… The wedding… We'll celebrate… With Allah's help… You'll give dear Sonia *Khanum* grandchildren…"

I lay silent, feeling so low. Poor Uncle Kerim. His golden Scheherazade's tongue could usually weave a pathway to the moon. Now he had a hard time putting one word in front of another.

"Thank you, Uncle Kerim." I pulled the gray blanket over my face.

There couldn't have been a worse dishonor than for an unmarried woman in Azerbaijan to get pregnant. And, even worse, to have an abortion. I'd managed to accomplish both.

At least, Communism had abolished the Sharia Law, and I wouldn't be *stoned* like the Saudi Princess Misha'al. She was nineteen like me.

Well, "Long live Communism!" I whispered sardonically.

CHAPTER 31

I came home from the hospital on Saturday afternoon. Soon after, I heard the long vibrato of a doorbell. Loud. Obnoxious.

I opened the door. Fatima the mailwoman. Panting like a red-hot bellows. A white hijab on her head was stained with sweat, more of it running in torrents down her face.

"Here, *qız*," she said in her gruff voice, reaching inside her mailbag, "I thought I better put it in your hands. So the boys from the back alley don't use it for their *həşiş* cigarettes."

Letter from Tahir?

Of course. How could I have ever doubted his love? I waited for Fatima to produce a military postcard with Tahir's scrawled handwriting.

The envelope she retrieved from her bag had an unusual appearance: neither a gray square like the military correspondence from Afghanistan nor the typical white dove of the Soviet mail service. Beige, sprinkled with cacao powder. With stamps and stamps and more stamps in different shapes and configurations and languages, none of them Russian or Azerbaijani. In place of the sender's address: "The London International Piano Competition."

"Thank you, Fatima *Khanum*," I said, rushing inside, surprised that the sting of disappointment failed to deflate the excitement swelling inside me.

"Let it bring solace to your wounded soul, daughter," she

muttered after me. "And remember, Allah always finds a low branch for the bird that cannot fly."

A low branch for the bird that cannot fly? Gossip had obviously been hard at work wagging its tongue around the city. Oh well. One weaves her own carpet to sit on. Mine was filled with holes.

I opened the beige envelope and read the golden letters embossed on thick textured paper:

Dear Ms. Leila Badalbeili,

At the request of Her Royal Highness, Queen Elizabeth II, Lord and Lady Harvey of Ashleigh are honored to cordially invite you to participate in the Queen's First London International Piano Competition on the seventh day of November, year nineteen hundred and eighty-three."

I read the letter again and again to make sure I hadn't misinterpreted the message until every pleasingly curved letter became imprinted in my head. No mistake—I was invited to join the international music elite. No more Siberian workers' concert halls with Lenin at their every corner.

I took a shower, washed my hair with iris water, smoothed it with saffron oil, put on my knitted coat-dress and black heels, and wrapped a shimmering Turkish scarf around my throat, still sore after the abuse of the breathing tube. Then, almost forgetting, I turned back, grabbed the letter from London, and ran out.

I ran into one of those magical days when the autumn sunset is too heavenly to believe. When you get drunk from looking at the wine spilled across the lavender of the sky and you smile at every stranger for no other reason than being alive. Renata was right in one respect—I did heal like a cat, feeling better and stronger than I had been in months.

As I entered the gate of Primorsky Park, I noticed a flock of young men crowding Mulberry Tree Alley, smoking, laughing, and joking coarsely. At the sight of me, their shouts became more intense and their gestures explicit. One of them, a thumb on scrawny legs, ran toward me and threw something. Mulberry juice splashed on my face, and a dark purple stain spread across my white coat.

"Hey, come here, Leila *fahişə*," shouted the thumb in a shrill voice. "I'll pay you five rubles to stick my *sik* in your *halva pişik.*"

Another youth with a flattened shaved head separated from the rest of the crowd and headed toward me, demonstratively unzipping his pants. Now I could see the ringleader, hiding and snickering behind the group, his one-of-a-kind bulbous nose so huge it seemed to push the rest of the features off his face. I recognized him. A son of one of Papa's oil engineers.

I might have felt weakness in my knees, but the rest of me seemed to grow chain mail. I shoved the boy with half-unzipped pants aside. He stumbled against a mulberry tree. Then, like a lioness, I smashed into the crowd, facing the ringleader, screaming, "I'm going to call your father and tell him that you've been spending his money on boys and *hashish*. He'll believe me. And, by the way, do your friends know your nickname?"

The boy's face turned into a ripe tomato, his eyes blinking nervously, begging me to stop. Papa told me that he had a problem as a child—wet his bed into his teens. So his father, appalled at having a son like this, called him *Bələkaği*. Diaper.

I could ruin his life, burn his tough *öndər* reputation into ashes, and scatter them over Caspian Sea. I decided otherwise. I turned around and strutted away to the beat of Beethoven's *Turkish March*. My victory march.

The square in front of the Music Conservatory was empty. The monument of the founder of Azerbaijani opera, Uzeyir Hajibeyov, the white column portico against the yellow stucco of the building—everything looked slightly different. Smaller, less impressive. Or had I changed—grown up—in the three months I'd been away?

The stairs to Professor Sultan-zade's studio on the third floor turned out to be a challenge. I had to stop at each landing to take a breath and calm my syncopating insides. I hated being a woman. How much better if I had been born some genderless creature. How much time and energy would have been saved. But no more. From now on I was eternally wedded to music, my only passion. That was the vow I took on Renata's kitchen table.

I leaned my ear against the door of Professor Sultan-zade's studio. Not a sound. I pushed it gently. Locked. I peeked through the keyhole. Darkness. And disappointment. I wanted so much to share my news with my professor. She had been at my side, unwavering. Neither a question nor a judgment throughout my hospital ordeal. She visited every day, bringing my favorite chocolate, Alenka. She sat with Mama and me, and shared our small talk, which must have been a task for her—Professor Sultan-zade and small talk lived on opposite sides of the Caucasus Mountains.

Then it hit me. Amid all my adventures, I had lost track of the days. Today was Saturday, and that's why the Conservatory, dimly lit with its granite and marble and cold, lethargic air, felt like an Egyptian sarcophagus. I was both frightened and thrilled to have this vast space all to myself. I rushed down to the second floor, each step echoing and multiplying into an orchestral arrangement as if a dozen ghost drummers followed me.

The door to the concert hall was closed but not locked. I hesitantly entered the dark auditorium. The Bechstein grand piano had been moved to the side for an orchestra rehearsal, its dark, polished wood gleaming from a janitor's always-lit backstage light.

I approached the piano, opened the lid, sat on the edge of the bench, took off my shoes, and placed the toes of my feet under the pedals. A quick glance into the dark auditorium, and I shut my eyes. I switched off my mind, leaving nothing but a blank canvas. A canvas waiting to be painted with the ever-changing palette of Rachmaninoff's *Piano Concerto no. 3*.

The dramatic opening of the third movement, "Alla breve." The frothy-mouthed demons of pain, anger, and shame galloped past me amid barren desert wastes and the brown scabs of mountains before disappearing into the black horizon, into the nightmare they had come from. The keys moved my fingers to the highest register of the piano, urging them into an effortless flight—a lyrical theme in G major as sheer as the chiffon wings of Zümrüd Quşu in Tahir's painting.

No, not Zümrüd Quşu. It was me he painted. Those were the wings he had given me. I waved them. Weightless and powerful, they lifted me up into the air, into the infinite ocean of the sky where I could sail freely, carried by the legato winds of the west. A starry portamento of strings drifted by, followed by the stormy gusts of horns and flutes. Then nothing but a soulful, nocturnal chorale. Oblivion painted in greens, blues, and violets. The colors of the flowers Tahir promised to bring me from the mountains.

And the colors of burning flames. Flames inside my heart, spreading throughout my body, reaching the tips of my fingers, striking the keys with a cascade of ferocious passages, splashing and smudging blacks and grays all over the skies. Forcing them to explode with white-hot snow—the apotheosis of Rachmaninoff's *Piano Concerto no. 3.*

The sound of clapping seeped through my heavy breathing. Then footsteps. Someone was coming toward me. Who? The janitor? The night sentry? I strained and squinted but failed to see through the darkness until a figure became clear.

"I didn't mean to scare you. Sonia *Khanum* told me you would be here."

Farhad. Was he here to try his chances with the easy virtue of a fallen woman?

He mounted the stage and approached me without his usual overbearing poise. Even humbly. A rather different Farhad wearing square glasses, dressed in a loose black sweater with a long mohair scarf wrapped around his neck, his hair wavier and longer than I'd ever seen it, giving him an uncharacteristically relaxed flair.

"I'm sor-r-rry if I intr-r-ruded on your pr-practice," he said.

"Oh no. It's all right. I just came here to play."

"I know. I've been listening to you. To your music. It touched me so deeply. You have a gift. A ver-r-ry special gift. And I can't let you r-ruin it."

"What do you mean by ruin it?"

Farhad leaned forward on the side of the piano. I could see the shadow of a new mustache. His eyes were moist. He wiped them—quickly, nervously.

"What I mean is London," he said. "The London Piano Competition in November. You've been invited."

"How? How did you—"

"I work at KGB headquarters, Leila. We monitor everything that goes to and comes from the West. I shouldn't, but I'll disclose classified information. Your Professor Sultan-zade bypassed the official channels and sent a private letter to her contact in London on your behalf. I held that letter in my hands. I was obligated to report to my superior. Instead, I gave it the green light. Your professor has taken a tremendous risk because she cares about you. And so do I."

A spotlight flashed, reflected off the piano, and died out leaving us alone in dark silence.

"We need to talk," Farhad said, "but not here. I told Sonia *Khanum* I'd drive you home."

Drive? Farhad had a car?

A brand-new green Moskvich waited for us outside the Conservatory. Farhad opened the door for me. We drove in silence, Farhad focusing on the road, making wide trajectories in each of his turns. The sign, Papa had once told me, of a new driver.

Outside, the streets seemed deserted, rain-soaked pavements glistening under the full moon, half of it veiled by a cloud. In the dim lunar glow, the Baku Opera House, with its Moorish pistachio-brushed domes and lacy carvings, resembled Scheherazade's tent.

"Are you hungry?" Farhad asked without taking his eyes off the road.

More than just hungry. I felt a breath away from fainting, my vision blurred by curly rings.

We ate at Baku Pearl, an open-air restaurant under a mother-of-pearl, shell-shaped crown, with the sea waves splashing languidly beneath our feet. The night air, crusty and tangible, kept me shivering, but I couldn't stop from devouring one plate after another—first, lamb shashlik, then lula kebab—as if I were trying to stuff myself for a coming famine.

Farhad whispered something to the waiter, a brown-skinned gypsy with a mane of unruly gray hair and a belly falling out of his slacks, and he brought a llama mantle and wrapped it across my shoulders.

"We have to talk, Leila," Farhad said, sadness melting in his eyes. "There is a matter that has come to my attention, and it's critical to your future. I'm talking about the implications of your trip to Afghanistan. The implications of your time...the night you s-s-spent with..."

Farhad faltered, his tongue refusing to pronounce Tahir's name, his index finger fidgeting along the line of his coming mustache.

"A traitor," he finished the sentence. "The implications of your involvement with a traitor, especially in light of the fact that the *person of your interest* has been reported as a deserter. Apparently, he crossed the enemy line and deserted to the American side."

I put my fork on the table quietly, my appetite gone. The last piece had fallen into place. Tahir didn't need me to defect. He had made up his mind long before I arrived in Kabul with my heroic proposition. I would have become an unnecessary burden for him. He desired his freedom much more than he desired me. I hid my face inside llama fur, watching the ribbons of city lights rippling in the mirror of the Caspian Sea sink down to its black bottom. Saying good-bye to the future that was not meant to be.

"Listen, Leila, I blame myself. For letting you make this awful mistake: to fly to Afghanistan, to put yourself in harm's way. And then to go through all the pain and humiliation you've been through since you returned."

Farhad reached out and took my cold hands in his, bringing them close to his lips, blowing gently to warm them. "You're naive like all artists. You're like a butterfly that flies close to a flame and gets her wings burned."

Hollow inside, stripped of my last illusion, I was losing myself in Farhad's words.

"Leila. My beloved Leila." Farhad's eyes glistened with tears from behind his fogged spectacles. "Life means nothing to me without you. Please allow me to be your protector. Allow me to love and cherish you. Leila, *ey vəfədarim*, my love! Be my lodestar. Be my bride."

CHAPTER 32

*The wedding caravan brought Princess Alsu to her groom's tent, where
he filled the palms of her hands with white lilies. In the morning, when
Princess Alsu opened her eyes, tears dropped from the lilies' petals, their
barren stems binding her wrists together.*

I struggled to breathe, gulping air in rapid staccatissimos. I was a
dummy laced up into a triangular corset, stuffed inside a mound of
white brocade and satin, my fingers and toes henna-dyed, my nails
blood red. The wedding veil covered my face and kept my feelings
out of sight, assuming there were any feelings left after I'd taken
Almaz's *elixir of oblivion*—a shot of opium with cognac—to numb
my heartache.

The squad of waiters in red *çuxa*, traditional coats, and balloon-
like trousers moved around in slow motion, carrying trays with
caviar and champagne. The hundred or more guests congregated
between the gilded columns of the Art Nouveau wedding chamber, sneaking furtive glances at their reflections in the cobalt-
mirrored ceiling.

The crowd consisted of two distinct groups. One was the
upper echelon of Baku society all in black silks, furs, and taffetas,
emitting the surreptitious scents of oud oil and jasmine, women
sparkling with their diamonds, rubies, sapphires, and emeralds.
Richard Strauss's crowd. Elegant, affluent, melodious like his *Der
Rosenkavalier* waltzes.

The other group—Farhad's relatives—loud, speaking with their hands, resembled an Azeri folklore ensemble preparing to perform a traditional wedding scene. I had to admit that Farhad had done an admirable job of disassociating himself from his flock. Fit and composed, wearing a jet-black tuxedo, he bore no likeness to his relations. Strutting around in gaudy polyesters and gold chains and stones too hefty to be precious, they trailed the tails of their multi-layered skirts, practically blending with the vibrant peasant images depicted on the wall murals.

Nevertheless, those people seemed to have brought with them the crystal air of humbling mountain summits and rapidly flowing rivers from their faraway village in the Caucasus Mountains—something so natural and feral it made me feel ashamed for marrying someone I didn't love.

At first, Farhad didn't want to invite his family. He hadn't been in touch with them in years. But his boss insisted. Apparently, his and Farhad's maternal ancestors came from the same area in the neighboring Republic of Dagestan. So Farhad invited his immediate family—his parents and three sisters—but the entire *aul* had shown up.

"One with a plow—seven with spoons," whispered Professor Sultan-zade to me as she passed by, slightly squeezing my forearm in silent consolation. She liked Farhad as much as she liked Richard Wagner. Once asked why she didn't attend a premier of his *Die Walküre* at the Baku opera house, she replied, "Why would I submit voluntarily to that fascist's torture?"

"Let me see the bride's face." One of Farhad's aunts unceremoniously lifted my veil. "Oh, she's *gözəl*," she intoned. "Our Farhadik *jan* brought a rose to our garden. A *halva* face."

"*Halva* makes the mouth sweet, but we'll see if it fills up our stomach," Farhad's mother replied.

She was an Amazon woman—tall and physical, with a healthy glow to her face, two thick black braids reaching to her waist, and catlike gray eyes—looking as young as if she had given birth to

Farhad while still in her early teens. Her husband looked more like her father. In his sixties, gaunt, with the dark, parched skin of a highlander and the same pitch-black eyes as Farhad, he seemed lost inside his suit. Chronic tuberculosis had been wasting his body away.

Finally, Farhad's boss, KGB General Tamerlan Jabrailov, arrived and made his way through the crowd—a handsome, personable man in his midforties with light skin, short-cut black hair, an aquiline nose, and the same hypnotic gray eyes that Farhad's mother had—a hereditary mark of people from the North Caucasus region of Dagestan. He wore a linen suit and a bright yellow necktie. He made me think of Papa, who had never yielded his eccentricity to the etiquette of dressing.

General Jabrailov approached us.

"*Salam eleykum.*" A brisk handshake with Farhad.

"Welcome to the family, Leila." He gave me a close, scrutinizing look through his glasses—identical to Farhad's. "I've heard a lot about you, but even the best of praises didn't make a fair judgment of your charms. You're a beautiful and inspiring young woman, and Farhad must be overjoyed to have you as his bride."

The ceremony started.

A middle-aged woman in a formal dark suit came in from the side door, thick kohl making her eyes pop out of her face. A dragonfly. Proceeding to the center of the room, her stilettos drum-beating the floor, she took her place at a table underneath the flag of Soviet Azerbaijan.

She'd make a good warden in the gulag, I thought to myself as she droned through the official marital lines in her book. "...Upon taking the responsibility of creating a new family unit to carry on and safeguard the principles of Communist ideology and morals..."

I glanced at Mama standing among the Richard Strauss crowd. Stylish as always in a black silk suit with a thread of black pearls, her strawberry-and-cream face pale, wearing a polite smile, her eyes seeking mine.

The warden reached the end of the official marital manual

and slammed the book closed. Spreading her stilettos wide, she took a breath, deep enough to support a coloratura note, and barked: "Under the flag! Of the Soviet! Republic! Of Azerbaijan! I. Announce. You. Leila. Badalbeili. And. You. Farhad. Abdul. Azizov. Husband! And! Wife!"

The party lasted into the night with endless toasts, lots of drinking, and two orchestras trading places. One played dance music; the other—a trio of *kemancha*, *tār*, and *dumbek*—accompanied a young *muğam* singer. Blind, his body swaying like a blade of grass, he sang a poetic ghazel, every line a stab to my heart.

> *Beloved, you lifted my soul to heaven, then plunged me into despair.*
> *My life is an infinite nightmare, but I can't stop longing for you.*
> *You treated me like a scented rose, then plucked me and threw away—*
> *A caught, unwanted prey, but I can't stop longing for you.*
> *Did her beauty blind your eyes? Did you take her to your skies?*
> *Oh, your cruel heart of lies, but I can't stop longing for you.*
> *Where are you, my sun-faced lover? Come back. Take pity on me.*
> *Without you, I'm dying in misery, but I can't stop longing for you…*

What? What had I done, Tahir? Why did you leave me here to suffer, to sell myself? To live like a serpent inside a closed bag, pretending, lying, waiting to coil my way out?

At midnight, Mama kissed me a sad good night. In accordance with the custom imposed by Farhad's kin, I wouldn't see her until we returned from our honeymoon. Then Farhad's mother, sisters, and a dozen of his female relatives led me to the bridal hotel suite overlaid with red roses, red symbolizing the blood of a sacrificed lamb—another custom. At least they didn't insist on slaying an animal here. Or maybe my sacrifice was enough.

Someone put a little boy in my lap—an Azeri ritual meant to help me deliver a male as my first child.

"Be with son," said one of the women.

"Be with son," sang along all others.

Mehriban, Farhad's youngest sister, patted my hair with rose water.

"Abundance and male heir." Farhad's mother placed a mirror with red ribbons in front of my face. An old woman in a ruby-studded kaftan sprinkled the mirror with donkey milk, chanting, "With Allah's help… With Allah's help…"

Pouring rice, silver coins, and sweets over my head and shouting the traditional "Aparmaga Gelmishiq" song, the women undressed and laid me under the blanket.

"Let the night last as long as the spring, and the pain pass as quickly as a flower blossom," they sang, kissing each other, sweeping their arms in wide circular motions, undulating their waists, dancing their way out of the bridal suite. Leaving me all prepared and garnished for Farhad.

My mother-in-law kissed me on the forehead and followed after them, closing the door behind her.

The women would spend the night in the lobby, waiting for the bloody sheet to sanctify the marriage and parade it in their village as a proof of my virtue.

Farhad arrived shortly thereafter, drunk. He sat on the bed, glowering at me. "Do you think I didn't see how you were looking at my family? With disdain. Why? Because they're not up to your *noble* blood?"

Reaching out to touch me, he abruptly pulled back, squeezed his hands into fists, shook his head, and stumbled to the window.

"I've been treating you as if you were a virtuous bride. I haven't touched you, waited for the wedding night. Sacrificed my pride for you. No one would dare to tell me this to my face, but I know what they're saying behind my back—that I've married a whore. Everyone knows that you've given yourself to that *pox yiyən*."

I pulled the blanket over my eyes, hiding from Farhad's swearing.

"What did he do to you? Huh? Tell me. How did he *atdirmaq* you?"

He threw the blanket out of the way and lowered himself over me, his body moving closer and closer, his knee forcefully spreading my legs. Then, suddenly, he stopped, grabbed my hair and twisted, watching me intensely, enjoying my pain. A jackal playing with its kill.

"Farhad, please stop it. It's in the past. I'm your wife now."

"Wife? No. You're my whore." He laughed drunkenly, breathing into my face. "My defiled whore…the thrown-away leftover of the Mukhtarov bastard."

"No, Farhad. Please."

"Please what? What do you want me to do, Leila? Tell me. Tell me nicely. I know you can be nice. Show me how nice you can be. Show me."

Did I have a choice?

I closed my eyes and dove into the stench of tobacco and alcohol. Into the swamp of stale sweat, seething lust, and the insatiable Napoleonic ego of a shepherd's son and a KGB rising star. Falling down and down. Down a rabbit hole of young male with wounded pride.

"Say you love me, Leila."

His eyes against mine, reflecting my shame in their black darkness.

"I love you, Farhad."

"Say it again."

"I love you."

"Again."

"I love you."

He fell asleep, still on top of me, a contented smile on his face.

I carefully got out of bed and went to the bathroom. My whole body felt raw and achy. Filling the tub with scalding hot water, I climbed inside, gulped the last vial of Almaz's *yatiştirici*, and lay back in the bath, slowly running my fingers through the water. The flow seemed natural, musical, blurring my bruises into a chromatic, Impressionistic palette of colors.

If Sergei Rachmaninoff could practice his *Concerto* on a silent keyboard, why couldn't I do it on the water? I drew the staccato arpeggio, my fingers moving fluidly, buoyed by the heat of the water. Then I gently submerged my hands, sustaining the chord in all its depth and sheerness. A pause—Vladimir Horowitz's pause— lightening the darkness with just a stroke of air.

I could breathe. My music surged with the new vitality, fueled by rage, the lightning tempos breaking through the clouds, scaring off the ghosts of the night. Windy passages lifted me off my fetters, driving me across the sky to a far, faraway island adrift in a sun-drenched turquoise sea.

I slept for a while in the safe music cocoon. Then back to reality, I cut the side of my leg with a razor and rubbed the bleeding incision against the sheet. My gift to Farhad.

In the morning, we left for our honeymoon at a resort on the Black Sea, a special resort reserved for the KGB elite. By the time we returned, Mama was gone. She had been appointed the director of a large children's hospital in Kuba—a provincial town 170 kilometers to the north of Baku—and given a splendid residence there.

Farhad moved into our flat in Villa Anneliese.

I hadn't seen Almaz since before my wedding, over a month ago. I knew Farhad wouldn't approve of my continuing friendship with her. On Monday afternoon, knowing that he would be staying at work into the evening, I called and told Almaz I'd stop by for some quick tea.

A few minutes later, the phone rang.

"I forbid you to see her," Farhad said in a hostile low voice. "You hear me?"

"Yes."

"That's it." The phone went dead, leaving me petrified.

At supper, Farhad acted as if nothing had happened. He cooked a delicious *shirin-pilau*—fruit stewed with sugar on top of rice—and served it on a tea table in Papa's smoking room, then sat on Papa's favorite lion chair, perched his feet on the lions' paws, and poured himself some sweet Georgian wine.

"To you, my love." He raised Papa's silver goblet. Emptied it.

I knew it was Farhad's call for me to pay attention to the lesson that would follow.

"Do you know why I love you so much?" Farhad began, wiping his mouth with a napkin. "You're irresistibly beautiful, gifted, artistic, and you're naive as a child. You're floating in your own sky, with the rest of the world contained inside the pages of your Rachmaninoff's *Concerto*. But even with all this, I didn't expect you to be *that* stupid."

Farhad poured himself more wine. Deliberately slowly, as if enjoying my anxiety.

"You embarrassed me today, Leila," he continued. "I had to be called from a meeting to deal with this situation—my wife and a whore spending time together. Didn't it ever occur to you that by marrying me you'd left your past behind and started living as a reputable woman and the wife of a KGB officer? That your running around with the filth of our society was over? Or is it some psychological need of yours to mesh with them?"

Farhad stared at me intently. "You're probably wondering how I knew about your behavior. Yes? Well, your girlfriend's been on the KGB list for the last two years, doing some work for us."

What? Almaz working for the KGB? No way. Farhad was toying with me. But then how else could he have known within a few minutes that I had spoken with Almaz?

Farhad chuckled. "Did you really expect that a girl, even one as worthless as Almaz, would be allowed to publicly parade around the city with foreigners in their fancy cars? Without experiencing any consequences? Of course not. She'd be marching at four in the morning to a farm field in some penal colony in Kazakhstan if we didn't put her talent to useful work."

"What talent?"

"Her between-the-legs talent." Farhad laughed. "Listen, sweetheart, that's what the KGB does—recognizes the talent in people and employs it for the good of our country. Your talent is in your musical hands; my talent is in my analytical ability to detect people's vulnerability. Why is my talent imperative? Because human vulnerability is the strongest weapon of control in the hands of the KGB. I shouldn't be telling you this, but one in eighteen Soviet adults are official KGB informers. The only ones we don't care about are talentless nothings who can do neither harm nor good."

Farhad grinned. "My boss once told me an anecdote. 'What will happen to the KGB when the Soviet Union reaches its full Communist phase?'"

Pause.

"Are you asking me?" I said.

"Yes."

"I don't know."

"It'll go out of business. Because people will be arresting each other." He burst into laughter.

I sat, unable to hold back my tears anymore. Did Almaz report my call to her? But why? It didn't make sense.

I got up to clear the dishes, but Farhad reached out, pulled me close, and pushed me into his lap.

"I don't like when you're sad, baby. And I didn't mean to hurt you. Not at all. I love you." He kissed behind my ear and whispered, "Almaz didn't betray you. No. It wasn't even necessary. You see, her apartment is bugged, and when a call came to her from the phone listed under my name, a friend of mine in the wire-tapping department next door informed me. That's how I found out."

"Then why didn't she ever tell me about working for the KGB?"

He gasped. "You're something else. Haven't you heard what I've been telling you for the last half hour? No one is to be trusted. Almaz is probably afraid that if she tells you, and you tell me, then

I'll report her for revealing confidential information and off she'd go to serve a six- to eight-year sentence for prostitution."

"Do you trust me?" I asked, out of curiosity.

"I did once. Four years ago. And I gave you the chance to prove yourself trustworthy. A chance that you failed."

"And you punished me by putting through the condemnation hearing and then appearing like my knight in shining armor to save me."

"Leila, I *am* your knight in shining armor, if you haven't figured it out yet. If not for being my wife, with your dossier, you'd now be playing piano somewhere in Far East Siberia, not preparing for the London International Piano Competition."

Farhad tightened his arms around my waist, pulling me closer. "You should be proud of your husband. I'm the youngest associate in the field of psychological domination, trained in ideological subvergence."

"Subvergence? What is that?"

"The science of altering the thinking and behavior of individuals, as well as the entire population. We don't use guns here. Instead"—he retrieved a small, square foil package with pills, broke the foil, and showed me a tiny aluminum cylinder—"this is the primal cutting-edge weapon. Works better than any gun." He put his index finger to his lips and winked. "But I didn't tell you that."

CHAPTER 33

On the morning of October 23, 1983, three weeks before the London International Piano Competition, General Tamerlan Jabrailov invited Farhad and me to his office.

He sat across the desk from us in his deep-buttoned leather chair. Behind him, dressed in a traditional Russian linen *rubakha*, Vladimir Lenin smiled at me from an oil painting encased in a gilded frame. Another Lenin—this one in formal coat and tie—surveyed me suspiciously from a black-and-white photograph standing on the General's ebony desk, alongside a wooden bust of Comrade Andropov—General Jabrailov's mentor.

Thick damask draped over two casement windows kept the room dark. The only source of light was a small dormer window with a white lace curtain fluttering in the wind, dispersing jaunty patterns of sunshine throughout the otherwise austere office of the head of Department A—the code title of the Department of Psychological Warfare of the Azerbaijani KGB.

The General, like Farhad, was a self-made man with a humble upbringing who had graduated from Moscow State University with a degree in ancient African civilizations. Later, he added a doctorate in psychology and a general's rank in the KGB, presented to him by Comrade Andropov himself.

"I hate these yearly reports. Damn waste of my valuable time." The General slammed the book closed and hurled his pen across the desk in frustration. Farhad leaped out of his chair and, with perfect timing, caught the pen in midair, ink splattering across his hand onto the edge of his starched white cuff, protecting the expensive leather inlay on the desk.

"That's why I keep him around. Always on the alert." The General winked at me and picked up a phone. "Olga, come here and get the files."

A young woman in a tight floral dress with long, blond hair and blue eyes glided over to his desk.

"Sweetheart, make sure everything is typed and labeled by ten tomorrow, will you?" The General smiled slyly.

"I'll work until midnight if I have to, Rafig Nazimovich," Olga replied, her voice unexpectedly low and husky, her false eyelashes flapping flirtatiously.

The General nodded, his eyes glued to Olga's back, reflecting every swing of her hips as she danced her way across the office and out the door.

"I need to talk to you, Leila darling." The General clasped his hands together on top of his desk. "It's a matter of our future. Our country's future. And for that reason, I'm going to let you in a bit on what your husband and I are doing here. Contrary to what everyone thinks of the KGB, only a small segment of our work focuses on espionage. James Bond is pure Hollywood whimsy, which, as a matter of fact, I'm a big fan of.

"But what we're really doing here is building the future of civilization, bringing the Western world to the cataclysmic point at which a Marxist insurrection can finally commence. And, thanks to Comrade Andropov, who's leading us forward and out of the Brezhnev era of stagnation, changing the old, rusty, bent rails under the fast-moving train of Communism before it falls off the track, we work on the ideological *subversion* of the West. Do you know what that is?"

I shook my head.

"I'll explain." General Jabrailov grinned boyishly, his gray eyes shining. "We're in the business of mind control, Leila. We are the champions of social conditioning. The moral corruption of the West—their counterculture of the 1960s with its sex revolution, drugs, rock 'n' roll, feminism—has been the work of our unnamed heroes. Over the past twenty-five years they have been demoralizing Western society, preparing it for the next phase of our psychological warfare—the destabilization and indoctrination of young Western generations with the ideals of Marxism–Leninism."

The General took a pencil and tapped it on the desk, shaking his head. "Unfortunately, the corruption of the West backfired. Our country is flooded with their Western music, their decadent ideals, their damned youth culture. I can't stop my own son from listening to their Beatles or buying their cowboy jeans on the black market.

"That's why we need to create our own stars—*sex symbols*—to attract the young generation. As you know, socially, our Bolshevik fathers 'eradicated' sex by substituting both male and female gender with a single hybrid label called 'comrade.' And the sex symbol cultivated by the KGB-controlled Novosti news agency for the last fifty years has been the same broad-shouldered, mannish milkwoman, whose breasts are decked with so many shining orders and medals that she looks as if struck by lightning."

The General laughed at his own joke.

"But it doesn't work anymore. We have to give our youth a new image. You know, Leila, what image I see? Marilyn Monroe. In her explicit gown. Walking across the stage into the spotlight, luscious as a peach, sparkling like a jewel, singing"—General Jabrailov closed his eyes and crooned in a low voice—"happy birthday, Mr. President..." He smirked. "Who can withstand the temptation? No one. And I'll tell you this—I saw you performing for that old buffoon Mark Slavkin, when you switched from Khrennikov to 'Body and Soul.' That's when I knew that you were the one."

General Jabrailov leaned against the back of his chair, stretching out his long limbs. "I see you, Leila, winning the London competition, playing for Ronald Reagan, for that bitch Thatcher, making the West fall in love with you, and becoming a spokesperson for our young Soviet generations. Someone they can look up to as their role model—for the girls wanting to be like you, for the boys wanting to be with you." He winked. "You'll be our own sex symbol—beautiful, intelligent, and internationally recognized. Well, not only do you combine all those qualities, but you're also one of us."

"But, Comrade Jabrailov." Farhad sprang out of his chair and leaned over the desk, his hands nervously rubbing its edges. "I can't allow it. Leila is not like some shameless *model*. She is a married woman. She is my wife—"

"Sit!" the General said in a low voice.

Farhad fell back into the chair and lowered his head, a flood of burgundy spreading across his face. I could only imagine what was going through his mind. To start with, he hated my success. Despised my music career. All he wanted was to lock the door of my golden cage, to keep me to himself and perpetually pregnant, but thanks to midwife Renata's deficient skills—or perhaps to sheer providence—I had been pronounced barren. And now more help was coming from this most unexpected source.

"Who do you think you are?" The General propped his body forward over the desk, staring at Farhad, an angry eagle eyeing his prey. "What do you think you are? Zeus? You think you can throw lightning? No. You have a long way to go before you can even light a small fire. So sit quietly, bite your tongue, and listen with your big ears. Do you realize the responsibility you have to the whole country? Your wife is a national treasure. And how do you treat her?"

A week earlier, for Farhad's twenty-third birthday, we had a party in the courtyard of Villa Anneliese. At one point, the General noticed me washing dishes and ordered me out of the kitchen. Later, Professor Sultan-zade, sitting at the table next to him, took the opportunity to complain that I had missed an orchestral rehearsal over the weekend. Why? Because Farhad, in a jealous fit, had locked me in the flat and gone to a KGB retreat.

"What do you say about all this, Leila?" the General asked, holding my entire being with mesmerizing power of his eyes.

By now, I had become well acquainted with KGB games. Like Johann Sebastian Bach's most elaborate fugues, they had layers and layers of counterpointed messages and traps. I had to think fast. The first thing to consider: the General had been grooming Farhad as his future successor. Second, and probably most important: the General had made up his mind about me as a sex symbol a long time ago.

"I love my husband with all my heart," I said earnestly, reaching out and touching Farhad's hand, "and as much, or even more, I love my country. With all my heart. And I will do whatever it takes to be—and to continue to be—her loyal daughter."

The General grinned, pleased, then narrowed his eyes and stuck his finger in my face playfully. "Go practice your piano and win that London competition. Don't let me down, Leila. You hear me? Don't. Let. Me. Down. I've got everything in place—no money spared and all our overseas manpower available—to put you on the covers of their *Vogues*. I've even pushed our Hollywood contacts to get you into the right circles. So. You must deliver the win. Period!"

He got up. "You can go now. Your husband and I have work to do. And by the way"—he hesitated—"not my business of course, but you two are like my own children so…" Pause. "No sexual intercourse before the competition. You know, in case Leila gets pregnant and doesn't perform at her full capacity. Anyway, that's my order!"

As Farhad and the General returned to work, I galloped down the grand marble stairway, out of the KGB headquarters, and into purifying, early autumn air spiced by a light rain. Little rainbows chased each other, and the sun sprinkled its gold stars on a blue polyphony of waves. I sat on a bench to gather my thoughts, shielded from the drizzle by the mane of a chestnut tree. A few droplets snuck through and landed on my head. If I could only shake my shackles off as easily as the rain from my hair.

I had three weeks left before the London competition. And the General had made it clear it wasn't about just music anymore. I had to win. Just like in the old *kalam*—"A winner sits at the lion's table; a loser sits on the lion's plate."

CHAPTER 34

"Come in, Leila."

Professor Sultan-zade opened the door, took my coat, hung it on a rack, and led the way to her living room. Recently, we'd had a few of our piano lessons at her apartment, followed by tea and conversation. These special times had become my escape from my own home, which had turned into a reformatory.

"Take a seat." Professor Sultan-zade pointed at a settee by the electric radiator. "Still no heat in the building. I'm freezing. Can't even bend my fingers. Would you like a shawl?"

"No, thank you. I'm not cold. Not at all."

It was quite stifling in her apartment. Maybe she had a fever?

"Would you like some tea?"

"If you don't mind, I'll make it myself. For both of us. May I?"

"Be my host."

I stepped inside the kitchen. Always tidy. Gzhel china behind the glass doors of the cabinet; silver trays and pitchers on a side table; a vase on a windowsill holding a single tea rose. I turned on the stove, boiled water, brewed tea, added coriander and honey, and carried the tray to the living room.

Professor Sultan-zade reclined on the settee, her head back, eyes closed. The crow's-feet spread from the corners of her eyes all the way down to the smoker's lines around her mouth. The bronze tint of her skin looked tarnished. A few strands of silver spilled out of her beehive. She no longer looked like Nefertiti. I placed the tray on the floor, poured tea in her *armud*, added three sugar cubes, and mixed it.

"I should probably take it easy on the sugar," Professor Sultanzade said. "I was seven when my mama had both legs amputated because of diabetes. And in my current condition I have to be cautious. It's not just about me anymore."

Current condition? I glanced at Professor Sultan-zade. Her long fingers flew to her eyes, concealing tears. Her lips trembled, trying to hold back sobs.

Unsuccessfully.

"I'm pregnant. Almost four months pregnant. How could I have been so stupid? I didn't even realize it until last week. I thought I was finished as a woman. And here I am. Pregnant with that double-faced, lying *donuz*'s baby."

"Double-faced? Lying?"

"This monster, this careerist Najafov, got engaged last week. In secret from me. Do you know to whom?" she asked, seeing my face.

"No."

"To the widowed daughter of the Third Secretary of the Party. She's twenty-five with two children. She's her father's darling. And she's my death sentence. Can you imagine what a scandal it's going to be when they learn that I'm pregnant with his child?"

I shook my head.

"They'll cut me out like a cancerous growth. They'll force my resignation from the Conservatory, the place I've built into one of the finest institutions in the country. That's it. How could I have been so stupid as to not see him for who he was—a liar and imposter? He needed me at the beginning of his appointment as a rector. He was nothing then. Nothing but a peasant *kemancha* player with a hundred-word vocabulary.

"That was the only reason they appointed him. A benign figurehead to temporarily fill the chair. And to stay, the weasel needed my unconditional support. He acquired it by playing a game no man

312

can ever lose. He used me, chewed me up, and spat me out like a rotten fig. Now, I'll be dragging my swollen legs across the corridors of the Conservatory, and the monster and his prized bride will be moving into a government building right across the street."

Professor Sultan-zade breathed rapidly, choking on her hurt. I nestled next to her and put my arm around her shoulders. If not for her daring endeavor, I wouldn't be going to London. She had risked everything to help me when I was at the lowest point in my life. Now it was my turn.

"Enough. Waste of time." She rose to her feet. "I've been thinking. It's not the first movement's ossia or the buildup to the toccata climax in the third movement that worries me. You've got enough technique to play them in your sleep. It's the opening theme that haunted me throughout the night. I don't think we've given it enough attention."

In her wide steps, she strutted to the piano, opened the cover, and lowered herself onto the bench. "Listen," she said, playing the first theme of the "Allegro ma non tanto," sharing single-note octaves between her hands, drawing clear-as-glass lines. "The melody here is so bare, so exposed, with nothing to work with, nowhere to hide. Imagine a lone birch tree in the middle of a snowy valley bathed in the moonlight. This is the mood of intimacy you need to establish, to draw yourself and the audience into the turbulent, unpredictable inevitability of what is to come."

A tear snaked down Professor Sultan-zade's cheek, leaving behind a black mascara trail.

I left Professor Sultan-zade and strolled down the street, aimless. The rain intensified. The stakes had risen. I had to win the competition at any price. For my professor—to give her the incentive to fight her enemies. For myself—to avoid burning in the hell of General Jabrailov's wrath. How could I take the pressure? I looked skyward.

No help there. The heavy, cloud-infested sky echoed the requiem of my soul.

I needed Almaz's opium. Ignoring Farhad's order not to see her, I headed to her place.

Almaz wasn't home. I waited, scouting around her new building, admiring the green cupola on top of its slick, glass-and-concrete carcass. Thinking. After all, we both hadn't sold ourselves *that* badly. With the KGB's blessings, Almaz's Turkish attaché had moved her to the most prestigious address in town and placed Almaz the Doll in the exhibition hall of the Baku Museum of Arts. And I had just been promoted to the role of the KGB's new "sex symbol." I spat on the ground and headed toward Taza Bazaar.

I hadn't been there in years, but it looked the same—scruffy, smelly, noisy antiquity, its usual cast of characters in place. A hairy midget juggled tomatoes, slicing them in midair with his bejeweled dagger. An old woman with the face of a Caspian tiger stuck a bunch of her greens to my nose. Turkish triplets in chadors sitting cross-legged on the ground guarded their burlap bags with nuts. The Rose Garden Fairy in a rabbit-fur vest hassled passersby: "Sunny day, with Allah's help. Don't you want to try my *halva*? My *halva* will melt in your mouth like rose sherbet. If you don't like my *halva*, taste my *pakhlava*. It will take you to Allah's rose garden."

I swept through the rest of the Bazaar like a sandstorm—past Tea Alley with the young man with his filthy stare, guarding a tea shop; past Fish Row with its deathbeds for belugas and sevrugas. Until I reached my destination: Beggars Corner, where Almaz had told me she bought her opium from an invalid nicknamed Genghis Khan.

I identified him right away. A hulking shaved head as if axed from the trunk of a tree, slanted Mongoloid eyes perched at the temples of his flat face, his torso hunkered down on a wooden cart with the wheels of roller skates. A brick on each side with which he pushed the cart against the ground. A sailor's hat full of coins in front of him.

"I'm a friend of Almaz," I whispered, bending over him.

"A friend of Almaz *Khanum* is my friend too." He raised his eyes at me. "How much?"

I held out ten rubles. "Is that enough?"

He grinned, baring his blue gums with a few rotten teeth, then retrieved a small package out of the breast pocket of his soiled military shirt. "My *tiryak* is smooth. All the way from the Khizi Mountains. Send my regards to honorable Almaz *Khanum*."

Clutching the package in my hand, holding my breath to avoid the revolting odors, I darted through the island of human misery toward the exit.

And there, as I reached the rusty exit gate of Beggars Corner, I saw Tahir.

Not the Tahir I kept seeing in my dreams: handsome and free with hair swinging in the wind, crossing St. Mark's Square in Venice, posing in front of the Eiffel Tower in Paris, sunbathing in Central Park to the sounds of Dave Brubeck's "Take Five." Oh, how I hated that Tahir, cursed him every time I woke up inside those dreams.

No, the Tahir I saw crouching next to a box with rotten oranges had nothing to do either with my dreams or with the Tahir I once knew, the boy who was ingenious and stubbornly unbeatable, cruising through a haze of *hashish* into skies of creative illusions and artistic breakthroughs.

I wanted to be wrong. I prayed that I was terribly wrong. That this comatose, hopelessly lost stranger couldn't possibly be Tahir. Couldn't be. Of course not. How could he? *My* Tahir had defected to the West long ago. He had been living in his America or somewhere else he always wanted to be, enjoying his freedom, his art, not even remembering my name.

But it *was* him. Inside that awful tattered clothing. Behind the wild shrubbery of his face. The same unmistakable eyes, intelligent and deep.

"Tahir," I called softly.

No response. And not a sign of recognition.

"Tahir, it's me. It's me, Leila."

I came closer and carefully patted his shoulder. My touch had the effect of a key turning on a wind-up toy. Tahir began to shake his head, rapidly muttering something incoherent. Then he gradually slowed down and returned to his detached stillness.

"Lover boy is high up." A crippled drunkard hobbled toward me, waving his crutch dangerously close to my face. "But I'm here. And I can do you better with one leg than this homo with no balls." His filthy laughter ignited the crowd. Other invalids oozed out of the cracks in Beggars Corner, flowing toward me from every direction.

"Tahir!" I shouted in desperation. "Just look at me! Please! Don't you recognize me? What have they done to you? What have they done?"

I reached to grasp his arm. Instead, I felt a hollow, empty sleeve. Where was his arm? I pulled my hand away in horror. Could he have hidden it somewhere under his shirt? I froze, my eyes searching, desperate to find Tahir's missing right arm.

"*Rəhmi*... Take pity on a veteran of two wars... Money... Bread... Allah... *Yaziqliq*..."

The sea of misery was closing in, the inhabitants of Beggars Corner almost upon me. Showcasing their stitched stumps and blistered skin, their festering lesions and empty sockets. Begging, cursing, confiding their wretched histories.

I pushed my way out of the circle, jabbing my elbows, shoving the horde aside. And I ran. Ran, out of the rusty iron gates of the Taza Bazaar. Ran, afraid to look back, as if the earth behind me might swallow me up. I could never have imagined this nightmare—a nightmare in which I played the two leading parts—villain and victim.

Suddenly I stopped. I knew what I was running from. But where was I running to? To the golden cage of Gargoyle Castle, with Farhad as my warden? To the win at the London competition so the KGB could parade me as their trophy?

Above, a caravan of clouds passed, veiling and unveiling the moon, her face luminous against the starless sky. Caravaggio's tenebrism—intensified lucidity of light against obscurity of darkness. Darkness held Tahir prisoner. Why? How did he end up there?

It didn't matter. He was there—beaten, maimed, and despondent. *My* Tahir. He needed me. But even more, I needed him. Because since I had lost him, I had lost myself, wandering the dark alleys of my destiny—my own Beggars Corner—clinging to my music as the only road sign. But even music could no longer give asylum to my homeless heart.

I turned back. I knew exactly what I had to do.

At about eight o'clock, one of the Taza Bazaar's guards, a brawny Russian woman in a rubber apron, lamb's wool vest, and tarpaulin boots, marched to Beggars Corner.

"All right, comrades *invalidiki*," she shouted, waving a massive key chain that could easily have knocked someone unconscious. "Take your crud and be gone, or I'll call the *militzia*. And if I see someone shat here—and I better not see it—I will kill with my own two fists."

As if responding to a military command, the inhabitants of Beggars Corner lined up along the fence. A well-nourished, animated man with a rumpled black beard came out of the alley, planting every step of his wooden leg in a wide sweep. A *vozhak*. One after another, the beggars handed him money. When Tahir's turn came, the *vozhak* unceremoniously tapped his hands all over his body, didn't find anything, spat on the ground, and pushed Tahir away. All the cache collected, the *vozhak* gestured to the guard with a smile, retrieved a stack of banknotes from his trousers, spat on his thumb, counted a few, and passed them to her. She hastily stuck the money under her apron.

"Good night with God's help," she hollered. "Good peaceful

night to you, poor souls. God is kind to those who sacrificed for Motherland." She waited patiently as the beggars shuffled out of the Bazaar, even helping Genghis Khan by pushing his cart with the toe of her boot when it got stuck at the curb, then soundly locked the gate and crossed herself.

I watched through the shattered glass of a telephone booth as the group wandered off. Tahir and a few others, including the one-legged monster who had threatened me with his crutch, slowly made their way up Bakikhanov Street toward the Circus Arena. I followed a safe distance behind, unable to take my eyes off Tahir's wobbly, shrunken figure. As they reached the Circus, they turned left and headed down toward Kubinka—Baku's most dangerous neighborhood.

Named after merchants from the town of Kuba who used to own this area at the beginning of the twentieth century, Kubinka was a haven of brothels and a black market. Crooked, narrow streets, sewers spilling into the roads, a havoc of broken bottles, scraps of food, and dog and human waste. Merchants and buyers never met in the light of the day. All transactions took place inside cramped stone-walled shacks.

Drugs, Marlboros, Kalashnikovs, fancy Western clothes, and fine objets d'art all exchanged hands there. The common saying was that if one could afford to buy a star from the sky he'd find it in Kubinka. Once, Almaz dragged me there to buy Caspian manna seeds for one of her love potions.

It looked much scarier now in the darkness. No streetlights. The only illumination came from the dimly lit windows of the shacks. I tried to keep track of the turns: one to the right, two to the left, three shacks and another left turn. The group stopped by a dark house, larger than most we had passed by, with someone guarding the entrance.

"*Salam!* Hello!"

"*Axşaminiz xeyir!* Good evening."

The door opened, and Tahir and his companions disappeared inside. I leaned against the wall of the next shack, trying to blend in without creating any shadows. My initial courage—or maybe it was just an adrenaline rush—had given way to panic. I was shaking, afraid to move. The distant lights of safe Baku twinkled three lifetimes away.

And yet, overhead, the vast, starlit tent extended from one rim of the sky to the other. Promising another chance. I tore myself away from the wall and headed toward the flickering cigarette light.

"I'm looking for my brother," I said to a man—a boy?—no, a midget. He stared at me.

"A brother?"

"Yes, a brother. My younger brother."

I had no money left in my wallet, and the midget's gaze promised trouble. I pulled my wedding ring off my finger and stuck it in front of his face. "Want it?"

Greed won. He grabbed the ring and opened the door.

The stench of mold, urine, sex, and hashish insulted my nose. I waited at the entrance and let my eyes adjust to the darkness. A single kerosene lamp swung overhead, dispensing more shadows than light across a long, narrow room. People sat along the walls, smoking, the lit ends of their cigarettes moving like fireflies in and out of the opaque blanket of smoke, the whites of their eyes following me as I walked through the room.

Tahir wasn't there, but as I reached the far end, I noticed a stairway leading downward. I stepped on one creaky step, then another. Ten altogether, leading into a small dungeon.

An opium den. I was inside an opium den. That's how they looked in movies about the West. I never imagined they could exist in Baku. A few human ghosts sat around a hookah, taking turns, gulping the fumes of the bubbling amber potion as if it was their last living breath. Tahir wasn't here, either. The room's stoned silence was disturbed only by the muted sounds of some commotion coming through another doorway. I pushed it open and peeked inside.

A pile of bodies—convulsing, jerking, moaning—copulated in the most repulsive ways across several cots, their deformed extremities, twisted heads, and patches of ashen flesh moving in a macabre dance. As if Francisco de Goya's dark, nightmarish painting *Casa de locos*, with its grotesque apotheosis of perversion, had come to life. Was Tahir among them?

No, I didn't want to know. I shut the door. The opium circle, submerged in the glow of the bubbling potion, felt like a safe haven. I sat next to a woman with a black scarf wrapped around her face.

The pipe traveled from ghost to ghost, ever closer toward me. When my turn came, I accepted it from the shaking hands of the woman, brought it to my mouth, and took a long, deep, hungry inhale.

"What are you doing here?" the woman asked, removing her black scarf and letting her gold tresses fall freely down her shoulders. She waved her hands in front of her face, blowing away the ashes, leaving her skin as pure and radiant as if it were made of milk and honey.

"Who are you?" I asked.

She laughed in a crystal clear coloratura. "Don't you recognize me?"

"No."

She leaned in closer, her breath emitting the scent of lilacs. "I'm Peri. And I've been guarding you for a while. Not an easy task, you know, with all the vicissitudes of your life."

Of course. How could I have not recognized her? The Peri Fairy—born out of fire and nourished by lilacs—from my *Legends from the Land of Fire* book. She looked exactly the way she did in the picture with long, golden hair and a veil of mauve silk.

I reached to touch her hand but my fingers went right through her flesh, feeling nothing but air.

Then I remembered. Peri had been banished from heaven and turned into a bodiless *xəyal*, a ghost destined to live between light and darkness, life and death, right and wrong.

"And that's what I've being doing ever since," she said, as if reading my thoughts. "Wandering everywhere, shedding tears, collecting them into my sack. Only after it is so full that it bursts at the seams, only then will I be redeemed. So, as you see, you and I are very much alike."

"How can we be alike?"

"How? I'm a fallen maiden, exactly as you are. I sold my soul to wicked Div for a pair of faster wings so I could be the first to reach the firmament of the sky. And you? You chose a path of conformism from the very beginning, with one compromise leading to the next, until your soul sank into the darkness."

"I didn't have a choice—"

"La, la, la, la, la... *I didn't have a choice*. An eternal excuse. Nothing other than self-indulgence. Evil tempts every soul, but a weak soul tempts evil. And you have done it not once but three times. First, when you signed your name under Tahir's death warrant. Second, when you woke up alone in that Kabul hotel.

"You know, I never stop wondering. It's kind of a mystery to me. If you really loved him, if you really cared about him so much as to fly to the war zone and save him, then how could you let your wounded ego blind you? Didn't it ever occur to you that your childish proposition to escape to the West could have been overheard? That the Kabul hotel room had KGB ears? That they were waiting outside the door to pick Tahir up?

"Of course you thought of it. But you preferred the role of a victim. With all the misery and diva melodrama."

Peri caught a tear sliding down her cheek and held it between her thumb and index finger, dropped it into a sack hanging on her neck. "And then your destiny presented you with the last test— your daughter."

"My daughter? How do you know it was a girl?"

"How? Didn't you give her the name *Ziya*—Light?"

"Yes, I did."

"Right before you butchered her."

"I didn't… I didn't want to… I was scared, terribly scared and alone. And mad. Abandoned and betrayed by the one I loved."

"I never betrayed you, Leila."

Tahir?

In his white tunic, freshly shaven, his lavender eyes a shade lighter than the sky behind, a sunbeam bouncing through his hair. "They seized me, the KGBs, the moment I stepped out of the hotel room," he said. "I thought I would surprise you with fresh flowers still filled with morning dew from the Kabul Mountains. Remember I told you—those greens, blues, and violets exactly like in Renoir's *Bouquet of Spring Flowers*?"

He smiled, opening his arms—both arms—calling me, inviting me for a long-craved embrace. So the nightmare in Beggars Corner, his missing arm, the opium den—all this had been just a delusion.

I rushed to him, yearning to disappear inside his embrace, to feel my body inseparable from his, to touch his eyes, his lips, his two healthy hands, to make sure he was real, that he was here with me. Forever. The old Tahir. The love of my life.

"I love you. I love you. I love you," I wailed, kissing his face and his hands, smudging my tears all over his white tunic. "Don't ever leave me again. I'm weak. I'm nothing without you, just a drained, empty *xəyal* living off the memories of those moments of happiness you gave me. I've shed enough tears. My sack is filled to the brim. The seams are bursting."

I felt a rapid, jolting motion.

"Get out of here." A pair of murky-gray eyes stared at me. "And don't ever follow me again. Do you hear me? We're finished playing your little princess games."

Tahir. He grabbed my arm and, in one swift, forceful movement, lifted me off the ground and dragged me out of the room and up the narrow, creaky staircase. Doing it all with his left hand while the empty right sleeve of his stained, discolored flannel shirt hung alongside his body.

"Please let's talk. Please," I cried, trying to stop him, to free myself from his hurting grasp. "Let me explain. I've made wrong choices. Terrible choices. But I never let you out of my heart. I've been a broken vessel for a long time. Scared, confused, brainwashed, blackmailed. I've lost myself. But I'm here now. With you. We need each other. Let me help you. Let me get you out of here. This is no place for you. I'll give up everything. I'll sacrifice everything to be with you. I need you for my soul. I need you for my music. I'm just a cracked, shattered glass. Tahir, please…"

Ignoring my cries, Tahir hauled me through the long room, its few remaining dwellers following us with their blank eyes. When we reached the door, he accidentally bumped his head against the kerosene lamp swinging overhead, swore coarsely, and released me for a moment to open the door before throwing me out. I tripped, lost my footing, and stumbled to the ground, landing in a muddy, trash-filled puddle.

"I could have forgiven you for betraying me," Tahir said in a raspy voice. "But I'll never—*never*—forgive you for marrying into the KGB for your fucking career. You—Badalbeilis—are our worst curse. Go away, Leila. I never want to see your Medusa face again."

The door slammed shut.

I had turned Tahir's heart into stone, and now he had returned the favor, stoning my heart.

I had no tears left to cry. I just sat in the puddle, next to a trench of sewage, and watched a stray dog and a rat fighting over a piece of garbage.

CHAPTER 35

The giant steel bird gleamed in the rising sun, waiting, her engines roaring impatiently, eager to soar into the cloudless sky. A brand-new Aeroflot Airbus A320, chartered for a once-in-a-lifetime nonstop flight from Baku to London, to carry—in first-class style—the delegation from the Republic of Azerbaijan to the International Piano Competition. The privileged group included the First Minister of Culture and his son; the Second Secretary of the Party and his wife; the rector of the Baku Conservatory of Music, Professor Najafov; as well as a large entourage of young but seasoned KGB stallions dispatched from the Moscow KGB office, camouflaged in relaxed, casual attire to blend in with the rest of the Baku artistic intelligentsia. But with their universal blond crew cuts and military bearing, they stood out like a convoy of white shepherd dogs amid our procession of pampered black llamas.

The message was clear. In light of the escalating, high-visibility defections, Moscow kept its vigilant eyes everywhere, even on the top echelon of its vassal territories. Within the last year, a pair of our Olympic champion skaters, Ludmila Belousova and Oleg Protopopov, husband and wife, had remained in Switzerland after the end of a tour. The son of legendary Soviet composer and Communist Dmitri Shostakovich had asked for political asylum in West Germany.

And the most embarrassing episode of all took place just a couple of months earlier when Leonid and Valentina Kozlov, the principal dancers with the Bolshoi Theater, disappeared from KGB radar in the middle of a crowded Los Angeles airport. The Soviet government announced that the dancers had been kidnapped by a Western spy agency, only to hear the couple interviewed on the Voice of America where they described how they outmaneuvered their KGB keepers. As a result, we were only allowed to bring one family member on the trip to London, the rest left at home as hostages to guarantee our return.

In my case, it had to be either Mama or Farhad. And until the last day—naively—Mama and I still hoped we'd be allowed to travel together. After all, I was their magical *utka*, expected to deliver a golden egg, and I needed maternal support to carry out my mission successfully. That's what I wrote in my application for Mama's exit visa. General Jabrailov promised it would come through. Farhad—oh, that phony Farhad—acted as if he was outraged over the visa processing delay, while Mama kept calling the Bureau of Visas and Registrations and hearing the encouraging message: "Your visa will arrive shortly."

It never did.

The same with Professor Sultan-zade, but for a different reason. Professor Najafov had trashed her request to accompany me to the competition and instead put his own name in her place as my mentor. To avoid any last-moment surprises, two days before our departure to London, he dispatched her to Stepanakert, a small town in the South Caucasus, to sit in the jury of a local piano contest.

I accompanied her to the terminal where she was to begin her 250-kilometer journey through forests and mountains on a decrepit, crammed bus.

"I hope I'm not carrying a scorpion there," Professor Sultan-zade said with her usual caustic humor, pointing at her five-month belly bump. "From that venomous *əqrəb*, I wouldn't be surprised."

"You'll have a beautiful baby," I said, wiping tears.

"I hope so. You know, where I come from we say: even a

porcupine child feels like velvet to his mother." She affectionately stroked her belly. "This is all that matters to me now."

"I'll do my best to win," I said, throwing my arms around her folded shoulders. "And if I win, they won't be able to touch you."

"No, Leila." She shook her head in disapproval, her lips pressed tightly, stubbornly. "I don't need your win for my job security. It's unlikely I'll be staying in Baku after the birth anyway. I have an offer from the Tbilisi Conservatory of Music. But it's not about me now. It's about you, the most gifted student I've ever had. I've taught you everything I know. I've seen you grow technically from a child prodigy into a world-class performer. It's your heart, though, that concerns me the most. It's like a broken tree, its leaves torn and blown by the changing winds of your destiny. So please hear me."

Professor Sultan-zade leaned closer to me, her lips against my ear, her breath as hot as the desert Khazri. "Time to heal your heart, drop by drop. Go to London. Win or no win—don't come back. There are plenty of Western impresarios who'd be keen to manage your career. You can even try to contact Rudolf Nureyev."

"Who is Nureyev?"

"The world's greatest dancer. He might remember me. We met many years ago in Leningrad. He had just joined the Kirov Ballet and I studied at the Rimsky-Korsakov Conservatory of Music. I played piano for their ballet classes."

"Are you getting in?" The bus driver impatiently blew the horn like a Morse code signal.

We hugged—a finale of Chopin's "Raindrop" prelude with its poignant acceptance that this might be the last time we saw each other.

I helped Professor Sultan-zade climb the stairs, and the bus grudgingly took off, lurching through the dusty fog.

Win or no win—don't come back.

"Why aren't you smiling?" Farhad squeezed my forearm, pulling me toward the TV cameras fighting for space in a small reception room of the Baku Airport.

I did. I smiled like a mannequin.

"We'll be back in just five days with a big laurel wreath crowning my talented wife's head," Farhad announced to the crowd.

Everybody applauded enthusiastically, except for Mama. She kept stroking my hand with her cold fingers, softly scratching my skin with her short nails. Making my heart sob. Yesterday, we took a long walk in Governor's Park. Something we hadn't done since… well, a very long time. Something I always wanted to do with Mama. We had tea inside a small *chaikhana* tent, surrounded by grapevines with clusters of ripe, milky-green sultanas emitting the nostalgia of autumn. Then we sat on a bench by a pond with lilies, admiring its still beauty, its greens, blues, and violets fading into the Impressionistic strokes of sunset.

"I've been thinking," Mama said, "over and over. There's no future for you here. Only hurt and humiliation. They don't deserve you." She swallowed hard, suppressing the moan in her throat but not the tears spilling out of her eyes. "I hate seeing you in this awful marriage. I hate seeing your youth and talent being used for *their* ambitions. Win or no win—it doesn't matter. All I want is for you to be happy. I want my daughter to be free."

First, Professor Sultan-zade. Now Mama. Why? Why now and not four years ago, when I could have saved my soul from burning out in the furnace of lies, betrayal, and survival. I wanted to scream. Zümrüd Quşu, her wings turned into ashes.

"Farewell from General Jabrailov!" Farhad shouted, clearing the path for his boss. The General took the spotlight in what was supposed to look like a spontaneous emotional message.

"Go, Leila, show the rotten, decadent West what a true daughter of Soviet Azerbaijan can do," he said, waving his index finger at the invisible enemy, planting the roots of his proudly conceived propaganda campaign. "Let them choke on their alcohol, their drugs and sex, together with their Marilyn Monroes and Elvis Presleys. Their so-called *idols*. We have our own star lighting the way for the young generation, and doing it in a wholesome, cultural, Communist way."

The lobby exploded with a storm of ovation, and the line of black llamas formed to thank General Jabrailov for the parting words and submissively shake his hand. The boss of the KGB was their boss, no matter how long and high their titles read. A squadron of Moscow KGB foot soldiers picked up the dignitaries' huge, half-empty suitcases—with abundant space left inside to soon be packed with jeans, sneakers, watches, Marlboros, and gum cartons—and headed toward the exit doors.

"Remember what I told you. I want you to be happy. And free," Mama whispered in my ear, leaving a trace of hot tears on my neck.

I buried my face in her gold and jasmine-white hair, breathing in the scent of my childhood. "*Mamochka*, I love you. I always wanted to tell you how much I love you. But every time I tried, you stopped me, saying those words were cheap. And you know, maybe you were right. Maybe these word are cheap, but not what is behind them. I love you. I love you. I love you. And I'll do my best to win, for all of us."

Mama took my face in her hands, her sad, cerulean eyes filling my entire vision, holding me in their power. "Be strong and bold. Your happiness is all I wish for."

"You're saying good-byes as if you're parting forever," Farhad said, pushing me aside and kissing Mama on both cheeks like a good son-in-law. "Good-bye, Sonia *Khanum*. And don't worry, Leila will be back. I'll be watching her. Won't take my eyes off her."

A black government Chaika waited for us outside. Together with the dignitaries, Farhad and I were driven across the tarmac and unloaded at the foot of the boarding stairs to the fancy Airbus. As soon as we settled inside its soft leather chairs, the steel bird soared into the sky.

The golden domes of the Baku mosques, the amphitheater of whitewashed streets over the cobalt arena of the Caspian Sea, the sunburned maze of Icheri Sheher, and the invincible bastion of Maiden Tower all began to sink into the heavy smog of the exhausted city. And with them, the last eighteen years of my life slowly dissolved into oblivion as the plane ascended into clear skies and headed northwest, playing hide-and-seek with the soft cotton clouds.

> *When my lips part to utter farewell, and my tongue is quick*
>   *as a dagger,*
> *I carve out the memories of hate and leave them behind in the*
>   *land of darkness.*
> *When my lips seal to withhold farewell, and my eyes swell like*
>   *a mountain river,*
> *I gather the memories, sweeter than honey, clearer than crystal*
>   *clear gems...*
> *And there is a farewell silent as snow,*
> *It goes with me wherever I go.*

The rain gushed across the window as our bus negotiated its way down the clogged, noodle-thin road out of Heathrow International Airport. Outside, nothing but a grim vista of empty fields, rusty bridges, and decaying, claustrophobic tunnels. Nose to the window, I waited impatiently for the glorious ramparts of Westminster Abbey to materialize. We passed by a succession of small towns with the same brick houses, darkened by damp and age, submerged in the dreary dusk.

"I'd like to have a talk with Comrade Badalbeili."

One of the Moscow KGB personnel gestured to Farhad to vacate the seat next to me. Unlike his cohorts, he had a distinct personality. He was short and nimble with an egg-shaped face, his nose a thin blade setting off Tatar eyes, and his dirty-blond hair layered stylishly. Farhad got up obediently. Dark, hesitant opening notes of Beethoven's *String Quartet of Transcendence* played ominously in my head.

"I'll be your personal assistant for the duration of the trip," the young man said in a soothing baritone, settling next to me. "So I think we should get acquainted properly. First of all, you should know that I'm a huge fan. I was at your last orchestral rehearsal. And I'll tell you—that Rach 3, it either makes you or breaks you. The original cadenza you chose for the first movement—*bellissimo*! *Mwah*." He swept his hand in an air kiss.

Something didn't feel right.

"How do you know so much about music?" I said.

He smiled, revealing two crimson dimples on his cheeks, his face turning boyishly perky. "You think that if I'm with the KGB I should be Ivan the Fool from the Village of Simpletons?"

"I didn't say that."

"You almost did." He smacked his lips soundly. "Let's put it this way. I'm an amateur pianist, and in my previous life, I studied at the Kiev Conservatory of Music. But I dropped out after the first year. I realized I'd never rise above the ranks of a music schoolteacher or, at best, an accompanist in some provincial Opera House. So, I switched to the Moscow State Institute of Foreign Relations. You see, during my childhood, I lived in many different places—Prague, Vienna, Baghdad. My father is still there in Iraq, in charge of security at the Soviet Embassy. So I've always been good with languages."

Where was he going with all this?

"How many languages do you speak?" I asked, forcing my eyebrows up to showcase the amazement.

"Let's see. Ukrainian is my mother tongue, so it doesn't count. The same goes for Russian, Polish, and Slovak. Then it's just English, German, French, and a rudimental Arabic. Now you know almost everything about me."

"I still don't know your name," I said, failing to keep nervous vibrato out of my voice.

"Oh, that's true. It's Ivan Vasilyevich." He gently shook my hand, placed it back in my lap, and leaned closer. "I should be careful with this precious jewel, shouldn't I?"

Farhad watched us closely from across the aisle, his face purple. Whoever sat next to me obviously had a considerably superior rank than my husband.

"I can't imagine why, but some people have nicknamed me Ivan the Terrible," my neighbor continued with the broad smile, "which brings us to the topic of this discussion—the nature of our relationship for the next three or four days, until our plane touches the ground, safely and soundly, at Moscow's Sheremetyevo Airport.

"Throughout the duration of our stay here, you will have no communications with anyone—anyone—outside of this group. Any requests, no matter what—music manuscripts, rehearsals, acoustics, lighting—will be made only through me. As I've mentioned, I'm your personal assistant and your voice to the outside English-speaking world. Your only task here is to win the competition, to smile prettily, and to keep your mouth shut. Understood?"

I stared outside, swallowing tears, as the concrete industrial blocks suddenly gave way to the astonishing view of the River Thames, aligned on both sides by white palaces, their reflections shimmering in the dark waters.

"Yes." I nodded.

"Bravo. And one more thing. I'm sure you're going to be a good girl, but with your dossier, unfortunately, I have been given an instruction to resort to Plan B in case of any unexpected action on your part."

"What is Plan B?"

"Oh, not a big deal." With the same happy smile, Ivan the Terrible reached into the inner pocket of his jacket and produced a tiny aluminum cylinder partially wrapped in a handkerchief, exactly like the one Farhad once showed me.

"You make a single wrong move, and I will have to jab you with a dose of *matreshka*. You won't make any more moves, and it will leave you quite paralyzed. But I'm sure it won't get to that, will it?"

He looked at me, the outer corners of his Mongoloid eyes raised, half testing, half teasing. "Of course not. So…relax and enjoy the scenery. There's no place like London. And by the way, there is the auditorium where you'll be playing." He pointed at a monochrome building with a boat-hull roof standing lonesome on the other bank of the Thames, looking like an abandoned factory. "Royal Festival Hall, *Her Majesty's* failed attempt at our Socialist Constructivism style. Honestly, they should have stayed with their moldy Victorian."

CHAPTER 36

The deceptive exterior of Royal Festival Hall didn't prepare me for what waited inside. An arena-like concert auditorium with three thousand seats, a peculiar canopy over the stage, zigzagged metal balconies and ceiling—all seemed to float inside an envelope, accessible by transparent foyers and flowing staircases. A smart palette of browns, reds, grays, and greens bestowed the feeling of a warm, cozy oasis. There was one major problem though—acoustics.

During the afternoon rehearsal, I couldn't hear the strings, and even worse, the lower register of the Steinway sounded muted, taking away any possible control over the dynamics, balance, and, most important of all, any emotional connection with the performance. But I was afraid to say a word. Not after Maestro Mstislav Rostropovich had been personally invited by the Queen to inaugurate the competition. In protest, the Soviet Ministry of Culture threatened to withdraw me from the competition.

Mstislav Rostropovich, the greatest cellist of the twentieth century, left the Soviet Union in 1974 for the United States. I heard him once when I was eight at the Baku philharmonic hall. He played Bach's *Suites for Unaccompanied Cello*. His bow flying, his deep, poignant tone carried the same sort of vulnerability I would hear later in Vladimir Horowitz's performances. I remembered how proud I felt that this genius was born and started playing music in Baku.

Two hours before my scheduled appearance, Ivan stormed into my dressing room.

"We're on," he declared. "Moscow has given us the green light to proceed. Get ready."

I zipped my sleeveless black dress and slipped on comfortable pumps with a tiny heel, to better manipulate the Steinway pedal that had a low, almost to the floor, position. Surrounded by a myriad of lights, I waited for the curtain call in front of a large mirror, trying to apply kohl along my lash line, failing to keep it straight, my hands shaking, poking my eye until it felt on fire. I gave up, wiped the residue of the black pen, and washed my face clean. My *Medusa face*. Could it ever be washed clean?

In a daze, I followed Farhad and Ivan the Terrible through a labyrinth of corridors to the stage. There we parted. Ivan the Terrible took his surveillance position on the side curtain, Farhad rushed back to join the rest of my keepers sprinkled strategically throughout the audience, and I stepped into the spotlight of the arena—a slave, a gladiator with music as the weapon, who had to bring victory to her masters.

"Ladies and gentlemen." A smooth bass came from somewhere high up in the metal ceiling. "Rachmaninoff's *Piano Concerto no. 3*. Played by Leila Badalbeili, the representative of the Soviet Union."

The announcer took an appropriate pause to allow applauding, but only a few polite claps swept across the sea of spectators.

"Leila Badalbeili was born in Baku, Azerbaijan," the imperturbable bass continued. "She studies at the Baku Conservatory of Music under the mentorship of Professor Mirza Najafov."

What? Not only had Professor Sultan-zade been left behind, but she had also been stripped of her credit for schooling me.

"Miss Leila." Maestro Klein, the Argentinean conductor, dashed over and led me to the middle of the stage for a bow. A vivacious little man with silvery temples and the sad eyes of a dove, he had great sympathy for Communism. After the dress rehearsal, when no one but my assistant hovered nearby, he told me how much he'd love to have the opportunity to engage in an extended contract with one of the Soviet Union's great orchestras.

The audience applauded with a bit more enthusiasm than before.

Or was it empathy? Could they sense that the symbol of the impenetrable nation could hardly place one foot in front of another? No, it wasn't stage fright. Instead, I drifted inside a bubble of detachment.

Maestro Klein, an authority on Wagner's music, waved his arms in what looked like a call to arms, and the full orchestra charged into battle. All I could hear, though, were clarinets, thin and muffled, but at least I had something I could count off.

Two measures in and my hands joined, playing in unison the plaintive diatonic leitmotif of the first movement, executing everything Professor Sultan-zade had taught me—a dark, ductile, seamless legato, an interplay between diminuendos and crescendos—increasing intensity for the broad passage that led to my lacing of sixteenth notes around the opening theme in violas and contrabasses.

Why weren't they playing? I glanced above the piano and saw them moving their bows fervently like in a silent movie. But the only sounds reaching me were the first beats played by the timpanis. Those were going to stop soon, and I would have nothing to hold on to other than the conductor's baton.

No help there. Maestro Klein's movements were too thespian, obscure, mostly exhibited for the strings and the audience. I resorted to tapping my foot for a count, the worst possible crime I could have committed against Professor Sultan-zade's recital ethics.

The poor acoustics probably had to do with the canopy, decoratively twisted in the wrong angles, dispersing the sound unevenly across the stage, but the glitch was obviously inflated inside my head. I knew the piece well enough to play it with my eyes and ears closed. I had to let the mechanics go and immerse myself in the music before the performance was entirely doomed.

I closed my eyes, letting my fingers do the job, visualizing the *partitura* of "Allegro ma non tanto" with its flying passages, encased with ties and slurs, crammed with flats and sharps demanding obligatory modulations, building up to the nightmarish climax.

No! Not yet! I almost screamed, stamping my foot, missing the pedal, trying to stop or at least slow down the devilish dance possessing my hands, my mind, the black-and-white keys bouncing up and down out of control across the hostile turf of the Steinway.

They obeyed. Letting me regroup, take a deep breath, disassociate myself from the human race before plunging like a wild animal into the tempestuous cadenza, smashing the barriers of tempo, racing ahead of the storm on top of the plummeting chords of the finale.

Then nothing. Silence. A fragile silence, transparent as the air, fragrant with morning dew, luring me away from the chaos of reality back to the safety of the dreams hidden behind Tahir's green door.

What a relief. Now I could let everything go and stay with my music, let *her* lead me back to my island of inspiration.

With my eyes closed, I rush through a long, narrow corridor, my hands brushing against walls with sporadic, impatient chords. Three steps down, and the passageway opens into a room overlaid with rugs. Ancient rugs with brilliant greens, blues, and violets spinning in the slow trance of the theme of the second movement "Adagio." Or is it Billie Holiday's haunting "Body and Soul"?

"...For you I cry, for you dear only," I whisper into Tahir's ear as he leads me through the dolce steps of our dance. Our Dance of Love.

A screeching mayhem from the strings—a razor through the tranquillity, forcing me to open my eyes.

To a blinding cascade of spotlight. And in this light, I'm dancing along with a corps de ballet of the dead cows, swinging to the rhythm of my music from an overhead rack. The stump of Tahir's arm in my hands. All soaked in blood.

"What did you think? That you'd just come back when it suits you and get your inspiration?" Tahir whispered, his mouth lopsided in a sneer, his atrophied face distorted by hatred.

I stopped in the middle of the arpeggio. The orchestra continued to play. The conductor—in total dismay—signaled for me to resume. On the side curtain, pale-faced Ivan the Terrible thrust his fist into the air. In the audience, Farhad sneered with malicious pleasure.

Be strong and bold... Win or no win—don't come back...

Now it was my chance to defect. My only chance. But how? I closed my eyes and saw it in a flash.

I jumped down from the stage and ran down the aisle toward the jury box with Maestro Mstislav Rostropovich. He would understand. He would help me.

Before I could reach their row, Farhad grabbed my forearm. "What the fuck are you doing?" he hissed into my neck.

Ivan the Terrible ran behind, screaming, "She's having a nervous breakdown. Apologies. Leila has a history of mental instability."

"Please. Please, Mstislav Leopoldovich, don't let them take me away. I want to defect like you. To defect!" I cried, feeling a pinch where Farhad squeezed my hand. A warm wave washed up my arm, numbing my body, turning me into a sponge.

No. I couldn't do it. I couldn't defect.

Like a wounded animal, with pools of sweat under my arms, I limped toward the side stage, accompanied by the sympathetic *oohs* and gloating *aahs* of an astounded audience.

Farhad stood by the window, framed by the drowsy lights of nocturnal London, emptying one bottle of cognac after another from the room bar, chain-smoking cigarette after cigarette, throwing the butts down to the street below. All in condemning silence. Was he taking pleasure in prolonging my suffering?

"I wonder, how would it feel to live in a big city like this?" he said broodingly. "To have a lot of money in the bank, to drive a fancy silver Volvo, to go on vacation to the Riviera on your own yacht?"

My heart paused. I'd been around the KGB long enough to know that not a single word ever came and went impromptu, even under the influence of alcohol. Especially in the case of such a fanatical careerist such as Farhad.

"No bugs here." He smirked. "They don't bug hotel rooms, you know. They just live, enjoy their lives. And we could have savored some of that too, if you hadn't fucked everything up. Anyway. It's a lost cause."

He took a long inhale from his cigarette, letting it burn all the way to the butt, then threw it out the window and emptied another cognac.

"The question is—what am I going to do with you now? Today you pissed away your princess tiara and departed from your little golden cloud straight into the gutter, pulling me with you. You're a complete embarrassment, Leila. You have failed the General, ruined a campaign that he was convinced had the possibility of propelling him all the way to the Politburo in Moscow. And the General is not one who forgets and forgives. So the right thing for me would be to get rid of you. To dump you like a used, secondhand whore."

He moved closer, his swollen crotch against my eyes, his hand hastily unzipping his trousers.

"I've had enough of jerking off into the toilet," he murmured angrily, bending my head for a convenient angle of entry.

"Ohhh…" he moaned, relieving his lust almost instantly.

"You see what you've done to me? All your fault." He pushed me away, trying to mask his disgrace. "For three weeks I had to be celibate so you'd put *everything* into practicing your fucking piano. For what? For no good reason at all."

He downed another cognac and looked at me with a licentious smile, rubbing his rising *chlen* affectionately. "Doesn't take long for me, does it?"

For what seemed like an eternity Farhad pleased himself, unleashing his bizarre fantasies, playing sexual games as specific as if he had spent hours scripting them in his head, celebrating my failure. The Firebird was safely in his cage now, watching silently as he plucked her golden feathers, teaching the new reality—Leila the pianist had died in the Royal Festival Hall. What was left of me belonged completely to him.

"Don't worry, I'm not going to divorce you," he said, breathing heavily, elated, still relishing the role of a pharaoh who had just disciplined, then savored, a naughty slave. "You're good in bed, no complaints here. And I'll deal with the General. He'll understand. He needs me. I'm his eyes and ears. He'll just have to accept it. And you know what?" He brought me up, his hazy eyes against mine. "I love you. And I want you to have my babies. I've got lots of them here for you." He patted himself with my hand. "I'll send you to Moscow. Let them fix whatever is wrong with you there. To the best clinic. Kremlin clinic. They'll put you back into working order."

I felt nauseated by Farhad's prospects for my future, a carousel of the cacophonous, mutilated, unmusical phrases and chords of Rachmaninoff's *Concerto no. 3* spinning inside my head.

"I'll be right back," I said, getting out of bed and heading to the bathroom.

"Just hurry back. I'm ready for the next ride." He yawned.

I closed the bathroom door and turned the water on. With my back to the mirror, reeking with the fumes of Farhad's smell, I was afraid to look at my face.

After a few minutes, I tiptoed back. He lay across the bed, asleep, drool slipping down one side of his mouth.

The suitcase in the corner. My shoes, together with all my clothing, were inside. The suitcase locked, the key hidden inside Farhad's locked briefcase. He diligently followed the safekeeping protocol.

I crept to the exit. A slight click, the door opened. I squeezed through the narrow aperture into the dim hallway.

The plush carpets swallowed the sound of my footsteps. Across the hallway, down the steps, past the sleeping doorman.

Panic. The entrance door was locked.

A green light on the side. I pushed the button. It worked.

I darted outside, stepping into an icy puddle, another one. The November rain fell at me from every direction.

The distant sound of a train. Or the echo of my sorrow?

No time to ruminate. Barefoot, in my silk nightgown, wrapping the towel I had stolen from the bathroom around my shoulders, I raced down the street. My destination—I'd seen it when the bus

took us on a tour that first day in London. Just a few blocks away.
With a red, white, and blue flag over its entrance.

The Embassy of the United States of America.

EPILOGUE

June 2002

Submersed in the twilight, I reached the conclusion of the "Finale" of Rachmaninoff's *Piano Concerto no. 3*, its majestic sequences of octaves and chords fading into the rhythmic mantra of the Pacific Ocean.

And then I saw her—Maiden Tower. The magical tower of my childhood emerging from the purple glow of the horizon. So close, just a short flight away on Tahir's magic carpet—sitting cross-legged beside him, sipping his pungent tea, drifting away on the clouds of his *hashish*.

And I knew that the time I'd resisted for so long had finally come. The time to make peace with the past.

Three days later, a British Airways flight unloaded me at Baku International Airport. As I walked from the plane to the terminal, bathing in an oh-so-familiar heat wave, I had the remarkable sensation that I had just returned home from a short trip. Well, twenty years short. And the spirit of the Azeri crowd in the waiting room, bursting with warmth and unquenchable energy, almost overwhelmed me at first. I'd succumbed long ago to the slow, placid, unemotional cadences of California.

"*Salam eleykum*," a taxi driver greeted me. A dark-skinned young man with a thin face and a thick black mustache, he opened the door of his silver BMW for me, then placed my carry-on luggage in the trunk.

"Where do you wish to go?" he asked in broken English.

"To Maiden Tower, please."

I'd crossed twenty years... Now only twenty kilometers left to reach the place from which I had taken my leap of faith—the crown of Maiden Tower.

Since then, the history of my country had been rewritten. In the nineties, the Soviet Union finally crumbled, the Iron Curtain came down, and the people of Azerbaijan grasped the opportunity to realize their own version of the American dream right here at home. From afar, I lamented having not participated in the excitement, in missing the chance to live in my country as a free person and an artist. But then, it was no longer my country.

Through years of repression, the accumulated craving for transformation was so vast that it hadn't taken long to change Azerbaijan into a foreign place. Oddly, while living in the United States, I remained an exile from the Soviet Union, walking among the ghosts of my own past, while the destinies of the people I knew and loved had taken them to so many unimaginable places.

Mama had been living in India for the last decade, heading the pediatric department at Bombay Hospital, operating in the company of her new husband and colleague, British-born Dr. Peter Javankar.

Almaz had fallen in love with some Chechen militant and borne him five children. After her husband blew himself up, along with fifteen innocent passersby on Tverskaya Street in Moscow, she hid her beautiful face behind a *niqāb*, moved to Iran, and joined the radical Islamic group Black Widows. No one had heard from her since.

My dear Professor Sultan-zade had succumbed to lung cancer in 1987, but she left her precious daughter, Eliza Sultan-zade, to the world of music. I met her last year at Lincoln Center in New York, where she performed Robert Schumann's *Carnaval op. 9*, her mother's favorite piece.

Even Farhad had changed—dramatically. Now an oil tycoon and a billionaire, married to a British model half his age, he had been living in London for the last six years.

Everyone had moved on. Everyone but me.

At first, right after my defection, the adrenaline ran high. My heroic flight out of the claws of the KGB—in the middle of the night, barefoot, in a nightgown—brought me instant fame, turning my fiasco performance at the London Piano Competition into the "triumph of an invincible spirit." The Western world embraced and glorified me as their hero—the new Rudolf Nureyev. I was given one of the most lucrative contracts in the twentieth-century history of classical music to record Sergei Rachmaninoff's four *Piano Concertos* with the London Symphony Orchestra for Deutsche Gramophone.

But unlike Nureyev, I didn't deliver. I may have left the Kingdom of Darkness behind, but the darkness followed me.

A month later, on the night before my opening concert at the Wigmore Hall in London, I had a visitor. Ivan the Terrible casually invited himself into my hotel room.

"You're doing splendidly well, Leila," he said, looking around my suite with its Steinway grand piano, nodding his head in satisfaction. "Just as we'd anticipated."

"What do you mean?"

He took my hand in his. Numb with fear, I shut my eyes, expecting to be stabbed with a dose of *matreshka*.

Instead, Ivan the Terrible kissed my fingers gently and released my hand. "I heard you rehearsing for tomorrow's concert. You'll be sensational—guaranteed. I've always preferred your Mozart over your Rachmaninoff, but who am I to voice my humble opinion?"

"What do you want?" I said, stepping back toward the door.

"I want you to relax, sit down, and listen. And please don't do anything irrational. You don't want your mother to spend the rest of her life in a psychiatric ward, do you?"

I shook my head.

"All right, Leila. Then down to business. I hate to do this to you, but that *heroic* defection of yours never would have happened if we hadn't *let* it happen. That's number one. Number two—you'd failed the London competition and along with it General Jabrailov's plan, so we've switched to Plan B. In accordance with which, you'll continue with a high-visibility international career—as our informer, waiting for directions from Moscow. Understood? And it'll be my honor to keep an eye on you."

The next day, I wrecked my Mozart performance at the Wigmore Hall, intentionally. And I did the same with the next few concerts, causing the organizers of my concert tour to cancel the remaining dates. Two weeks later, I packed and left London behind along with my music career. It was the most difficult decision I'd ever made—to give up my music and become a *nothing*. But it was the only way to free myself from my KGB masters. As Farhad once said:

"The only ones we don't care about are talentless nothings who can do neither harm nor good."

For a while, the music managers approached me, offering to revive my piano career. But gradually the world forgot about me, leaving me to drift between earth and sky, flapping my broken wings.

Until Tahir's painting found me and drew me back to the place where I had left my heart.

The taxi pulled up to let me out at the entrance to Icheri Sheher, a few steps away from Maiden Tower. Still the same as I remembered her—mysterious, austere, majestic tower—but now restored to its ancient glory as a symbol of free Azerbaijan.

I bought a ticket and entered the Maiden Tower museum. Miriam Mukhtarov's large photograph was exhibited in Coronation Hall, in a place of honor over the Mukhtarovs' clavichord. She lived to see the day when evil was wiped out, when she proudly pressed the key of Maiden Tower into the hands of the government of the new Democratic Republic of Azerbaijan. Her tragic life had not been in vain after all.

And Tahir?

I found him rather easily—Professor Tahir Mukhtarov at the Azerbaijan State University of Culture and Arts. I called and left a message asking him to meet me.

Would he come?

I mounted the spiral staircase to the top and stepped onto the crown of Maiden Tower. The city of my childhood lay sprawled beneath my feet. So much the same as I'd seen it in my dreams throughout the years; a maze of cobblestone streets encircled by the ancient walls of Icheri Sheher; the ornate Mudéjar carvings atop the limestone mansions bordering glorious Neftchilar Avenue; the aquamarine of the Caspian Sea sprinkled with oil derricks looking like giant seagulls taking wing into the blue satin of the summer sky.

But the signs of change were everywhere—in the mustard-hot rays of sun reflected in the new futuristic glass-and-steel skyscrapers, in the exuberant atmosphere on streets dotted with Western cafés and clubs, in the fusion of the traditional "Bayati Shiraz" *muğam* and Missy Elliott's "Hot Boyz" blasting out of neighboring teahouses. This was definitely not the city I had buried in the deep vault of my heart twenty years ago.

Click, click, click…

A group of Asian tourists, their fancy cameras cocked and loaded, acted like a firing squad on the command of a vivacious, toothy, smiling young guide who spoke in broken English: "You are standing at the crown of Maiden Tower—the soul of our Azerbaijan. From here, you can see the whole city of Baku. To the right, the fifteenth-century home of the Azeri rulers, Shirvanshahs' Palace"…*click, click, click*…"Eleventh-century Synyk-Kala Minaret and Mosque"…*click, click, click*…

"Leila."

I turned. And at once time stopped, vanished, evaporated, rewinding back to May 1979.

A thin and lanky man with wavy hair reaching to his shoulders, dressed in dirt-streaked, bell-bottom jeans and a white tunic stood behind me, his intensely violet-blue eyes locked with mine. He made a slow, uncertain step toward me. Then another. Now I could see the netting of fine lines on his sun-kissed face and the strokes of silver in his long chestnut hair. But the eyes were the same, mirroring every passing emotion—both his and mine—from the fear, anguish, and fatalism of Tchaikovsky to the nostalgia, longing, and timeless harmony of Chopin.

"I haven't told you the ending of the Maiden Tower legend," Tahir said softly, dreamlike, reaching out for my hand and leading me toward the edge of the crown, where, on the last day of summer 1979, he had told me the Legend of Maiden Tower. And once again, his hand against mine ignited the same electric glissando that had connected us into the same circuit, making us one, a long time ago.

As the powerful Khazri lifted us into the air, taking us farther and farther from the shores of reality, Tahir told me the rest of the Legend of Maiden Tower, about Princess Zümrüd and the Knight in Lion's Skin. His own story. How the Knight in Lion's Skin continued to dwell in the dark dungeons of his soul, long after his beloved Princess Zümrüd turned into the Firebird and left for the skies. How his splendid Lion's Skin turned into rags, his besotted mind lost its sight, and his unforgiving heart grew a shield of anger and pain.

> *Once the pain became so unbearable that the Knight—like a mad man—ran to the top of Maiden Tower to hurl his useless life down its ramparts. But as he stood at the edge, asking his Princess Zümrüd for forgiveness, he heard the Firebird crying for help, crying out her sorrow, her loneliness.*
>
> *The Knight turned his life around, determined to find the lost Bird and bring her back home. But how? How could he trace her through the vast sky? There was only one way left—to paint her the way he remembered her: a spirited, gifted, powerful half maiden, half bird.*

We sat silent, entwined in destiny, alone under the infinite tent of the darkening sky. A soft breeze blew from the sea, bringing the familiar taste of our childhood—hot, thick, and buttery air saturated with the aroma of black gold and made fragrant by the fresh bloom of *zùmrùd* jasmine.

How could I have lived without it? I closed my eyes and slowly, hungrily, blissfully inhaled.

READING GROUP GUIDE

1. The novel begins with Leila visiting an exhibition of Azerbaijani art in Los Angeles where she sees and recognizes herself in the Maiden Tower painting as "*a lonely princess—half human, half bird—standing on its crown, her wings reaching into the dome of the wakening sky.*" The novel ends with Leila returning to Baku and climbing to the top of Maiden Tower. Why did the artist paint Leila in this way? And why do you think that the author choose to frame the novel with those scenes?

2. Soviet Azerbaijan in 1979 was supposed to be a "classless" society, but there are several indicators that this is a fallacy (for example, Leila belonging to the Communist royalty—*Nomenklatura*). What did you think about this "classless" society? Do you think it's possible to have a society without class designations?

3. The novel is filled with descriptions of Baku on the crossroads of Turkish, Persian, and Russian cultures. How does the author create the imagery of this city using music and legends rooted in those cultural traditions?

4. In the novel, we see Communism fighting a "two-headed hydra"—religious fervor coming from the East and toxic hedonism (or the perception of such) coming from the West. We

commonly think of those two ideologies warring against each other, but not against a third party in Communism. Discuss this unusual battle that takes place in Soviet/Islamic Azerbaijan—the last outpost of European Communism as it makes its way farther into Asia.

5. How does the author transcribe music into words using metaphors, fine art imagery, colors, and emotions? Are there any examples that particularly stood out to you?

6. Comrade Farhad sends Leila to spy on an American mole and his music shop that is supposedly a cover-up for anti-Soviet activities. Instead, Aladdin's shop becomes Leila's haven. Discuss Leila's transformation from a dedicated young Communist into a free-spirited artist.

7. Leila's mother describes Azerbaijan as the "kingdom of crooked mirrors." Everyone in this novel seems to live with lies. Are there some lies that you forgive more easily than others? If yes, which ones are they, and why are they more easily forgivable?

8. The fairy tales and legends of Azerbaijan often serve as emotional references and metaphors throughout the novel. Discuss how the storyline mimics the Maiden Tower Legend; how the Legend of the Stone Heart mirrors Leila's fear of being rejected by Tahir; how an encounter with the Peri Fairy reveals Leila's guilt-torn soul.

9. How do Leila and Tahir unveil the ambiguities between music and art, friendship and love?

10. Leila betrays Tahir and later marries into the KGB—all for the sake of her music career, only to fail miserably at her most important final performance in London. Why?

11. Much of classical, jazz, and traditional Azerbaijani music flows throughout this novel: Chopin's *Ballade no. 1*; Czerny's *The Art of Finger Dexterity*; Beethoven's *Sonata Pathétique*; Mozart's *Piano Concerto no. 20*; Rachmaninoff's *Piano Concerto no. 3*; Tikhon Khrennikov's *Five Pieces for Piano*; Billie Holiday's "Body and Soul"; Nina Simone's "Strange Fruit"; and traditional Azerbaijani *muğams*. Listen to these musical works and discuss their depictions in the novel. Does the author's musical/literary palette resonate with your own imagery?

12. What do you think of the novel's ending? What do you think will happen with Tahir and Leila after the novel ends?

A CONVERSATION
WITH THE AUTHOR

The Orphan Sky is the first novel about Azerbaijan written in English by an author born in Baku and published in the United States.

How much of *The Orphan Sky* is rooted in your own past?

Just like my heroine, Leila, I grew up in Baku in the seventies when it was part of the USSR. My mother was a well-known pediatrician, my father headed the engineering department in the subway system, and both my sister and I began studying classical piano soon after we were old enough to walk. My family didn't belong to the Communist oligarchy, but we lived comfortably. My transformation from a dedicated Lenin Pioneer to a young person fascinated by Western culture began when I was twelve, when a tiny music store with a green door opened across the street from my school. Everybody warned us: "Don't take a single step inside that place. The store sells poisonous albums from the black market, and the owner is a sorcerer or an American spy."

I remember walking by the store for months before I worked up the courage to go inside. The man in the store wore a turban, and he looked like Aladdin. He also had a poster of Liza Minnelli on the wall. As I stood in front of it, mesmerized by the energy exuded by that half-naked alien woman, the owner played a vinyl recording of her singing "Maybe This Time." The music seemed to come from a different world—unknown, beautiful and free. The world outside my own. The world I became determined to discover.

Music plays a major role in *The Orphan Sky*—from traditional Azeri to jazz and classical. Your main character, Leila, is a child prodigy, whose classical piano excellence eventually provides her with a path out of the Soviet bloc. You too are a well-trained musical artist who took a similar path. Is Leila's relationship with music a reflection of your personal journey?

Yes and no. I started as a classical pianist, but the encounter with the "poisonous music shop" ignited my passion for jazz that led me to a local musician: Vagif Mustafazadeh—the father of Azerbaijani jazz. From him I learned the ins and outs of jazz improvisation, along with the intricacies of *muğam*, our traditional Azeri music. Driven by a dream to sing jazz in America, I applied to the government for permission to leave the Soviet Union. So naive. Instead, I joined the "black list" of dissidents, with no hope of ever seeing the world beyond the Iron Curtain. I moved to Moscow, studied composition at the Conservatory of Music, performed with the Jewish Music Theater, recorded a children's album that sold over three million copies. I toured with two major jazz orchestras across the Soviet Union, far and wide, with its red banners, Lenin monuments, and pig fat for food. Just like Leila. But, unlike Leila, I didn't have to defect.

I came to America because of a lucky occurrence. In the summer of 1989, I was singing at a Moscow club across from the U.S. Embassy one night when the American entrepreneur Armand Hammer came in to celebrate his birthday. His entourage included lawyer Mickey Kantor, who would later become the campaign chairman for Bill Clinton. During the break, we struck up a conversation, and I confessed my desire to get out of the Soviet Union. A week later, a telegram summoned me to the U.S. Embassy, where I was told that my son Sergey and I could emigrate to America.

Soon after Leila defects to the West, she gives up her music. Was that true of you as well?

I almost did. My son Sergey and I arrived in the United States—in Norfolk, Virginia, of all places—with two suitcases and three hundred dollars. My ex-husband, a high-ranking officer in the division of Soviet Electronic Warfare, wasn't allowed to leave the country. And my dream of a music career in the West quickly drowned in the reality of what I was facing. I had to buy food, pay rent for a cockroach-infested apartment, and never show my disappointment to Sergey. So I took a job at a manufacturing company, gradually bringing music back into my life—teaching theater and voice at the Old Dominion University, performing with my jazz orchestra Selah, later moving to Chicago and coaching actors and singers at the Center for Voice. Then tragedy struck—my son Sergey was diagnosed with leukemia, and the next two and a half years we spent together in hospital rooms, moving between incredible highs and lows, writing poetry and songs together, hoping to record them some day. After Sergey died, I had nothing to hold on to, except those songs, our music... Music was my only way to remain connected to Sergey's spirit. It still is.

You grew up speaking Russian and Azeri, and now you're writing fiction in English. Where and when did you learn English? How challenging is it for you to write in a literary fashion in a new language?

My parents hired an English tutor for me when I was five years old, and later I studied English in school. But my real coaches were Billie Holiday and Ella Fitzgerald. I learned the words and their meaning through their musical expressions—a truly universal language. And because of that, my process of writing in English is similar to composing music. Words are my musical notes, formed through melody. I follow its rhythm, syncopations, harmonies, dissonances, climaxes till I reach that sacred place of creative freedom where I can pour my heart out on paper.

Is the Maiden Tower legend something you grew up with?

Maiden Tower is Baku's most celebrated and mysterious monument. I was about six years old when my mother took my sister and me to the tower for the first time. Standing on its crown, she told us the Maiden Tower legend about the Shah who decided to marry his daughter. Hoping the Shah would change his mind, the girl, who was secretly in love with a young knight, asked her father to grant her one wish before their wedding: to build a tower that would reach the sky. The Shah didn't change his mind. When the construction was finished, he confined his daughter in the tower until their wedding night. But the knight killed the cruel keeper and rushed into the tower to free his beloved. Hearing heavy steps echoing through the tower and thinking it was her father coming for her, the princess waved her arms like wings and threw herself into the Caspian Sea. A heartbeat later, her knight reached the top of the tower. All he saw was his maiden's veil carried away by the wind.

After I heard that legend, I became determined to save the princess. I kept going back to Maiden Tower, time after time, climbing its steep stairs, hoping to change—to fix—the ending of the legend. Many years later, I finally did it in my novel, transforming the princess into a magical Firebird, giving her and her knight another chance.

Where do you draw your inspiration from?

From life. I've been fortunate to live and travel around the world. Every place adds another dimension, another spark to the creative process. Whether I sit on my balcony in Laguna Beach watching the sun dip into the Pacific Ocean, or drive on Lake Shore Drive along the Chicago skyline, cross the Pont Neuf in Paris, climb Gaudi's cosmic creations in Barcelona, wander through the museums in the presence of Goya, Caravaggio, Renoir, Miro… And then, after all those experiences, I lock myself away from the world in my loft and write and compose, with the soundtrack of Vladimir Horowitz's piano, Billie Holiday's voice, Maxim Vengerov's violin, and London rain tapping overhead against my skylight.

ACKNOWLEDGMENTS

My eternal gratitude—

To my family: Stuart, Micah, Inna, Nick, Jim, and especially my father, Pavel—you are my home, wherever I am…

To Don Heckman, my patient reader and encouraging friend.

To my agent, Jeff Kleinman of Folio Literary Management—you tamed my wild imagination into a phenomenon called *author*.

To my editor, Shana Drehs of Sourcebooks, Inc.—your keen intelligence elevated my Maiden Tower draft into *The Orphan Sky* book.

To Anna Michels, Heather Hall, and Heather Moore of Sourcebooks, Inc., for taking this book out into the world.

To my homeland, Azerbaijan, whose sunshine sustained me through the darkest of days.

ABOUT THE AUTHOR

Ella Leya was born in Baku, Azerbaijan, and received asylum in the United States in 1990. She is a composer and singer and lives in Laguna Beach, California, and London. *The Orphan Sky* is her first novel.